A Daring Resolution

Celia Boyd has written *First Fashionings, Social Conditioning in Georgian Children's Fiction* and *Young Ravens*, a novel for children set in the Midlands during the Second World War - being published in Summer 2007 by *Graficas Books*. She has contributed to *The Cambridge Guide to Children's Books in English*, and has had two articles published in *Signal, Approaches to Children's Books*.

As Celia Mason, working for the West Midlands Probation Services, she wrote *Are You Here for the Beer?* an in-cell, self-help guide for prison inmates, whose criminality stemmed from alcohol abuse. For this she received the Butler Trust Award. She currently writes full time, and is working on the third part of A Reason from the Stars series, entitled *Act of Rebellion.*

Author's Note

I would like to thank Margaret Banthorpe and David Crane for their patient and helpful readings of this text, and that of the first of the series *First Dry Rattle.*

I have had recourse to many works on the English Civil War, but none has been more informative for this particular novel than Howard Clayton's *Loyal and Ancient City. The Civil War in Lichfield*, which I have found invaluable. I would like to dedicate *A Daring Resolution* to Howard Clayton's memory.

In researching mining on Cannock Chase, I found a description of the Pelsall Hall Colliery Disaster of 1872. I hope I will be forgiven for using the surnames of two or three victims of this disaster for the names of the men Lord Hastings fetched from Cannock to mine for Prince Rupert in Lichfield on April 9th 1643. It is likely that the same families were living and mining on Cannock Chase over two hundred years before the terrible tragedy of the Victorian age. My hope is that by using their names, their sacrifice will be remembered yet again.

Many, many friends, and my son and daughter-in-law have been extremely kind and encouraging, and Graficas, my publishers, a.k.a. Tom and Jane have never been too busy to help and advise me. Without them I wouldn't have the impetus to continue.

I would also like to thank Douggie for being living proof that in 364 years journalists have not changed.

Celia Boyd

A Daring Resolution

The second book in the series "A Reason from the Stars"

Graficas Books

First published in 2007,
by Graficas Books, Cwmbach, Glasbury-on-Wye

Set in Classical Garamond by
Graficas Books

Printed in Great Britain by
Biddles Ltd., Norfolk

ISBN 978 0 9554834 1 7

A Daring Resolution

Being the second of the Thomas Fletcher papers, entitled *A Reason from the Stars*, a first-hand account of the late civil disturbances endured by our unfortunate country, undertaken by royal command in 1668.

"The King Enjoys His Own Again."

"There's neither Swallow, Dove, nor Dade,
Can soar more high or deeper wade;
Nor show a reason from the Stars,
What causeth peace, or Civil Wars."

Matthew Parker d. 1656

True Intelligence from Lichfield

It is apparent that Prince Rupert hath alwaies been fince the firft beginning of these Warres, and at this prefent doth continue very active in promoting, countenancing, and perfonally executing thofe defrtructive, difhonourable, and fo much detefted defignes of pillaging and plundering the inhabitants of this Kingdome, alwaies expreffing his valour where he finds, or expects the weakest opposition, otherwife he had not fo valiantly affaulted Cirencester, had not his ods in number, and times advantage given him A Daring Resolution.

London.
Printed for Thomas Watson 1643

1

January 2nd 1643

The farmer stood on the slight rise, gazing at his ruined turnip crop. I prudently dismounted some distance from him and led Jupiter along the hedgerow, avoiding as delicately as we might, the few undamaged plants. As I approached, he turned.

"And what might you be wanting?"

I knew something about farmers. I found my purse and took out a sovereign. "A meal. A bed. To set me on my way."

He did not reply but turned again, beard jutting angrily at the grey horizon, surveying his ravaged land. "First, last September a whole drove of Essex men they call themselves loiters along the Way there from Northampton I heard say. "Sing hey for old Robin" says they. "Sing God rot old Robin," says I. Then the whole of the King's army troops crossways my land. Baggage trains, pikemen, horsemen. I think they've gone for good and all - and then the next day the bastards trail the guns over - calivers, drakes - bound for London the villains claimed but it seems only to Banbury. We could hear them roaring and banging away last backend October time. Then the evil Bulgarians are back. Not all together this time but in groups of seven or eight, stealing my turnips - no word, no offer of payment. This time they say they're for King and Parliament. They even tried to shoot the dogs. Where you from then?" he asked, suddenly not taking his eyes from his land.

"I'm from Worcester. I'm returning thither."

"What you a-doing so far from home then, you great yard and a half of broom handle?"

It pleased him to make merry at my expense. A man cannot help his height. I gave my best dog-fox grin.

"I was doctoring the troopers during the battle." He tuned slowly to look at me. I presumed that to him I was just such another "evil Bulgarian" I had misjudged the distance from Moreton in the

1

Marsh. I judged it was another five miles to Broadway. I should have stayed at Moreton where there was a friendly inn, (and what inn is not well disposed to the traveller with gold in his pockets?), but I longed to see my home again. I felt lonely for my own house, for my own people, even though I now had no family in Worcester. Against my better judgement I had set off too late in the day even to reach Evesham. Now a horseman alone, if I was lucky the farmer would set me on my way with nothing more inhospitable than a curse and a stone.

He continued to regard me with deep suspicion. He spoke at last. "If you can doctor my littl'un, you can bide the night for nought."

I agreed to try. We walked along the hedgerow track in the January twilight, he before, I leading poor Jupiter who was finding the going hard and the wind keen on these high Cotswold ridges. As we stooped under the lintel of the low gray homestead my host roars out: "Nance! Here's a fine barley bun gentleman must needs seek bed and board with the likes of us. What peckage have we? Now then, Master Quacksalver. Here's Tobias. He's been ailing for a day or two now. Can you help him? Do so, and you've paid your shot I'll look to your horse."

Tobias lay in a truckle bed near the fire. I approached him with caution as I feared the plague, but his skin was clear, if pallid and sweating. He was however racked by a terrible cough piteous to hear and complained, he told me, of a "crumbling chest." I put my head to his thin little body and could hear great gobbets of phlegm shiver and tremble in his lungs. If we did not move it, he could choke. He had the croupe, that commonest of childhood ailments, easy to cure but fatal if neglected. In Worcester I had all the necessary tinctures and potions ready to hand. As it was, I had to fight the ague on two fronts, and it must be fought now. The child had a shadow of grey darkness below his eyes. His next journey would be to his grave unless I could devise the means to lower his fever and clear his chest.

"Have you a willow near by?" I asked. The farmer's beard jutted. "Ay by the duck pond. You're not proposing to take my boy…?"

"A paste from boiled willow leaves will deaden the fever. There may well be a few green leaves, under the ones shed in the autumn," I told them, and Nance ran from the room wiping her hands on her apron. "God grant she fall not in the pond now it's full dark" the farmer blustered. The wind of the door opening and closing behind his wife echoed his tone and the fire belched out a great cloud of smoke.

"There!" I told him as his coughing near rivalled his son's. "'Twas well done to house Tobias near the fire for the warmth but the smoke troubles him sorely. He must be kept warm to break the fever. You can see that the body sweats to force the evil humour out from him. That is very good, but each draft of smoke infects his lungs, makes him cough and each bout of coughing weakens him still further. We must move him from the smoke into purer air. If you have large clean stones, I will undertake to heat them in the embers through the night. Then," for the poor man looked mighty perplexed, "if we wrap them in clean linen and place them round him, we will keep him overwarm so that the fever will break with his sweating."

Nance came back with the leaves; dirty and old though they were, they were thankfully still green. I had seen that their water was from a well and not a noisome stream. Even so I made her boil the precious leaves, break them down in mortar and pestle and form a paste, a kind of liaison as she would understand from her housewifery. I then gave Toby a few drops in some honey.

"Now, for the phlegm." In my pack I had a root of elecampane - that old, old remedy. When boiled and crushed, it can clear the blocked passages of the nose and chest to allow untroubled breathing.

I raised Toby and held him in my arms to breathe in the vapours from the boiling infusion. After five minutes I made to lay him down again but then he pleased us all by suddenly sitting up and coughing up a great gobbet of phlegm. "How do you now, sir?" I asked him. "Very well, sir," he replied politely. I laid him down again and asked how far the cider must had fermented.

"Scarce bubbling at all," said Nance. "We were late with the harvest and then the dratted soldiers - But we have good small beer and he will have some of his Merry-Go-Down hidden about the place somewhere…"

I interrupted her. "'Tis not for me but for Toby. He must have a soothing cordial that will quench his thirst and bring back his strength."

She hurried off to the brewhouse with bowl and ladle and returned with a good supply. I tasted it but as it was cloudy still, I ordered her to boil it. There was a good supply of honey, "from my sister in Burford," she told me.

When it had cooled I drained some off and mixed it with the honey: "Here's some special cider for a poor sick soldier," I told him.

Tobias smiled weakly, but drank thirstily of my posset. I placed hot stones around him to bring out the fever and had the willow extract ready.

"Well, Nance," said her husband, "you'll know what to do again in a pinch." He lit his churchwarden pipe and began to puff contentedly. "What's to eat then, little wench?"

As they were the epitome of Jack Spratt and his wife, she could hardly have deserved this epithet. "Mutton pies and carrots Joseph," she told him, "and show more respect before the good gentleman doctor."

"I fear that for your son's sake I must now show you disrespect, good Master Joseph," says I courtly to the last. "But you do him harm, sir, if you will smoke near his bed. Indeed you do. He must have pure air."

Without a word he doused his pipe. After we had eaten very heartily, I told them I would sit up with Toby to dose and treat him as the need arose, tending the fire and keeping him furnished with the hot stones. I told them that the Master's great chair would serve me well. If they would find me a blanket I would be snug as a pig in pease straw. At first Nance demurred, but when Joseph reminded her she had not slept the night before because of her son's plight, she thanked me very graciously and they trooped off to bed.

Toby woke and coughed again. I gave him more extract of willow. His head was much cooler, and the deep breaths that he drew over the elecampane infusion now had a boyish element of bravado, signifying, I hoped, the departure of the hated phlegm. Again he coughed up the wretched substance - though it was a good colour-yellowy white with no blood streaks, which made me hopeful that he had not strained his lungs. "Master," he whispered, "What is that stuff?" He pointed to the parings of the root. "That is elecampane," I told him. "A most useful medicine and a brave yellow flower."

He mumbled something to himself. "What do you say?" I asked him.

He repeated: "Here come I, the doctor with my little bottle of elecampane. Here Jack Pour it down thy tip-top. Then rise and fight again."

"When did you see the Mummers then Toby?" I asked him delighted both by his memory and by his humour.

"Just before Christmas. They came here in the night all the way from the Broadway. All night they went roundabout - and Father Christmas an' all." He remembered more. "I hope old Father Christmas will never be forgot."

"I hope so too," I told him. "So, another drink?"

"Ahh!" he said, for all the world like a Cotswold clodhopper, "Oi sall have another good zup o' moi zoider!"

"Here you are then!" I held it out to him. He gulped it down then settled himself among his nest of blankets.

"It's you what's the Doctor in the play, Master," he told me, "with your elecampane to make me well again."

"Say you so?" said I. "And are you St George soon to fight again?" A decided shake of the head. "What?" I cried, "You are bold Slasher, the Turkish knight, come to give St George another crack of the head?" Another shake. "Who then, are you?" I cried, "Father Christmas?"

He gave a pretend roar and a gnash of his teeth in the direction of my hand. "The dragon!" he hissed in delight. Five minutes later he was asleep with cool brow and even breath. I slept too, waking every so often to tend him but I slept well enough for all that.

Once I woke and found his round brown eyes gazing upon me. "I likes you, master," he told me pleasantly.

"Do you so?" I replied, pleased beyond belief that a child could find it in him to like me. "I likes you an' all," I told him in the vernacular with scant regard for the grammarian's sanctions.

"Tell us a riddle-me-ree then," he instructed me, as if his compliment had earned such a reward. I searched my brain and suddenly remembered my mother's voice as she dressed me, when I was no older than His Worship here.

"What's this then? - Four stiff standers;

Four dilly-danders

Two lookers, two crookers and a long wig wag."

"I know that," he proclaimed. "It's our Daisy."

"Who is Daisy?" I asked all innocence. "A duck?" He laughed so much I feared he might wake his parents. Then all he needed was another drink, another cough, and another sleep.

In the morning it was obvious that the fever had broken and Tobias was himself again, although it had been a close fight. He was still pale and weak, but the terrible shadow had gone from below his eyes. He demanded milk with sippets of bread and more of "his cider". All seemed well with him but I begged them both to keep him warm in bed.

"I am afeared that his throat is prone to irritation," I told his parents. "If the air round him is heavy, he will make overmuch phlegm, be short of breath and then the fever could come again. It would be unwise to burn green wood if you value his health as I know you do."

For answer Joseph silently threw his churchwarden pipe upon the fire, looking at me almost in defiance as he did so.

"I would like to make him a present," I told them, whilst Tobias was helped to the jakes by the cook-maid who came in daily from a near-by hamlet – Blockley - as I recall. "I would like you to take this for my keep and buy him books of rhymes and tales. Tom Hickathrift, and so forth. Tell him if you will it came from Father Christmas."

I laid four guineas on the oak table. Neither spoke. Joseph slowly picked them up whilst Nance watched him like a hawk.

"Well, master" - he began but got no further for she flew at him. "Oh, no you don't, Master Pinch-Back-Belly-Penny," she screamed. "Never will we prey on this good young gentleman." The guineas had rolled into the corners. She scrambled after them, gathered them up and pressed them back into my hands. "We owe you our son's life - or very near it. If you had not happened upon us, we might this day be paying the priest. That'un," and she shook her finger at Joseph, "would take money for his nose drippings, the miserly old turd."

Joseph stood still as stone through all of this. With infinite dignity, he turned to me and said majestically, "Young Master, I was about to thank you and to return your coin. I was prevented by this - this hoydenish slattern," he went on his voice rising to a roar. "Woman, you should think deep burning shame. I wear my arse to

6

a rat's prick to keep you in your gay finery and you speak slander of me before our guest. Now pack commons and small beer for the good young gentleman. What might your name be, sir?"

I told him, "Thomas Fletcher, Surgeon of Worcester." Suddenly I liked my name and my calling. It had a good ring to it. As if I was a man of substance and not a nineteen year old mackrel-back, orphaned and deserted.

Nance came up to me and kissed me soundly - all lavender, sweat and moistness but none the worse for that. "This is your home Master Fletcher, should you need it ever." She hustled together a parcel of food, and gave me two bottles of her own brew. "What again is the name of the root that cleared his chest?"

I laughed. "Don't trouble to remember it. Your young master knew it from the Mummers' play. I would ask in recompense that he learns his book. 'Twill not be a chore for him."

"He shall have books a-plenty," she promised me with a withering glance at her husband who was gazing at the sky.

"Yes, 'tis a fine day for Worcester travel," he proclaimed as if we had been speaking pleasantly of the weather all this while, and indeed the small rain of yesterday had disappeared and the day was bright and clear. Toby like his mother kissed me soundly, and then settled down to sleep again. His father shook me warmly by the hand, told me I was a good hand in a dead lift and promised me he would make shift to find a few pence for a chap-book. "A few pence!" burst forth Nance, but I left before she could again give him another ear thrashing. They came out to bid me Godspeed, roly-poly Nance and Joseph his beard pointing my way homeward towards the west.

Toby suddenly called out loud and clear from inside the house: "Our Daisy's not a duck, master." I needed no further proof that he was well recovered as I waved Farewell to his parents from the end of the barton and led Jupiter, much refreshed by his night's rest, carefully back to our road.

Within an hour it seemed we had reached the edge of the Cotswold escarpment. Below us was the straggling village Toby called the Boadway, and far away in the distance were the Malvern Hills. The great vale of the Severn stretched before us, under the pearl grey sky. Slightly to the North West, I could just make out the tiny fingers that were the two great towers of the Cathedral. My father had died for that building. As we carefully made our way down the wandering track frequently diagonally and on the bias I allowed myself to drown in the nightmare thoughts and memories that surrounded his end. My mother had died in the plague outbreak of 1637, six years ago. This had been as hard a loss as one could conceive for my father and myself, and yet it was one we accepted with a degree of fortitude. A fifth of the town died. Every family was burying a loved one. We accepted her loss with despair, true, but as a loss decreed by God and Nature. Even now I was hard put to hold back the tears at the memory of her gentle Welsh voice but my grief for her rose only out of my love. Whereas my father had died horribly for another man's whim. When Essex occupied the town with his drunken Parliamentarian hotheads at the end of September - on the 24th in fact - my father, Amyas Fletcher, respected citizen and Master Butcher of Worcester - felt that for love of the Cathedral, he must needs go to Essex to complain at the monstrous treatment, (a stable for their horses no less), such a holy edifice was receiving at the hands of Essex' Godless troopers. My father took it upon himself to do this - where were the overfed unctuous prelates who should have carefully explained to the rebel Essex that the Cathedral had no part in the politicks of men but was a living testimony in stone to the faith and dedication of our forefathers. Where were Bishop Prideaux and Dean Potter, when Essex on that terrible Sunday ordered my father hanged as a spy? Well, one thing was certain sure, they were not there.

It may now seem like a terrible heresy, damning me to eternal perdition, but I have been hard put to it to find the workings of the Almighty in our lives since my father's death. Men, (aye and women too), seemed to be lurching from one crisis to the next without forethought, without purpose. There are no reasons in this age of civil war. I saw again, in my mind's eye, the cold indifferent stars above the Rollright Stones. In the moments before Brigstock and his evil cronies captured me, the stars had gazed stonily down. They had no message, no prophecy. I was alone, without parent, without ally, without friend. With the loss of my father, I had lost my faith also.

But there had been a kind of envy in the eyes of my new companions, Edward Holte and Lucius Carey. They had longed for a father like mine, loving and supporting, encouraging me in all my little enterprises, once we had ascertained, he and I, that I was not suited to follow him in the butchering trade. It was my father who even now prompted me to laugh at myself. I had a tendency to take myself too seriously, to be somewhat sententious in my advice giving. I thought of my sermonising on the subject of smoking to poor Joseph and blushed at my audacity.

We trotted through the Broadway at a fair pace. Jupiter today seemed to take good heart from the January sun, in which there was the faintest trace of warmth. The Lygon family had built themselves a rare fine house close to the road near the Green. I dismounted to look at it, and to give Jupiter a drink from the horse trough. Christmas Roses were pushing their heads through the frosty grass and nodding in satisfaction at the sight of the pleasant mansion behind them, built in the warm stone of the district, pink as the flowers. It was, of course, as nothing beside Sir Thomas Holte's palace at Aston, but then I do not think he would have been troubled to plant flowers, either to please passers-by or himself.

I promised Jupiter good provender in Evesham if he would continue his good paces and we set off on the wellworn track. Wellworn indeed! It was this route that Essex men had followed to invade Worcester. I cursed myself again. I could not keep my thoughts from the horror of that day, no matter how I tried to fill my mind with other matters. As we cantered through Childswykem, I gave both Jupiter and my memories free rein.

I thought of my brief encounter with the King. He had seemed concerned, nay, conscience–stricken by Edward Holte's plight, had remained by the crude fire, with wounded men both Royalist and rebel whilst I had tried to save Edward's leg. He had sent wholesome food to us all, as all the common soldiery had empty bellies. In this, he acted like a kind father to his subjects. But I could not deceive myself. The terrible war had begun because he demanded more and yet more money from his poor subjects. My people, the middling sort of people, were not to be drained and squeezed of all the honest profit that we might make from our many trades and skills. If a King is father to the nation, this was not the action of a loving pater familias to his children. I knew too that there were disputes as to what the Church could teach, and there had been cruel punishments for men who resisted Archbishop Laud's dictates as to what one might believe. Not yet burnings in the market-place for heresy, nor yet the traitor's death of hanging and disembowelment, but now no doubt after the rebellious taking up of arms, such endings could be the lot of men like Robert Burghill

My stomach twisted at the thought of such a death for so good a friend. I reined in at the side of the road and for a few moments gave myself up to bleak despair. I could see no way forward with either faction. Lucius had encouraged me in my belief in my own "fierce neutrality" and bade me hold fast to that viewpoint. I remembered a conversation we had had when there was yet good news and bad, in November for the King's army had had great success in Brentford but had been turned north again by apprentices at Turnham Green. Lady Letty was deploring the rebel action against the King and I perhaps with some daring as I was lodged very well in a royalist house, had felt that I must try to redress the balance: "To me, dear madam, the blood of a rebel runs as red as that of a King's true servant. If he is sick, or wounded, to me, he is none other than my patient, no matter what the colour of his sash."

Lucius turned to me with tears in his eyes. "Tom, you say well. Enough, Letty! Whatever our loyalties we know, yes, you as well, madam, you know the King has flawed judgement. It has all continued long enough. We must soon surely come to sanity." And he walked from the room in depression, saying softly to himself: "Ah, peace, peace, when will you come to us again with all your gentle blessings?"

The moment passed but now I felt acutely all the Viscount's anguish. I looked around me. I had descended from the Cotswold heights to the great vale with the town of Evesham lying ahead of me. Poor men were in the field near to me. They had paused in their ploughing to gaze at me. Poor fellows, one could scarce descry them from the earth they toiled in, their garments were so mud engrained.

At Evesham we found an inn near the great field where Simon de Montfort had challenged his king. I wondered if the town's inhabitants were then wholeheartedly Parliament men out of respect for their local folk hero. Not so. When the landlord knew I had ridden in from the East he and his cronies wanted news of the King. I was able to tell them he was in good heart and that he had made his makeshift court at Christchurch college amongst the Dons and scholars in Oxford, that he had celebrated the Christmas feast with such jollity as he might muster given that his lady and our Queen still stayed in Holland.

"God bless him," said mine host. "Amen" said his cronies. "And a pox on all mangy Puritans that seek to set him about with discord, the Prickeared Quakebreeches. Oh, be you a-going so soon, Master Gregg?" as a tradesman - a baker I think - with a hunted expression, rose, set down his tankard and slunk from the room.

So was it in the world that Winter. Treacheries, betrayals, desertions. And Ben, my cousin, nay, my brother, my teacher, my master had left me. I still found it hard to conceive how he could have had the heart to do so, so soon after my father's death seeming to forget all we had undergone together as a family. But then he had found his true father, Isaac Nunez, and had felt that he must dwell with him and love him for the rest of his life. God knows, if my father, risen from his grave, had been trotting towards me along the bridle way from Evesham, even now, I would never leave him. So I could not resent Ben's departure, merely grieve for it.

We had set out half an hour after noon on the last lap of our journey. We would travel through Pershore and I hoped to reach Worcester just before the light left the sky. Jupiter was so good a pad-nag, I took great pains never to tire him unduly, then if it came to a pinch he would not fail me I hoped. He had been Ben's horse and was as old as myself, both of us deserted by our past master. Now he went with a will along the flat track that wound through the orchards and gardens - the lush lands that bordered the Avon.

We cantered over the old bridge outside Pershore. Home now was in his nostrils. Nonetheless I bade him halt and watered him in the town square of Pershore. After he had drunk his fill, I came round to him and caressed him, stroking his nose and finding an apple in my pack from Dame Nance's orchard. It had seemed over the months since my departure from Worcester on Monday 17th of October last year that Jupiter was all I had to remind me of who or what I had been. But I was surprised to learn what respect a good horse and a purseful of gold will earn a man, be he never such a bumpkin. Joan had insisted that I "rob" my father's store. "To buy your way out of danger," she warned me. "It is a better means of currency than those ready fists of yours."

"Well then old friend," I whispered to my horse. "Shall we make a last gallop for our own stable?" He nuzzled my shoulder, which I took to be an argument for swiftly covering the last few miles. As we clattered out of the Market Square I thought for a moment I heard my name called. I looked around the groups of stall-holders and housewives, all of whom seemed totally engrossed in their affairs. No-one seemed to be interested in my coming or going so I judged that I had misheard. But then it came again: "Tom! Tom Fletcher! Hold your horse!"

I wheeled about and saw running and stumbling from the inn in the corner of the market square, a dear good friend of my father's, whom I had always called John Barleycorn. He was a man who spoke much and laughed even more than he spoke. Now he laughed in pleasure at the sight of me, but tears stood in his eyes. As I dismounted he paused in his run towards me, but then came to me and held me and buried his face in my shoulder. "Oh, Tom! Tom! Dear lad! That it should come to this! The best man in the world!" I could not keep back my tears, and for a moment or two we wept together. I had noticed that after such moments, grief diminishes a little and happier memories crowd sorrow out of doors. And I had many happy memories of my father and this good man.

I had known him all my life. He would bring his beasts from Pirton, where his farm was, into Worcester for slaughter. His arrival was the signal for my father to kiss my mother soundly and ask leave to visit John Barleycorn. Our visitor was also a John and in my infant mind the two persons merged, so that when this same farmer appeared in the shop door, I would call out in glee to my father: "Here comes John Barleycorn!" His name was in fact John Appleton, but much to their delight, I had it in mind, that my father counselled and aided this same John Barleycorn, whenever he appeared in our shop…. although I puzzled as to why it was always necessary to administer such counsel and help on the premises of an alehouse at the Port Key on Keyn Street. After my mother's death I began to understand the jest of this mild subterfuge and occasionally had accompanied them for a draught of sweet cider. After such little indulgence I had cause to wonder why the air off the river was quite so sharp and why the cobblestones of Cooken Street on the way home were quite so uneven.

Now John Barleycorn as I could not but think of him, wept in my arms for his old friend, in the middle of Pershore market whilst butter women stared and yokels seeking hire gawped. "Such good times! Such a good old friend! Poor boy! Such a hard fate!"

"Come, sir," I asked him. "Let us sit in the inn rather than in the public gaze."

But of a sudden he collected himself. "Listen, neighbours!" he cried out to the interested spectators. "This poor young man is one of the first to suffer the gross injustice of this Devil's War. His father, Amyas Fletcher, was.... was slaughtered for nought in Worcester Market as you have heard. Let us have no more schisms and divisions, good neighbours. Can we not live in peace without this turmoil?"

There were murmurings of agreement. I liked not being the object of attention, and least of all, of the pity of strangers, but the good will of John Barleycorn was hard to resist. "Indeed, and so shall all here live in peace, good Master Appleton," called out the innkeeper. "Come you back here, and pray bring in the young Master Fletcher and drink your fill."

So it was in mid-afternoon I disengaged myself from the good wishes and good will of all the good fellows of Pershore, with the promise to John Barleycorn that I would visit him at his farm in Pirton. I resolved to give him my father's bible or some such keepsake. In truth I felt to some extent ashamed, in that I had forgotten that a man's death does not merely affect those close in family. Friendship also has its dues, and I had neglected or ignored those ties, my father had forged.

The climb up Windmill Hill was long rather than steep, and I was dozing and fuddled somewhat from the toasts I had drunk to my father's memory and found the upward track endless but at the summit I could see again the great square tower of the Cathedral, much nearer now. I gave the horse his head and from a canter he lurched himself forward into a gallop.

At the crossroads where the way from Alcester joined the road down into the city I paused again, glimpsing the river winding below and the plain stretching towards the Malverns and the setting sun. As we trotted down the Sidbury hill to the cathedral I had to decide where I would go first. In truth I had a great wish to see Joan and Adam. Jacky and the butchering could wait. I trotted down Friar Street, turned into Baxter Street. I found I could not look right to the Corn Market or the Corn Cheapen as some called it. I could not look where my father had been so brutally.... murdered, ...but rode steadfastly past Swithins and into Goose Lane. Then a short

13

canter down Broad Street and I turned under the sign of the Mortar and Pestle, which we had adopted to advertise our trade. It is always strange (and sobering) to return to familiar places and find them unaltered by our absence. For me at that moment there was a slightly grating sensation.... a feeling of disappointment, almost, that life continues smoothly even if I am not there to oversee its quiet flow.

For indeed all in the courtyard seemed as usual I could see Roger, his back to me, forking hay in Hector's stall, Joan's voice came from the kitchen, shouting instructions to someone in another part of the house, and a beautiful girl in a becoming green gown, that set off to perfection, ringlets of the russet of autumn leaves, came from the dairy, hastening to gain the warmth of the house as the evening was setting in with January chill. They had none of them seen me until the lady in green who had I noticed the slightest limp, screamed most unladylike at the sight of the tall horse, blocking the street archway.

"Why, Tom! It's Tom! Joan, he is returned! Master Tom is here!"

2

January 21st 1643

A fortnight or thereabouts passed and one morning I lay musing in my bed watching the filigree pattern of a wintry sun coming and going on my ceiling. It seemed strange that I, who had thought of myself as no more than a workaday apothecary and bonesetter, could have had to do with such noble causes and company in the shires of Warwick and Oxford, but such a short time ago. Indeed now I was hard put to it to believe that after two or three short weeks or so, back on home ground that I had ever been away. My Worcester patients had barely noticed my absence, and it was in fact for Ben's magic touch that the merchants' wives and the rich tradesmen's daughters still yearned. Short shrift had they with Joan's bony charms! But yet she was proving a popular and lucrative apothecary now she lived in Worcester and as a herbalist she had no equal, (Roger secretly told me he thought his mother was well content. "No-one challenges her now, Tom. She's in heaven!")

I had learned during my four years with Ben how to treat wounds, extract foreign matter and I had set nigh on a hundred broken limbs, many of them the Sunday night after Edgehill, in circumstances that Ben would have found deplorable. I smiled to myself. Bone setting was an unpleasant, unpopular yet vital skill. I had heard more colourful curses after the battle than ever were uttered during its passage.

It was becoming necessary to replenish our stocks of the tinctures Ben had devised, and it would be on Joan's knowledge of the whereabouts of certain plants and simples in the area that we must now depend. Why had Ben gone from us? I refused to allow myself to travel that well worn path. At least the methodical manner in which he had conducted his practice was an excellent legacy on which we could build. We had all his receipts for the tried and tested remedies that were proving so necessary in these troubled times.

15

Every night since I had been home, I had burned my candle, pouring over his treatment notes to glean as much knowledge as I could. I was aware that much of his learning.... and hence my own.... came from skills and practices taught him by a Damascene Doctor in Bologna University. This same Doctor was an Arabian whose ideas had run counter to many of our dearly held notions of past years. For instance this same Doctor Iqbal had refused to let his students bleed their victims or rather patients. He had pronounced that men and women were not so much living meat to have their precious ichor spilt in a libation to the surgeon's ignorance. Ben used to say he had never in his life seen a man or woman improve in their condition through bleeding, but he had seen many die from weakness after it. Ben had also insisted on clean water supplies, again a dictate of Doctor Iqbal's. I suddenly thought, Josef, my friend the brown pedlar.... he was an Egyptian. I should have asked him what he knew about doctoring.

It was a tincture of Ben's that had saved lives at Edgehill, not my skill, though it had been pleasant to reap the credit for it. I had barely enough for Edward Holte's wound. I must obtain further supplies of those particular herbs, Woodruff, Kings Clover and Water Betony.... a liaison of these, caused flesh to halt in the process of decomposition. I was terrified of encountering again the Ferret's condition, the necrosis of a limb. The only remedy when faced with a gangrenous mass of corruption is amputation. "The pain your patient is in, is of such extreme," Ben had told me coolly, "that he will almost certainly consent to that procedure. And if he has had the strength to endure so much already, it may be that he will survive your saw."

I shuddered. It was an experience that I, as a doctor, hoped to avoid. If the war continued and Edward Holte who was privy to the King's mind, was of the opinion that he would never.... could never.... give up his cherished belief in his divine right to rule both Lords and Commons, then 'twere foolish optimism to suppose that we had seen the last of battles and bloodshed.

With these concerns, I lay between sleep and waking. I must set about the replenishment of Ben's stocks. The future presaged much need for doctoring. I must today check all supplies and send order to a merchant who had begun to import roots of healing from the New World.

How strange it was that I who five months ago had been the greenest of green youths, in search of such wild oats as presented themselves in this staid city, was now head of a large household, managed for me in recent weeks by Joan. She now encouraged me to take control. I pulled the bedclothes up round my ears. In the Spring, she had explained to me, it would be most pleasant for her to have leisure to walk with Adam along the river path, so she would wish to begin to relinquish her duties in my favour.

But all contributed their portion to the smooth running of both households. Adam, though blind, still had much strength in his upper body and could help with maintaining the two houses, provided all his tools remained within the grasp of his sensitive fingers. Roger took care of the horses and mended our cart, in which I travelled to outlying villages, either to collect herbs or in response to a plea for assistance. He had also taught himself to cut hair.... and from the results one would have thought we had firmly espoused the Roundhead cause. But he was skilled with figures. And even his mother admitted he could be trusted to calculate our profits and losses accurately.

Jacky and Matt had maintained the butchering trade, although Jacky complained daily of Sir William Russell who insisted Matt must leave his work with other able bodied apprentices to assist with fortifications against any future Parliamentarian attack.... although I believed as many others did, that it was somewhat futile work. If Essex wished to enter again, he would not allow a few earthworks to prevent him. The city spilled beyond the old walls now. But Sir William, for all his zeal, had spared us the quartering of King's men. Whether this was from an awareness of my father's recent tragic death, or from the knowledge that two Staffordshire King's soldiers had been butchered horribly by Essex' Lifeguard, whilst staying in my father's house, I know not. Townsfolk will talk. Perhaps the master butcher's shop had gained an unfortunate reputation for King's men seeking shelter.

The butchery business continued to prosper. Our customers remained faithful to us and Jacky slaughtered and Matt was now able to dismember and joint the carcasses. I who now had no fear at the sight of my dead fellow men, could still not contemplate lambs for the slaughter, and kept well out of the way on killing days. The most my father had been able to teach me was skill in wringing chickens' necks.

"If 'tis a botched affair, they suffer much and all know when they sit down to table for the tenderest young pullet will be tough eating, if it met its end without love and charity."

I started from my bed. It was as if he had been in the room, explaining his theory. I heard his voice commenting on a multitude of issues almost daily. Yet if I asked him for advice, he was silent. After death as in life, the wisdom of our elders is never there when needed! I smiled to myself. It almost seemed as if I had just shared a joke with my father. Again each time I heard his sage counsel in my head, it seemed as if he was less dead to me, a strange non sequitor.

I seized his velvet lined bed-gown that I had adopted for myself and lurched from my bed to break the ice in the bowl set ready for me in the corner. As I did so I glanced out into the courtyard, where the frost glinted in the early sun. Phoebe was coming into the yard from the street. She had walked well wrapped up in her worsted cloak to get the daily milk and cream from a farm in St. John's parish across the river. Now in true milkmaid style, she carried her yoke across her shoulders. Her appearance was much improved, perhaps with Joan's advice and assistance. Her hair whilst not red was of a russet brown close to crimson, which now flamed against the frosty yard. Certain sure she worked hard for her living, proving of great worth in matters domestic and with our customers. She had a quick brain for a girl of fifteen, a lively wit and a gentle manner with those who sought our help. If she had not been afflicted by her palsied limb, she would have been.... she seemed to sense my gaze, looked up, and smiled. She laughed.... I read her thoughts.... better laugh than wave.... and cry over spilt milk.

Later that morning Joan and I were reassuring Mistress Gardener who being great with child, was afraid it would be born covered in fur, as she had been frightened the night before by a tom-cat leaping from their brew-house. "Certain sure, Master Gardener's first born son" (for so she had spoken for seven months of her expected offspring), "gave a great kick to my ribs, and at that moment I had a terrible presentiment that I might give birth to a cat.... What think you, Tom?... e.... Master Fletcher I should say." She faced me, and could not see Joan's face behind her, which was the epitome of impatient scorn. But when Joan spoke it was with studied and com-

18

forting courtesy.

"Good Mistress Gardener, your babe is well protected from these minor upsets of mundane life by the great bag of waters, in which he... or she....swims at ease. I beg you fear not. The babe still moves gently and is well content. I have a tincture here which will strengthen you and your dear child, and which will prevent any abnormality. Pay now only for your consultation with Master Fletcher, but when young Master or Mistress Gardener emerges into this world, healthy and hale.... and without an unnatural compliment of hair, then please you to pay us five sovereigns. That will be a separate account from our midwifery attendance."

Bet Gardener took her flask of redcurrant cordial away with her well pleased. Phoebe stood aside and curtsied to her as she heaved herself through the narrow door of the room in which we entertained daily patients.

"Give you good day, Mistress," said Phoebe, to her pleasant as a princess. "Tom, there is a young man to see you. He has come in from Stratford."

It was Elijah! I had told him that if his mother could spare him, I would gladly employ him. Now he came with his few possessions wrapped in his Sunday shirt. It seems he had walked to Alcester from Stratford through the frost yesterday, paid for a place by the fire in the King's Head there overnight and had travelled the rest of the way in style on a farmer's cart full of winter cabbages. He had bought two with his last pence from the farmer and now held them out to Joan.

"Why, you good lad, that is wholesome eating in a white winter," she told him, well pleased with the gift.

"Tom," he turned to me, "I have no money to buy indentures. I gave what you and Master Tovey gave me to my mother to keep her while I am gone from her..."

I led him into one of the withdrawing rooms where a great fire was roaring half up the chimney. He looked around in wonder at the oak panelling, the Knowles family crest of beech leaves surrounding the dove, with the olive branch, carved above the fireplace, and the settle and the fine chairs still cushioned with my aunt's needlework.

"Yes," I told him laughing. "This is my house and worse is to come. I have anotherdwelling in Fish Street, my father's house and butcher's shop…but 'tis not so grand as this. This was my aunt's house, that I inherited from my cousin by deed of gift last October."

There was a flagon of wine on the dresser nearby. I poured some into two Tickney bowls, and motioned to Elijah to sit which he did although it was as if he sat upon a dragon's back, so carefully did he dispose his person on the oak settle.

"Listen, Tom…. Master Tom, I should rather say…. I am come hither with nothing. Since Father died, Mother and I are poor. And compared with this, our house is as naught. I hated to leave her for the Parliament men keep threatening from Warwick Castle. But she wanted me to come. She thought I might be taken up to serve with the Parliament if I stayed in Stratford, and she thought it was a good chance for me to work for you."

"Not for me, with me!" I told him.

But he still looked unhappy. "I thought you were a poor boy like myself…well, perhaps not so lamentable poor as me…but nonetheless not rich. It must seem to you that I am come to fasten myself on your hospitality and your goodness."

"It seems naught of that," I cried, "and cease your ramblings. I have great need of more assistance, have I not, Joan?" as she entered with bread, cheese and onions…. my favourite commons for the middle of the day. "Come. Fall to! Joan, do we not need more help about this dispensary? Elijah had to turn his hand to anything and everything at the battle. What say you, Joan? We can surely use his talents and teach him what we can."

Joan surveyed Elijah critically. "You seem a good enough youth, Elijah. And if what Master Thomas has told us is true about your holding up through the long night after the dreadful battle, then surely there is work and board for you here, and welcome if that is what Master Thomas wills."

I was well content that Elijah had sought me out. We had had marvellous happy times with Edward and Eliza and the Careys at Great Tew. I pledged him in the Canary wine and thanked him for his friendship and for his zeal at seeking me out at first jump. He pledged me in turn and we began to speak of the strange days of Advent that we had spent, taken by our good friends to the King's skimble skamble Oxford court. The Canary was not of too poor a quality so we tasted a little more and then drank healths to Eliza

Holte and to Lettice Cary, our kind gracious hostess. Then we remembered the November night at Great Tew when one bought news of the King's victory at Brainsford or Brentford or some such sad southern flea-pit…and the music and talk and laughter that followed. And we drank to the memory of that merry evening. Then we drank confusion to all the scurvy apprentice lads who by standing in their Trained Band ranks had outfaced their King and "turned him" at Turnham Green. That seemed a monstrous pretty quibble to me. I explained it again to Elijah but he had drifted into a nap.

When Phoebe came in to clear the board, I rose to greet her and to pledge her, but then sat again in a discourteous abrupt fashion. Elijah snored a little after his early morning ride with the cabbages, he was fatigued. I tried to explain this. Phoebe giggled. I realised with a shamefaced awareness that we were somewhat "well to live."

"Prithee, Phoebe," I asked her "If you love me, do not tell Joan that we are drunk as rats."

She coloured but agreed. Afterwards I realised that such a spoken condition was not seemly from a young man to a young maid, but at the time I could not apologise. Indeed all I could do was sink into slumber beside Elijah. And so we rested for perhaps an hour or two well into the afternoon until suddenly at about three I must needs relieve myself.

I wandered out into the yard but the jakes had moved. I asked Roger who had mysteriously multiplied into two "fac similes" of himself where it had gone and he fell to laughing so much that he was hard put to direct me. "Why, Tom" cries he, "I never in my life thought to see you so wamblety. Here you are, where it always was."

As I was emerging, being careful to be nice and secure about my person, a large cob clattered under the arch, ridden side-saddle by Catherine, the buxom wife of the Ledbury apothecary, Owen Lloyd with whom I stayed last September.

She saw me and called immediately: "Master Fletcher, I have ridden the twelve miles from Ledbury without halt nor comfort. In the name of God, help me down and to the privy."

"In the name of God," I replied "That will I, mistress, and right willingly for I am well advised of its whereabouts. This way please."

Somehow I had forgotten we had a mounting block. I went straight to her and pushing her petticoats aside, began to pull her

21

down from the horse by her fat little feet, but Roger, seeing the outrage on her face, pushed me aside and led the great cob to the block. Joan hearing the anguished squeaks of Mistress Lloyd came out wiping her hands on her apron. She immediately took her into the house, where she had insisted there should be a private retiring room for ladies, but not before she had given me one of her looks, which have made strong men fall instantly to prayer. I stood feeling rather foolish, looking at the sky that presaged snow, so purple-black was the welkin. Roger came out to me after a moment.

"It's you she has come to see, Tom. Now what do you say? Have I not begged you for a draught that will sober a man up swiftly? Now you know what a case I am in, after I come in of a Friday after I have met my fellow Trojans."

I suppose I must have looked at him very foolishly. "Oh, Tom!" he cried, "Come with me." He led me round to the barber's shop, where he had ensconced himself comfortably.... away from his mother. He had a stoup of cold water that he heated for shaving customers. Now he poured some in a bowl and suggested I splashed my face with it, until I felt sage and sober again, as befitted an elderly nineteen year old, with my responsibilities.

"Believe me, Tom," he cried, slapping me on the shoulder, "I am right glad to see you so bumpsy, for you are such a monstrous, serious, long-faced fellow. At least now I know you can be as much of a bellshangle as the rest of us, when the drink is in you."

At length, I felt sober enough to enter the kitchen, where the ladies were sitting, drinking elderberry wine and eating Phoebe's almond cakes. I made my bow, with Roger's good counsel ringing in my ears: "Say as little as you can. Much the best policy when you are foxed!" In fact it would be a brave, determined Jack Bragger, who could get in many words with Mistress Lloyd, but her story was disquieting, especially for me as it concerned Eleanour.

I had always hoped Eleanour Lloyd would have been my bride. When I had seen her last September just two days before the action at Powick Bridge, I had thought once or twice during my stay with her parents that I might still be the man for her, but she, something of a Gill-flirt and wayward with a man's affections, spoke overmuch about a relative, one Ralph Truscott of Lichfield, a cousin by marriage to a connection of her mother. This same Ralph was to spend some days in Ledbury with the Lloyds, his distant relatives, at the end of September. I went off from Ledbury in something of a bad humour, but consoled myself with the notion that I would see pretty Sal Beckford, the landlord's daughter at the Inn at Welland. To my shame, I had felt irritation that Phoebe was now also in my care. I even forgot her, when I had to make a swift escape from Welland. Now she sat with the older women, as nice as a little nun, gravely accepting their thanks and compliments for her sweet cakes.

Mistress Lloyd was explaining to all that I had gravely misjudged Eleanour's inclinations. She wept a little as she told us that her daughter had been heartbroken when I had set off still unpledged to her on that fateful Thursday, last September. Why had I not declared myself and spoken for her? It was despair that caused her to accept the advances of Ralph Truscott.

"Are they then betrothed?" I asked.

"Betrothed? They are fast married in St Michaels and the Angels at the end of October last. He had so many enterprises at his command in Lichfield or thereabouts, so many concerns.... an inn here, a chandler's there, and a thriving wagon-makers in a town to the north of Lichfield. He told me and her good father, he could not afford to wait overlong, as his attention is so needed in a multitude of places."

"You are to be congratulated then, Mistress!" said I on my high horse. "Fair Eleanour will want for naught."

"So thought we, I declare to you, but all my worry and all my care is for this, Master Tom. We have heard nothing from her since they went off in their wedding finery with his parents at the end of October last. I have written by carrier many times. I have enclosed golden guineas under the seal, so that she might the faster reply post-haste, but I swear to you - not one word. Her father and I are at wits-end. I am come to ask if you would accept this purse and ride over to Lichfield to put our minds at rest. The twelve mile from Ledbury to Worcester is as much as I can manage, and I am sore afeared of footpads. And Master Lloyd has this past winter been much afflicted by the rheumaticks and 'tis profound torture for him to attempt to mount aught these days." (There was a muffled snort from Roger. I did not dare catch his eye for fear I too should break out a-laughing).

She continued: "So I must needs seek help from good friends that have youth and health to sustain them. To tell truth, I heard a prophecy from a preacher lately that made me think 'twould not be labour wasted to come hither to prevail on you. What say you, Master Thomas? Will you undertake the task?"

I could not reply for a moment. If I was honest I did not want to leave my comfortable home in the midst of winter. Also, there was an element of outrage in my mind. Why should I help find her wayward daughter?

"Mistress, think you there might not be a degree of pain for me in such a quest? I was not indifferent to your daughter as I think you know. When I last saw her, she made it clear that Truscott was the man for her. She hardly ceased to speak of him to draw breath."

"'Twas but a ruse, dear Thomas, a stratagem I suggested to make you jealous and to provoke you into a declaration."

Phoebe suddenly left her chair and hurried from the room. She had lately bought some hens and was very anxious that none should stray from the coop, Roger had built her.

Catherine Lloyd continued, "In truth she cared nothing for him, when you were by, Tom. It was only when she feared that she had lost you, that she contemplated a union with Ralph."

"If there is such scant affection between them, then 'tis fortunate indeed that the young man has such a multiplicity of financial enterprises as recompense," said Joan dryly.

"Indeed and you are in the right of it there, good Mistress Bailey," Catharine rattled on. "We have spoken of that many a long night this past December. I and her father have comforted and sustained ourselves in the knowledge that at the very least she will want for nothing."

I had not liked Truscott when I had first heard of his many perfections, from Eleanour's rosy lips. I liked the sound of him even less now. But she! To speak continually of another man, merely to make me jealous! That was sure- fire certain to send me packing. "If she think not well of me, What care I how fair she be." My father sang in my head, a poem he had heard somewhere.

Finally I made some sort of an answer. "I think, mistress, I will need time to consider if I should commit myself to this journey. It seems to me strange that you ask the spurned suitor to ascertain that his lost love is safe and well. Sure, you must have great faith in my attachment to your daughter if it transcends her marriage to another man."

I felt rather proud at this response, but poor Catharine began to weep noisily into a scrap of linen. Joan kindly began to comfort her, shaking drops of lavender water onto her sodden little rag. Phoebe returned suddenly. "It's snowing!" she announced gleefully, brushing great flakes from her cloak. Catharine sobbed again and lay back in her chair, as if she were about to faint and Phoebe, ever the kindest of girls, suggested that I fetched gentian root from the dispensary, to revive Catharine's low spirits.

I walked straight into Elijah, who must have gone out by the street door and was now standing outside the kitchen, perplexed, lonely and no doubt with something of a headache, if he was in like case to myself. Embarrassed and snow covered, his knuckles were poised to knock, but he was seemingly frozen both by cold and uncertainty.

I gave him no more time for any of his poor-proud humours. "Swiftly, man, I need your help." I hustled him into the dispensary and instructed him to prepare an infusion of gentian root, a sovereign remedy for preventing faintness in females. (Partly I believe because it is so bitter that they dare not faint again, for fear of another dose being administered.)

When we returned with it, Elijah carrying it carefully over the snow-covered yard, neatly covered with a snow-white cloth, Mistress Lloyd was explaining to the company why she had been named Catharine. "Yes," she expounded "I was named after the blessed Catharine Audley, kissing cousin to Edward the Second. Did you know that, good sir?" (This to Adam who sat bemused and silent in the chimney corner.) "This same Catharine, noble and bred to high matters, walked to Ledbury, for she had heard a prophecy that she must walk until she came to a tower where the bells are rung by no human hand. And that place was Ledbury. Strange is it not, Master Bailey, that she was not canonized? That means to be made a saint, mistress."

Joan was not impressed. She sniffed and replied something waspishly: "Strange indeed, mistress, for 'tis true the old monks would sanctify anything that was one step above the Devil, and even though this blessed Catharine seems to have done precious little of practical work to benefit her fellow humans for aught I have heard tell, at the very least it seems she was a good walker! Here, swallow a little of this tincture, mistress. 'Twill prevent further attacks of female weakness."

As Catharine sipped and spluttered, Joan continued: "Doubtless you had planned to remain at an inn this night, but I know that dear Tom will not allow such an old friend as yourself, to sleep this night amongst strangers. If you will excuse Phoebe and myself, we must heat up coals for warming-pans and prepare linen, beds and rooms for you, and for Tom's young friend and journey-man, Elijah. And Roger? What of Mistress Lloyd's mount."

She bustled out attended by Phoebe, leaving Catharine in a sad state, torn between politeness and gratitude for the hospitality enforced on her, and distaste for the bitter medicine, both liquid and verbal that she had been constrained to swallow.

The snow was now falling in great flakes against the darkening sky. Jacky and Matt came in shortly afterwards, brushing great flakes off their shoulders, to take their evening meal with us as was their custom. Old Gill had retired to her bed betimes with a posset, as she feared to walk on snow-covered cobbles. Venison had been culled lately from Sir William's estate, and those who could pay, could buy. Mistress Catharine's eyes widened at the great haunch we had on the gridiron. Peppered winter cabbage made a meal fit for.... if not for kings, at least for a fat Ledbury wife to know that if her daughter had seen fit to throw in her lot with me, she would not have starved. All but Elijah and I drank small beer. We drank water with our meal for some reason I cared not to examine.

Suddenly Adam spoke: "I have thought for some time about Mistress Lloyd's request, and about Thomas' response. As one who knew his father well, I know that Amyas would wish him to ascertain that all is well with your daughter, Mistress Lloyd. In fact I have heard a prophecy that indicates that he should do so," (and here a gleam of humour played about his sightless eyes), "for sad it is indeed that parents should let a daughter out into the world and have no reassurance that all is well with her, that she is cherished and beloved not just by a new young husband, but by his parents also."

He paused. Roger and I looked at each other. Joan had made no secret of the fact that she heartily disliked her eldest son's new bride. "The Whore of Babylon" was one of her milder terms for the poor young woman. Now she looked somewhat conscience stricken I thought and bowed her head as Adam continued:

"But Amyas would not have wished Tom to leave his home again so soon for several reasons. The weather has it seems set in, and all ways will be foul. If there is snow on Severnside, 'twill be inches deep elsewhere in the shires around. Secondly, Tom has but today taken on a new young journey-man who will need time to adjust to this, his new calling and his new home, in which I know I speak for all here when I tell him he is heartily welcome. Thirdly, Mistress Lloyd I would remind you of the old adage: "No news, good news." If your daughter had met a tragic end, be sure you would have heard ere this. And fourthly her treatment of Tom smacks something of the hoyden, if you will forgive me, madam, but perhaps she should not be blamed, as it seems those who should have known better encouraged her in this. Fifthly and most important, poor Tom has suffered much in recent months and whilst he is well capable of undertaking what you ask, he needs more time to recover from his father's dreadful passing (of which I am sure you have heard, Mistress), and to grow accustomed to his new responsibilities. So, Mistress, on his behalf I say to you: 'Not quite yet!'"

There was a silence. Catharine began to cry again and this time I began to feel pity for her, as she clearly yearned for her daughter. Joan gazed at her husband with love and devotion in her bright eyes, and Roger clasped his father's hand, saying, "Well said sir!" Jacky wiped his eyes again at the mention of my father: "Such a good master!" he muttered to himself.

My father in my head, spoke quite clearly to me: "By the masskins, Tom, why have all here their arse in their hose? Tell them to cease their burbling and drink about."

I could not help but laugh at the force of his words (or his memory) and told them: "I know that my father does not wish for long mourning or for long faces. Let us drink to his memory and dwell on happy times. Master Adam, thank you for your wise summary and Mistress Catharine, I will seek out your daughter, if the ways are clear and you have still heard nothing in a month's time. At the end of February I will set out for Lichfield, come Hell or High Water."

"And if this weather sets in, we shall have both of those," said Matt, as the wind blew hard specks of snow against the window, and we cleared the board and drew nearer to the fire.

3

The snow which had imprisoned Catharine with us for twenty four hours, had melted enough by the following Monday, and Roger had ridden back with her on a day of rainbows sparkling from the steaming trees. She was not sorry to leave us but glad enough to have extracted my promise that in a month I would set off to find her daughter. After seeing her safe in Ledbury, Roger had ridden through the hills to his old home by the Severn and stayed there for one night with his elder brother and his new sister-in-law. On his return, his mother studiously avoided enquiring after their progress, but Roger drawing me into his barber's shop told me that Betsy had made a marvellous tasty rabbit pie: "as good as anything She can cook," he said disrespectfully of his mother. "Do you wish to return thither?" I asked with apprehension.

"God help me Tom! No, never by my faith as long as you grant me bed and board here. Mother is right in that. It is monstrous hard work in those leaden fields. But James has bred two healthy foals. If what you tell us is true about the sad slaughter of horses during battles, he and Simon are like to make their fortunes whilst the war lasts."

This was the first relatively innocent instance that I had heard of our bloody war putting money in a man's pocket. It was not to be the last.

When the weather improved and became humdrum, dull, sunless and totally without interest, Elijah decided to travel back to Stratford with the carrier, and retrieve the horse, Mercury, which I had bought him after Edgehill. Mercury had lodged with his uncle outside Stratford and had apparently gained a reputation, totally deserved, for biting his innocent equine fellows. Elijah returned, redfaced and somewhat out of patience with his wayward mount, the following day.

So it was in mid-February that I went to Ledbury with Elijah, to discover if there had been any news from Lichfield, but the Lloyds had not received a word from Eleanour and were much reduced in spirits. Poor Owen sat hunched in his chair looking pinched about the mouth, and said very little at first, except to ask how Phoebe did. When I asked for the address to which they had been sending letters and money, Catharine gave it as the sign of the Magpie in Boar Street: "or perhaps 'tis Bore Street," she added.

I asked for more information of Ralph's parents. Catharine's spirits rose somewhat as she could not forbear to boast yet again, telling us that they were well-bred and affluent and that Mistress Truscott's gown was a miracle of the seamstress' art.

Owen would have none of this. "This is all your frowardness!" he accused her bitterly. "I liked them not at all!"

"Why so, sir?" I asked him.

"You said nothing of that at the time, husband!" said Catharine peevishly.

"How could I, madam? You brooked no rivalry in gob politick, then as ever." Poor Catharine began to weep again and he softened, realising that at heart, she like him, was as sore perplexed in this haggling time. "Come, madam, this avails us naught!" he told her, gruffly reaching across for her hand. "No Tom I tell you, they tried to impress too much. They were all show, pewter dressed as silver, all huff and ding."

We left the next day. Catharine followed us into the yard and insisted that I took a purse of guineas. Her argument was that as I was an honest youth, I would be more likely to perform my quest conscientiously if I had been paid. I wanted to spurn her purse but before I could argue that a noble knight, righting a wrong does not act for a wage, she told us: "Make sure that Mistress Phoebe accompanies you. Eleanour may well have need of female support. I had rather be set in the stocks than that she should lose her reputation."

"But how then will the reputation of Lady Phoebe Stanhope survive, madam, if she must travel alongside two such lusty blades as us as far as Lichfield?"

She had not thought of that. "I am sure you and Mistress Joan will contrive accommodations to the credit and repute of all," she said doubtfully. "That purse will ensure good beds at the very least."

She looked so down in the dumps and desolate, in the muddy stable yard that my heart was touched.

"Dear Mistress Lloyd, I will bring back news of your daughter, though the Devil says me Nay!" As if in echo, Mercury neighed. "There, madam, a prophecy!" I shouted as we clattered off over the cobbles.

And so, on Friday the 24th of February, Phoebe, Elijah and myself set out from Worcester, like knights in an old tale to right wrongs. Joan had given us many instructions pleading with us not to sleep in damp beds and Adam suggested that the motto on my shield should be "Think first, fists second!" We would ride to Stratford in our first day, as Elijah was concerned for his mother. Joan had heard in the marketplace that the citizens of Stratford had had all their weapons confiscated by one Colonel Needham for Lord Brooke, who was now commanding the Midlands for Parliament.

It was a good day's ride of twenty five miles, and with my known dislike of ill using the horses, the dull afternoon was waning as we clattered down Wood Street. We turned into Henley Street where I had heard tell of a good inn. I bespoke clean rooms for Phoebe and myself, stabled the horses, and then we went with Elijah to his mother's home, a small cottage over the river by Clopton Bridge. As we walked over the bridge, we noticed that a group of soldiers, King's Men, I decided by the Sergeant's red sash, were completing their day's work on what seemed like fortifications on the far bank of the Avon. They told us that they were the Earl of Northampton's men.

Their sergeant rallied them, calling out: "Come on now, brave lads. We must to the Market to meet Colonel Croker. The Parliament dogs shall not take Stratford. God save the King." And with that they shouldered their spades, and set off over the bridge. But when they had got barely halfway, some young trooper cried out: "The pikes! We have forgot the pikes!" At this the harassed sergeant sent back some six men who rushed to two carts loaded with pikes and swords, and pushed them over the narrow bridge with great difficulty as there was no room for a man to walk beside the carts. This alarmed Elijah. "If my mother should be stranded in her home on this side Avon, away from friends and neighbours, it could go hard with her at time of war, alone and friendless."

However the case proved far otherwise. Elijah pushed open the door and cried out: "How now, Mother? Here's fine company for you!"

At first sight it seemed as though Elijah's mother was from home. But a pot hung from the hook over the fire, and the fragrant smell of beef braised in beer, filled the cottage. A flagon of wine, with two bowls, covered by a white napkin was standing ready on an oak coffer. This simple but wholesome repast evidently awaited the persons whom we could hear in the next room, in joyous concourse, for the gasps and shouts that came from that inner chamber could be no other than the sounds attendant upon those who are completing the act of generation to their mutual satisfaction. It was clear that they had not heard our arrival.

We stood for a moment, uncertain what to do. I was for going swiftly and returning at a more convenient time for Elijah's mother. But from his face, which had an expression of stunned disbelief, it was perhaps more loyal to remain and pretend naught was amiss, though I confess his last description of his mother: "alone and friendless" seemed somehow inappropriate.

The joyful noises subsided and the door opened. A large man, naked as a cuckoo at Christmas, came out, humming gently to himself, his organs of procreation hanging limp and redundant. When he saw Elijah, he stood stock still, his jaw dropped, and his eyes widened in dismay. Bereft of the powers of speech, he had at least the presence of mind to seize the linen napkin from the coffer and attempt to bind it about those parts of his person, which had so recently been actively employed. Sadly it was too small or he was too large.

"Is all prepared, Samuel?" called Mistress Bridges, Elijah's mother, from her bedchamber.

Elijah as if in a dream moved to the fire, picked up a skewer that lay in readiness and poked the braising beef. "Aye, Mother. 'Tis done to a turn," he called out.

There was a stunned silence, a scream and scuffling noises. Within thirty seconds, Mistress Bridges emerged, black of hair, bright of eye and buttoning of bodice. "'Lijah, son, who would have thought... and this must be Master Thomas... and his sister... well, God bless all here, say you not so, Parson Worthington?"

The naked man gulped, his whole being suffused with a fiery red hue, which must have had its origins in embarrassment, for after all, it was February.

"Good Parson Worthington came hither to.... to assist me to read your letters, 'Lijah." Mistress Bridges explained, "You know what a poor hand I am at lettering and figuring, and he was about to read a budget that came from you by the good carrier this very morn."

"Indeed, had he had the leisure to do so, madam, you would have been appraised of our arrival here today," I said, smiling like a brewer's horse. "If you will excuse us now, madam, Lady Stanhope and I will return to our hostelry and return for Elijah tomorrow betimes. Good day, madam and to you too, sir." I swept them a bow and Phoebe managed a curtsey. I stood aside to allow her to precede me from the cottage, and we uttered no word until we were over the bridge.

A sound came from Phoebe, something akin to a snort. Before we knew it, we were clinging to each other like deranged lunaticks. "His face!" Phoebe spluttered.

"Indeed, his face for one could not look elsewhere!" I replied which set us off again. The passers-by of Stratford must have thought us demented, as we tottered down Henley Street. Then the name of the inn, the Maidenhead, caused us further mirth, and it was with a poor grace that I gave the order for supper to be laid for us. I heard the hostess mutter that, "Worcester folk must be wamblety in their wits." It was a good meal much enjoyed by the two witless Worcester folk, our rooms were well appointed and we slept soundly, so soundly that when I awoke, pale sunshine such as follows rain was warming the room.

But when I came down to find Phoebe, that day took on the flavour of a bad dream remembered. Lord Brooke's purple men of Parliament were suddenly everywhere. As we were eating matchet rolls dipped in honey to break our fast, the room was suddenly full of troopers, eying our meal with envious desire. I would not say that they snatched or forced our food from our hands, but we felt that perhaps they had greater need of it and abandoned our meal as swiftly as we might. It seemed that there had been a battle in the grey rainy dawn under the Welcombe hills just to the North East of Stratford and Lord Brooke had chased the King's men out of Stratford. I wondered if this time they had remembered the pikes. The purple troopers were a detachment from Warwick, Lord Brooke's headquarters, sent to scour the town of the enemy.

"And who are you, sir?" their Captain asked me, as I stood.

Better to tell the truth. "We are bound for Lichfield, to see if a close friend is living or dead," I told him.

That was not enough. "I did not ask whither you were bound. I asked you who you were," he rattled back at me.

"I am merely a Doctor, not a fighting man," I told him, hoping I looked modest and unwarlike.

"This good youth has come to see me!" an imperious voice announced. We all turned to see a stately lady dressed in blue or purple sateen... I know not what for her gown changed colour with the grey light from the windows. Her white hair was fashionably dressed in a multitude of ringlets. "You must be the Doctor of whom I was informed. This way, Master Doctor." She disappeared into the street.

I beckoned to Phoebe to follow me. The Captain caught hold of my arm as if to detain me. "A word I pray you," he barked at me, but I hurried away.

"Did anyone know of my calling?" I whispered to Phoebe. "Nay, I have said nothing of it!" she told me wide-eyed with apprehension. The silkshot lady led us swiftly from Henley Street, down the High Street and to Chapel Street to a fine house which, the lady explained, was New Place, "left to me by my illustrious father."

"Now, sir. Here are my husband's notes. I pray you examine them at your leisure." She had led us to a magnificent reception chamber. There were rich hangings on the wall, one of which I noted was of Christ raising Jairus' daughter. On a handsome table, lay two volumes, which contained the "notes" of which she spoke.

"You must know, sir, that he treated the Earl of Northampton, aye, and Lady Tyrell. And on his death, he was termed "Medicus peritissimus", I may tell you."

She rattled on but I could not listen as I was delighted to have the opportunity to read the actual remedies of another doctor. I had scanned a few pages and was speaking to Phoebe, bidding her remember "Watercress, brooklime and yellow rocket," when there was a knock on the door. The Landlady from the Maidenhead scurried in, extremely frightened.

"Mistress Hall, Lord Brooke's surgeon is here. 'Tis Master James Cooke of Warwick."

She was followed by a very angry young man, who came straight to me, ignoring the gracious lady who had invited me there, stood in front of me and told me: "Sir, you are an imposter and a charlatan."

Adam's advice rang in my ears. I clenched my fists and asked him mildly: "How so, Sir?"

"You are not me!" he shouted.

"I confess it freely!" I said as gently as I could. "Who are you, good sir?"

"Who am I? I am James Cooke, Lord Brooke's surgeon of Warwick and the Castle, invited here by Dame Susannah Hall to view her husband's casebooks."

"What?" said the shotsilken lady, "But surely you are James Cooke!" she accused me.

"No madam. I am a surgeon, but of Worcester not Warwick," I told her, smiling in a manner, which I hoped was conciliatory. "You assumed I was this gentleman. Certain sure I am a doctor, but you did not ask my name."

There was a silence, during which everyone looked at each other and then at the ground. James Cooke then remembered his breeding and swept a bow to Mistress Hall. "Madam, forgive me." She inclined her head graciously and then another person bustled in, attended by the Captain who had spoken with me previously.

"Good day, dear madam. 'Pon my honour a slight misunderstanding." He was a portly gentleman, somewhat stouter round the waist than is convenient for brisk activity, but clad in a peach velvet doublet, and clearly a man of some substance. He came straight over to me and clasped my hands.

"Dear Doctor Cooke, we meet at last. I assure you I have long awaited this honour."

All was to do again. "Dear Sir," I told him "Alas, I am not Doctor Cooke. This is the gentleman you seek. I am a Doctor, but of Worcester."

He dropped my hands as if they were burning coals, and turned to Doctor Cooke. "My dear sir, how can I apologise? I am Richard Court, Apothecary of Stratford, and had the honour to be in the confidence of this dear lady's lamented spouse. To say he was a genius is to praise him too mildly."

The Captain became impatient. "I care not who is Cooke, Court or Country Clodhopper," he cried, "I have a man like to die who cannot catch his breath. In the name of God and Parliament, will one of you help?"

"Indeed I will, but for the love of God and good health" I told him, "Parliament can go hang if there is a sick man or woman to cure. After, will you allow us to travel on to Lichfield?"

"With a right good will," he cried, hurrying me out of the room "The young man in this case is my nephew. I might as well set myself in the pillory in Warwick, if I return thither with his corpse."

"Where is your invalid?" I demanded, following the Captain through the house.

"We laid him in the Market Hall, merely a step from here. He is my sister's only child - her one ewed lamb as folk say. I would not give a farthing for my life if he...."

Phoebe went with all haste to the Maidenhead for my case of medicaments, promising to meet us at the Market Hall. The Captain and I hurried down a narrow lane and of a sudden we were in the market square.

"Has he had attacks like this before?" I asked the Captain.

"As a child, yes. Again and again, through winter evenings. This is the first time since he has come to manhood."

We fairly ran into the Market Hall, which was packed with Brooke's purple troopers. The Captain roared for them to make way for him, and we followed him towards the back of the main hall, where his nephew lay on his back, gasping and floundering like a landed fish, surrounded by anxious but misguided comrades. His skin was already the blueish tinge which it assumes when breath cannot reach the lungs.

"Away from him!" I shouted. They were impeding recovery by crowding him. The air was thick with the fumes of tobacco. A bench and some barrels stood near. "Come, sir. Up with you! Sit you down here." I made him sit down and pushed one of the barrels beneath his elbows, bidding him to take his breathing easy.

He seemed faintly relieved to be upright but still found breathing out, a painful and tortuous process. I made him lean forward slightly, resting his arms on the barrel, his hands clasped before him. But light suddenly dawned for me. His breastplate caused his flesh to bulge unnaturally round his neck and waist and was constricting his lungs most grievously. "Let's get this fearsome thing off!" I cried out to his uncle and together we managed to remove it. As his chest expanded, freed from its needless torture, his colour straightway began to improve. His fellows pressed around eagerly and I swore at them again, using oaths I did not know I knew.

"Get these bastards away from him!" I shouted at the Captain. "Can't you see he needs air?"

In a moment the hall had cleared, except for a few old veterans, determinedly taking their ease, smoking, eating and drinking, near the stairs to the upper storey. A tall handsome man came bustling in, most impressively dressed for war, wearing a gleaming cuirass with vambraces over his purple coat. His helmet was of singular design with five struts protecting his face. All gave place before him. After a glance at the Captain, he encouraged them to leave the surgeon to his task.

"Tom!" a voice screamed. "Thomas! Whatever are you thinking? Get out! Get out, you fools!"

To my total amazement, it was Phoebe. She was standing at the door under the cloisters, clutching my chest of medicaments. When she saw she had my attention but that I was bemused by her behaviour, she rushed into the Hall towards me in her bundling way and shouted: "Gunpowder! Can't you see? Barrels of gunpowder and they are smoking!"

The Captain started and ordered the soldiers out immediately but even as I hauled his nephew to his feet, I saw that one of them was actually knocking out his clay-pipe, on the side of one of the barrels. He must have just lit it, as a shower of sparks fell to the floor near where there was white powder, clearly spilt from the barrel.

Phoebe screamed: "No!" and ran over and stamped on the sparks with her clumsy uneven shoes. By this the troopers were out in the market-place, and the tall Commander and the Captain were with them, clearing a passage for us and shouting warnings. Phoebe ran to me, thrust my chest at me and pushed our patient through the door by the small of his back, but I tripped over the threshold and measured my length half in, half out of the building. She screamed yet again: "Tom!" ran back, and pulled me over the low step out of the cloisters into the market-place.

A series of bangs like cannon-shot came from behind us, and the crackle of a fire. Then a terrible rumbling and crashing. The market hall even as we watched, collapsed in upon itself in an ugly heap of tiles, plaster and beams. A terrible dust fell, encompassing us so that we looked like nothing so much as the snowmen, children fashion in the winter when the world is white.

For some reason, our wan faces amused our invalid mightily. He was in like state but of course could not see himself. His half crazed laughter rang through the shocked silence. The citizens of Stratford who had gathered in the Square looked at the ruin of their fine town hall and groaned. The Commander who I gathered from Captain Cross was none other than Lord Brooke himself, spoke to them most cheerfully explaining they should not grieve for a building for his good men of Parliament had escaped death in the ruin by a hairsbreadth. Still I had the strong notion that the citizens set short store by the miraculous escape of his soldiers and would rather have had their fine new Market Hall as it had been barely five minutes ago.

"Why, Phoebe! What a virago you are become to be sure!" I told her teasingly.

"A virago? Nay, she is a heroine." And Lord Brooke was beside us again. He had that unusual capacity of being everywhere at once. "Madam, we owe you our lives."

But at that moment, a messenger brought news of a gathering of King's men somewhere in the fields towards Snitterfield and Lord Brooke was off again, calling to Captain Richard Cross to learn Phoebe's name and residence so that the Commander could thank her as behoved a great earl to a humble maiden.

"How did you know it was gunpowder in the barrels?" I asked. "It might have been salt fish."

"Those are budge barrels, used only for gunpowder," she told me loftily. "My father had to use it in his mine to blast out new tunnels. One must treat gunpowder with respect and care."

"So did you know they were there?" I asked her.

"Mistress Hiccox at the Maidenhead told me not to let the Parliament men steal them, as it seems they belonged to Colonel Wagstaffe, who has very recently embraced the King's cause. Anyway," she said with some satisfaction, "no-one can steal them now."

Word of our involvement in the destruction of the new Market Hall had flown like wild-fire through the town. Mistress Hiccox was not pleased at all with the news that the Market Hall was no more and as for Colonel Wagstaffe's carefully hoarded gunpowder, on that she was inconsolable. She informed me that Lord Brooke would hear of it. "Lord Brooke was there, Madam," I told her somewhat angrily, "and heartily glad that none came off worse than we did. He and Colonel Wagstaffe are at odds, madam, bitter odds. As for me I care naught for either of them, so long as I come out of this hocus-pocus with as clear a conscience as is possible. All my concern is with the sick. The gunpowder was most carelessly stored. Any Stratford urchin could have blown himself to kingdom come, it was so ill guarded."

I noticed that our saddle-bags were at the stair bottom, none too tidily packed. I went on, "I see you are all too ready to speed the parting guest, madam. Perhaps you feel that my money is tainted, and would prefer that we went our way immediately, as the loss of Colonel's Wagstaffe's gunpowder has grieved you so much that coin of the realm no longer has value for you. Come, Phoebe!"

But it seemed her sensibilities could accept that there was a debt to be paid. She did not offer water to clean our faces nor a brush for our clothes, but took three pounds for our bed and board, insisting on the full rate, even though our breakfast had been rudely interrupted. Then when we went to the stables, the boy tried to extract even more payment for the stabling from us. By this I was beside myself with rage and made as if to cuff him about the head, but Phoebe stayed my hand and gave him a shilling from her little purse.

I had to manage two horses across the bridge. Phoebe rode ahead on Cleopatra and I followed on Jupiter, leading Mercury, as wayward as ever. He respected no-one. He followed us over the bridge, on the leading rein, trying to bite Jupiter's tail and nether parts. As there were more of Brooke's soldiers waiting to cross, and the bridge was scarce wide enough for one mounted man, I felt that I must not change horses midstream, as it were, but grit my teeth until we gained the opposite bank. Mercifully Mercury began to bite the leading rein and we reached the other side without mishap.

More irritation and delay awaited us. An altercation had broken out outside Mistress Bridges' cottage. Elijah was arguing fiercely with a Quartermaster, very well accoutred with ribbons on his legs and a plume waving majestically above his pot helm. He was flanked by several other Parliament men. It seemed that they had all decided that Elijah was a likely recruit, borne to carry the pike for Lord Brooke.

"Tom! Thank Christ you are come. Tell this man that I cannot go with them. I am not a soldier, nor have no wish to be."

I dismounted and approached the quartermaster. "Certainly, he cannot. He is my journeyman. We are surgeons and we are bound for Lichfield."

"Lichfield?" The Quartermaster looked at a Corporal behind him. "Does Lord Brooke know of this?"

"Lord Brooke? Indeed he does. It is he who has bidden us thither. And I was asked to tell you that he awaits you now in the Marketplace. Did you not hear the mighty explosion? That is some develry of the King's Men and you are wanted instantly."

"And are you then, Master Cooke of Warwick?"

"Indeed I am, and expressly bidden by Lord Brooke to ride to Lichfield." The Quartermaster looked again at the Corporal who shrugged, and slowly mounted, bidding the rest do the same. Still gazing at me suspiciously, the two officers trotted towards the bridge, followed by the rest of their detachment, about ten or eleven men in all, in single file. As the last one came past me, he reined in and leant down to me.

"You are no more Master Cooke of Warwick, than my grandam!" He touched his nose knowingly, winked and followed the rest.

"Pray God he keeps his gob shut," said Elijah piously. His mother had reached home a few minutes before us. She had been buying lamb collops from a stall in the Market square and had seen our plight. With many sympathetic words, but much practicality, she brushed us down and put water on the fire so that we could wash. Phoebe longed to wash her hair but time was pressing and Mistress Bridges helped her comb out the plaster dust so that at last, the beautiful chestnut hue of nature prevailed. Elijah told me that my white hair gave me a gravitas and seniority that became my status, and which was otherwise lacking.

I knew not what to make of that and decided to press on as it was by now nearly noon. We bade Farewell to Elijah's mother and who should we meet on his way to Clopton as we trit-trotted across the bridge yet again but Parson Worthington. He called out a most civil greeting, blessing us and wishing us Godspeed and explained he was engaged to accompany Mistress Bridges to a prayer meeting. Elijah seethed and could not speak to him, thinking his mother seduced and deceived by the "wolf in black fustian," as he called him. I asked my companions to ride on and stopped to speak to the parson.

I dismounted and asked him politely whence he came. There was a flash of caution in his eye, and he began to untangle a knot in Jupiter's mane, but he replied civilly enough, "Something to the west of here, dear sir." And then, as if to change the subject, "Alas, I am not well liked by the citizens of Stratford. They seem to resent my preaching to them at the Market Cross."

"Then why cast your pearls before what must seem Stratford swine?"

He laughed inordinately, far in excess of the jest's deserving. "Sadly it is my calling, sir. Some few pence are donated by those who are of the Presbyter persuasion and that enables me to live.... and help the poor."

He might perhaps have been speaking of himself as one of the poor. His black gown was almost threadbare. He was a large man with abundant brown hair which hung loose over his shoulders.

"Mistress Bridges seems a most kindly and compassionate woman," I said, and he replied in an undertone for the first time in a manner which I could sense was sincere.

"Dearest beloved Patience. What would I do without her?"

"Well, Master Parson, I trust you will enjoy your prayer-meeting," I said, it must be admitted, with my tongue in my cheek. It seemed to me his specious piety was only skin deep. Was he a rascal, a vaillain? Certain sure, he was not what he seemed.

"God speed, Master Doctor," and I spurred on, both of us, no doubt relieved at our parting. I had an instinct, a feeling, an intuition, call it what you will, that he was playing a part. He was certainly not a convincing Puritan. Yet I was content that he meant no harm to Elijah's mother. I did not think he was a dishonest womaniser. Rather he seemed to be a man in love, who would fain marry had he the means.

We would have to strike northward from Stratford and I realised with joy that there would be a warm welcome for us at the Swan in Henley.

I told them with a hint of superiority: "There will be much rejoicing to see us there for I delivered the future landlord of that hostelry."

"What from?" asked Elijah.

"From his mother's womb, numbskull!" I retorted, my dignity again in tatters. But it was as I had predicted. I could hear my namesake protesting about something from the street. He must by now be four months old and it seemed he was hungry. So were we and the landlady's Mother, God Bless Her, sat us down and regaled us with blackcurrant wine, gingerbread and gossip. Young Thomas was brought down, rosy and half asleep, by Marian, who thrust him at her mother so that she might the better embrace me.

"But Master Thomas, your poor hair. Oh dear God! The Battle! It has turned your lovely black curls white overnight!"

Before I could reply her husband bustled in, hearing from the ostler we had arrived, and started back at the sight of me.

"Tom! God love us! You are married, clearly! White as snow with worry and expense already."

I finally managed to explain that the new Market Hall had exploded that very morn and had covered Phoebe and myself with plaster dust. To my amazement, they began to crow with laughter.

Marian seeing our blank faces explained, "We have heard nothing from the good people of Stratford but what a wondrous edifice their new hall is! Every merchant, every farmer, even the tradesmen come to find honest work in Henley, have had to tell us not once but many times what a wonder it is and how we in Henley are backward country cousins because we do not have such a fine new meeting place."

Elijah, a Stratford youth borne and bred, felt impelled to speak. "The old hall was a tumbledown pig-cote so perhaps they took an unnatural and tedious pride in the new one."

"But in any event," I pointed out, "it was monstrous careless of whoever was guardian of such a civic amenity, to allow gunpowder to be stored there without warning."

Walter and Marian seeing they had ruffled Elijah's feathers slightly were at pains to mollify him. Walter remembered his father, who it seems, had been a gifted carpenter, and asked kindly how his mother was thriving, and I asked if I could have hot water to wash my hair. They were immediately all concern as to our welfare, and as they bustled about to accommodate us, I had thrust upon my lap, a round eyed, redheaded personage who gazed at me with an expression somewhere between astonishment and disdain. We regarded each other in silence until Phoebe, telling me I did not know how to entertain a baby, seized him and began to play a bouncing game with him upon her knee, at which he seemed to smile.

Marian's mother excused herself to attend to the evening meal, and Nat, who could not forbear reminding me of the adventure with the apprentices from Morton Bagot, told us the best route to Lichfield. It seemed we did not need to travel much further west but could strike up to the north, skirting a fine house called Packwood and then up to Dorridge, Knowle and Hampton in Arden. When we came to Coleshill, we must ask for the Lichfield Road, which ran due north and was a good high road with wide views, east and west. In all he told us he thought that the distance from Henley to Lichfield was a little over twenty five miles. There were a few good inns in Coleshill should we wish to cover the ground in two days instead of one. I asked him how he knew so much about the roads around and he told us that before Walter had befriended him and employed him, he had been a drover, and knew most of the highways of the Midlands. Perhaps that was not all the truth as a knowing glance passed between the two men.

After an excellent meal of jugged hare and plum pie, while Walter thoughtfully smoked his pipe by the fire and Elijah went out to see that all was well with the horses, Nat asked me abruptly:

"Come then Master Tom! What is your memory of the battle?" So I told them all my tale and how I came to be, by default, the official surgeon of Bazil Lord Fielding's regiment at Kineton under Edgehill Ridge, and how a joint stool saved my life - the strangest of coincidences, since it was a treacherous joint stool that near caused my death a few months before my sixteenth birthday, three years before, when I attempted self-slaughter. But I did not tell them that - merely of my dealings with Brigstock. At some point in my narration Elijah retuned bringing a breath of cold February air into the warm comfortable parlour where we took our ease. I mentioned only in passing Brigstock's insinuation that he had known I had stayed here at the White Swan. Indeed the sound of young Thomas' healthy bawling when we clattered into the inn yard today had been the sweetest music to my ears.

"You have had more than your cross to bear," said Walter gravely. "It is dreadful and terrible to hear of your poor father, God rest him. Pray God that the rest of your life is easier."

Suddenly it seemed to me that I needed to shrug off somehow the tragedy of my life so far. I had always tended to take a ponderous view of things and yet I could make merry and be a man of as good wit as any gamester. I passed my cup for another generous potion of Her Mother's blackcurrant wine, and listened and laughed as Walter and his younger brother made mock of each other's skill at Nine Men's Morris.

We slept well and were up betimes. Marian's mother gave us cheese and bread as well as the White Swan's own cider in a flagon. I tried to pay Walter for our good cheer but he would have none of it.

"But for you, I would have lost both wife and son. Money will never pass between us, Thomas," he said, gripping my hand, "This is your home, whenever you need it."

I had dimly heard young Thomas voicing his desires in the night. "Alas, Walter, you have the sleepless edge of that bargain," I told him, and we parted as we had met this time, with merriment and good humour.

As we skirted the grounds of what must have been Packwood House, Elijah said thoughtfully: "May I ask a question of you, Tom?"

"Ask away," I told him.

"Truly I do not know how you made such a recovery. Your poor father hanged for naught and then the horrors that villain Brigstock forced upon you. What sustains you? Is it faith in God?"

"I must think long and hard before I can answer such a question," I told him. "But it heartens me that you think I am "recovered"."

"In truth" he went on, "when I heard what you had suffered at that farm, and then when we were there after the battle and you refused to allow me to go in with you, well, I should not have listened to you. I should have tethered Jupiter and followed you immediately. I have a good sharp knife in my pocket, see here. You had no weapon and yet like a fool, in you went, devil may care. And like a fool, I stood there until Simon Croker bid me follow him down the path. Truly if I am your journeyman I must share your ills and not be protected like a silly babe."

"Yes, Elijah," I said meekly. "You are right perhaps and I thank you, but I cannot chose but laugh when I remember that Simon

Croker caused me more harm than Brigstock... or at least his kitchen fender did. I had known somehow that I would have to encounter Brigstock again, and that there would be violence between us. I did not think it just to saddle an innocent like yourself with the horror that this man has caused."

He said simply, "Your ills and sorrows are for me to share now."

I thanked him and we journeyed on. We stayed that night in Coleshill and then struck North again for Lichfield. Nat was right about the road. It was high and well drained and afforded us wide views of the surrounding country.

Phoebe who was a very careful rider, whose eyes and thoughts were always on the road ahead, suddenly asked me a disturbing question.

"Tom, who was the gracious white haired lady who invited us into her house?"

I told her I had no notion and wished with all my heart we had never met her. We and the Captain's nephew might have been out of the new Town Hall well before its destruction though certain sure that would have happened, the Parliament men so wretchedly careless with their pipes.

"Tom, I think it was Shakespeare's daughter!"

I nearly fell off my horse. "What? How so?"

"Well, she spoke of her illustrious father and her house was called New Place, was it not? And I heard tell she married a doctor."

I was silent. Had I indeed been in the presence of the daughter of the man whom my father admired above all other Englishmen, whose words once heard, echoed in my head like angelic song from heaven? What a wasted opportunity! But she had seemed a worldly, practical woman, not "poetical" at all.

"I doubt it, Phoebe," I told her. "All her discourse was on her dead husband. Sure, Shakespeare's daughter would have spoken more memorably." And so we left it.

Lichfield we could see about an hour and a half before we reached it, the three spires of the cathedral pointing into the grey sky. As we got closer the town itself seemed dwarfed not simply by the Cathedral but by the great walls some worthy bishop had built to enclose it. We were directed to the George in Bird Street, which was a large fine comfortable house.

As Phoebe wished to spend some time mending a portion of her dress that had been ripped by a stirrup, and Elijah had found Mercury something of a handful to control and wished only to sleep, I left them to their own pursuits. I asked the landlady about the sign of the Magpie in Bore Street. She did not know it but directed me to Bore Street and I wandered out to see the sights.

I looked carefully at the dwellings in Bore Street but could not see the sign of any Magpie There was an area given over to market stalls before the Church of St Mary. Butter, eggs, cheese and cabbages - it seemed there was no shortage of victuals. I stood near a pedlar who was extolling his farings for ladies, wondering if Phoebe would like some pink ribbons, when suddenly a balladmonger, in a shabby black velvet doublet, tapped me on the elbow.

"Wondrous strange marvels, sir!" he told me. "Nostradamus is proved true yet again. A calf with two heads, a talking pig, aye and one that can count and a woman in Stafford delivered of four infants at the same birth."

I knew that Elijah greatly loved these news-sheets and ballads. "Oh, if it must be," I said with a bad grace and felt about in my breeches pocket for my purse. At that moment a slatternly woman, joined the balladmonger.

"There, I have sold all the diurnals, Ralph," she told him, "and one man cursed me that I did not have more for him to take to...." She ceased abruptly at the sight of me and her jaw dropped. "Oh Jesu, Thomas!" she said in consternation. It was Eleanour.

4

R alph Truscott, looking at me intently all the while, placed his bundle of news-books in Eleanour's arms.

"So you are the paragon, the nonpareil beside whom all other men slide into oblivion. Well, Eleanour, I must tell you that perhaps you have exaggerated your would-be lover's good points. Is he so very much my superior, dearest heart? Tall, certainly, but handsome? Debatable!" All this was said in something of an actor's voice, slow and careful, every syllable weighted and drawn out.

I laughed partly at his way of speaking but more so at the notion that I had displaced him in Eleanour's favour, since they had been married.

"Nay, sir 'tis I who am the sad bumpkin beside yourself. When I last saw Eleanour, she was intent on extolling your every virtue. I am sure she has married the better man. Can we agree on that and shake hands on it?"

"With a right good will!" he said clasping my arm. "Come wife, you have done excellent well today. Give Ralphie the money, like a good little sweetheart and let us see about refreshment for Cousin Fletcher."

Through all this Eleanour had said not a word. Now she said, in a somewhat wrangling tone: "What refreshment can we offer, husband? May I not keep this money to buy a quart of wine? We have naught at home, but crusts and dregs!"

"Oh, my dear, what will Cousin Tom think of our cheer? Can we not make holiday with him? He has come from Worcester, is it not? To resolve if you thrive, my dainty duck. If not, he will magic you back to Catherine, Kate of Kate Hall. Is not that the purpose of this most welcome visitation? "Crusts and dregs" indeed!"

He was shepherding us back to Bore Street, looking round always at the Lichfield citizens, most of whom seemed to know him.

At the vintners he stopped and searched his pocket, into which he had stuffed Eleanour's takings, only minutes before.

"Have you by chance four pence, Cousin Tom? That will buy us two pints of good claret. Alas I have but large coin and this man is a rare cozener and will not give back the remainder. He profits by me daily. He is a notable fellow and should be set i' the stocks for his ill-dealing."

I had four pence and then Ralph suggested that I went into the shop alone, as he feared that honest Master Froggatt, the vintner would keep him talking. He pointed to a yard across the street and told me: "Thither is the humble homestead where we lay our heads. We shall await you with empty cups and thirsty expectancy, Cousin Tom. Come wife." And he hurried her across the way.

"Was that the Magpie I saw dawdling at my door? Tell the varlet he'll get no more credit here until he pays his debts." The vintner was a somewhat sourfaced fellow, as broad as he was long with a very loud voice. It seemed as if he wished Ralph and indeed all the town to hear his displeasure.

"The Magpie?" I asked bemused.

"Aye, that's what he calls himself. He'll kick the wind before he's much older. What were you wanting?"

I asked for claret and he asked me to place my four pence on the counter before he drew the wine from the cask. When he saw my coins he grudgingly obliged me, and then asked for another penny for the battered wooden jug into which he poured the wine.

"Mind you, that is to be returned, well washed in pure Lichfield water," he told me sternly. "And let me tell you, you're in luck for the old'un up in the Cathedral Close sends for all my best vintages. He don't know about this new cask. As soon as he does, he'll swallow the lot."

"Is it a Bishop of whom you speak?" I asked humbly.

"A Bishop? No, not so Master Longshanks! 'Tis the Earl of Chesterfield, God rot him!" He came mincing round his wooden counter and presented me with the wine with a courtly bow. "I hope you did not think it is one of the common sort who holds Lichfield for the King, and feeds fat on our victuals? No 'tis Baron Stanhope, Earl of Chesterfield, and the sooner he takes himself back to Bretby, the better will us poor citizens thrive."

"I thank you, sir," I said courteously, and was about to follow

Ralph and Eleanour, when in a softer tone he asked me: "So what is your calling then? You are not one of that heathen tribe of ballad mongers and penmen, are you? "

"No, Sir. I am a doctor, bonesetter, surgeon, what you will," I told him.

"Are you so? But not of these parts, I think."

"Of Worcester, sir" and my catechism completed, he nodded me away.

Ralph and Eleanour laid their heads in a very sorry habitation. The yard, which he had indicated, seemed to be the place where farmers voided the vegetables they could not sell in the market, and there was a dismal stink of rotten cabbage. As I stooped through the low doorway, it seemed as if there had been some sort of hasty bustle on the part of Eleanour to make all tidy, but that task would have been Herculean. Heaps of clothes and papers lay about and a very handsome painted lady was curtseying to me, and a man, clearly Ralph's father by his appearance was inviting me to sit in one of the few chairs. A strange squeaking noise, like kittens seeking the mother cat, was coming from an inner room.

"Master Thomas, welcome! Welcome, indeed!" said Master Truscott. He made it sound as if he was conferring a knighthood on me. "I understand that you are connected to our dearest jewel, our pearl above price, our beloved Eleanour."

"Good day to you, sir," I said slowly. "Connected? Only in that we have known each other from childhood."

"Ah, yes, a blessed time. I see you now, gambolling like lambs in her dear father's orchards. Can you not envisage such a delightful scene, my love?" This to his wife, who sat in a bronze coloured satin gown, smiling at me graciously.

I suddenly remembered Eleanour viciously pulling my hair over a pet rabbit that I would not allow her to hold. I glanced in her direction. She was standing near the door whence the strange noises were issuing, her hands clasped before her and her eyes lowered.

Mistress Truscott was speaking: "I fear you catch us somewhat unprepared for noble company such as yourself, sir. But fear not. Our son promises that we shall shortly be transported to a dwelling of which we need not feel afeared for your visitation." She spoke English very slowly and carefully as if she had been unused to the language.

Ralph came abruptly from the inner room, speaking over his shoulder to an unseen presence in an unknown language. He swiftly reverted to English. "Yes we need more of the woman who gave birth to four. If Hans can print, sweet Eleanour can sell. Can you not, my flower? Cousin Tom, I beg to present my mother, Cornelia, and my father, Gabriel Truscott. Now, Tom what of the wine?"

I passed him the wine jug and in a moment or two we were sampling the excellent claret from battered pewter goblets. The vintner was right. It was indeed a supernaculum vintage. I noticed that Ralph and his father, after a toast to " Good Fellowship and Cousin Thomas", had emptied and refilled their glasses marvellously swiftly. After the day when Elijah had arrived in January, and I had made us both drunk as brewer's dogs, I have been careful with spirituous liquor, and sipped like a modest virgin, whilst Ralph and his father gulped like horses at a trough.

"So, Tom, what of the journey? Saw you aught of the King's loyal followers or of Parliament men, ready to defend their thoughts with blows?"

"Yes indeed, we did," I told him. "In fact we near escaped death when those same Parliament men under Lord Brooke, blew up the new town hall in Stratford with sparks from their pipes."

"What?" cried Ralph, forgetting to drawl. "In Stratford you say? When was this?" His father rose abruptly and called out to the person in the inner room: "News! News! Hans, smoking hot by God."

"But two days ago. I had been called in to the Hall to tend a man who could not breathe....." I stopped amazed, for from the inner room came forth a dwarf from the old tales, and yet 'twas not a dwarf, for he bowed graciously to me and when he straightened himself, I could see 'twas but a marvellous little man, stunted in growth perhaps. His face was a mass of wrinkles, like an old russet apple. I rose and bowed to him, and made as if to shake his hand but he laughed and showed me the palms, black and wet with some strange liquid.

"My father, sir," said Mistress Truscott, "and my Ralph's grand-sire, and that on his hands is the mark of his calling. 'Tis printers' ink."

Her father was smiling and nodding to me.

"God save you, sir," I said.

"Bless you, Cousin Tom, he cannot understand you. He speaks

only the tongue of the Low Countries. I have to learn from him and devilish hard work it too. Take a look."

He opened the inner door and beckoned me over. A most noisome stench came from the small room, which was obviously where Hans laid his head. A large machine with a great screw rising from its centre took up most of the room. I shook my head in bewilderment.

"It's a printing press!" cried Ralph with a hint of impatience in his voice. "It is our alpha and omega, our servant and our master, our provider and saviour that will make all our fortunes. Eleanour, be ready with your quill, dear heart. Now Tom, the explosion in Stratford if you please."

So I told them the circumstances and explained that Lord Brooke had proclaimed Phoebe a heroine for her quick thinking. Eleanour listened intently, writing the occasional word of my narrative on her tablet.

"But where is this heroine? Where is this Joan of Arc, this Boadiccea, this Maid Marian, the most swift thinking of all her sex?" cried Ralph's father. "Surely her firsthand tremors at the knowledge of the danger must be sought, my boy, to embellish this moving tale of rescue."

"She is resting at the George in Bird Street," I explained. "May I bring her to greet you? Perhaps later this evening after we have dined....?"

"If I may, dear husband," said Eleanour with a degree of firmness, "I would wish to accompany Tom back to the George, to pay my respects to Phoebe. When I met her before, I did not treat her as she deserves."

This was a new Eleanour indeed. Her white dress was stained with black, her finger nails were inky halfmoons and her pale hair was no longer curled in ringlets but drawn straight back from her brow and tied with a dirty ribbon. And yet she spoke confidently, no silly miss now but a young woman who knew her mind.

"May I come with you, my pretty maid?" said Ralph. "You say true, father. Her immediate memories of this terrible event must at once be recorded for posterity and, only think, the woman's touch. You are right, father. It must not be forgotten, nor forgone."

If Eleanour could be generous then, so could I. "I have a better notion," I told them, "Come you all to the George, and I will bespeak a good dinner this night for us. There is Elijah, my journey-man who likes nothing so much as news-books and chapbooks. 'Twill be as good as a play to him to meet you all."

The enthusiasm with which my proposal was greeted was prodigious. "Ah, blessed day!" Ralph's father clasped his hands and raised his eyes heavenwards. His mother rose and claspt me to her bosom. As I was sitting down, this was a somewhat suffocating experience, but when I emerged, Ralph and Hans were grinning from ear to ear.

"Come Tom," said Eleanour, briskly with a note of impatience, "At the very least I may set him on his way, dear husband? He has, no doubt of it, news of my parents."

After we had regained the street after promises for a merry meeting some few hours later, she said, "So tell me Tom, how does my mother and my poor father? He will be sore beset without me."

"Then why did you not send them news? Did you not get your mother's packets, with gold under the seal?" I asked her with something of irritation.

"Oh, aye, I got them. Even held the gold coin in my hand for a moment or two, before Ralph purloined it. Without money I had not the means to write."

"Eleanour!" I cried stopping short as we turned into the corner of St. John's Street. "Are you telling me that Ralph begrudges you the money to write word of your situation to your parents? This is tyranny, indeed."

And for a moment I saw myself as a latterday Sir Galahad, galloping back to Ledbury with Eleanour clinging to my waist, rescued from want and privation and endlessly grateful.

But she too had stopped, "Tyranny?" she laughed. "No indeed! I am integral in Ralph's great scheme, his - what does he call it? …magnum opus. It was my dowry bought the press and Hans from Amsterdam. We are saving every groat, every farthing to pay him back, so that he can return home and Ralph will then become a Master Printer, and we will be rich."

"So your mother's gold coins?" I asked her.

"Went into our coffer. I scarcely thought of it. Indeed, Tom, I have too much to do, am too needed by my husband and his dear parents."

This I could not stomach. "Madam," I hissed at her "What of

your own parents? Do they not deserve your news at the very least? I have had to travel fifty miles to ensure that you still lived, so that Owen and Kate could rest easy. You are their only child, God help them. Your poor father is not half the man he was and your mother had to mount up and ride to Worcester through bitter cold, to ask me to come all this way to find you."

"I had not thought they would be so anxious," she said, shame-faced. "I am sorry Tom."

"You are sorry. What would I not give for my own parents, living and breathing and caring for me?" But at that my father in my head, spoke to me softly as was his wont. "Now son, too strong, too strong by half. The poor maid did not deserve that."

"Oh come, Ellie, I am sorry," I told her, using the old childhood name. "I should not have spoken so. Forgive me. All can be set to rights at once this afternoon."

We had reached the George, with its handsome sign of the Saint, one foot on the Dragon's neck. I sent a passing maidservant to fetch Phoebe and told the girl to tell her to bring down paper and quill. We seated ourselves and I asked if the landlady had some elder-flower wine or some cordial such as women drink. She produced a flagon of perry, and three goblets. And at that moment Phoebe came down the inn staircase as slowly and stately as a little queen.

"Mistress Eleanour," she said, "I am rejoiced to see you well." No word then or ever of the unpleasant behaviour of Eleanour to her in Ledbury, a scant five months before. It seemed as if the insult "hobgoblin" had never been spoken. Eleanour arose and came round to her, seized her two hands and held them to her lips. She said but two words "Forgive me," which Phoebe said she did with a right good will.

Within half an hour, a goodly letter was written to the Lloyds, entreating their forgiveness and explaining something of her husband's plans. I asked her to tell Catharine that Elijah and I would be swiftly following the letter, as all was clearly well with Eleanour. She did not request more money, but gave a clear account of her Ralph's great scheme. The missive, which was long, was signed and sealed and given to the landlady to entrust to the next carrier, who travelled south.

"For people need news," Eleanour told us with a gravitas un-known before when she had been but a green girl. "When we are printing a new Corranto, men - and women too - will stand in line to buy." I found this hard to believe but Elijah who had joined us, told us that in Stratford he had bought from a pedlar, a news-sheet telling of ghosts seen after Edgehill. The pedlar had sold all his news-sheets in minutes. I bit back my retort that if Eleanour was so anxious to provide news for strangers, why had she had no thought for her poor parents, starved of tidings of their daughter.

It was now about four in the afternoon and Eleanour rose to depart. "I trust you will not take it amiss, dear Phoebe," she said humbly. "If Ralph and I question you about your bravery in Stratford, so that your heroism can be immortalised in print."

And she left us, outwardly a different young woman from the simpering impertinent miss, we had encountered in Ledbury. She was certainly better skilled in the art of pleasing people. Whether her reformation came from herheart, it was impossible to say.

I enquired of the landlady if she could provide a handsome meal for eight that even. Somewhat grudgingly she asked for proof of payment, but when I showed her my purse she became all smiling courtesy and explained her problem.

"The old bastard up in the Close is eating us out of hearth and home. We're thin as willow wands, master, since he and his damned King's devils took the Close and they pay with promises. Now I ask you, sir, how will the goodwives in the market selling fowls and lambs, how will they like to be paid with promises? For that is all I have from the old bastard and his so-called paymaster. But rest easy, good young sir, you shall have roast leg of lamb with carrots fit for a king this day even. Eight of you, you say, sir? And Betsy shall make you her baked apples, the pride of Staffordshire, though 'tis her mother that boasts indeed."

I broke in to say that would be excellent fare for us and she promised all would be done in about three hours. I went quickly to Bore Street to tell them to come to the George, when they wished, and surprised Ralph and Eleanour at the pump among the rotting vegetables, washing and shivering like two half dressed trout. She was attempting to clean his arms and hands, and even his back of the ink that stained his person. I called to them to come when they wished, for Phoebe was ready to tell them her tale.

And so we dined excellent well, late in the day 'tis true, but the Landlady, by name Mistress Emily Hill and her daughter seemed to think nothing of their labours for I had prudently paid beforehand with the guineas from my store. As they cleared away our platters I made bold to ask the landlady how long "the old bastard" had disported himself in the Close.

"Just before New Year he came with some of the King's men hereabouts. They kept open house at first. But now, their womenfolk and little ones as well, all sleeping on floors in the bishop's palace, and living hand to mouth as if they cannot walk freely about, like Christians. Who constrains them, I ask you? 'Tis madness I tell you! That old bastard has more hair than wit, and not much of that either! 'Tis said he was no stranger to the dock at the Assizes in his youth!"

Ralph and Eleanour now began to question Phoebe on her experience in Stratford. I noticed that Eleanour was as sharp as Ralph in her ability to ask what was to the point. She it was who made Phoebe explain why she recognised the barrels, as containing gunpowder.

"Remember, husband, we saw such "budge barrels"…call you them? In the Cathedral, but last week. We went thither to sell news of the King and his court at Oxford."

I could not forbear but to mention modestly that I had visited that same court in December, and had made my bow to the king with no less a person that Lucius Carey, whom the King had appointed his Secretary of State.

"Tom, dear cousin Tom, you are a veritable goldmine!" cried Ralph. "You must tell all of this, if you please, and to us, your dear kinsmen, not to any other long-eared, prick-brained cozener."

So I told them of Lucius' plight, how he seemed torn in two by his loyalty to the King and his awareness that the King did not, nay, could not rule well, because though pleasant and kindly to his friends, he could not accept any challenge or slur on his Divinity as King. I remembered Lucius' words of despair: "Surely the terrible death of Verney and other loyal subjects at Edgehill must show him that God is impervious to his claim. God supports whichever army is better at killing."

I had become moved myself remembering poor Lucius' dilemma. What a good friend he was to all he met and so divided in his soul. Ralph gazed at me intently.

"No, Tom! That we cannot print! Your friend is in the right of it but you must know that both King and Parliament have God in their vanguard. I must be careful not to invoke the Almighty. Both sides would have me in the pillory, if I so much as questioned Jehovah's loyalty. But something of the world of Christchurch, now that you could supply, and we could print. What furnishings, what food, what wine, what did the King wear, what does Prince Charles to wile away his leisure time? That is what will sell our wares without recourse to violent reprisals."

I promised I would remember what I could, and he turned to Phoebe. "And Phoebe, Mistress Phoebe, in Stratford was there no bloodshed, no wounds, no terrible imprecations of the townsfolk at the loss of their fine new building?"

"There was no bloodshed, Sir. Indeed there may well have been complaints, but we did not stay to hear them. Rather we were hustled from our lodgings without benefit of assistance. We were both covered in plaster dust and had Elijah's mother not helped us, we would even now appear like these same ghosts at Edgehill, about which Elijah has read so much."

The conversation turned to those phenomena that cannot be explained by natural laws. Cornelia, Ralph's lady mother, told us that she had heard from her gossips in the market that the ghostly figure of St. Chad himself, had been seen walking into a house of ill repute in Lichfield on more than one occasion. "No doubt to chide and bring destruction on those sinful hussies!" she explained. "How they can still display their bosoms without shame I know not."

This set us all heartily laughing, though Elijah, eyes wide, pleaded, "No more o' ghosts, if you please. Such tales bring on me shudders and goosepox."

"The blessed saint was perhaps celebrating his birthday, somewhat prematurely," said Ralph "A pious lady told me this very afternoon that it is but two days off. On Thursday next."

"But certain sure it is," Cornelia insisted, "and I have heard it sworn as truth that one Edward Wightman walks in the market place, all on fire, near our lodging."

The Landlady had just come in to see if we wished for further refreshment. "Oh aye, masters and mistresses," she broke in, on hearing the last pronouncement. "Poor twice burned Wightman. And him mad as Jack Adam's tomcat as we say round here. Or if not mad, too wayward and braggart to hold his tongue."

"Twice burned, you say, Mistress Hill?" I asked her.

"Aye, indeed, for the first time they set him on the faggots, as they burned up, he cried out he would recant and many of the good citizens of this city rushed forward and pulled burning branches away from him, getting themselves sorely scorched as they did so. But all was to do again for he would go on, proclaiming himself the son of God and all such moonshine. So again he was for the faggots and this time, scream as he might, there was no reprieve".

This terrible tale cast something of a blight on our merriment. "And do you know who was that same Bishop's Chaplain here in Lichfield thirty years ago? This same William Laud, the Archbishop, who even now infects the King with his poisonous slanders. He, it was, decided poor Wightman must be burned for his heresies. My poor husband saw it all, a child of seven he was, and his father and grandsire had blistered palms for many days."

I rose quickly and closed the door of the parlour where we sat. Eleanour, eyes wide, laid her finger on her lips in warning. Master Gabriel said quietly: "Have a care, mistress. You may trust all here but who knows where eavesdroppers might lurk."

I had scarcely sat down again when there came a sudden thunderous knocking on the street door. "Oh Jesu," cried our hostess, "Think you some sneaking varlet heard me speak ill of Laud?"

"They would be spring-heeled Mercury to get the Watch so swiftly," said Ralph. "Here mistress, sit down with us. My father will deal with whoever knocks."

And Master Gabriel had risen, looked around at the company and declaimed "Tis not for naught that I played the comic interest so often in the Scottish play," and going into the hallway called out majestically: "Who knocks?"

A voice that I had heard before that day, called out "Froggatt, with the Earl's men. Is Longshanks there?"

Gabriel flung open the door and the vintner came bustling into our parlour, flanked by two troopers. I had just time to note that they were armed, much like Robert's men, helmets, breastplates, and with the long wheelock pistols. They came in as if they were indeed rooting out a nest of traitors, and the hostess and Cornelia shrieked. Their sudden appearance out of the night into the decorous atmosphere of the parlour was, no doubt of it, somewhat alarming.

"That's him!" cried Froggatt, pointing at me.

I know not how I kept my head. Truth to tell I was sore afraid, but I was also angry and the anger was what I vowed they should encounter.

"What is this?" I asked. "Why this rude interruption?"

The older of the two soldiers stept forward.

"Might you be a doctor, Sir?" he snapped at me.

"What if I am?" I snapped back.

"Then you are to come at once with us to doctor the Earl."

I looked at Froggatt who looked excessive craven and guilty.

"I had orders to take that barrel what you know of, up to the Close. The Earl said he would not pay me for that and other vintages I've supplied unless I could find him a leech. He's in vile pain, no doubt of it."

"But what is that to me?" I asked them. "Why should I break up this meeting for an Earl I do not know, and if he has the manners of his minions, one that I can assure you, I would not care to know."

They seemed surprised by my answer. "He is an Earl, sir," said the younger soldier.

"Is he so? Then until he and his servants learn courtesy he must remain for ever untreated.... by me."

I could feel that my guests were being made uneasy by my response. Elijah came and stood beside me, but I had the notion that if Ralph could have done so he would have gladly slipped below the table's edge.

"Ah, well now," said the younger trooper, looking something askance at his companion "He's used to folk jumping when he cries "Jump". 'Tis what he is used to, sir."

"What law has been passed that enjoins one man to do another man's bidding, at his command, be he belted earl, or loud-mouthed churl?"

I felt proud of my response. The two soldiers looked at each other in dismay and Froggatt groaned. Gabriel who was something of an equivocator came round the table and spoke softly to me. "Dear Tom, whom I love as if you were my own child though of precious short acquaintance, 'tis the law of expediency, sweet youth! Troubled times, my boy, troubled times!"

And to the soldiers, he asked: "What ails the Earl?"

The younger who seemed to be the self-elected spokesman: "'Tis the gout, Sir. Wracks him something cruel. The man who doctors the Lichfield folk is from home, good sirs, else we should not now break up this merry meeting."

I turned my back on them. "I and my assistant who knows a good cure for his malady will be with him and you in the Close tomorrow betimes. Fare you well."

In faith I was mortal tired. Phoebe looked somewhat worn and I had noticed that Elijah's eyes had closed, involuntarily over his baked apple. It seemed an age before that we had set out from Coleshill that very morning. The three interlopers had to be content with my promise. They departed, the landlady ensuring that she would direct me to the Close in the morning early.

Hans anxiously now held out a great key, clearly the key of their lodging. "My grandsire fears for his press." Ralph explained. "Until we have paid for it, he is sore frightened of knaves and caitiffs. As far as is known Lichfield is free of rufflers and robbers but we had best be gone."

The guests rose to go with many words of thanks and gratitude. The landlady locked the door securely after them and pronounced me a rare good fellow, who could be trusted to treat the Earl's demands as they should be treated when he came ordering honest folk to do his bidding will they, nill they. I thanked her for her excellent roast lamb and so we picked up our candles and went to our beds, well fed and contented and with scarce a thought to spare for imperious earls, belted or not.

When I came down to break my fast, Phoebe had preceded me by some hours. She had been in the fields near Stowe Church she told me and had found multitudes of comfrey, and had with her little trowel dug up several roots - enough to make compresses for the Earl. She had with Emily's assistance, shredded some roots into boiling water and the resulting unguent would, she was sure, relieve the pain but not the condition: "For you and I know, do we not, dear Tom, that claret and other red vintages, are as poison to a man with the gout. I will make him an infusion of apple and chamomile which he must drink instead of those dangerous tinctures."

"Yes, Phoebe," I said humbly, with a trace of sympathy for the Earl. The wine in question was very good indeed. Elijah at this moment wandered yawning into the parlour where we sat and I told them both that as our mission was accomplished, that as Eleanour was clearly happy and fulfilled with a valued place in the Truscott household, we could begin our return journey to Worcester that very afternoon. Elijah's face fell.

"Tom, can I not see how the news-books are made? I would dearly love to learn how one man can reach so many by printing the words that come into his head. His own words, i' good faith, not Bible words."

And I was bound to confess that I too would like to know something more of the mystery of Ralph and his family. His father must surely have been on the stage. There was something familiar about the way he carried himself, and his voice, I felt instinctively, I had heard before. In any event we must bid them Farewell. So I agreed that after noon we would visit the Magpie again and take to our horses early tomorrow morn.

And so, leaving Elijah to make holiday wandering through the town of Lichfield, we set out to walk the short distance, into Bridge Street and thence over the bridge which was not so much a bridge as a causeway dividing two bodies of water, the Bishop's Pool and the Minster Pool. The sentries at the South-West Gate, guarding the portcullis and drawbridge, after a cursory glance at what we carried, and hearing who we were, waved us into the Close with little ceremony.

The high stone walls enclosed the Cathedral in the centre and sheltering under the walls themselves, there were fine old houses, and a soldier coming from the Cathedral, directed us to "the Palace", in the North-East corner. We walked carefully round the great edifice, marvelling at the richness of the stonework, and at the multitude of statues which decorated the West Front. The Palace when we reached it seemed to have been taken over entirely by the military. We could see no sign of churchmen. I commented on this to Phoebe, who replied somewhat caustically: "They are following Demosthenes."

"Why, Phoebe," I told her "How learned you are! What said Demosthenes?"

She recited: "He who fights and runs away. Lives to fight another day." Substitute 'praying' for 'fighting', Tom, and all is explained."

Sentries at the door on learning who we were, commented wryly that they wished us well, but to be sure to duck swiftly if any utensil was hurled in our direction. "Fear not," one said, in friendly manner. "His aim gets monstrous poor." And as we entered the great hall, we were soon aware of the cause of their cautious words. Several servants were gathered round a man seated before a great fire. A small table was at his side on which was the remains of a meal. He was arguing loudly with one who stood with a white napkin over his arm.

"And I tell you, numbskill, that the bread is stale. 'Tis yesterday's baking. How can I defend the liberty of you all without fresh bread? Uh? Tell me that, you Jack Sauce? The devil knows I have paid and paid for all your comforts and you fob me off with a stale roll. Uh? Go ask this Master of the Rolls if he will vouchsafe us the pleasure of his company and furnish us with an explanation as to what means this abomination of the baker's art!"

We had to walk forward the length of the hall, whilst the Earl continued raging against the unfortunate steward. As we came nearer he turned, looked at me, and shouted out: "And who the devil are you?"

One of the soldiers who had visited us last night stepped forward: "'Tis the leech from the town, my lord, come to cure your affliction."

"I hope so indeed," the Earl snapped, "or I would not give much for his future success in his profession! Uh? I'll make him drink his own potions, by the Rood!"

And then a voice came from beside me, loud, imperious, used to command, that same clear voice that emptied the Market Hall in Stratford, issuing from the same small person.

"Oh, come now Great Uncle Philip. You know you do not mean a word of what you threaten."

It was Phoebe who had spoken, Phoebe who now walked forward to confront the Earl with all the grace, all the confidence, and all the poise of a nobly borne Lady, smiling as graciously and as joyously, as a Saint at the door of Paradise.

5

The Earl slowly stood up and then grasped the arm of his steward, not taking his eyes from Phoebe's smiling countenance.

"And who the devil.... who are you? Is it Lewis' girl?" He peered at her, his eyes keen under great reddish eyebrows. "But you.... they told me you are dead."

"It is Lewis' girl and I am far from dead. I am come to cure you with my good master Thomas Fletcher. Come now, sit down again and let us relieve your pain."

"Little clever Phoebe! Little misshapen Phoebe!" He sat down heavily and to my amazement could not hold back his tears. Phoebe stood beside him cradling his large hairy hand in her two small ones and holding it to her cheek. "But Gell swore to me that you had perished..... and Isabel with you." With his free hand he snatched the napkin from his steward and wiped his red face. Then noticing that Phoebe too was weeping for joy at their reunion, he tenderly wiped her tears away, and kissed her white brow.

"My great niece!" he shouted at his servants, still with his hand on her shoulder. "As clever a little piece of Evesflesh as any of you will meet in your misbegotten lives!" His servants were all grinning broadly and came forward to congratulate him. It seemed the Earl's bark was all sound and fury, and his bite nothing.

As we doctored him, he asked of Phoebe's story and she answered. When she told him of the treacherous servant who had robbed them in Tamworth, he shouted out, "That was Gell's doing by the Rood! There is not a man here he has not approached with promises of gold. Am I not right, my true Derby rams?" and there was a chorus of agreement. When she told him of her rescue from the evil youths who had stoned her in the village near Malvern, he grasped my hand and thanked God for me.

While I anointed his toes with our comfrey root ointment, he continued to tell his henchmen of Phoebe's prowess as a child. How Greek and Latin were to her as easy as her native English, how she was assisting her father with his accounts before her tenth birthday, and how her mother had declared there lived not her equal when she was needed to assist in the still-room. "And Isabel dead in such sadness! Well, she was always sickly! But you my maid. Warm and living! But have you grown apace? You were a little Jill-o'Lent before. This Doctor you call Master is a miracle worker!"

I could not take the credit for Isaac Nunez' intelligent contrivance and told the Earl how he had ordered a special built up shoe for Phoebe in Worcester, and how it brought her height up to that of a small but regular woman when she wore it.

"Blessings on you! And on this Spanish conjuror you tell me of. So what now, Phoebe? You had better ride to your Great Aunt at Bretby. But perhaps not now for I've heard that whoreson renegade Brooke is up to mischief. But back to Bretby you shall...."

Suddenly he ceased his oration. "By the Rood, 'tis gone!" he roared.

Phoebe and I looked at each other, wondering what was to follow. Had he lost some coin, some jewel? "The pain, the pain!" he shouted. "Gone! Gone! God bless you, niece and you, good sir. Sit you both down now and let us drink to your future prosperity, Master Doctor. Uh? And to she who was lost and is found!"

"Now, dear Uncle, I have a word to say to you about that," said Phoebe firmly and she explained that the very liquor that he had felt confident numbed his pain, was in fact a deadly potion for him and would enflame the delicate tissues of his feet. I nodded gravely and observed the "delicate" yellowing, large, somewhat noisome feet in question. He must from now on drink wine only sparingly if he wished to be free of his ague, Phoebe told him firmly.

"But you can doctor me as needed, now that you are.... reincarnated. Uh? Is it not so?"

"Alas, dear uncle, I must return to Worcester with Tom. I have agreed to help him in his practice and those same still-room skills you speak of, believe me, have been well recompensed. Next year, when there is peace I will come and visit you, I promise."

"Peace, you say? I doubt it, wench. This Parliament faction are all either long faced Presbyters who hate good living, or men who use every instance to make money. That hell-hound Gell is one such. But a scant two years ago there was no more worrying a terrier, snapping after Ship Money for the King, than Royal tax gatherer, Gell. Now the bastard has turned his coat and harries us for Parliament. I, and Ferdinand had to leave Bretby for our lives. My Lady stayed but now as I hear has barely the clothes she stood up in. He should be hanged by the heels for this outrage from Chesterfield spire, for that's as crooked as he is, God rot him!"

"I have no love for him, that is certain sure, Uncle," said Phoebe slowly. "He killed my father or at the least stole his wish to live. But sir, my travails have taught me never to repine. I look forward now, with joy to every day on which my eyes open. And Tom must go now, Uncle Philip, for he has come hither to Lichfield to find the lost daughter of friends and although we have found her, I know he wishes to learn more of her husband's calling, so that he can describe to her parents how they earn their bread."

She gasped for breath and indeed for Phoebe this was a long speech.

"But you can stay with your uncle, today, Phoebe," I told her, "I will come for you later. We have found not only Eleanour but also a most illustrious member of your family." And I bowed, humbly reflecting on my churlish refusal to come to the Earl last night.

I left them then, as they remembered old times when the Earl had been a constant visitor to Lewis Stanhope's small manor house, near Wirksworth. When I reached the Magpie's nest, I was invited to join Elijah who was watching old Hans and Ralph engaged in composing a page of print.

"Look, Tom, what Ralph has to do here. He must select these letters by their shanks, but then follows a near impossible task. He must read every word backwards for the letter moulds, when they press upon the paper, would read nonsense if the printer did not place them backwards. He must think topsy-turvy, Tom, and Ralph has to understand Hans' instructions in Dutch. Believe me his task is monstrous difficult. It is the world turned upside down!"

Ralph stood modestly by during this paeon of praise. In truth, I was in no doubt as to his cleverness. He showed me how the great screw was turned so that it would press on the paper that had been inserted between the screw's weight and the letters, placed backward in their platens or grooves made in the shape of a line.

"But even more difficult is the measurement of the ink into the hollows of the letters." he told me. "Too much or too little, all is labour and time lost."

Hans here said something in his own tongue, which ended with a chuckle. I looked questioningly at Ralph who told me that his grandfather often reminded him how fortunate it was he was well grown as, if they had been printing in the Low Countries, an apprentice was commonly whipped for any mistake. For a moment I thought of my own apprenticeship with Ben who never whipped me but who had such a store of good old English invective and abuse, that I felt when he scolded me as if I had been whipped indeed.

"So come then Ralph," I asked him, "what is your story? What trade did you and your father follow before you married Eleanour?"

He laughed: "I followed my father into his calling. Tom, do you perchance have a few pence about you that I could borrow? I want to drink your health and Elijah's too in an alehouse hard by. My father is already there. I think."

The alehouse though crowded, seemed a friendly place, welcoming all comers. Gabriel was ensconced near the window, telling some tale to his cronies gathered there but broke off to welcome us to his circle.

"My dear boy, and Tom and young Elijah borne hither by a fiery chariot, I make no doubt." (Elijah grudgingly smiled the tired but polite grin he had to give at this tedious jest.) Gabriel continued: "Can we drink about, son?"

I asked the serving wench for ale and Gabriel continued his story. "So, my friends. Ancient Rome. There am I about to render Mark Antony's most famous speech, when the audience fell a-laughing. The stage hands had forgotten to wrap the supposed coffin of Caesar... Caesar I should remind you, played by none other than my excellent good friend John Lowin, and to his horror and mine also, his supposed coffin as I say, unwrapped and the bare wood visible, made from an old inn sign and alas! the legend, "Pig and Whistle" clear for all to see! How the penny stinkards roared! Then if you please, adding insult to injury, a whoreson stagehand in his dirty jerkin and soiled hose enters in amongst our snow white togas and tries to wrap the coffin in the purple cover. This is enough for John who rises from the coffin like Lazarus from the dead, saying to me. "By your leave, Mark Antony, Bury me some other time when my hearse is suitably prepared," and he stalks off to the howls of the groundlings."

"What did you do?" I asked.

"What one ever does, dear Tom. I carried on. The play must go on. ...And we made a tolerable attempt, I think to carry it forward. Although when poor John appeared as Caesar's ghost at Phillipi, some low fellow shouted "What price a cup of Canaries in the old Pig, Caesar?"

"Prospero!" suddenly I shouted. "You are Prospero!"

Gabriel looked at once both modest and proud. "Well! Yes, dear lad I have undertaken it many times. May I enquire at which hostelry we had the honour to entertain you?"

"The old Talbot in Worcester!" I told him. "But you were magnificent! My father was in tears when you forgave everybody. And Miranda, so pretty and enticing."

Ralph rose and bowed with a rather shamefaced expression, stroking his black moustache.

"Behold, Miranda!" said Gabriel with pride. "But in truth, Thomas this was some years ago, eleven, or twelve perhaps. When my poor boy's vocal chords grew heavy, we could no longer dress him in petticoats."

"And thank the Lord for that" put in Ralph. "And so, Tom I grew into Romeo but Hamlet I could never master. My fate was always to be Horatio and never the Prince of Denmark. But Father's Claudius was praised by the King himself."

"Did you act for the King?" I asked them much impressed.

"Act for him? Indeed we did. We were his Men, our expenses undertaken by him at Blackfriars for many years, and the sweet Queen was patron of her Men at the Cockpit. T'was not a fortune in remuneration, but 'twas enough, dear Tom. But can you believe this, Tom and Elijah and my good friends of this noble city of Lichfield, on the 6th of September last, Parliament men, a group of backbiting, sermonising, hammer-headed caitiffs, came into the Blackfriars, climbed up on the stage, if you please and I in the middle of my Tamburlaine, and announced that they had arrived to close the theatre. They claimed that they acted for Parliament and the King, saying that he had been much deceived by evil counsel. The churls announced this on the stage, my stage! Can you begin to imagine my distress!"

"So, what did you do?" I asked, again mouth agape no doubt.

"Why dear Tom, I gathered my wits and leapt as it were to the end. "Farewell, my boys, my dearest friends, farewell!" says I wringing the cursed soldiers' horny hands each in turn, much to their consternation. "My body feels, my soul doth weep to see / Your sweet desires deprived my Company," and here you know I sank to the ground, most affecting, was it not, son Ralph? "For Tamburlaine, the scourge of God must die." And so I died, while they stood, like so many claybrained clodpolls, whilst the audience whistled and hooted. At the very least the Laurels of Victory were wrested from their grasp and adorned my brow.... In short, I upstaged the churls!.... But no matter," he concluded, his features truly sad and regretful "Blackfriars was closed for all that."

"So what then?" I asked.

"What then? We thought that if we travelled North, Ralph and myself might make a modest living from performing extracts. So we travelled hither to Lichfield with my most gracious dear good lady wife, thinking perhaps that we might again encounter the King. But 'twas not to be. And I alas, cozened of my calling by these Parliament base Trojans. But then my dear boy, my Ralph, my scion from the tree of Truscott reminds me of my family in Gloucestershire. I have a cousin on my mother's side in whose acquaintance you rejoice, in that most salubrious town of Ledbury. Perhaps we deceived, somewhat, I know not. But my boy and their daughter. "No sooner looked but they loved: No sooner loved but they sighed... They are in the very Wrath of love," and none could part them now dear Tom. We went thither and when sweet Eleanour looked favourably upon my boy, and he was dazzled by her beauty and her attributes, we could see a way forward. He had seen how the populace craved the News, were mad you might say for News. As soon as we had arrived back in Lichfield, my sweet lady wife travelled to Hull and took ship for Amsterdam. Miracle of miracles! Her dear father still lived, earning his bread, printing the news. And so my dearest love returned to Hull, with her father, and with many of the smaller precious parts of a printing press. Between us Ralph and I contrived the grosser parts and now we eke a living as corrantoes, penmen, printers what you will. People want News, we supply it! We write, we print, we sell."

"But if you had told Owen of your plans," I told him, "He might well have supported you. You were not open with him."

"We did not know that we could have counted on his support and indeed, that is just conjecture on your part, Tom. Our scheme had not taken wings as now it has. Would he have given his daughter and her dowry to mere travelling players?"

"And consider Tom," he went on, "as actors we were "The brief chronicles of the time" but brief in truth. Paper endures longer than air, than spoken words. Parliament closed the theatres, but both sides need news, the written word carries all before it. See here."

He gave me a news-book. It ran: "Lamentable Newes from Stratford...... being the true Copie of an account from a learned doctor, of the dismal carnage and tragic outcome, of the firing of the New Town Hall in Stratford and the heroic actions of an unknown ladie, in warning the citizens of their peril, when Brooke's Purple Pulpit Bangers set the building alight....."

I did not read further. "But Ralph," I told him, "Believe me it was not so. Thanks to Phoebe there was no carnage."

"Yes, but there could have been, Cousin Tom, and where is Phoebe? I could wish her to read of her brave exploit."

I explained about the happy reunion that had just taken place, and that she was even now in converse with her great-uncle the Earl, whose younger brother had been her grandfather. The effect of this titbit of information was alarming.

"What?" cried Ralph, leaping to his feet. "Father, by your leave. Quickly to work. This second edition must be changed. So she is Lady Phoebe Stanhope you say? The old bastard her uncle?"

"He is not so old nor I suspect a bastard." I told them waspishly. "He is more to my liking than some of the well-borne popinjays that I have encountered, and yes she is Lady Phoebe Stanhope as you could have learned yesterday, and as anxious to be spared your written notice as I am." But I spoke to the air. He and Gabriel were out the door, helter-skelter, leaving me to settle the account. I found I had treated several tradesmen of Lichfield who were clearly used to delight in Gabriel's tales of his theatrical past. I sighed and dug deep into my purse.

I bought Elijah and myself two capons' legs and a stoup of wine and then I thought that it was time to return for Phoebe. Elijah came with me, thinking that the Bishop's Palace might be hung with cloth of gold. It was hard to disappoint him. Everything he encountered was a new delight.

"Oh, Tom, Tom, look at all these saints and kings!" he cried as we passed the West Front. "Who are they all?"

"I think their names are carved beneath each effigy." I told him shortly, wishing to find Phoebe.

"Indeed they are, young Master!" a young woman, heavily pregnant, stopped beside him, resting her hand on her back. "If you can read you can make their names out clearly enough. And look, here is the blessed Saint Chad, whose day it is tomorrow. You are come to Lichfield in very happy time. His feastday should be celebrated in the Cathedral tomorrow."

She had pointed to the statue of a stern bearded old personage, who held up two fingers in perpetual blessing or reproof.... it was hard to tell. Elijah thanked her politely and to my consternation, looked round and seeing we were alone, apart from his new friend, swiftly crossed himself.

"You are a good youth, my duck. God strengthen all of us in these terrible times," and she went on her way.

"Elijah!" I hissed at him. "Don't do that! Don't cross yourself!"

"But look Tom," he cried, with a sweeping gesture at all the saints and kings in their niches on the West Front. "They are marvels, created for us all to wonder at, and praise. Don't you feel that there is something miraculous here for us?"

By this we were nearing the Bishop's Palace. "Well, never mind that now!" I told him "I'll tell you what I think later and it involves keeping a whole skin!"

"Oh there you are Master Doctor!" said the Guard at the door. "You are stayed for. The Earl thinks that the sun rises from your backside, aye and the moon as well!"

Our welcome was courteous indeed. Phoebe was sitting beside her uncle, holding his hand, but when she saw us, she came quickly towards us, and whispered: "Thank God, you are come. I thought I would never escape!"

"Master Doctor Fletcher. Come you here and let me thank you again for your chivalry towards my sweet niece, the cleverest wench in Christendom, is she not, my boys?"

There was a chorus of "Oh Aye, me Lord." and the poor steward who had been so scolded earlier in the day ventured to comment:

"Clever indeed to turn your mood, my Lord. Will she not remain with us? My Phillipa is near her time."

"Do you think I have not asked her, Jonathan? Begged her, by the Rood? But No she will go to her calling, and though we, poor boys all, are intent on saving this great church for God and King, back to Worcester, she will go!"

"I would be but a sad companion for you, sir and for Great Aunt also. I am too shrewish and used now to going my own way. You would find me froward and difficult."

"A perfect companion for my wife, if that is true," said the Earl heavily. "It has seemed a blessed holiday here in the Close, apart from my affliction, and the endurance of these silly knaves, who smilingly accept my curses."

The steward laughed: "We could fare very far indeed, my Lord, before finding a better master than you."

The Earl winked at us. "You see how I am beset with fearful rogues. Well, well, off with you, Phoebe, sweet girl. And mind you treat her well, young Master Doctor. And who is this young saucer-eyed tow-haired rapscallion?"

I introduced Elijah, and we waited for the fiery chariot jest, that almost always followed the first mention of his name. But it was not forthcoming. Instead the Earl commented, "A good name for these evil Presbyters. Are you such a one, boy?"

"Indeed, no, my Lord, and my father, God rest him, held to the old religion. There were some few citizens of Stratford who refused reform."

"Did they so? I see you have a good loyal journeyman, Thomas. Fare you well then and God bless you all on your travels and after. Phoebe, one last kiss for your uncle."

She kissed him heartily and so we took our leave. "Did you know this fearsome Earl whom everyone abused, was your relation, Phoebe?" I asked her as for the last time we passed the glorious West front.

"Do you know Tom, I wondered if it were he. I did not hear his name mentioned but hearing of the gout and of his propensity for liquor, thought that perhaps it might be. There are, after all, not so many Earls in these parts."

I still felt guilty about my reluctance to treat him on the previous night, but reflected that at the least his steward, Jonathan, now knew which roots to prepare to alleviate his suffering. Phoebe seemed to catch at my thought as she remarked somewhat harshly for her: "The mischief is, in that he now knows how to relieve the pain, he will see it as a licence to drink all the more. He is a good man, no question, but good living will be his downfall!"

"What a little Puritan you are, Phoebe!" I told her for she sounded such a miniature soberminded preacher "You constantly surprise me. Your husband will be the most fortunate of men, for you are never tedious like so many women."

She stopped short on the corner of Bore Street. "If women are tedious then believe me, it is men who make them so." She set off again, with her pretty head held high. Elijah and I looked at each other and shrugged. She was hurrying away in front of us so fast that we had to hasten to keep up.

We went to the Magpie's nest to bid them Farewell and discovered that they were printing off a single sheet about the Earl of Chesterfield's reunion with his long lost great-niece. It was wondrous affecting informing the reader with a Biblical zeal how the Earl clasped her to his bosom (which he would have been hard put to accomplish as his great belly would have prevented it) and exclaimed "Behold, she that was lost, is found!"

And so we parted from them. I was sorry. I had never met so entertaining a family, and I hoped with all my heart that I would encounter them again. The three of us dined quietly at the George, thinking of tomorrow's journey and Phoebe complaining that her head ached somewhat, went early to her bed.

I took the opportunity of talking more to Elijah about his life in Stratford. "I did not know your father was a... a... recusant. Surely your mother does not hold to the old ways."

He said, disparagingly, one word: "Mother!" and then gaining courage went on: "Do not mistake me, Tom. I love my mother dearly."

"I know you do," I assured him.

"But she accepts whatever doctrine she hears. Or rather she believes the creed of the last man she.... converses with. If that ape Worthington told her that the King had two heads, she would believe him. My uncle, my good father's brother, despairs of her. Uncle George is a farmer and inherited the farm as eldest son. He offered to take me on with him but explained that as he has ten healthy children, six of them boys, there was no hope of my ever being more than a favoured hired hand. As I showed some gift with sick cows, he gave me money to follow the soldiers, "and bandage them, after they had banged each other about." And so I met you Tom. I am very grateful to you, Tom, as is my wayward mother."

"No, no, Elijah, and I would not describe her so," I told him. "It is I who am grateful to you for accepting my crochets and cranks. But why did you come to Edgehill, alone and friendless, and why did you ally yourself to Lord Fielding, who was for Parliament? You plainly prefer the King's High Churchmanship."

He blushed and looked at his feet. "Master Tovey told me I would be serving Lord Fielding. I did not know until the end of the battle that we were serving his son who was for Parliament. I thought the son was his father."

"And do you think there is a notable difference between a Parliamentarian broken leg and one of a King's Man?"

"No Tom. And I am grateful for that lesson. I have heard that some doctors would not treat men on that battlefield unless they could pay. And I was pleased indeed that you stopped for me on the Ridgeway, and let me ride Jupiter. Edgehill was a day of terror but it was fortunate for me."

"And for me," I told him, "for you are the best of journeymen. But for sweet Jesu's sake and I choose my words, Elijah, no more crossing yourself. Believe me, I share your love for our great cathedrals, as did my father, but keep your Papist ways inside your head, so that it does not find its zealous way into a noose. Circumspection is our watchword. You read the News sheets and the Corantoes with much interest. Did you not read of the horrors in Ireland?"

He said slowly: "But perhaps both parties were equally guilty."

"No doubt, no doubt!" said I, like some opinionated old grey beard. "But, I beg you to observe caution, and indeed, my friend, I am grateful that you let me know your heart, and I say again I could not have a better journeyman."

"Nor I, a master," he told me. And so in this flood of mutual gratitude, we took our candles and went up to our beds.

I was in a deep, comfortable dream in which I was assuring my mother that although she was dead I was very grateful to her, when through the vales of sleep, I knew that someone was knocking far below me. A moment later our hostess was knocking on my door.

71

"Master Tom!" she cried "Pray you awake! Master Tom!"

I heaved myself out of my dream and my bed simultaneously, and called out, "What's the matter?"

"They are saying that they need a doctor desperate bad in the Close. Will you go?"

I sighed heavily, pulling on my clothes. "Very well," I called. "Is it the Earl again?"

"They are saying it is a childbed matter."

I groaned to myself. I had left the practice of midwifery to Joan since she and Adam made their home with me. I had studied Ben's notes and knew what was to be done, had delivered several babes alone, once even twins but the process was hedged with perils. I had even heard of a doctor being beaten because the babe was yet another girl and the father had set his heart on a boy.

I wondered whether to wake Phoebe but this was a skill about which she knew little. I picked up my box and for some reason, put on my riding cloak, lest the night was cold and took some guineas from my purse, lest we might need medicines from the apothecary's store.

Downstairs, two men from the Close waited for me. One was the soldier who had been the spokesman yesterday. As we trudged over the bridge, I said waspishly: "Twice in two nights called to the Bishop's Palace. Thank God I shall be gone tomorrow."

He said meekly: "They will be monstrous glad to see you, sir."

The sentries motioned us through, and to my amazement the Earl himself was standing at the door to meet me. "Tom, Doctor Tom, I am rejoiced to see you, by the Rood." I realised I had never seen him stand before, let alone walk but now he almost ran up the nearby staircase, calling out as he did so: "He's here, Jonathan. Now all will be well, I promise you, my boy,." and ushered me past the steward who stood chalk-white at a bed-chamber door.

One moment's examination of the poor wretch upon the bed convinced me that all was far from well. Two women were trying to soothe her, by mopping her brow and moistening her lips. The crown was visible but as the contraction ended, it was as if it were reabsorbed into her body. They exhorted her to push again as the next contraction started. Her screaming was pitiful to hear.

"How long has the crown been coming and going?" I asked the women.

One of them looked at the steward: "About an hour or so. It seems the babe is reluctant to be borne."

"He cannot be borne," I told them, "as things stand. I fear that the cord is round his neck. Each time she pushes to expel him, the cord prevents his journey."

"What can you do?" asked the Earl.

"Well one thing is certain. He must be borne for his mother's sake. We could lose both babe and mother if this continues. I fear the child may already be dead as the tightness of the cord may have strangled him. I need goose grease and clean water. If it has been boiled over the fire and is now lukewarm, that is good. I need both now," and turning to the women I told them, "Do not tell her to push again. With every push she destroys their chances."

They already had clean water in a pail. I poured some into a bowl and washed my hands like a latterday Pilate. I had a piece of soap in my chest and a brush and I scrubbed and scrubbed as Ben had insisted. A maid brought in a vat of goosegrease and I approached the poor woman on the bed. I was not entirely sure what I could do but one thing was certain. I could not now make matters worse.

She screamed again as a contraction gathered force. I plunged my right hand into the grease and as the spasm faded managed to insert it alongside the head.

"Please be still, madam," I muttered. "I mean you no harm or disrespect. I must find the cord."

As I had surmised it was round his neck. With my other hand I pushed him back a little further and found I could hold the cord in my two fingers. Did something brush the back of my hand? I held the cord while I pushed still further on his mother's stomach with my left hand and pushed his head through it. I withdrew my hand as gently as I could.

"With the next contraction, I think now we may expect the head," I told the women.

And so it transpired. By my intervention, I had given enough leeway for the infant to complete his journey. One of the women helped me support the little head as it emerged. I could see at once that the child might not be for this world. There was a blueness about him and the cord which should have been his lifeline could have caused his end before he had in fact a beginning.

One of the women began to weep at the sight of him. Well, I told myself in for a penny, in for a pound. Thinking it was a useless duty, I took clean straws from my box and cleared his mouth of mucus in the way Ben had taught me, sucking it out into the straw and blowing it away. I lifted his chin and tilted his head backwards, listening all the time for the slightest breath. There was nothing. I would try the method Ben had learned in Bologna. I placed my mouth round his tiny mouth and nose and blew fast little breaths, counting one two three for each one. I was aware that everyone in the room watched me. The chest began to rise and fall with my efforts but I knew that could be merely my exertions, not the infant's life returning. I knew I would have to give up after two or three minutes to attend to the mother who was weeping and crying possibly because she had not thought to see her babe half eaten! I decided to cease this attempt at ventilation. There was one last manoeuvre I could try....

But suddenly the baby coughed, took a deep breath and began to howl fit to wake the dead. I cursed myself in that I had not followed Ben's instructions. He had told me, to look constantly for a lessening of the blueness. The child was now an acceptable shade of pink. I cut the cord, with a knife I kept wrapped clean in my box, lifted him carefully from the bed, and after giving him to the women to wrap in clean linen and place in the drawer made ready for his reception, I realised to my shame that this whole resuscitating process had taken place between his mother's legs. And she, poor soul, still had to expel the afterbirth.

But not merely the afterbirth. Whilst the new-born had taken centre stage as it were, she had been "labouring". To my surprise and that of the women, there was another crown appearing. I remembered that something had brushed my hand. This babe was intent on following the established procedure. As the womb was already dilated, she emerged with her head already facing her mother's left leg. First one shoulder and then another appeared, and she lay blinking at us, with quite a knowing look on her face. Another drawer from one of the Bishop's fine old oak chests was immediately purloined, his holy small clothes scattered and the little girl washed and ensconced therein, side by side with her brother.

I turned to the patient who had yet to dispel the afterbirth. The poor mother seemed bewildered by the swiftness with which events had taken place. I confess, green youth that I was, I felt an embarrassment to look her in the face, having had so close an acquaintance with her other areas. But she, poor wretch, lay back, caring not at all for fine manners, whiter than her sheets, with a dark shadow below her eyes. Suddenly I knew her. She was the kind woman who had blessed Elijah that afternoon. As the afterbirth appeared what had been a trickle of dark blood became a stream. I wished I had woken Phoebe. She would have known instantly the herbs, that would cause the blood to clot. I had to assume that her womb had been torn by her son's exertions before I had loosed the cord. I tried to staunch the flow, by propping up her lower half on a couch of pillows.

There was a commotion outside the door. Jonathan came in, glancing in horror at the spectral form on the bed. "Is all over?" he whispered to me. "Will Pippa live? The midwife is here. Do you wish to be relieved of your task? It is not seemly for you perhaps?"

"Why is the midwife so late in her attendance?" I asked. "If she had been here before she could have helped me, or I could have helped her, and, by the bye, you are a father twice over."

"God be praised!" he said and clasped my hand briefly. "But what of old Mary here. She is something outraged that you, a male doctor, should have been called. But we could not wake her. She is somewhat "well to live", and enjoys her brandy wine." Indeed a somewhat rich aroma was permeating the atmosphere of the sick-room.

I flung open the door, and glared downwards at a very angry old woman, who stood aggressively with her arms folded. "What do you here, young puppy? This is the realm of womankind." She hiccoughed and steadied herself on the lintel. "What do you here, you young whelp?"

"More to the purpose than you, you old bitch!" I snarled viciously. "I have delivered two babes, one like to have killed both his mother and himself and his unborn sister by straining against the cord which was strangling him. I need nettle and bistort to stop her bleeding. If you wish to be of help, tell me where I can get them."

She sighed heavily, looked at me something askew and asked me, somewhat more civilly: "Bistort? Do you mean snakeweed? Nettles there are aplenty, growing hot and strong where the men void their urine. Let me see her!"

I stood aside and she staggered into the sick-room. She cast a cursory glance at the two newcomers and ordered one of the women to fetch a mother whose babe she told me she had delivered three days ago.

"She has milk a-plenty," she told me grudgingly.

"Listen, madam," I ordered her sharply as she was swaying like a ship about to founder on the rock of the bedpost. "Help me, and we may yet save this poor soul. Have you such a thing as a clean sponge?"

She caught only the last word, "Who is a sponge?" she demanded. "Mind your manners, puppy!"

I ran to the door and called for the Earl. He was sitting with his steward, near at hand, comforting the man as best he could. They came quickly at my summons

"My Lord," I pleaded with him, "I need a clean sponge - or one that can be rendered clean, more hot water in a pan or cauldron and bistort which I think you call snakeweed. I might still save her."

The steward ran back down the stairs. I could hear him shouting in the kitchens The Earl stood bemused, "Snakeweed? What the devil.....?" but one of the women, understanding the urgency of the situation, picked up a candle and ran to the door. "I have seen those roots in the still-room," she cried and ran down the corridor.

"But I cannot manage with this harridan," I told the Earl, who gaped at me in disbelief at my lack of respect. "She reeks of the ale-house and the gutter. Get her away from the sickbed."

He came in behind me prepared I think to manhandle the witch away but she had collapsed in an unseemly heap beside the bed. The earl averted his eyes gallantly from the poor patient in her up-ended state and told me that the Midwife, one Mistress Mary Bellison, was well spoken of, and was known for her ability for delivering live children: "Oh, aye, my Lord. She boasts that one in three of her charges is born alive," the remaining woman informed us. I stared in horror. For Ben ever to lose one child was not a matter of course, but a tragic rare exception. At this point the drunken jewel of the midwifery profession gave a loud belch and fell to snoring.

The water and a sponge were brought in. I poured some water into a vessel ready to make a decoction and fell to washing the sponge with my soap, like one demented. To my joy, she who knew the whereabouts and contents of the still-room returned with a flask of powdered root... a wise precaution when it is needed speedily to stay bleeding. I mixed some with the water I had prepared and soaked the sponge in the luke warm decoction. Now to insert the sponge. I heard Jonathan gasp at my effrontery but when there was a plain choice between life and death, propriety and decorum must give way. I waited a little, withdrew the sponge, soaked with dark blood, quickly washed it and soaked it again in my decoction and continued to do this until only a faint pink tinge stained the sponge. We left her upended, covered her over and to my joy, she sighed, reached for her husband's hand and fell asleep.

The twins were taken to the wet nurse. Jonathan did not know whether to accompany his offspring or stay with his wife. I advised him to stay with her, and thanked the woman who had known of the snakeweed root, saw a chair and sat to rest for a moment.

As I sat I reflected that Ben would have been pleased with his pupil. "Resourcefulness!" he often used to say, "Next to knowledge, resourcefulness is your greatest talent." I wondered for a moment what he might now be doing.... doctoring the great men of Parliament in London.....

I woke with a start. The room was full of sunshine, Jonathan and Philippa still slept, the old crone lay a heap of soiled rags, by the bed, snoring softly. There were shouts coming from downstairs and amidst the tumult I could make out the voice of the Earl, swearing vociferously.

I ventured to the head of the stairs and saw a scene of what at first seemed to be panic. The Earl's soldiers were carrying out great planks of wood and a few servants were scurrying in with baskets. He, himself, was directing operations, and whilst there was much noise, there did seem to be some method in the mayhem. He glanced up, saw me standing there, and shouted up to me.

"Thomas, Doctor Tom. Alas, I must keep you here with us. The drawbridges are up and we are reinforcing the great doors. Brooke is here. He arrived last night with all his scurvy knaves and they camped a mile south of this town. There is a small detachment the other side the moat as we speak. Good lad, good lad," this to a boy whom he patted on the head as the grinning child staggered past him carrying a basket of loaves. "Doctor Tom, I have just ordered the doors closed. We are besieged, my boy. And I must look to the lives of all here. It is God's blessing you are here to help me!"

6

The chilling dismay I felt must have been evident in my expression. The Earl ran nimbly (for a man of his girth!) up the stairs and grasped my hand. "Cheerly, dear Tom. 'Tis only young Brooke and his band of purple poltroons. There are some of the best marksmen here in the Close from two counties."

I gazed at his cheerful countenance. "Have you been in a battle, Sir?" I asked him courteously.

"I was judged too young to go with Essex to Ireland, and chose not to fight the Scots two years ago. But then we all chose not to fight over a prayer-book. Why do you ask?"

"I was at Edgehill, tending the wounded." I told him. "I did not care for it. I, and Elijah stayed on the battlefield until the end. I cannot describe the horror of it, and God, I am sure, was not present."

He frowned. "Well, we must do what we have to do. Will you care for my poor boys, if any of them fall foul of Brooke's cannons?"

"I must do what I have to do." I said echoing him, and then as his eager face fell at my lack of zeal, I told him: "Aye, my Lord! And with a good will, Sir!"

"Good boy!" he told me. "Come and eat." And indeed as I followed him into the great hall and contemplated my position, I could see that perhaps it was as well that I was not in the town. I had, after all, deceived the soldiers at Clopton Bridge in Stratford as to my identity. Phoebe would be safe. Brooke himself had deemed her a heroine, but I felt uneasy as to Elijah's reaction if he was forced to witness the desecration of churches.

My fame had gone something before me, as the Earl's followers and servants knew that both babes and their mother had survived, and I was patted and praised, "like to swell my pate," as my father would have said, "and make you a rare Hogan Mogan." It was pleasant to hear their adulation but I had no doubt that Phillipa's recovery was due to the Bishop's maid, whoever she was, who had powdered the snakeweed roots, and the clever wench who had seen it in the still-room. Some of the Earl's soldiers had resisted the oncoming Parliamentarians in the town at dawn, but had hastened back to the refuge of the Close, unharmed. Now they spoke loudly of their escape, looking to the Earl to be sure he could hear of their courage.

I sat and ate bread with a smear of bramble jelly, and then returned to the new parents. Jonathan still slept but Phillipa was awake and asking for the babes, as her bosom was aching somewhat. As I examined her, the little ones were brought back, and were now in contrary mood, as Little Miss was bawling and my Young Sir regarded us all with the round eyed wondering gaze of infancy. The midwife slept on, snoring occasionally. Ben had chastised me verbally once for speaking disrespectfully of such a one,.... "a roynish rude old trot," had been my epithet as I remember.... but he had told me, "She might know the life saving herb, you need. You are right to forbid her contact with the sick, if she is dirty or drunk, but if she has the knowledge you lack?" But as far as I could see, Mistress Mary was unclean, drunk and ignorant. I judged she could do least harm if she was left......

The air was suddenly rent by an appalling explosion! The nightmare of the first hour of Edgehill flashed into my memory. Jonathan, who had been dozing in a chair, leapt up and ran from the room, but the child continued to suckle and the midwife to snore.... an unspoken homily from womankind as to the madness of men.

Phillipa sighed deeply. "It begins!" she said.

"How do you, madam?" I asked her.

"Well enough, I suppose, but it is a cruel fate to have gone through all for these two, only to see them torn asunder by.... I know not what. And you, Master Doctor. A rare good doctor as I hear but to what purpose if we are all to die?"

And she began to weep, as women do after great stress and strain.

"Comfort yourself, Madam. The Earl is....."

But another great crash drowned my words.

"I'll find out what is happening." I told her, "I'll return shortly." The clever girl who had found the snakeweed was returning, with a bowl of bread and milk for the new mother. I pushed past her and leapt down the stairs in time to see the Earl, running outside into the Close.

Shards of stone and wood lay about the ground and a few of his soldiers were making for the Cathedral. They ran with the Earl for the West door as another frightful boom shattered the silence, coming from the gate by the Minster Pool.

"The bastards have a cannon, a demi-culverin. Get the side doors unlocked, Jonathan. We must have quick access," the Earl panted. "They are trying to destroy the gate. Come on, Tom!"

For a few silly moments I thought we were entering the Cathedral to pray. How misguided I was! As I passed below him I glanced up at St. Chad, and silently wished him good fortune on his feast-day, then hurled myself after the Earl and his soldiers who were running through the nave. I followed them as they turned aside and rushed through a low wooden door. We ran helter-skelter up a narrow stone stair, which twisted as I thought, for ever. I was the last as we scurried upwards. Unused to this kind of exertion, I was quite out of breath when suddenly I burst into the sun, and the wind, far, far above the town of Lichfield.

I staggered and yelled out in panic and pressed myself against the wall, which rose for many feet still above us. We were at the top of the square tower from which the tallest spire of the three soared into the blue. The soldiers who seemed unmoved by the terrible height, spoke cheerily to me, telling me that Brooke's harquebusiers could not reach us here. In fact I would not have cared if Brooke, Essex and the Devil himself had shot me through there and then, I was so monstrous terrified of my position. I had not known how much I hated heights. What had I thought when I ran like a rat up the spiral stairs? Why, that we were bound for some chapter house or upper room where perhaps a Council of War would take place. But the Earl was this day a one-man Council, a father, a general, and an inspiration to his men. (Alas, I was to learn to all our costs that he was a man without foresight, excellent in emergency, but useless as a planner.)

One of the soldiers had brought bread and meat for a sad looking fellow, who sat like me, his back to the spire and who nursed the longest gun that I had ever seen. A small pile of lead balls lay beside him. I was clutching the stones on which I sat and slowly understood that the purpose of our upward flight had been to observe the actions of Brooke's gunners. The cannon that was causing the noise and mayhem below was stationed at the end of Dam Street. The gunners were firing across the causeway to the gate in that corner of the Close. One man rushed hither and yon with a long matchlock stick and shouted instructions.

"Are they in range, John?" the Earl asked the man with the long gun. Rudely to me it seemed he did not speak, but tested the wind with a wet finger. Then he aimed his long weapon at the gunners. There was a sharp crack and to my amazement I saw that he, far below, who had been so busy, lay powerless. He was not dead and bravely continued to shout for some seconds, but then overcome by the pain in his leg, he lapsed silent and lifeless upon the cobbles. His fellows pulled him out of the range of John's fowling piece as the other soldiers beside me on the tower levelled their muskets and a rain of shot fell beside the besiegers.

"That's given them a lesson!" The Earl came and stood beside me as I cowered on the ground out of the rushing wind that would I was sure blow me down to perdition if I moved. "Nay, Tom, you are safe from the rogues here, I promise you. Come lads to the gate! They should have half the planks in place by now."

And to my dismay, they stood in turn to enter the stairs and left me alone in Hell with the dumb sad fellow with the longest gun in Christendom. He looked sideways at me, smiled slowly, and gestured to the bread which lay on the stones beside his leaden balls. I could no more have eaten than I could have flown and was powerless to move and so we sat, silently for perhaps half an hour. I forced myself to look at Lichfield spread before me. There was little sign of the townsfolk..... this was a marvellous fresh news budget for Ralph, I thought to myself. But the rogues clad in purple were everywhere. Slowly I began to think, if I shuffled along the wall, still seated I would reach the door of the staircase, but then the horror of standing up to open it with nothing to grasp to steady myself, overcame me and I resolved to sit a little longer, keeping a silent vigil with my dumb friend. Through all this time, his gun had been primed on his shoulder, ready to fire. We could see some little way down into Dam Street, which seemed deserted.

Suddenly he stiffened and looked below to the cannon that had been reaping such havoc on us. We could plainly see the muzzle moving through a few degrees of an arc. And then it fired again at the great gate of the Close. We only saw one of the rogues for a second, as the hideous tumult echoed around us. I could not see the gate, their target, but my companion leaned forward to my horror and made a clicking sound, indicating displeasure. There was a confused noise of hammering and shouting, rising up to us from within the Close. Another great booming thunderous explosion shook the world. And, this time not a glimpse of one of them. Curses and swearing rose from the ground below.

Someone shouted from the town. I could not hear the words plainly, but caught "Halt" and then, "My Lord". My companion had his gun trained now onto the town, which was quiet and deserted as ever. But there was the slightest of movements! Someone was looking round the corner of an entry which gave onto Dam Street. As I watched he drew back swiftly, but I had seen the helmet he wore before in Stratford. It had a distinctive five bars protecting his face. It was Lord Brooke.

In that moment the wind dropped, Lord Brooke, his helmet pushed back, once more peered round the corner at the cannon, and my companion fired.

And Lord Brooke dropped, dead as a stone.

As far as I could tell, he had been struck in the face. He can have felt nothing, I told myself. My companion of the air, grinning like a living gargoyle, indicated to me by pointing at the door that I should go below to report this triumph. I shuffled on my bum towards the door and realised that I could no longer delay, standing up. Mercifully the door had a great round iron knob, which I grasped as if it was the holy grail itself. Clinging to this I edged my craven person round into the stair well and launched myself onto the first step. My right hand swept the smooth round wall beside me. Nothing! No comforting hand hold or rail! But then I began to reflect that five or six common soldiers had clearly descended with the portly Earl, half an hour before without obvious hurt to their persons. I held myself upright, resisting the temptation to bump myself down on my cowardly arse, and slowly took another step, seeing the stairs sweep round and away from me, under the bright sunlight from the narrowest of slit windows.

And so I crept down, slower, far slower, than I had ascended. The sounds of my fellows began to leak up to me and gave me a little more courage. I felt less alone and after what seemed like an hour although was probably no more than five minutes, I had gained the door into the nave. I took a deep breath and gathering around myself the shreds of my dignity hastened through the cathedral. I cannot describe the happiness and confidence with which I again strode out onto our Mother Earth.

I judged that the Earl was probably commanding the battening of planks against the gate that had been so pounded and splintered. He was leaning against the high Close wall taking his breath when I found him. "At least ten minutes since the last cannon!" he was saying in disbelief to a Captain, a Sir John Harper I later learned "Why, Tom," he cried at the sight of me, "have you seen a ghost?"

"No, my Lord," I told him, "Not a ghost, but a death."

"Whose?" he demanded. "Not honest John Dyott."

"No, my Lord," I told him, "I left him, at his post on the Tower, munching bread and meat. Honest John shot Lord Brooke through the eye. As far as I could see, he was instantly killed."

The soldiers around me raised a cheer fit to rouse the Dead at Doomsday. The Earl threw up his hat, which was caught by one of the small boys who clearly had been assisting their fathers.

"This gives us a welcome respite. Come, good boys all. Let's take refreshment. Come on, Tom." And he led the way back into the Palace.

I must confess the notion of a cup of wine was welcome. Although I tried to walk tall and courageous, there was still a "wamblety" feel about my legs. After a bite of bread and a sup of Canaries, I felt better able to treat my patients. All three were dozing peacefully and the hideous old crone of a midwife, still slept on the floor, a bundle of dirty rags.

Jonathan and the Earl followed me into the bedchamber. "Look at this!" I said loftily, pointing at the old woman.

"Is all well with her?" the Earl asked, gazing at her sleeping form with something of compassionate alarm in his look.

I bent down, and tried to hear a heartbeat, my ear pressed to the filthy gown that had seen not better days, but better years. There was nothing. I lifted her hand and chafed it, but it was cold as Death. And Death indeed had claimed her. Whilst Brooke's gunners had been observed and the Close fortified, she had slipped into oblivion.

"I would judge she died about the same time as Lord Brooke." I said, standing away from the stiffening carcase.

"Well, there's a moral lesson for you, Doctor Tom!" said the Earl, quietly. "Robert Greville, Second Lord Brooke stands outside the gates of Paradise, in company with a friendless old midwife. Something more of charity, my son, and perhaps less of over-niceness."

He spoke exactly as my father would have done, and had I been a child, I would have hung my head in shame. I turned my face to the window, and hoped none would see the tears that were springing from his gentle reproof.

He came over to me and clapped me on the back. "Come, now, dear boy, you are a good lad for all of that. Jonathan will see Mary Bellison disposed of, and if these three thrive you must help me. I must figure what we have, and get some notion as to how long we can hold out." He led the way to some store rooms, and thrust parchment and a quill with an inkwell at me. "You write what I call out. We'll begin with the absolute essentials. Half a barrel of best Claret. Write it down, my boy."

And so we passed the rest of the morning. To satisfy my curiosity and to ensure that there were adequate supplies in the event of many of the Earl's soldiers being wounded, I made a careful mental note of the conrents of the stillroom. It was very well stocked. At the back were several wooden boxes and crates, which could have contained food.I asked the Earl what they contained.

"Alas, nothing useful to us in our present state" he told me regretfully. "Merely the Cathedral treasures, Tom."

I knew little of housewifery but to claim that the stores in the Close were sufficient to feed his three hundred followers, for more than two or three days would have been foolhardy indeed. Everything had been bought in daily from the tradesmen of Lichfield. And when the ready money had given out, the inhabitants of the Close had continued to live on daily credit. Indeed apart from a few haunches of salt beef and some cabbages, there was very little to withstand a siege.

"At the very least, we have a good supply of candles," he told me with some satisfaction.

"Sir, we cannot eat candles," I said "We have hardly enough food for two days."

He wearily sat on a bench outside the Hall and looked at me in consternation. "Three hundred of us!" he said, sighing heavily. From above came the wailing of one of the new-borns.

"Three hundred and two." I reminded him. He smiled. The bombardment had ceased, although there was the noise of shouts and hammering, coming from the town. There was an ornate old market cross, near the Magpie's Nest, covered in saints that would not suit well with Puritan notions. I hoped that Elijah would not play the hero and attempt to reason with the troopers. This could be one of the surest routes to becoming a saint himslf. But there was no further bombardment of the Close.

Until, at about three there were shouts from the soldiers, watching with the dumb man, John Dyott on the tower. Scaffolding had been constructed behind the gate, which had previously suffered so much battering. The Earl climbed the ladder to the rude platform that ran a short distance along the Close side of the wall.

He took a swift look towards Dam Street, and cried out in alarm. "Oh, Sweet Jesu!" he moaned. "Tom, look at this. By the Rood, they should burn in Hell for this."

I carefully climbed the ladder and had to assume an ape-like posture at the top. I overtopped two yards in height, so my head would have been a useful marker for target practice, had I stood upright. I knelt beside an embrasure and peered around it.

In the market place, a large crowd had gathered. At the point where Lord Brooke had been shot, there was a group of people, who were all chained, one to another. They were in range from shot from the Tower, and I could see white faces, turned in fear ever and anon in that direction. Behind them were Brooke's purple coats aplenty.

And then I saw that the small figure at the front of the captives was Phoebe. Behind her there were women carrying babes and small children, with a few old men. All were chained together. The Earl was shouting imprecations and threats and had so far forgotten his safety to stand in full view of the musketeers in the Market, who were jeering and mocking his rage. They had not the range of the gate yet, but sent a few balls over the heads of their captives. "Father!" cried a voice from below. "What are you doing?" It was young Ferdinand, the Earl's youngest son, whom I had met earlier. He was about thirteen.

He swiftly climbed the ladder and clasping his father round the waist from behind, pulled him down onto the platform. "That is madness, sir. What would we do, all, if you should perish." The Earl looked at him and slowly nodded, sitting with his back against the Close.

"I think this is proof positive that Brooke is dead." I said slowly. "He told Phoebe she was a heroine for saving Parliament lives in Stratford Market Hall. And also....."

"What?" the Earl asked.

"I do not think he was a man who would have countenanced a slaughter of innocents."

The Earl nodded slowly. "You are right. He would not. There was something of honour in him although he was an irreligious renegade."

"Who will be the commander now, then if Brooke is dead?" I asked him.

He shrugged. "They will have sent for someone by now. But meanwhile...."

There was a new and confused sound from the market. I risked another glance round the embrasure. The citizens were howling abuse at the soldiers and screaming at them to free the captives who now were being forced to walk across the causeway towards the Close. The Parliament men huddled behind, using the wives and fathers and little children of the Earl's followers as a human shield.

"Tom, get back, you fool!" Phoebe's scream suddenly alerted me to the danger I was in. As I dodged back behind the stone battlement, lead shot whistled into the aperture where I had poked my curious head. Phoebe had saved me again. And "Fool" I was in those days. Even though I felt gratitude for my life, I was not sure that I relished being screamed at by a woman, even when it was poor crippled Phoebe.

But now a hideous and familiar sound mingled with the crying of the little hostages. I risked another look. Parliament men were being carefully selected on the Causeway by the Earl's snipers on the Tower, and systematically wounded in thigh and leg as they crept bent double towards the Close. The hostages were as yet unharmed, but their pitiful weeping mingled with the groans of the wounded men. The neutral citizens of Lichfield continued to screech imprecations at dead Brooke's foolhardy harquebusiers, as more of them crowded onto the Causeway. Shots continued to rain down on these unfortunate Parliament victims, blood staining purple doublet and hose. The noise was indescribable.

The Earl was on the Tower. "Unchain them!" he roared "Get back, you rogues! Unchain them!"

The advance headed by the prisoners had ceased, as their captors were too demoralised to continue. Most of the poor fellows lay in their blood, gasping and screaming for help. The shower of lead shot from the Tower continued with the Earl exhorting his men "to make every ball tell, and wing the bastards!" Through all of this I kept stealing glimpses of poor brave Phoebe. She was now much nearer to the gate. Two children clung to her skirts, weeping as she stroked their heads. I climbed down the ladder wondering if I could in some way rescue her and bring her into the Close. But this idea, though gallant, was totally impractical. The Earl and his men had effectively shored up the gate from within.

Suddenly there was a frenzied screaming from the town. "That's the officer down. That's their bastard colonel who ordered this!" said one of the men gathered at the foot of the ladder, gazing through the gap left by the hinge. And all firing ceased for a few moments. But then another shout came from the town, drowning the terrible screaming and wailing of the wounded men on the Causeway and the sobbing of the captives. This voice was comfortingly familiar. I had heard it in Stratford. It was Captain Cross and he was ordering his men to retreat from the Causeway. I peered through the gap in the side of the Gate. He was waving a white flag over his head and walking through the wounded and shouting up to the Earl. The firing from the Tower ceased and the Earl shouted again: "Unchain them!"

The Captain shouted: "Yes, my Lord." Still waving the flag he walked to the captives and told them - I heard him say it…. "You have nothing now to fear!" He ordered them to return with him. They picked their way back among the wounded, their chains now clanking in the silence, the women horrified at the carnage, the children crying in distress. Some of the elderly had to be assisted back by the Captain's men, who now came onto the Causeway to carry the wounded back into the town.

The Earl shouted as he neared Dam Street: "Who ordered this?" Through the slit in the gate I could see the Captain turn and pause.

Then he shouted up: "Peyto. But I am in command now. Peyto is like to die."

And indeed the Parliament men had gained nothing from their cowardly exploit, but wounds, and pain and death. I wondered whether Elijah and Phoebe would now be pressed into service, dressing the savage serrations of the musket balls. Some of the Earl's men had descended and were crossing the Close from the Tower, among them John Dyott, who was receiving the congratulations of his fellows with a modest smile. They trooped into the Palace for refreshment and I followed, turning aside up the stairs to see how the twins and their mother were faring.

One would be forgiven for thinking that nothing more could happen on this endless of days, St Chad's Day, 3rd of March, in the year of our Lord 1643. And so I hoped, returning to the Banqueting Hall, having seen that all were well in the bedchamber. The Earl told me to sit near him whilst he consulted with his Captains. No-one was wounded and all were in good spirits at the discomforture of Brooke's minions. All but Jonathan. He kept interrupting the Earl's council with the solemn words: "But, dear Sir, we have nothing to eat!"

"Alas, Master Jonathan, nothing to eat…. a difficulty indeed, but might there perhaps, My Lord, …might there be something to drink?"

The Earl laughed. "I am a neglectful host by the Rood!" he vowed and sent Jonathan for the Bishop's goblets and some claret from the barrel. The thirsty man, who had asked for a drink, was clearly deferred to in all things military. He was broad rather than tall, of plain features with the gift of making that which was courteously said, sound saucy, and that which was rude and impolite sound seductive and captivating. When he spoke, all fell silent to listen.

They began to discuss how best to defend the North Wall, where the lie of the land would have afforded much easy access to besiegers. A tall fellow like myself could jump down the seven feet or so at the back of the Close. Why the Parliament men had not approached from this vantage point was a matter for speculation, although the shooters on the Tower would have been equally able to pick them off, by the simple expedient of moving around, under the spire.

It was finally agreed by all, that Brooke's followers had not known the geography of the Close and that the townspeople, more in awe of St Chad than either King or Parliament had deemed it wisest not to tell them of this easier access. I started to think that maybe I could escape back to Phoebe and Elijah by the simple expedient of dropping down the back wall and sauntering back into the town, unnoticed, and had decided to ask the Earl for permission to rejoin his niece, when rather than dropping down any wall, I dropped asleep.

I woke from a hideous dream, in which Parliament men were using my twins as crashing cannon balls. I started up on the bench where I had dozed to find it was dark, the Earl and his men were gone and cannon or guns were roaring. Still with the horror of my nightmare in my eyes and ears, I rushed upstairs to see if all was well. Mother and babes slept soundly but Jonathan stood at the window trying to see whence the firing came.

"Are they firing again from the Tower?" I asked him wearily.

He looked at me and frowned. "Pray God we are being relieved!" he said finally with a heart felt sigh. "A King's force under some gentleman has ridden into town, and is giving Brooke's men a run for their money."

I returned to the Gate where our viewpoint had been earlier and cautiously climbed the ladder. There was nothing to be seen but bangs and flashes and I began to fear profoundly for my companions. If they had been asked to remove musket balls from thighs and shins, in a hail of shot, then the doctors would be in as bad a case as their patients. I smiled to myself imagining with what delight Ralph would have fallen on each new happening, transforming it into print and news. Today would have been a red letter day for diurnals. Perhaps St. Chad was after all disposed in friendly fashion towards Magpies and those who peddled news. I breathed a silent prayer that he might also look in kindly benevolence on all doctors and surgeons.

I climbed down the ladder resolved to ask the Earl for permission to decamp over the back wall. I found him with Ferdinand, about to begin their supper of.... salt beef and cabbage. They insisted that I sat and joined them and indeed none of the inhabitants of the Close seemed much perturbed by the noise issuing from the town.

"What is happening, sir?" I asked him.

"We think it is mad blind Hastings," he told me, "God knows where he learnt to fight like this. Somewhere in High Germany, no doubt." He peaceably speared up some cabbage and indicated to me that I should serve myself, which I did, finding myself monstrous hungry though fear for Phoebe and Elijah took the edge off my appetite.

"I take it Hastings is for the King?" I asked politely.

"Oh, aye, be sure of that. No man more so! But the devil is, he won't stand fast. He'll harry 'em like Old Nick and then after he's peppered their arses, he'll be gone again."

"Do you think I might escape over the back wall and go and find your niece and my journeyman?" I asked him.

Suddenly the firing and banging began from a new direction, something further away, but none the less disquieting. The Earl smiled and shrugged: "Hastings does not shoot women and boys. It is one of his boasts. Nor does he attack the wounded. My guess is that your charges are safe enough. They are too valuable to that Captain to hazard their lives. But Hastings' cavaliers could easily mistake you for a whoreson renegade if you go skulking through the streets at this hour."

There seemed nothing for it but to address myself to the cabbage and salt beef. The instant my plate was cleared Ferdinand produced his chess board and as the shots and explosions had now died away, I played to placate him and to pass the time, although truly I had little liking for the game. He was a scholar from Oxford and took pride in his ability to beat anyone foolish enough to agree to play him. He won the first two games with consummate ease. To my surprise and his distress, I won the third game and was ready for the fourth with growing enthusiasm, but Ferdinand elected to make for his bed. His father grinned and winked at me as his youngest son collected his pieces, shouldered his board, and bade us Goodnight somewhat resentfully.

"You did him a service there, Tom," said the Earl. "Setbacks are good for the soul!"

"Alas, I have never found them so, my Lord. Perhaps that is why I am not a chess player," I told him.

"Well, I greatly fear we will be checkmated tomorrow. With Lord Brooke dead as mutton, and Peyto destined for death it seems, that Captain will have to send for the nearest great man of Parliament. And you know who that is?" I shook my head. "Sir John Gell. Believe me, he'll be here tomorrow, slavering at the bit, in the hope that he might dishonour my corpse. Anyway get you to bed, good boy. We'll see what the morrow brings."

And the bright morning "brought forth the adder." I ate a piece of stale bread in the Banqueting Hall as the sun rose and then heard an outcry from the gate that had seen so much action yesterday. The Earl was there, shouting up to John Dyott and the marksmen who were already on the Tower.

"Silver lace edging, if you please, the cursed popinjay! If you get him in your view, blast away."

I found a knot hole in the gate above the planks. Dam Street was full of soldiers, Lord Brooke's purple coats augmented by buff leather and orange sashes but as a couple of shots whistled down among them from the Tower, they retreated in disarray, until there was no-one in sight. Invisible captains rapped out some orders and then a voice shouted:

"Are you there, Chesterfield, you fat old bastard?"

"Don't reply, father!" hissed Ferdinand, "Let him shout!"

But this advice went unheeded by his father. He roared back: "Aye, Gell, I hear you, you loathsome slippery toad!"

"I spent the night with your niece, Chesterfield, here at the George and Dragon. What do you say to that?"

I feared that the Earl might have some kind of a fit, his visage turned purple as a Brooke's man, but before he could reply Jonathan and the loyal knights pushed him away and back into the Hall. I could not envisage Captain Cross allowing such a dishonour to take place and besides Phoebe would have been engaged all night in bandaging the wounded.

I told the Earl that Gell's comments were so much wind and piss. Sir Edward Deering agreed. "You know how he is, sir. He will ever use false information to unman us. There is news on the Tower of action at Stowe Church. Will you come up and view the proceedings?"

"Come on, Tom!" the Earl was halfway to the Cathedral as he called to me to follow. I swallowed hard, some stale bread in my throat no doubt, and went after them, with more circumspection than I had last hurled myself at the Tower staircase. Again at the top I was like to become a cowardly pissabreech. Again I sat down heavily, but as Stowe Church must be viewed from the east side of the Tower, I must needs shuffle a foot at a time, away from the friendly door and round to the left. There was the Earl, with Sir Edward and Sir John Harper gazing keenly at the little church, about a mile away. There was much activity in the open space before it. Drilling, of Brooke's men, marching of others whom I was told were Staffordshire men come south to augment Gell's Derbyshire yeomen, and pikes, thrusting forwards and stepping backwards.

"But look behind all that." said the Earl. "What are they piling by the church?"

Ladders were being carefully carried to a growing pile that the pike drill had been positioned to hide. It was clear that this was some kind of plan or trick which the Parliament men were hoping would go unnoticed. There was a keen wind blowing on the top of the Tower. The earl looked at me and said pityingly: "Down then, Tom, poor boy! You are green as grass!"

Sir Edward kindly went first down the stairs, I after and then the Earl followed me. "Why Tom," cried the Earl when we were only about half way down, Sir Edward disappearing from our view, "And you a lad from Worcester! Did you never explore the roof of your great Cathedral?"

"No, I did not!" I told him firmly, "And a school friend whose father was a steeplejack begged me to employ him as an apprentice butcher. He could not stomach his father's trade and I well understand why."

"Well, well!" he gasped, more out of breath than I as we neared the foot of the Tower, "What a man you are, Tom, already, and not yet twenty! A doctor and a butcher! There are some that will say the two trades go hand in hand."

"I tell you, my Lord, I would give all my wealth for my good father, alive again. He was a master butcher and something of the manner of yourself...." I could not continue.

"Dead, you say?"

"Hanged in error as a spy by Essex in Worcester."

"How you must hate the traitors!"

I thought sadly as I crossed the Cathedral nave that if I did hate the Parliament men, my life would be blessedly simple. How cursed are they who clearly see both sides of a question.

We went back to the Banqueting Hall and sat to discuss what we had seen. I considered wryly as I was motioned to a chair that if I had ever wished to be a man of the cloth, these few days imprisoned in Lichfield Close would surely cure me of any such spiritual pretension. But not merely the life of a churchman. The soldier's lot was worse. Boredom, discomfort and sudden barbarous violence. This was the pattern of civil war. No wonder then that God if he existed, chose to be elsewhere.

"I think we can be sure that the ladders they were trying to hide are to scale our north wall," I heard Sir Edward saying.

"You're in the right of it there, Ned," said the Earl. "Now how to prevent it? Sergeant Peabody? What say you?"

The broad man who had asked for a draught of the Earl's claret yesterday, replied slowly, "Well, your Grace, how are they to reach the North Wall if not along Gaia Lane. And Gaia Lane has high banks and thick hedges. How if we waited for them either side of the Lane and....."

"Asked them courteously to chose another way?" said the Earl, laughing heartily, "Let's about it, then, lads."

If I had hoped to be excluded from this venture, my hope was swiftly dashed. The Earl looked me in the eye and said; "And Tom will go along and help with any injuries you might sustain."

Master Peabody went among the two hundred or so loyal henchmen, but he had already marked me out as one who could advise others as to the best way of descending the wall, due to my height His scheme was that I and another tall fellow would drop down first and then lift and encourage down our comrades in arms. Except I had no arms, only a dagger.

"Can you use a sword?" asked Sir Edward.

"No, Sir." I said humbly. And then I remembered a schooldays' triumph. "But I was the school champion with quarter staffs."

At this such a roar went up that it seemed I had made a wondrous keen jest. "Why, 'tis Little John come amongst us !" shouted Master Peabody, "We'll send you in first, and you can ask for Robin Hood and give them a few friendly buffets, whilst we blow their balls off."

I would probably have never held up my head again amongst these martial heroes, but there was suddenly a shout from the Tower. We ran to the drawbridge and applied our eyes to the knot holes and cracks. To my horror, the self same trick was being played again. Phoebe led the same sad tired group, hurrying themselves along, the women anxious, the children tearful. I was glad to see that Elijah was with her this time, supporting her by the arm and this time they were not in chains but pushed and cursed along, so that the soldiers behind them would be the targets for the marksmen on the Tower for as little time as possible. Sure, whoever had ordered this had little respect for human life. Had not Captain Cross told Sir John Gell how the Parliament men were easy pickings on the Causeway from the Tower?

"The faster we attack, the less of them we face," the Earl declared. "Gell cant get many of them at once on the Causeway. Can we prise away the planks behind the drawbridge swiftly?"

The hostages had reached the drawbridge and were warned by the Parliament men to stand well to the side under the shadow of the Close wall. These same men who had followed behind them had pots of blazing tar which they meant to set down at the foot of the drawbridge to burn it open. But the Earl's men on the Tower shot away at the Parliament troops and one or two with fiery torches fell into the Minster Pool. Some who had gained the Causeway thought better of it and ran back, but about thirty of them had reached the safe ground in front of the drawbridge. We could see them through the cracks and holes and could smell the fire they carried. They were attempting to set light to the planks at the bottom of the barrier before them. The Earl had ladders placed so that stout fellows could climb behind the drawbridge and gather the slack of the chains in their arms. The battening planks were quickly prised away and then came the word of command.

"Let her go, lads!" roared the Earl. The drawbridge crashed down and about fifty or so of his men swarmed out onto the Causeway. Some few of the Parliament men were grievously crushed by the sudden monstrous weight. As they rushed past the hostages, cowering at the side, the Earl's men shouted, "Get in! Get in!" and the women, children and four or five old grandfathers stumbled and staggered into the Close.

The action was over as swiftly as it began. The Earl's men chased the Parliamentarians back, banging at them with the flat of their swords. Where any had already been picked off from the Tower, they kicked them into the water. When the Causeway was clear and all fire threats had been doused, they came running back, unharmed to a man, and the drawbridge was raised again so all was again "tight as a drum!" as the Earl proclaimed.

But we could not rest upon our laurels.... not that I had gained any. We had quickly to ready ourselves for the sortie to the lane between the Close and Stowe Church. The word came down from the Tower: "They are drawing up to march with the ladders." I had less than a moment to embrace Phoebe, a back-breaking experience for me and a neck-straining one for her, to grasp Elijah by the hand and tell them I rejoiced to see them, but Peabody must needs have me over the North Wall. There was a narrow path on which we landed. I was shouting up instructions telling them to face the Wall and let themselves down to the uttermost length of their arms, and then to drop, letting their knees give gently, as their toes touched the earth. Peabody, as broad as he was long, made heavy weather of a simple athletic procedure. That sort of man will stand until they are dead on their feet, but ask them to be supple and duck and dive and as well save your breath. He landed in an uncomfortable heap, and as I assisted him onto his feet, I could not resist observing that practice with quarter staffs would have stood him in good stead. He burst out laughing and made to cuff me in jest as I danced aside. His hands were the size of trenchers.

About a hundred of us ran to the right along Jayes Lane which was the name of the path which bordered the north side of the Close. It widened slightly and became Gaia Lane, leading straight behind high banks to Stowe Church. Peabody, in charge, divided us into two groups, and we made our way silently through the bushes on each side of the deep lane, looking down onto its rutted and ridged surface.

At last we reached the deepest point and Peabody ordered the men to stand and thread their muskets through the bushes with their mouths trained down on the lane. "Not across it!" he hissed. "Spare your companions!" Then they knelt in readiness upon the muddy ground. I crouched behind the group to which I had attached myself. Peabody gave a last instruction, "When I shout "Now!" give the bastards a loving leaden greeting."

We were only just in time, as we could hear voices and marching feet pounding along. I could see glimpses of the troop as they fell silent, so as not to give the watchers on the Close, warning of their approach. There were about forty troopers followed by a great lumbering cart, on which the ladders had been piled, drawn by two great horses, one following after the other. The carter seemed to need encouragement.... two or three men hung on the side, urging him on.

Peabody bided his time. We had the element of surprise and the first men were level with the hidden muskets when he shouted "Now!" That volley wreaked hideous carnage. Every man in the lane seemed to have been hit or had fallen over his fellows. The carter, his face a white rictus of fear, leapt from his seat, ran up the bank, charged through Peabody's musketeers and ran pell-mell, across the field to the little hill behind Dam Street. Another Parliament man jumped onto the cart, and gathered up the reins. This was his last action. He fell dead between the shafts.

The screams and shouts of the Parliament men must have been heard back on Stow Church and in Lichfield itself. Peabody waved a red scarf at the Tower. There were answering cheers from the marksmen.

None of the Earl's men had sustained as much as a scratch and had no need of my services. It occurred to me, craven sawbones that I was, that if Gell finally took the field and he had a great advantage in numbers, that if I had tried to help his men, I might get free passage home. But Peabody would have none of it. Ordering me to stay on the bank and do nothing for the wounded and dying in the lane, he had the resourcefulness to have two ladders carried back with us to facilitate our return over the wall of the Close. He set loose the two bewildered horses and fired the rest of the ladders, piled on the cart. As he performed all this, he shouted, "Get back! Back to the Close!"

The groans of the wounded were pitiful to hear. Those who were still conscious were trying to rise to escape. If they succeeded in standing, they could not prevent themselves stepping on their fellows and damaging them still further, New screams arose from the poor broken victims. The scene resembled nothing so much as an old print of Hell.... only we had been the devils. I stood uncertain for a moment on the bank, torn between my calling and the need for retreat. Sir Edward saw my dilemma. "Tom, you can do nothing for them. Leave them. Their own surgeon will come for them."

I followed him down the bank and was horrified by the injuries we had caused. Some who writhed in agony could be helped with the right attention, but some were dying. One man called to me, "Sir, I beg you!" I picked my way over to him. Edward stood guard looking down towards the Church, "Come on Tom! We aren't safe here!"

"Help my boy!" the man who had spoken passed his hand over the body of the man next to him. A man? A boy! Perhaps five years younger than myself. He was bleeding copiously from his shoulder and there seemed unnatural swelling around his ankle. I thought no more but scooped him up in my arms and followed Sir Edward.

7

Sir Edward hurried ahead with my box and I followed with my burden as fast as I could. He reached the North Wall before me and was calling up to the soldiers who had already regained the safety of the Close to let down a hammock. As I appeared Peabody's red, angry face was glaring down at me.

"What in Hell have you there, Tom o'Bedlam?"

"You make war against children, do you, Peabody?" I asked as brave as I dared. Two soldiers were letting down a hammock and I laid the child, for he was not much more, as gently as I could into its linen curve.

"For Jesu's sake, pull him up softly. Don't bang him against the wall!" I implored them. I climbed the ladder after Sir Edward, one handed, steadying my patient away from the wall with the other. As I launched myself over the wall at the top, the ladder was swiftly pulled up after me, and we could hear the men from Stow Church shouting in anger at the burning cart. I suddenly felt quite horror-stricken. Suppose the flames from the cart should spread to the helpless wounded?

The Earl with a thunderous expression was suddenly beside me as I knelt beside the boy. But good Sir Edward, ever my friend, spoke for me.

"Both Tom and I could not leave this boy, my Lord. See, he is no more than a child.... with a look of Ferdinand."

I had stripped away hose and shoon from the injured leg. The knee was undamaged, but the ankle had been, it seemed to me, broken.... when he fell with the ball in his shoulder and then his foot had been horribly bruised when a fellow soldier stepped on him when he was down. But I did not think the bones of the foot were damaged irreparably. The break was I was certain above the ankle, where there was bruising and swelling, independent of the foot. I ran my hands ever and again over the joint and could feel the broken bone, jagged under his skin, just above the ankle bone itself. I judged that recovery would be best effected by that old painful skill of bone setting, and as he still had not totally regained consciousness I looked round for Phoebe and Elijah, to hold him whilst I tried to knit the bone together. "Remember!" Ben used to say: "There is only ever one attempt. Your patient will drag himself about, a cripple, rather than chose to go through that agony again."

Elijah was beside me with clean water. "It has been boiled, Tom," he assured me. "Moisten his lips, Elijah, and talk to him about anything you like." I told him.

"He's not with us." Elijah told me "But breathing well, for all that."

I continued to stroke the area softly, feeling where the bone must go back and lock into itself. The swelling was spreading upwards. I too began talking about nothing in particular, soothing myself as much as the patient, preparing myself for that sudden outrageous jolt of unbearable pain.... a firm hold, a twist, a gasp and a moan from the unconscious boy and the leg was straight again.

"Phoebe, a poultice, as cold as maybe, and comfrey. What think you?"

"Rosemary and thyme also," said Phoebe, bandaging with cold wet cloths.

Now for the shoulder. "I need you, Elijah!" I told him "Remember Edgehill!" The child was slowly gaining consciousness, which I did not want. As Phoebe would be busy macerating her herbs for the foot and ankle, I needed a woman's tender voice, telling him all would be well as we opened and cleaned his shoulder. Suddenly Phillipa was at my side, hastily clad.

"What can I do, Doctor Tom?"

"Speak to him gently. Tell him all will be well. By the mass, I hope it will, mistress. How do you?"

"I am well recovered, Tom," and she began to stroke the boy's brow. Elijah meanwhile had been cutting away the felted coat and linen shirt that covered his wound. Fortunately I knew we had a good supply of Pares Lotion in my box and the good young serving girl ran up to the Bishop's still room to search for lavender. I began to clear the area where the ball had lodged, removing shreds of clothing and flesh also. I wanted him to lose as little blood as possible I pulled aside the sinews and caught a glimpse of the ball, a grey sphere in among the muscle and white fat. Fortunately I judged that whilst there would be a terrible stiffness and soreness for many days to come, the ball had come to rest in the fleshy area, where children in particular have slightly more fat than adults, just below the shoulder and away from the chest. If we could remove it cleanly, he might recover.

"Fold out the cloth, Elijah, and match with the holes. You know what to do. Remember Edward."

I poured some of the boiled water into a bowl and washed my hands again. My long callipers always to me seemed excessively cruel, but they were undoubtedly effective. I had to be careful not to damage further any ligaments or muscle that the musket ball had dislodged. With infinite care, I pushed aside the outer fold of flesh and inserted the callipers. There was no difficulty. The ball was easily caught and I began slowly and painstakingly to edge it out. Slowly.... but suddenly there was a crash of firing from the town.... and I lost the ball. It disappeared and all was to do again. I became terrified lest I should pierce his lung. Carefully I pushed the callipers into the void and found the elusive ball again. This time I vowed nothing and no-one should distract me. Inch by inch.... perhaps it was a four inch cavity.... I pulled the callipers back from the wound and held it up to show Elijah and Phoebe, perhaps with a little pardonable professional triumph. I did not realise that the Earl and his men had gathered in a circle around me and at the sight of the ball, a sigh of quiet victory was audible. But now the whole area must be anointed with the Pares Lotion. I looked at Elijah's shreds of cloth, and peered again once more into the cavity. Then I saw it. A tiny shred of cloth behind which the ball had lodged.

"Elijah, there's still a piece in there. Can you hold the flap? The big callipers won't do. I must use the small ones." I would not be able to see my way clear without assistance, now. Blood was seeping into the cavity. I must act quickly. Elijah came opposite me and knelt steadily holding open the wound. I took out my small pincers. They had been wrapped in clean linen and I took them in my right hand. I had a clear view of the piece of cloth and neatly and cleanly this time was able to draw the shred out of the terrible gash.

Now for the Pares lotion. It prevented the agony and stench of putrefaction. I spread it around and was happy to see that there was

101

only a minimum of bleeding. "He must lie on his back." I told Phillipa. "Where can he go?" Phoebe was busy binding up his shoulder.

"We set aside a small bedchamber for if there was need to isolate a sick man.... or woman for that matter," she told me. She made as if to lift the sick boy but I prevented her.

"You should be resting," I instructed her, Master Doctor to the life. "Phoebe, have you seen the twins?"

She nodded, smiling. Women always love the sight of small babes. At this moment, our patient gave a clear groan, and said plainly: "What.... what's the matter?" Again the spectators sighed with what I thought was relief, and one or two gave faint huzzas as if this had been a wrestling match.

I carried the boy into the Palace. The banging and firing had started again. The Earl followed me inside. I carried my patient upstairs, made him comfortable and turned to the Earl.

"Yes, my Lord?" I asked him.

"I must speak with you, Thomas. Let us say that I speak for your dear father. Given his intolerable ending, how can you waste your skill on these traitors? This.... (he pointed at the boy).... this is one of Essex' creatures."

I sat down wearily, and then leapt up again, realising there was only one chair in the room.

"My Lord, a vicious madman, a vile devil misrepresented my father to Sir Samuel Luke and Essex. At Powick Bridge, I helped anyone who needed my help. Two poor Kings men were cared for, in my father's house and I prevented the untimely burial of Sir Robert Burghill, one of Essex' trusted captains. You will grant it was untimely, given the gentleman was still alive. He spoke for me after my father's death or we would surely have made it a family occasion on the gallows."

"And what of the vicious madman?"

"Oh, I killed him, after Edgehill, with a stool."

He flinched in horror. "What? Oh well, you devil doctors think nothing of using the sweepings of the Ajax. I had hoped that such witchcraft had gone with the old King."

I suddenly realised the ambiguity and now I could not forbear from laughing heartily. I sat down, shaking uncontrollably and Elijah came in to see if all was well.

"Tell him, tell him how…. how Brigstock died." I managed to splutter.

The Earl must have thought us a pair of warlocks from olden times, but as Elijah explained the horror that awaited me in the farm kitchen, on that Monday morning in late October, he too began to laugh at our verbal misunderstanding.

"Phoebe will reassure you, my Lord. We do not use excreta. Not even white do!" I managed to gasp out as she came into the small room, carrying my box of medicaments.

"Well, enough!" said the Earl though it was clear he was afraid that perhaps he was in the presence of unmitigated lunacy. "Jonathan?" he called out. His steward had been hovering in the corridor outside and now came forward into the little room, which was becoming intolerably crowded. "What's for dinner, good Jonathan?" the Earl cried. "My poor stomach rumbles fit to wake the dead!"

"There is nothing, my Lord!" said Jonathan, looking the Earl straight in the eye.

"What?" the Earl roared.

"Nothing!" Jonathan repeated. "There are a few cabbage leaves, picked up from the kitchen floor for which the men are dicing downstairs. The children who came in with your great-niece have eaten the windfalls, every one. There is nothing."

The Earl looked discomforted. "Greville Brooke's coming so suddenly surprised me," he explained.

"Nay, my Lord, surely it was his going so suddenly that surprised him!" I answered with a rare burst of wit. He laughed and clapped me on the shoulder.

"Well, there is still that cask of Bourdeaux, by the Rood. At least I can pledge you, Phoebe, my child. This is one blessed outcome of today's happenings. I may enjoy your company a little longer." And he bustled off downstairs, followed by Jonathan.

We at last had leisure to compare our experiences of the last few days. Colonel Peyto himself had knocked on the Lichfield doors to collect his hostages, on the first occasion that they had been driven across the Causeway. Phoebe had been alone in the Inn parlour and Elijah had escaped as he had been feeding the horses. ("What of them?" I interrupted. "All well," Elijah reassured me. "Cared for by the ostler at the George.") The second time when Sir John Gell had collected hostages, they had been in the Magpie's Nest, where they had gone to ask Gabriel's advice as to what they should do to make contact with me. It seems Sir John had recognised Phoebe and realised what a useful pawn she would be. Elijah had gallantly refused to be parted from her.

"And what of the Magpie?"

Elijah's expression, usually open and trusting, hardened somewhat. "He discovered that he, his wife and parents had always cherished an unshakeable loyalty for the cause of Parliament. And when Sir John learnt that they were even then setting up a diurnal for printing entitled Glad News from Derbyshire, he was pleased to allow them to continue with their task."

"Oh, he loves to be in the news!" said Phoebe. "They were talking of him in the town. He's a rare turkey cock of the dung heap and thinks he's irresistible to women. I swear he is as irresistible as a dead donkey!"

Elijah and I fell to laughing again and were surprised suddenly by a voice from the bed behind us. To my shame I had forgotten we were in a sick room. The poor boy was asking for water and Phoebe hastened to get him a drink.

When she returned and I held him up so he could drink more comfortably, I asked his name. He whispered something that I could not hear and slept again so I accompanied Phoebe to the kitchens, to see what she could contrive. There was flour, two large bags of it, and cinnamon. Suddenly she remembered.

"Tom, there is a brewhouse where the small beer has been made. Perhaps I can steal brewer's yeast and we can all feast on cinnamon rolls."

"Well bethought, Mistress." And one of the maids scampered out. Within an hour the kitchen was fragrant with the smell of new bread. The Earl, prompted by his stomach and the aroma of fresh cooking, looked in on us poor scullions. I sent Elijah to watch the injured boy and congratulated the Earl on the intelligence and practicality of his talented great-niece.

As she dropped lumps of her dough onto the greased tray, I told him: "Phoebe is a Mistress of the Rolls, my Lord. She is a Cook, sans pareil."

"How long must I wait?" The Earl asked, picking up and dropping a brown hot roll cooling in a basket.

"Now, Uncle Philip!" and Phoebe aimed a blow at his hand. "Hot will cool, if Greedy can wait!"

The explosions and firing began again in the town. "Is it Hastings again?" I asked. "It is indeed!" the Earl told us. "What sort of a way to fight is this? Tell me, Phoebe, how did you escape him?"

"Just as everyone escapes him," she explained wisely. "Lock up doors and wait until he and his madmen tire of their banging about. Last night he had heard that Gell was here and shouted out in the streets for him to come and meet his Maker. But that was an invitation Sir John felt bound to refuse!"

"They fear him, though." Elijah who had returned, scratched thoughtfully at a flea-bite. "It is his ability to come and go so swiftly and be everywhere and nowhere that confounds them. I heard that there are perhaps not more than thirty in his troop at this time, but any poor Parliament man who is unaware of his coming in the town is shot to pieces before he can run for cover."

"Don't speak of that!" said the Earl. "Or Tom here will be out over the wall and doctoring the knaves as fast as Hastings can kill 'em!"

I went upstairs to see my patient. He woke when I came in and asked again for water, which I gave him, and again I asked his name and this time I heard it. It was Zacharius and it seems he was a nailor's son from a place I had not heard of, Duffield, a village somewhere to the north of Derby. I was afraid that he might be feverish but apart from a terrible stiffness in his shoulder and a persistent ache in his leg, he told me he was well enough.

"You're Kings' Men here, aren't you?" he suddenly accused me.

"I'm my own man. I'm a doctor. If a man or woman is sick, I treat them. Often I heal them."

"Aye. That's right and tight for you, Mister. You're gentry like. But Father 'll have to give Gell back his money. It were for our Lizzie to get wed. She's in family way and chap won't touch her without five guineas."

"I'll see what can be done," I promised him. "Sleep now."

I went down and told the Earl that Zacharius and his father had joined Gell's regiment to earn enough to enable his sister to marry. I thought it unlikely that the finer points of politicks and faith had moved them nearly so much as Gell's bribe.

"He was no doubt, her seducer and despoiler, the evil bastard!

105

What town are they from? Duffield you say? That's one of the mean little mill villages that line the Derwent. The populace are so poor that they haven't a pot to piss in between 'em, let alone guineas for a daughter's dowry."

"Why are they so poor?" I asked curiously.

"Gell and his rich Curzon kin from thereabouts tax them to the hilt. First it was ship money. Now he's turned his coat, he'll be bleeding 'em dry for Parliament. You know the King excused the Derbyshire leadminers what they owe him and one thousand of them fight for him now as his Life Guards."

Phoebe sniffed. "Somewhat too late in the day for my poor parents."

I excused myself and went to find Sir Edward. He was with the other knights and invited me to join them. "Come, Tom, don't stand on ceremony but sit on this bench." I declined at first but then saw Peabody taking his ease with them like any gentleman, and so accepted.

"Your actions today have given us pause, Tom," he told me.

"Why so, sir?" I asked him.

"John Tichaber and I are of a mind. We do not care for the notion of killing our own people. We are knights of Derbyshire. The men we ambushed today were poor workmen of our County, bribed by Gell in their ignorance and poverty. Loyalty to our King is one thing, but perhaps there is a greater power on high whom we serve very ill by killing His creation."

Strangely I found I could not speak for a moment. I looked down to hide the tears that had sprung to my eyes. The ambush had been an atrocity.

"When one considers that not one of the hostages picked by Peyto and Gell had been harmed, it seems an extreme revenge." I said finally.

Peabody snorted: "Do you think John Gell is so nice in his notions, gentlemen? Empty bellies and bare backs cannot afford consciences."

"And we shall have empty bellies a-plenty here, cooped up like chickens in the hen-house! What does the Earl intend?" asked another of the knights.

Phoebe and the serving girls came round, distributing a cinnamon roll to each of the men sitting hopefully round the tables.

"So, mistress," asked Peabody "what vittles have we for the morrow?"

Phoebe paused. "Why sir, there is nothing else in the kitchen. I fear it is a case of considering the lilies of the field and trusting in Providence."

"And Peabody is a very comely lily!" Sir John Harpur jested.

"Indeed, Mistress," said Peabody with a chivalry I had not known before. "I verily believe you could make soup from a sausage skewer."

"Alas, I cannot, Sir, but I thank you for your good opinion." And she passed on to serve the children, who crowded round her, clutching at her skirts.

"A brave and lovely woman," said Sir Edward, as he saw me looking after her. "Your sweetheart, perhaps?"

I could not reply. I was suddenly embarrassed. "Perhaps I would be aspiring too high. I am after all only a butcher's son."

He snorted. "So was Wolseley!"

Sir John Gell was perhaps familiar with the notion that a momentous deed may be executed as well on the Sabbath as at any other time. Next morning, Sunday the 5th we were woken by a great booming explosion, followed by a tremendous splash. The Earl who was on the Tower betimes came down with the news that a great mortar-piece had been mounted in one of the gardens of Sadler Street, overlooking the Minster Pool, and facing directly onto the south wall of the Close. Gell's men must have burnt the midnight oil, and worked like dogs through the silence of the night. They had raised protective earthworks, so that all we could see was the huge muzzle of the great black gun. Even as we watched from the Tower, empty and chilled, the muzzle swung back and with a terrifying roar, a great cannon ball shot forth....to fall harmlessly in the Minster pool with a great fountain of water. The watchers on the Tower gave an ironic cheer, but decided discreetly to descend. Even dumb John Dyott seemed suddenly to prefer the comforts of terra firma.

"Ferdinand?" the Earl shouted, leading the way back into the Palace. "You know this jabberment, this calculating cant. How long before their reckoning reaches us and gives us a grievous headache?"

Ferdinand, who seemed unperturbed by most crises, climbed the ladder to the scaffolding behind the drawbridge and peered through the embrasure. His father and I followed him. Another great cannonball crashed into the Minster Pool, its path somewhat lower than its predecessors, landing nearer to us. In fact a shower of drops moistened our clothes, on our precarious platform.

"Well, they will find a trajection which will pass over the wall of the Close. If there had been one there who could use a quadrant, they would not have to waste all this time and effort in experimentation!" he concluded, seemingly irritated by their profligate misuse of resource.

"Well, pray God there is not!" said the Earl, "Pray God if such a scholar exists, he sits in the stocks, reaping the rewards of over indulgence. We must hope they expel all their granadoes into the Pool."

We descended to the Close. Many of the woman and children were standing silently, waiting for a service or prayers as it was the Sabbath. The children forbore to play, not because of the sacredness of the day but for very hunger. Two women came up to the Earl, but before they could plead with him for food or escape, he told them waspishly: "Yes, yes I know, sweet ladies. We are all hungry. I hope to rid myself of this great gut of mine with this enforced abstemiousness. Where is James Audley? Let us have some music."

A lute player was sent for. He sat himself in the door of the Palace so all, inside and out could hear him. First he played the old French tune "Mon Desire" but when the Earl's soldiers asked for something rather more roistering he gave us "Bobbing Joe". Sergeant Peabody and one of the Sir Johns began to dance, with the Sergeant taking the woman's part, gracefully wafting a handkerchief he had hastily borrowed. The men lustily sang the chorus: "And canst thou dance the bobbin jo!" and the women and children laughed heartily, with some of the little ones forming their own round dance.

But all was to end in chaos and sorrow, though thankfully not in the loss of life. There was yet another great boom from the town, a terrible splintering crash and we were showered with shards and tiles. One of the granadoes had pierced the roof of the Cathedral. Our music ended abruptly and the Earl ordered all into the Palace. Two of the soldiers were injured, one with a cut to his arm and the other with a graze on his brow. They were not so badly injured however but they made it clear that they would have preferred their healing ministrations at the fair hands of Phoebe, rather than from me and Elijah. Phoebe, bless her, had kept a stale cinnamon roll by her and now fed it to the invalid, Zacharius, as sippets in some precious sour milk.

Ferdinand bustled up to his father, a great grin suffusing his features. "There you see, Father, at last they did find the right projection. I knew they would in time."

"Yes, my son, I thank you for your learned counsel!" said the Earl, somewhat heavily.

"But good cheer, father!" went on the indomitable Ferdinand. "The Cathedral acts as a mighty bulwark."(There was another boom and a crash and a shower of broken tiles cracked against the Palace windows, causing the woman to shriek and the children to cry.) "We are safe here. They will have to raze the Cathedral to the ground before they can hurt us."

"However," said his father, "Let me remind you, Ferdinand, beloved youngest son, the last fruit of my loins and your mother's blessed womb, that if it is all the same to you, I would infinitely rather they did not destroy the Cathedral. It is the sacred symbol of our King, our Church and our Saviour. If the Cathedral is destroyed, then we are as good as dead, whether we live or die in this flesh." Those around him agreed heartily, and I heard Elijah murmur, "Well said, my Lord." as he bathed the broken brow. I must confess, that whilst I did not share Ferdinand's pragmatic view of the Cathedral as a fortress, I was not whole heartedly behind the Earl in thinking it was worth all our lives.

Ferdinand seemed slightly crestfallen. "Oh, well. It will take them many assaults, before total annihilation occurs."

Jonathan spoke: "Well, let us be glad we shall not live to see it. We will all be dead of starvation, before even a tenth of the Cathedral is destroyed."

"How am I beset with long-nosed Puritanical pulpit punishers!" cried the Earl "Has no-one a cheering word for me? Tom, tell me a merry tale, if you please."

So I told the company of my escape from Worcester, much to the amusement of all. I was surprised that the notion of me lying on the floor of the inn at Holt Heath, covered in pease pudding and snoring like a lewd drunkard whilst Lord Philip Wharton and his troop stepped carefully over my legs, should provoke such mirth. I could only surmise that they had thought of me only as a grave unsmiling young doctor. When I told them of Lofty's tale of Essex' fictitious mistress, devised to save my horse from sequestration, their laughter knew no bounds. One of the knights made the old jest of Essex not knowing his prick from his pipe, and another mentioned that both his marriages had ended in disaster.

The Earl sighed heavily: "Lucky man!"

Phoebe was swift to upbraid him. "Come now, Uncle, that is nonsense. Your marriage abounds in blessings. Here is Ferdinand, I swear, one of the cleverest youths in England. Who could not be proud of such an offspring, the fruit of a most happy union?"

"Cousin Phoebe, will you play chess with me?" asked Ferdinand, encouraged anew by her praise.

"It is a game that Elijah here has long wished to learn." Phoebe stood swiftly to give up her seat to my unfortunate journey-man.

As the day progressed I became aware that the children were beginning to show the first signs of extreme hunger. They had not the energy of yesterday and hung round their mothers, sometimes asking for the impossible, but more often clinging to their skirts and gazing wide-eyed at their elders, puzzled by this sudden deprivation of what they had always taken for granted. The granadoes became less frequent…we realised that they were bombarding the Cathedral on the hour, and by turning up the hour glass we were able to calculate almost to the moment when the next assault would come.

Another hazard presented itself. After the noonday cannonade, one of the men cautiously patrolling the walls smelt burning. He ran to the Cathedral shouting to his fellows to bring water. The latest granado lay smoking, a line of match or tow smouldering on the flagstones. Water was thrown upon it and the device made safe, but guarding the Cathedral was now fraught with danger. Having made an aperture in the roof, Gell was using the same trajection to try to fire the building.

The Earl, ever an excellent organiser, even though his planning abilities left much to be desired, now arranged fire watch teams. As Sir John Gell was kind enough to continue to fire his granadoes on the hour, six of us would be ready in the Cathedral porch every sixty minutes under the critical unwavering gaze of St. Chad. We held buckets of water, and as the great hourly cannon ball crashed into the nave, we ran as swiftly as we might, to extinguish the smouldering line of match, protruding from it. It was dangerous work and I had surprised myself by volunteering to be with every fire party after noon. I told the Earl if anyone was injured I would be on hand immediately, my box ready in the porch, but I confess that my deep reason was profound boredom, imprisoned as we were in the Palace. The hourly granado at least marked the passage of time. Although I had been enclosed with the Earl for a scant few days, (I had arrived in the small hours of Wednesday morning to deliver the twins) it was now Sunday and I felt as if I had been in Lichfield Close all my life. It is a matter of some wonderment how mealtimes break up a man's life. Do away with them and time becomes eternity. This was clearly felt particularly by the Earl whose predeliction for belly cheer was obvious.

It may have been hunger... his own and the visible effects of the gnawing inner pangs of others, or it may have been his fear for the Cathedral or it may have been the fact that the women constantly assailed him, pleading with him to let them leave with the children as they were sore afraid of the possible effects of the granadoes, that made him call a meeting.... a Council of War or Peace.... on Sunday evening. The only cause we had for rejoicing was that with the dusk, the bombardment had ceased. He ordered myself and Elijah to be present, and Phoebe also attended, to ensure that he did not punish the Bourdeaux to excess. One or two of the knights and Peabody tried to persuade him to hold out a little longer. But Sir Edward asked: "What would that achieve other than a further trying of their patience and more destruction of the Cathedral. What do you hope for, Sir?"

The Earl said with a broken voice: "Hastings, perhaps? If he would but stand we could assist him." But the wailing of the babes reminded all of us that even their source of sustenance would soon be exhausted. It was agreed that on the morrow Sir Edward would act as herald or emissary. "And do you go with him, Tom," the Earl ordered.

"Why me, sir?" I asked bewildered.

"Because I know you are not completely with me for the King. Because you insisted on bringing in the child from Duffield and putting to rights the havoc we had caused in his young body. And because your linen is the whitest of any man's here, which is saying little. We are all so many scarecrows but you are the cleanest having joined us so recently."

My fear must have shown in my face. Sir Edward attempted to reassure me. "We are heralds only. Messengers. Sir John will not harm us. He will want us to report his mind truthfully. He is a rogue, a cozener and a seducer, but he does not kill for pleasure."

It was arranged that the King's red insignia should be struck and a white flag of surrender flown from the tower, as soon as dawn coloured the East. A trumpeter would stand before us on the Causeway, until we were bidden to approach the town. I must confess I slept little that night. Elijah had the notion that as his treatment would end shortly, Zacharius should at the least have the means to enable him to stand upright. He spent most of the night fashioning a crutch from wood that had fallen from the Cathedral roof. About an hour before daybreak, Peabody with a face as black as midnight's arsehole, as he would have said himself, organised the removal of the planks from behind the drawbridge gates. They had been replaced after the sortie onto the Causeway when the hostages had run into the Close.

"Well, Tom, to stay up late is to be up betimes," the Earl was beside us with a sup of wine. "I do not think you have slept this night." I admitted it. He had had fashioned two white tunics which we slipped over our heads.

At that moment, the final planks were removed and the drawbridge crashed down. The trumpeter, a young relative of Jonathan's came and stood before us on the Causeway, blew a few notes and then ran behind us back into the Close. We stood looking towards the town, Edward holding high a white flag. I remembered the terrible tale of twice burned Wightman and in my mind's eye could see very clearly our two corpses, dangling and dancing from a gibbet in the Market Place before the Guildhall.

A great voice hailed us from the town: "Walk forward and be recognised." We walked slowly along the Causeway. Edward stole a quick glance up the nearest Tower. "John Dyott is watching for us," he murmured to me. "If anyone thinks to shoot us, he is a dead man."

"But so will we be!" I managed to whisper.

He laughed. "Ever a man for a timely jest, Tom." I forbore to tell him I was not jesting.

As we neared the end of the Causeway, four men approached us. They held white scarves which they tied round our eyes. I knew one of them. It was Captain Cross, but thought it might be better not to claim acquaintance. He gave no sign that he knew me. We were led firmly but not roughly. I could tell from the smell of cabbages that we were crossing the Market Place. There was some shouting and jeering as we walked along. We were then turned to the right and led to one of the houses on Market Street. Or Sadler Street as some citizens called it. We were hustled down a hallway and into a large room, where we stood waiting for perhaps five minutes. Then Captain Cross spoke: "They are not here yet. Sit, gentlemen." And I felt the edge of a chair pushed against the back of my legs.

"I thank you, Sir." said Edward and we sat and lapsed into silence. After perhaps ten minutes, there was a rustling and movement and it seemed as if three or four persons had brushed past us and sat down. We were not bound and at any time I could have pulled off my blindfold but fear, craven and all encompassing, tied my hands like a vice. I became aware that there was a fragrance in the room and as that seduced my nose, I knew that the scent was perhaps to mask Sir Edward and myself. We stank.

At last one spoke. It was a pleasant voice, redolent with the soft sounds of Derbyshire to which I had become well used in the Close.

"Well met, Sir Neddy!"

I could tell from his tone of voice that Edward was smiling. "Give you Good Day, Sir John."

"Here's a rare dog-trick that Chesterfield has played on you. Lord Brooke is come hither to listen to our conference. Will you stand and do him Courtesy?"

"Willingly, my Lord." And Edward stood and bowed. I judged that I too should stand although I did not know where "Lord Brooke" was supposed to be sitting. I made a bow hoping it would encompass all the company, alive or dead, although my nose, strangely alert now, was well aware that there was no corpse in the room.

"Who is the bean-pole?" asked Sir John.

"He is a good young doctor from Worcester, who travelled here with the Earl's great-niece. He does not support either King or Parliament."

"Does he not? I'm sure we will persuade him.... at length.... to embrace the great cause of Parliament. The rack is a great remover of scruples. Well, what of your terms?"

Briefly Sir Edward asked for safe passage out for all in the Close, to include goods, arms, horses and servants. His various points aroused laughter and even I unversed in the art of warfare could see that no opposing commander in the ascendant would allow his besieged foes to retain their weapons.

When the laughter had ceased Sir John spoke again. "Sir Neddy, ever the pleasant jester. You will be lucky indeed to obtain free quarter. I will visit you myself this day and take possession of the Close, when we will decide how best finally to dispose of you all. Be prepared for my visit. Any resistance and you are all dead men, and your women will be reduced to whores, begging their bread in the gutters. That concludes the matter."

The soldiers behind me grasped my arms. I knew I had one chance to remind Captain Cross that Phoebe and I had saved Parliament lives in Stratford.

"May I address Lord Brooke?" I asked and the guards paused.

"Well?" said Sir John.

"I am rejoiced that his Lordship took no hurt from the explosion in the Town Hall at Stratford. He will remember that I, and my assistant constrained his regiment to clear the Hall when she saw that gunpowder had been spilt. As I, the last to leave tripped over the threshold, the Hall collapsed behind us."

There was a long pause, so long that I wondered if they had all crept out and left us alone. Then Sir John spoke.

"Lord Brooke is suffering from a slight ague, young man. His voice has disappeared. But be sure he hears you. Good day to you."

We shuffled out, led by our captors. As we went across the Market Place, I heard a familiar voice, calling my name.

"Tom! Tom! Has Lord Chesterfield capitulated? Have you been eating cats and dogs? Will your lives be spared? Give me some indication, man. And I can print all by the afternoon!"

I stopped in my tracks. "Captain Cross?" I called. He was behind me.

"Yes, Doctor?" he asked civilly.

"Of your charity, keep this treacherous gadfly away from me, or I swear I shall break his pate, blindfolded or not."

114

He laughed and there was the sound of swords being drawn. The Captain removed our scarves and I had the pleasurable sight of Ralph running through the Market Place pursued for perhaps twenty yards by two sturdy musketeers. The Captain suggested that we could remove our white tunics and so we came to the Causeway. The soldiers walked halfway over with us, then politely bade us Good Day and marched back to the town.

"Well, there you see, Tom, we both still live and breathe. But what a masquerade to pretend Lord Brooke was there! I think Sir John is hoist with his own mortar piece. He dare not tell the Warwickshire men that their idol is dead or they would disband straightway."

"Why does he not use our killing of Lord Brooke to punish us?" I asked innocently, as we waited for the drawer bridge to be lowered.

"Because he has stepped into his shoes and clearly finds they are a good fit! You do not know Sir John. If you can offer him money and power, then he will use you gladly to achieve his own ends. He likes to be spoken fair and he likes women. I do not think he intends our deaths, for all his threats today. I think too that there were other great Parliament men with him whom he wished to impress."

"You were devilish well controlled when he called you Sir Neddy!" I congratulated him.

"Controlled? Why should I mind that? My mother calls me Neddy." And we passed into the Close.

Sir Edward spent some time persuading the Earl that in spite of Lord Brooke's death and the ambush fatalities, he believed that Sir John had more to gain by sparing us, than slaughtering us. The Earl's rents and those of his knights would be confiscated. Almost certainly they would be imprisoned. "But better to have tried to support a great cause and failed, than not to have tried at all." Sir Edward argued. The Earl nodded reluctantly.

What was necessary was for us to be as cleanly and nice in our persons as was possible so that we did not look, for all the world, a collection of raggedy Queer-coves and Quaedams but could conduct ourselves like dignified prisoners of war. Buckets were drawn from the well and the water heated in the kitchens, soap was produced from the still room and a procession of men, women and children slowly entered the kitchen to be cleaned. I was called upon to deal with a few head lice, and was myself pleased to wash my itching head and anoint it with lavender in spite of Peabody's lewd comments which compared me with a whoremaster from a House of Easement. He of course would have no part in such foppery he told us, but would merely wash himself free of the Close fleas which he wished to donate to Sir John.

As the day advanced, the Earl suggested that we drew up our company, knights, servants, guards, musketeers and women and children, so that we could at the least face Sir John with dignified courage. Sir Edward agreed but thought that where there were families, they should group together, father, mother, children and in one or two instances, grandparents also. It was agreed that Peabody should stand with the single knights who undertook to stop his mouth, should he feel moved to insult Sir John. I noticed that the Sergeant in spite of his comments pouring scorn on our "foppery" had somehow managed to change his linen.

Zacharius, excited at the prospect of leaving his bed, was hoping against hope that his father had survived the Ambush. "Could the boy stand with us?" Edward asked. Elijah thought if he were helped downstairs, he could use his crutch, but Phoebe volunteered to stand beside him and support him.

So we assembled in the Close. Trumpets sounded from the town and the Earl, his face, revealing his lost hopes and bitter disappointment, signalled for the drawbridge to be lowered.

There was the sound of marching feet upon the Causeway. All eyes were turned to the gate and the word of command to the Parliament men to halt was given. And Sir John Gell strode into the Close.

8

I had never seen anyone with such large staring eyes, like an owl. He gazed at us, ranged up before him, the Earl standing alone in front of everyone. Then Sir John smiled. His grey eyes seemed to take the measure of everyone, but value no-one. His expression was not so much hard, as calculating. Then he motioned to one behind him with a great basket, to follow him.

He moved forward towards the families, standing with their backs to the south wall of the Cathedral and stopped beside a group, comprising a musketeer, his wife and their little girl. The mother instinctively drew her daughter to her, but Sir John bent towards the child and asked sweetly: "Do you like sugar plums, my poppet?" Without waiting for a reply, he motioned to his servant to present the child with a sweetmeat from the basket. There was instantly a murmuring of apprehension amongst the children. He moved on to the next family, which rejoiced in three small boys. His question brought forth the rapturous response. "Yes, please, Sir."

"Good boys!" he told them, patted their heads, distributed the sugar plums and moved on to the next group. In all this he did not speak to any adult, but confined his attention entirely to the children, to whom he spoke gently and in as friendly a manner as one could wish. Ultimately some of the older boys, of ten or eleven years of age, left their families and followed the fascinating basket. Soon the little boys and the girls began to follow him too, understandably for they were all desperately hungry. They had had no food since Phoebe's cinnamon rolls.

When he had given a sugar plum to each child, he turned towards the Earl's followers. "Why, Sir Neddy!" he cried. "Well met again, by my troth! Can I tempt you to a sugar plum, or are you now too gravely adult to crave such sweet jellies?"

"I thank you, Sir John and I assure you I do not count myself too grave a man under your compassionate governance as not to savour such a jelly from Sir John Gell," said Edward, all smiles, wit and courtesy. "But here is one of your own, whom we have tended for you. I know he would relish a sweetmeat." He indicated Zacharius whose eyes were undoubtedly at that moment, bigger than his belly.

"One of my own?" said Sir John.

"Doctor Tom felt he was too young to lie wounded on the ground in Gaia Lane and brought him into the Close to tend him."

"And have you had good treatment from this Doctor?" and while Zacharius caught his breath and tried to answer, he asked: "From Belper, are you?"

"From Duffield, sir. And aye, he's trussed me up like a Michael-mas goose. And this feller made me this, so's I could leave me bed." And he indicated the crutch and Elijah in one gesture.

Accepting this as a recommendation, Sir John turned to me with a smile. "I see you think as I do, Doctor Tom. It behoves us to nurture, nourish and care for our young, whatever our policies." At that moment he caught sight of Phillipa, standing by Jonathan behind the Earl. Husband and wife held each a babe.

"Why, Mistress Goodhead, Good day to you. I see you are the lighter by two stalwart citizens of Derbyshire. And what beautiful cherubs! Twins? A boy and girl?"

"Yes, Sir John." And Philippa with a degree of courage I did not know she possessed placed the girl in Sir John's arms.

"This is the little maid, I vow. In time she will be as beautiful as her mother. And her name?"

"Rosamund, Sir John. And the boy is Philip John Chad Thomas."

I had not known that Philippa could be so cunning a diplomat. Sir John, gave her a sidelong glance and uttering gentle sounds, replaced the babe in her arms and turned to the children who still followed him.

"Back with you to your parents," he told them. "Perhaps later there will be another sweetmeat for you all." As they made their way back to their families, he stood waiting. When all was quiet and still again he gestured to the captains of the troops who had followed him. Captain Cross came bustling up at the head of a group of purple clad harquebusiers.

"Gentlemen, I must command you. Drop your weapons before you."

There was a prolonged sigh. The Earl's men had known that the price of life would be to be turned off defenceless. Swords and daggers were produced and let fall and the musketeers dropped their firing pieces. A great clatter rang out as all were given up at once. I had only my small dagger, which Captain Cross picked up with a raised eyebrow.

"I use it to cut up bandages for the wounded," I told him.

"I doubt Sir John will wish to deprive you of it," he said returning it to me. "Keep it. I will answer for you."

The Parliament men moved amongst us collecting the weapons, which were passed down the Causeway to the town. I noticed that although dumb John Dyott was standing looking steadfastly at the ground, his duck gun was absent. Well, what Sir John did not know about, he could not miss.

Their task completed, the victors formed a grim line facing us, swords drawn, seemingly daring us to object to what was to follow. An ominous silence fell. Sir John walked slowly to the front of the Earl, who through all this had glared fixedly ahead. Though the two men were of a height, perhaps both four inches below myself, there the resemblance ended. Sir John was richly dressed, perfumed, clearly nice in his person, his hair which was abundant was curled in a multitude of ringlets. The Earl looked hardly better dressed than any beggar at the town gate. He had, I think, found his least soiled linen to try to assume a brave show. His doublet and hose were wrinkled and stained and stinking.

"Well, my Lord Chesterfield!"

"Well, Sir John." The earl seemed to speak through clenched teeth.

"I have a sugar plum for you, my Lord." He gestured to the front rank of the regiment, standing in the postern.

"Now then, my Lord Chesterfield!" said Sir John. "Here is your sugar-plum!"

There was a creaking sound and a hideous contraption was wheeled up the Causeway into the Close. It was a moveable gallows. Five or six men pushed it until it stood directly in front of the Earl, full in his line of vision.

John Gell who had not left his place directly in front of the Earl,

119

took his leather gloves, trimmed with delicate silver lace from the loop on his sleeve. He wafted them in front of his face as if to remove the Earl's bodily stench from the air he breathed, stepped closer to the Earl, and smartly struck him with his gloves on each cheek. The Earl did not flinch but I knew that an outraged growling coming from the far corner was Sergeant Peabody. No-one else made a sound or moved. The earl's life seemed to hang in the balance, a grisly jest if ever there was one. My innards churned. Sir Edward must be wrong. Sir John was going to hang the good Earl, the man who in some ways reminded me of my poor father. I choked back a sob.

Sir John took a step back. "Well, then, Chesterfield. Why should I spare your life? What reasons can you give me?"

The Earl spoke at last. "None. I have no reasons why I should be spared. I expect you to hang me. At least I acted soon enough and surrendered before these for whom I was responsible began to starve."

This was clearly not the answer for which Sir John was hoping. He looked sidelong at the Earl as if to catch him in some deception. Then he made that strange noise we English make at the back of our throats when we do not know what to say, a strange humming note. "Hmmmm!" said Sir John.

"Well, gentlemen and ladies too. Let me invite you to give me your reasons why he should be spared."

Ferdinand pushed fearlessly through the troops and knelt at Sir John's feet. He was in tears. He was not after all very old. "I beg you, Sir John. You have sons. You would not wish them to be thrown fatherless upon the world."

"Very pretty!" said Sir John. "Who is next?"

One by one the knights came forward and spoke of the Earl's many kindnesses, his care for his people, when they were old or sick and he could no longer exact his dues from them.

Then Phoebe stepped forward. "Well, Lady Phoebe Stanhope! It is you I think. You travel so close to the ground it is easy to overlook you."

"That may be so for you, Sir John, but with my mode of transport I miss nothing, and I ask you to be very sure that you administer justice, as in the great Day of Judgement we must all hope for mercy."

Phoebe's example so fired me that I felt I must speak. "May I address you privately, Sir John?"

"Is it the bean-pole? Well, aye. I am curious as to what one whose head is so close to the clouds, might have to say."

I drew him round the corner of the Cathedral towards the west front. We paused near the statue of St Chad.

"Sir John," I said in an undertone, "The King could win the conflict!"

He looked at me as if I had told him the man in the moon had come down and was selling cheese in Lichfield market.

"Nothing is certain in this life," I went on. "Perhaps you are right in your opinion that the great cause of Parliament must prevail. In that case there can be no threat if the Earl lives on, without followers or weapons, but if the King does take the ascendant, at least Lord Chesterfield will remember your mercy and not press the King for your death."

He began to laugh. "Are all Doctors from Worcester this adept at chop-logic? What sort of moralising, whey faced philosopher are you? As I understand it you have known the old blackguard for only a few days. Why such passion?"

So I told him of my father's fate, and how the sight of his "sugarplum" had caused my stomach to knot and my mouth to turn to a dry chasm.

"No matter! What of the men of the true Parliament cause who died in the ditch back there? Gay Lane is it? No, the old bastard must atone."

He walked back round the corner and told a black gowned churchman who had followed the gallows: "Prepare him!" The cleric approached the Earl and mumbled something of the church ceremony at him. If he hoped for the resurrection of the body and the life after death, he must now confess his sins.

"I decline to do so in this company. Time enough in all eternity!" The Earl proclaimed in a clear loud voice.

Sir John gestured for the execution to take place. The Earl was led to the platform and instructed to stand upon a wooden block that was placed below the noose. A black hood was placed over his head and the loop lowered round his neck.

I had nothing in my stomach to void but I could not prevent myself from retching violently. My father and his fearful fate crowded in on me. When I closed my eyes all I could see was his dear, dead face. The Earl's people began to murmur amongst themselves, and I think I groaned aloud, but Sir John with a gesture of his hand, ordered silence. He placed his finger on his lips, gave us all his sidelong look, and winked conspiratorially. The Earl stood straight and blind waiting calmly for death. When it did not happen it became clear that we were witnessing a grim jest, a charade, a masquerade. The servant with the basket moved to the children again and gave each another sugar plum. All of the adults were at a loss as to how to conduct themselves in the face of Gell's cruel duplicity. Any objection and the noose could be instantly pulled tight and the block kicked away. If they laughed at his joke as perhaps he wished them to do, he might on the instant change his mind and the Earl be hanged in good earnest.

So we stood waiting for perhaps fifteen minutes. Some of the older boys began to grin and snigger, hoping perhaps by so doing they were playing the same game as Sir John. Some of the little ones began to cry. The sight of the Earl alone was terrible indeed but their tender stomachs would also even now be attempting to digest a sudden invasion of rich sugar, and they would be in the grip of painful cramps.

Finally Sir John, perhaps tiring of his jest, ascended the gallows and pulled off the black hood. "It seems, Chesterfield, that mercy is the watchword. Against my will, I will condemn you to life. We are at one in that we have both in our time been the victims of calumny and vituperative scandal. You in your youth and I now when I am trying to save my shire. And indeed I confess I should find it difficult and tedious to have no-one to hate." In a dramatic courtly gesture he assisted the Earl to descend.

The Earl allowed him to assist him and then with infinite courtesy, bowed to his captor and said: "Your servant Sir John. I must ask you to excuse me for a moment." He went into the Palace followed by Jonathan, who told me afterwards the earl had gone in to seek privacy to relieve himself, ever the human need in times of great stress. They returned a few moments later with the barrel of Bordeaux. "Allow me to pledge you, Sir John," said the Earl. "A pretty jest indeed."

I could see that the Earl was controlling himself with great difficulty. The more pride and dignity he displayed, the more John

Gell would seem a crude lewd rudesby. Not even Phoebe had the heart to scold her uncle for his recourse to strong liquor after his ordeal. As for Sir John, he looked somewhat discomforted, as he accepted and sipped a goblet of wine.

The gallows was wheeled away. I hoped I would never see it again. Some of the ladies asked permission to sit, which was readily granted and indeed some of Sir John's men brought benches for them from the palace.

Sir John addressed us again, "Well, my Lord Chesterfield, I fear this will be the last merry meeting you will have with your friends and followers for some time. I regret that you are a prisoner for King and Parliament, until such time as His Majesty turns from his evil counsellors. You must go first to Wingfield, then to London. Your son and these gentlemen knights will accompany you into prison. You will be dealt with as befits your status but you will comprehend that the treachery you have committed might make your captors and guards somewhat antagonistic towards you. However, Sir Thomas Lunsford who now controls the Tower...." he paused dramatically and there was a gasp from his followers.... "is a man of humane principles and Christian charity. Indeed, my Lord, it must be the Tower. I doubt there is a prison in Derbyshire large enough to contain you."

Sir John's soldiers smiled grimly at the jest, but the Earl, dignified and composed, asked for permission to address his people. Without waiting for any formal response he turned to the assembled company and spoke immediately.

"My friends and servants, for if you are the second I trust you know I count you as the first. I thank you, all of you, of whatever degree, for supporting me in this enterprise. I am sorry that my lack of forethought has caused it to miscarry. Sir John will, I know, deal with you all, mercifully. As for me, have no fear. Was not Elizabeth, our Queen, of blessed memory, imprisoned in the Tower by her own sister and did she not emerge from there, unscathed, eventually to take the throne? The thought of our merry days of friendship and goodwill here in the Close will sustain me. Do not fear for me...." for some of the women were weeping by this.... "We must hope and pray that right will prevail. I thank you all from my heart. Farewell and God bless you all."

He and the knights were marched away immediately, down the

Causeway and into the town. I heard later that they were given bread and small beer in the Guildhall, before the five knights, the Earl and his son were mounted and hurried east to Wingfield Manor, where I had heard that the ill-fated Scottish queen Mary was once imprisoned. And so he was gone, out of our lives. I had known him for less than a week. He had faults, no doubt of it, but his absence depressed us sorely. And now Sir John addressed us.

"You are all free men and women, after the payment of a small fine. The foot soldiers, if any, may pay one guinea, the musketeers, two guineas and any dragoons may pay three for their freedom. Good Sergeant Peabody, for a man of your military experience, I must ask you for seven guineas."

The soldiers came forward, and meekly stood in line. To my surprise, coins were produced, not merely from pockets but from the linings of coats.... my dagger was borrowed to slit seams.... and from small pouches hung round their necks. Peabody slammed down seven guineas on the table where Sir John's secretary was collecting the money and walked out of the Close without a backward glance, following the rest of the soldiers into the town. I had the impression Sir John regretted he had not asked for more.

He now instructed the women and children to follow their husbands and fathers. I noticed that he looked carefully at the women as they passed him, on their way out of the Close. He called one over to him, the clever pretty girl who had helped us find simples from the still room. I did not hear his question but could guess at it from her answer, which came pert as a partridge. "Alas, Sir, my monthly courses are upon me, grievous heavy, or nothing would give me greater pleasure." And with that she tripped out of the gate.

He asked nothing from the Earl's servants but asked Jonathan and Phillipa where they would go. They told him to Bretby Hall to serve the Countess.

"Ah, yes, indeed. A formidably noble lady," he said with something of a shudder. "Pay her my best respects. It grieves me much to separate husband and wife. But no doubt the Earl will embrace his fate with fortitude." And he bade them Farewell.

Only the three of us remained with Zacharius. Sir John's men, perhaps about a hundred of them, were sitting and taking their ease. He called to two of them: "Escort this youth down to the Hartshorn, to his father." And Zacharius hopped off gladly without

124

a word of thanks or a backward glance. Before Sir John could turn back to us, a messenger came in from one Lieutenant Colonel Russell.

"Do we have your permission to enter the Close, Sir John? The men are tired and need to sleep."

"Oh, aye. Pray enter now. The clerics as ever keep their distance. The Earl did not meddle with them. I suggest we do not. The populace revere them."

I had not thought of the churchmen who inhabited the Close. I remembered now the occasional black gown whisking out of sight. Their peace and tranquillity must have been grievously shattered by the granadoes. Now dragoons and cavalry could be heard trit-trotting up the Causeway. The Earl had paid for his horses to be put out to grass and I wondered where Colonel Russell's men would stable their mounts.

In a moment the Close was crammed with horsemen. Sir John motioned to us to accompany him round to the porch. There was a small oasis of quiet, under the great arched doorway.

"Come," he said. "We'll go inside."

My heart was in my mouth, lest Elijah began to cross himself or mumble the Latin mass. However he was silent and worried, as were Phoebe and I, fearing our fate.

"Your apprentice?" asked Sir John.

"My journeyman," I told him.

"He is over young," he commented.

"Nevertheless, he helped me at Edgehill. It was a baptism of fire for us both."

"I take it you would wish to return to Worcester," said Sir John with one of his sidelong looks.

Hope sprang in my heart. "Indeed we would, Sir John," I replied, and the other two nodded eagerly.

"Hmmmmm!" said Sir John "Lady Phoebe, if you have twenty guineas, you have leave to depart, on the instant. But you two young Trojans, alas, at this pass, I fear you are too valuable a commodity to allow you to slip through my fingers. I must detain you. Let us say I will give you leave to go in three weeks after you have spent time repairing some Derbyshire arms and legs and let us say, your freedom then will cost thirty guineas for the master and twenty for the man."

When an enemy offers terms, it behoves one to behave with circumspection, even though the prospect is bleak "May we discuss how we can best accomplish your command, Sir John?" I asked politely.

"Willingly," he replied.

We moved a little distance from him. "I have more than twenty guineas in the George in my saddle-bags." I told them, "and three guineas here in my pocket and some crowns, but I do not have the fifty guineas needed for our release."

"I have eighteen in my purse," said Phoebe, patting her bosom. "It seems wise and politic therefore for me to return to Worcester and come back with your ransom money."

"Phoebe, you cannot go alone. For all we know the horses may have been sequestred."

I asked Sir John if we could go to the George to recover our properties and suggested that two of his men accompanied us.

"No need of that. You would not be able to leave the town," he told us. "Be with me again at sundown." So we left the Cathedral through the South Porch, the other two preceding me. As I closed the great door behind me, I gasped. Horses were trooping into the church by the North door. I thanked God Elijah had not seen this sacrilege.

We left the Close, as I had first entered it, through the South West gate. Our horses were safely stabled at the back of the George, healthy and well fed, and pleased to be spoilt by tasty carrots we found in a pile by the hay loft. The Spring air seemed pleasanter and more wholesome out of the Close, but we could not give the horses the exercise for which they clearly longed, as we were loathe to draw attention to their presence.

We entered the inn through the door, which gave onto the stable yard at the back. I called out "Good day, mistress." And the landlady came from the kitchen.

As she saw us, she clutched her bosom and leant against the wall. "Oh Jesu!" she cried out. "Oh, Jesu! It did not happen. Oh, thanks be to God!" She clutched Phoebe to her person, and grasped the hands of Elijah and myself. Somewhat bemused by her reception of us, I determined to turn her delight in our reappearance to our advantage.

"Could you give us something to eat, mistress?" I asked her. "We have had nothing for two days in the Close. That is why the Earl had to relinquish it to the men of Parliament."

She brought us bread and meat and a frumenty pudding with large raisins in it, cream and small beer. Our need for conversation lapsed for some while, although the landlady obviously felt bound to remain with us and encouraged us to eat and drink our fill. Then as I pushed back my chair, she asked a question which brought dark horror to my heart.

"So, Master Doctor, you received your bags safely from the Magpie?"

I stared at her, dumbfounded.

"From the Magpie?"

"Aye, he swore yesterday that you were to be hanged at Sir John Gell's command.... all in the Close, said he. But poor Doctor Tom went only to deliver a child, not from conviction, says I. No matter, says he, all are for the noose and his wife, Eleanour, for old times sake, to be bequeathed such goods and money that you have left here."

This was too much to be borne. "What?" I roared, springing from my seat. I sprang smartly down again for I had forgotten the low beam that ran the length of the dining parlour, and had cracked my head upon it.

"Why did you believe him?" finally I managed to ask when my brow had stopped stinging, and the room had stopped swinging and a lump the size of a pullet's egg had emerged.

"Well, all that he says has the ring of truth. He sells the News after all," she said defensively.

"Do we look dead? Do we look hanged? Does that have the ring of truth?" I shouted.

"No, indeed, Doctor Tom, and God be praised!" She burst into tears, and wiping her eyes with her apron, ran to her kitchen.

We searched our rooms. He had not merely stolen all my money but had also removed every article of our clothing. My spare shirt and doublet, hose, Elijah's small clothes, patched and darned though they were and Phoebe's best green gown, and the saddle-bags in which they were packed. We returned to the dining parlour. I could feel fury, hot, violent and uncontrollable, rising in my heart.

"We had best pay our reckoning," I said to Phoebe. "See if she will reduce our debt, given her stupidity." I could not speak to the landlady. The first rule of a good inn. Never allow anyone other than the guests who have bespoken the room to enter it.

"At least we still have the horses," I said gloomily to Elijah.

"Only because he didn't know they were there," he replied.

"I beg you, Elijah, do not let me kill Ralph Truscott. When Phoebe has concluded this, I am going to his filthy Magpie's Nest where I will tie his arms in a knot behind him and remove his entrails with a rusty knife."

Phoebe returned from the kitchen. "Well, that at least is something. I have only had to pay for the horses and they may remain for another week for nothing. She is weeping, fit to drown the cat and all her kittens."

"So she should be!" I said darkly. "I think Elijah and I must lodge with the Derbyshire regiment, but can you stay here this night? I'll arrange for your travel tomorrow."

It seemed the poor landlady would let Phoebe stay till the Day of Judgement, if she so pleased and us too if we wished. "And after all," said Phoebe wisely, "She did see Ralph treated as if he were as a trusted friend by us, when you kindly feasted them. It was only Tuesday last when we had that merry meal with them."

"Oh, very well!" I said churlishly, and went to the kitchen. "Madam, forgive me. I spoke angrily out of concern for my two dependants. I will endeavour now to recover my money and clothes from this wretched cozener."

"Nay Doctor Tom," she said sniffing, "It is for you to forgive me. I am a numbskull. What sort of innkeeper am I, that I would be such an addlebrained hussy? It is these wars! They set everything at sixes and sevens!"

"Never fear, dear madam!" I said patting and comforting her shoulder, as she wept against my shirt. "All might yet be well. I will see if I can find this caitiff."

It was no distance from St John's Street to Bore Street. Elijah and Phoebe followed me as I turned into the rubbish-strewn yard, calling Ralph's name, and kicked open the door. The room was empty. Everything, the piles of papers, old rags, broken chairs all had gone. I went to the inner room where the printing press was housed. Nothing. It was as if old Hans and his amazing contrivance had never been. But there were the deep grooves in the earthen floor where the four corners of the press had rested, and there were a few stray smudged and spoiled pages of past diurnals.

I came out to Cabbage Court and looked at my friends. "They have flown the coop," I told them. "Perhaps they needed to escape other debtors!"

We wandered out into the street, unsure what to do. And there, waiting for us, his hands on his substantial hips was Master Froggatt, the vintner.

"Ah, now then, 'tis the fine young Doctor, who would not take my advice about this cozening shakebuckler of a Magpie."

"Do you know where they have gone, Master Froggatt?" I asked as politely as I could.

"I might at that," he said. "He still owes me."

"He has stolen all our money and clothes whilst we were unable to leave the Close."

"He is for the bastinado, if there were anything like Justice to be had in this craven town." And he called down the hole, which led to the cellar under his shop where the barrels were rolled down.

"Hodge! Hodge! Come here with you!"

As we stood waiting for Hodge to appear, someone clapped me on the shoulder. I half guessed who it might be fore the affectionate gesture nearly knocked me off my feet. It was Sergeant Peabody, who smiled graciously at the company, bowed to Phoebe and gave a civil Good day to Master Froggatt.

"Is all well with you, Doctor Tom, in this town?" he asked pleasantly.

"Alas, no!" I told him. "We are the victims of a thief!"

"A thief?" he asked, swaying slightly, "Is this the thief?" as the smallest, dirtiest most miserable urchin, heaved himself out of the cellar opening.

"No, indeed, it is not!" I cried out. "Master Froggatt, who is this?"

The vintner looked somewhat discomforted. "This is the child of a fellow Guildsman. He and his wife died of the plague last year and what does the Mayor and Aldermen do, but make me responsible for him and his sister." Another child was crawling from the hole, a tiny girl.

"It does not seem as if you have taken that responsibility very seriously," I said, remembering my father's good efforts on behalf of the orphans of fellow butchers in Worcester.

"I feeds'em, don't I?" Froggatt shouted. "Do I feed you?" he cried, leaning down to the children. "Do I feed you? Yea or Nay?"

"Yes, sir," whispered the boy.

"Oh, aye, we can see you feed them, Master Froggatt. The evidence of that is on their clothes and faces, and has been there for many a long day!" Lady Phoebe Stanhope was at her most aristocratic.

"And in return for their food and their blankets in the fine dry store here, below my shop, Hodge watches what goes on out here. So when did the Magpie and all his lot.... when did they go, Hodge? Tell the kind gentleman. Don't be afeared!"

"Yesterday, when it got dark," Hodge told us. "They had a cart for all the.... all the.... wooden bits."

"Oh, God's blood," I cried "They could be miles from Lichfield by now."

"No, they could not, Doctor Tom." Peabody shook his head. "I tried to follow the Earl to Wingfield. To leave town requires a dispensation from that lecherous devil, Gell. What are the wooden bits?"

"The printing press he has been using for his news sheets."

"Is it worth money?" asked Peabody. I nodded. "Then depend on it, Gell would never let it slip through his greedy clutches. There are guard posts on every road out of town. They may have moved house, but they could not have left Lichfield. Gell loves the diurnals. He'll probably employ this Magpie villain for his own purposes."

"Which direction did they go?" I asked little Hodge. Distressed, beyond measure, and now addressed harshly by something resembling a tall, dark Maypole, the poor child began to cry. Phoebe took a clean cloth from her pocket and began to wipe the children's faces, which were stained with age-old tears and snot. "Leave me with them for a moment," she ordered us, again in that piercing dominating voice she could assume at will. "These innocents are surely not yet five years old, and their condition is disgraceful. Vintner, you should think deep burning shame for their mistreatment. Tom, use your brain. This little fellow cannot understand words like "direction". Could you, at five?"

Elijah and I, our tails between our legs, moved somewhat down the street towards the ale house. When Phoebe assumed her Ladyship status, the effect was arresting. Master Froggatt seemed to wish to accompany us but Peabody delivered the final thrust of the knife.

"This sorts ill, Master. The children of a brother vintner? Whatever one might think of Gell, should he hear of this, it would go hard with a Guildsman who maltreated children." He bowed to Phoebe. "Lady Phoebe Stanhope. Your humble servant. I await your commands." He followed us into the alehouse, where we slaked our thirst.

After some moments, Phoebe appeared at the door with the children and beckoned. "All is understood. They have moved into the house of these two poor waifs. It is in Frog Lane, at the sign of the Barrel. Eleanour befriended them, telling them she would care for them there, as their new mother, if they would tell her where their empty house was."

Peabody shook his head. "This is outrageous. To steal your clothes and coin is bad enough, but to purloin the birthright of these two.... I would like to meet this Magpie."

"I beg you, Sergeant, and you Elijah, do not let me kill him. You should see what I did to Ensign Billiard." I remembered my rage, my knuckles tingling.

"Well, shall we go?" said Phoebe. "I am for deeds now, not words!"

And a formidable little troop we must have looked as we turned into the narrow street called the Conduit, which led into Frog Lane, Phoebe carrying the little girl and holding the boy by the hand, Elijah as determined as I to retrieve, if not his money for he had not much of that, but at the least his small clothes, myself still red-hot with fury, and Peabody as broad as a church door, and somewhat less welcoming.

As we rounded the corner, little Hodge pointed and there was the sign of a barrel, suspended still over the street door. We approached the house silently, and I bent and listened at the keyhole. The unmistakeable whirr of the great screw and the crash of the press onto the platens. Then I heard Ralph's laugh and that was enough. I kicked the door open, marched in, lifted him off his feet and sat him atop the printing press that sat conveniently near against the wall.

"Tell me why," I shouted in his face, "I should not ask my friend Sergeant Peabody here to rearrange your lying features!"

Gabriel rose from a table where he had been seated with the

ladies. "Tom, my dear boy, you are alive. You are all here, well and hearty. Praise be! I wondered whether dear Ralph was somewhat too hasty, in his prediction that all would hang."

"Somewhat too hasty?" I repeated his words. "Indeed, he was, Master Truscott, but then so were all of you. Where is my money?"

"And may I ask, mistress, what you are sewing?" Phoebe spoke to Eleanour in that voice which could be heard across a large manor court-yard, aye and beyond!

There was no need for Eleanour to reply. The green fabric was clearly Phoebe's fine gown. It had been my father's last expressed wish that Phoebe should have new clothes. Eleanour crouched down in her chair, clearly wishing she were some leagues distant. I shook Ralph like a terrier with a rat.

"I say again, caitiff, where is my money?" I had a firm grasp at the front of his doublet and felt a round, hard object, a money-bag under his shirt. I pulled it away from his chest and coins clattered and fell all over the floor.

There was a long silence. But then Cornelia rose from the table. She began to shriek in her native tongue and for a moment I feared that she was screaming and howling imprecations at me, who had attacked her precious son. But not a bit of it. She pushed me aside and with her clenched fist, punched her son hard on his chest so that his head banged against the wall. She drew back her hand again to repeat the blow, but by that that time Gabriel was beside her restraining her.

"Cornelia, my own, my dearest, forbear I beg you." He held her in his arms but she screamed even louder, clearly calling for her father, who timidly poked his head round a door and entered.

He had perhaps been trying on a new shirt, as that was all he wore. Except it was not a new shirt but Elijah's, altered hastily to fit him. The tail hung down below his sad little arse, but the hem at the front had still to be unpicked. He saw the gold coins on the floor and hearing from his daughter in his own tongue that they had been hoarded by Ralph, he picked up a broom that lay on the floor and seemed unsure whether he should sweep up the fortune that lay around us, or use it to beat his grandson.

Gabriel, envisioning the possible early demise of the only fruit of his loins and the support of his old age, began to intervene. "Cornelia, my heart, No, No! There must be an explanation!" and as

Hans became more vehement "My dear Papa! I pray you! A boy only! A child! Misguided, unwise but not a thief, surely! Still our dear boy, Ralph!"

"For Jesu's sake,Thomas, get me down! She will kill me!" Ralph pleaded with me. I looked away. Let her kill him for all I cared. It would save me the task.

But what I saw caused me even more disquiet, than Ralph's craven cowardly visage. The two little children, meanwhile, seeing golden counters spread about the floor of their old home, had begun to play with these shining new playthings. As their house was well-built with fine wooden planking underfoot, as I watched, one guinea rolled inexorably down the crack between the floor boards, followed closely by another to the children's whoops of delight.

"No!" I shouted, bearing down on them, and attempting to push them away from the treasure. They both immediately began to howl pitifully, Cornelia thumped Ralph again and Hans, began brushing the coins into a heap, whilst dancing about, attempting to hide his shrivelled old organs of generation.

I do not know how long this chaos would have continued, had it not been for Peabody. He helped Gabriel steer Cornelia to a chair at the table, put his large red face close to Hans small yellow ear and shouted loudly "Put. On. Breeches!" ordered Elijah, (who by this could not control his hysterical laughter), and myself to collect and count the coins, which we piled on the table, found in a chest in another room, a moppet and a wooden horse which were received with cries of delight by their rightful owners, and finally assisted Ralph to climb down from the printing press.... the great screw on the top precluded any kind of comfortable sitting.... and sat him at the table with his wife and parents. He stood behind Ralph's chair in the manner of a gaoler, defying him to slip from the room. Finally when the coins were all collected, when Hans had found acceptable clothing, and when Cornelia had stopped screaming, he indicated that Gabriel should begin some kind of interrogation.

"Ralph, my son. You knew that your grandfather has wished to return to Amsterdam for weeks, nay months, now. Why have you withheld the price of his journeying when he has been so kind and good to us? He is miserable here and needs his own people. You had the means to set him free, not merely to cure his sadness but also to preserve him from the dangers of this terrible civil conflict?

Why have you imprisoned the poor old man?"

"I needed him still," Ralph muttered.

"Needed him? You have the skills of the Press off pat, thanks to his teachings. And Doctor Tom and his companions? Why did you tell us they were hanged? That was a heinous crime and then to take their property, and tell us Eleanour inherited it. Tom had feasted us and stood payment for ale I remember. Why treat him so shabbily, son Ralph?"

Ralph could not reply. I looked out of the window, a handsome casement with leaded panes, and saw that the day was waning.

"And these two babes, Ralph. You promised to give them a home. You not only broke that promise but you have stolen their house. I would surmise that your parents know nothing of that duplicity. Elijah and I have now to meet with Gell, or we may be hanged indeed. About half of this money is mine. Phoebe will take charge of it, and our clothes and Sergeant, can you go with Phoebe to the Mayor tomorrow to explain that the children have removed back to their old home. I would suggest that Gabriel stands as their official guardian in law now." And as he began to protest.... "It is the least you can do, man. These innocents have brought you a fine home. Who knows what exploitation of them, your son and daughter-in-law planned?"

Gabriel looked broken and deeply ashamed. "Perhaps we should go back to the old Court?" he muttered.

"Not if there is proper stewardship assumed for these two, sir," said the Sergeant. "Anything is better for them than living in a hole in the ground. No doubt, that Frog-spawn has been pocketing a good sum of rent at their expense. But meanwhile what of this thieving wretch, Doctor Tom? What will the aldermen say if they know a convicted thief is proposing to profit from the inheritance of two of their wards?"

"A convicted thief? Oh, No! Tom you could not be so cruel!" Eleanour had found her tongue at last. "They will whip him at the cart's tail. I have seen such punishment in this town. Tom, I beg you for the old times. Here is restitution," she pointed to the piles of coin. "Have pity on us! Believe me I thought you were all dead." She seized my hand and held it to her lips.

"Nay, Eleanour, I assure you, the old times mean nothing to me. If you thought we were all dead, would not a short period of mourning have been fitting rather than altering Lady Phoebe's gown on the very day after her supposed demise?" I shook her off. "If you are to come out of this, with any degree of credence, let me tell you, it is these two who have bought your future for you." I went over to the children and knelt beside them. "What is your name, sweeting?" I asked the girl. At first she seemed like to cry at the sight of the giant from Jack, the Giant-Killer, crouched beside her, but as I tenderly pushed her curls from her eyes, she gained confidence.

"Lizzie" she whispered.

"Lizzie, short for Elizabeth, and Hodge, no doubt short for Henry." The little boy nodded. "Right royal names for two excellent good children."

I painfully stood erect. "Peabody, will you and Lady Phoebe arrange this with the Council tomorrow?" I took what I judged to be the amount stolen from me off the table. "And Phoebe can you retrieve our clothes and return to the George with them. Sergeant Peabody can you escort her? Stay there this night and I will attempt to arrange travel for you tomorrow. And now, listen, Ralph, Magpie, bird of carrion, and you too Eleanour, light as the king's groat, that you are, who could not even be concerned enough to write to your good parents, for I hold you complicit in this whole sorry bedlam matter, that your villainous husband has devised. Your report is indeed blistered, madam. Listen well! These two babes are your surety, your only means of avoiding the pillory, the bastinado ... whatever is the penance here for thieving. And listen well again! Sir John Gell rules in this town now and if there is one crime he hates more than another it is cruelty to little children. So love them and treat them as a prince and princess. They are your saviours. Come Elijah."

And we stalked out with as much dignity as we could muster. The sun was low in the heavens, slanting golden over the Minster Pool as we hastened back to the Close.

"Let us hope to God that he has remained here and not gallivanted off to some tun dish in a Pushing School," Elijah panted.

"God's death, Elijah!" I pretended profound surprise. "How comes it you know such words? What would Parson Worthington say, confronted with your knowing vulgarity?"

"Parson Worthington may.... make his bands into his own noose and kick the clouds!" said Elijah viciously, as we emerged into the Close. There was Sir John, in conference with a man whom I assumed was Lieutenant Colonel Russell. The two commanders were taking their ease, in the last rays of the westering sun, sipping wine from silver goblets.

We bowed at a distance but Sir John came over to speak.

"Are your properties safe and intact, then, my good physicians?"

"Thank you, sir, they are now, but were somewhat at risk and needed our attention," I replied.

"Good!" he smiled his sidelong smile. "Thieves abound everywhere! Well, now tomorrow, Doctor Tom and your young journeyman, I must ask you to give your best attention to the poor boys that Chesterfield left dying in that ditch. They are housed in the back rooms of the Hartshorn in St John's Street, down from Bridge Street. Two more of my Derby boys died today, I think from loss of blood. Others will surely fester and are like to die, if the putrefaction is not stayed."

I sighed heavily. "Sir John, Alas! I should be with them now, not tomorrow. I know we are both tired and troubled but perhaps Elijah and I should go now. And as it in St John's Street, Lady Phoebe is lodged hard by in the George and will help us with her apothecary's skills. Believe me, I ache from fatigue but the sooner the Doctor can treat a wound, the better chance there is of recovery."

The sidelong look again, but he was clearly pleased with my reply. "Good boy! Your father would be proud, God rest him! Very well then. You are to have food and beds for yourselves at my regiment's expense, and any medicaments or comforts for the poor boys that you may need. You are in complete charge. I have appointed two fine wenches to minister to their every need" He winked lasciviously. "If they do not cure them, no-one will. I went today to cheer them but I fear the smell drove me away."

I sighed, fearing what lay in store for us.

"Sir John, here is the twenty guineas for Lady Phoebe's parole." He signalled to his secretary who came swiftly to appropriate the coins. "She will help us for a day or two but is needed back in Worcester."

"She is free to go whenever she wishes. She is a noble young lady and I regret the treatment she and her family received. Perhaps you would ask her to forgive me."

"I can ask," I agreed doubtfully. "And thank you, sir. We had better go."

In the fading light we left the Close again by the western gate, passed down Bridge Street and down the length of St John's. As we passed the George, Elijah ran in and left word for Phoebe to follow us, if she could.

And so we came to the Hartshorn, and passed through to the back rooms, which in those first hours, proved to be Hell on Earth.

9

The stench was fearsome. I stood on the threshold of the first room and let my nose absorb the odours. I calculated as today was Monday still.... an endless day it had been.... and the attack on the narrow lane had been two days before on Saturday, gangrenous infection would be beginning but could be halted. No, the odour was nothing more nor less than excrement, and underlying it the smell of blood.

There were two rooms, lit by a generous supply of candles. Seven men lay in each, on the bare earthen floor. They were the fortunate ones in that they had not died immediately from the leaden bullets, which hailed upon them from point blank range in Gaia Lane. I could assume therefore that heart and lungs for the most part had escaped. They moaned piteously, asking for water. Elijah began to move between them, helping them gently to drink. Laughter came from somewhere nearby. I saw the tail of a rat whisk out of sight behind a pile of clean straw bales. Clearly there had been no stinting of supplies at Sir John's command but there seemed to have been no-one, however, with the humanity or intelligence to put fundamental care into practice. I walked through both rooms trying to gauge the extent of the injuries. All were serious.... none yet hopeless.

"Please, master. Will you help us?" A voice came from near my feet.

"That I will, my friend, and as speedily as I can," I told him.

My first outraged question: Why, when there was clean straw at hand, were the injured lying on the filthy floor? The sound of laughter grew louder. A further store room led off the second larger room. The door was closed. I flung it open.

A man and two women whom I could only surmise were the young harlots Sir John had mentioned, were engaged in playful concourse. The man was toying with the breasts of one woman, while the other girl paid lewd attention to his enlarged member. The scene resembled nothing so much as the picture of a Greek sculpture I had seen, where stout warriors wrestled with snakes. Arms and legs were everywhere. If I am ruthlessly honest, it cannot be denied that a touch of envy fired my wrath.

For the second time in two hours I lifted a man bodily by his doublet. I threw him out of the store room. Fortunately he landed some yards from the nearest invalid.

I turned to the harlots. "Sir John is paying you to care for these men. Why are you not doing so?"

The girl nearest to me, whose bosom was set out for sale, wrinkled her nose.

"They stink," she said.

I hit her. A stinging blow across her painted face. "They stink because you have done nothing for them." I controlled myself with an effort. If I gave full vent to my anger, treatment for the wounded would be even further delayed. "Elijah, see if they have press beds that they can move down here. Tell them Sir John commands it."

I turned back to the shameless bawd. I could feel the grease from her painted visage on my hand. Her face was smeared and angry now as she wept tears of rage. But I gave her no time for complaint. There were lives to be saved. "You brainless hussies can begin filling sacks with straw, for these poor men to lie on. We need feverfew in the sacks to repel insects. Do you know that herb?"

Their mouths dropped open. "We ain't witches!" said the one who had so far not spoken.

"I see you have bewitched this fool of his breeches. Who is he?"

"One of the potboys from the inn," said the one I had hit.

"Indeed!" I lifted him from the floor where he was cowering. "Then he and I shall go at once to the innkeeper with whom Sir John has made a contract for the care of his wounded soldiers. There will be money to be repaid, ladies, as I see you have feasted yourselves without stinting." There were wine stoups and chicken legs aplenty in their haven. "Come, sir!" and I grasped his collar and pushed him to the door.

"Please, sir, don't, sir. They'll turn me off, no doubt of it. I'll come back and help you for naught, sir. But don't tell Master and Missus we was a dallying, sir! That'll be the end of me."

I dropped his collar and resisted the temptation to kick him, as he ran to his breeches and struggled into them. "Go, then!" I told him, "But if you don't come back, your position is forfeit."

Elijah came in with two other men from the taproom. "Jackie, there you are!" One looked keenly at the would-be seducer. "Where have you been hiding your arse? Missus has a rod in pickle for you, no mistake."

I decided that I would have Jackie as a friend, rather than an enemy.

"He was just explaining that in spite of Sir John Gell's instructions and generous payment to your mistress, it has proved difficult to move the press beds in here for these poor broken fellows. But now that difficulty is resolved. You have all come to help them. Please bring the beds at once. There are rats running over my patients."

They stood gawping at me, gobs agape. I towered over them.

"Why do you wait?"

Within a few moments, makeshift beds began to appear. Meanwhile the College of Harlotry with many pouts, shrugs, sighs and carping began to fill some meal sacks, clearly left for the purpose, with the clean straw. I made the potboys use one of the bed frames to lift the poor sick soldiers carefully one by one onto their resting places.

"Now I need a plancher, planchett call it what you wish. A high table, a trestle so that I can begin to remove the balls of the wounded."

There was a gasp and a giggle from behind me. I turned swiftly. One of the whores had found my comment amusing.

"You laugh, madam? Have no fear. Your trade is not in jeopardy. I speak of musket balls made of lead which are lodged in the bodies of these poor sufferers. Is that a jest for you? I gather it must be, for you have done nothing for the poor fellows for two days!"

My voice rose in volume. The woman seemed to shrivel.

"Well, men, a trestle, a planchon. About it if you please."

I found some fresh rolls in the storeroom where the fustilugs had been disporting themselves and sent Elijah for bowls and fresh milk from the kitchens. Phoebe arrived with my box and agreed that we must put feverfew and lavender in the sacks to prevent infection from fleas and lice. The groans and moans of the wounded began to lessen as their backs were no longer in contact with the hard floor. Elijah and Phoebe helped them to sit and eat bread and milk so that they would be strong enough to withstand the horror of my callipers. A trestle was brought in and I moved the sconces around it so that there was light enough for me to treat them. I ordered the whores to bring fresh warm water from the kitchen so that they could assist me in cleaning the men of the filth in which they had been lying. Phoebe went back to the landlady at the George and bought a supply of old linen sheets and shirts, for cloths and bandages. The woman I had hit wrinkled her nose again as we began to make the men easy.

"Oh, forgive me, madam!" I snarled, catching her expression. "I forgot you have never before seen a man's genitals.... at least not for half an hour."

If a look could have killed, I would have been a cold lifeless corpse. I laughed and allowed them to continue with their cleansing under Elijah's supervision. Jackie reappeared, looking at me furtively. I ordered him to help the other two potboys to remove the clothing of the wounded men, as gently as maybe, so that I could have quick access to their wounds.

Two men were close to death and I resolved to deal first with them. One had stopped a musket ball just below the breastbone, in the area above the stomach. It was not deeply embedded but had wreaked havoc with his breathing, which was slow and laboured. I judged he was winded and his stomach nerves were in chaos. I thought that two ribs were broken on the left side. I was in fact surprised that the lung on that side was still unpunctured. I did not dare probe for cloth fragments and there was much blood from the stomach cavity but I thought his liver was intact. I could only do what was possible for me, and wished I could hold the flesh together so that we could avoid infection. We bandaged him up as well as we could and as he was a small man, I lifted him myself and set him upon his bed, Phoebe holding and protecting his head. "He must lie absolutely still," I ordered. "Any further movement and his lung could puncture."

The next poor fellow had two musket balls, one in his right leg and one in his left and was clearly in desperate pain. One ball was in the calf, one in the thigh. The thigh was easy enough.... I removed the lead ball swiftly, made sure no cloth remained and hoped and prayed the sinews and tendons would reknit. The leg might again one day take his weight. But the calf was more complex. The tibia was shattered, the fibula intact. I searched my memory for Ben's instructions, picking away all the time, removing not merely fragments of cloth but one or two fragments of bone. Bone will mend, and does if it is reset skilfully but it cannot stretch itself across chasms. As I peered into the wound, Elijah holding a candle close so that I could see, I resolved that all I could do was improvise. I had to ensure that the two broken ends of the tibia met and with some slight twisting, and a small piece of clean wood, incorporated into the gap of his tibia, I forced some kind of a liaison. He would not walk straight but he might walk.... Somehow.... if he did not die from the terrible stress he had endured.

As we bandaged his calf, he seemed to come to himself. "Moisten his lips," I ordered Jackie. "How do you, sir?" I asked him.

He could only groan and shake his head slightly. At least he would now be more comfortable. As he was replaced in his bed, he grasped my hand for a moment. I doubted whether he would last the night.

I now had to decide whom I should next treat. One young man whose arm was clearly sorely injured, continued to groan and complain, so I thought perhaps if he were treated he would prove less troublesome to his fellows, some of whom were trying to doze. He was able to describe what took place. He had not been shot in the lane, but had been violently knocked over by his friend who had fallen on him, stone dead. He could not straighten his elbow, which was swollen and sore. He had fractured his radius. As he was conscious I explained to him that I could cure this by resetting the bone and then it would cure itself if he would rest quietly, his arm strapped comfortably at his side. I explained that I had to feel his broken bones and that this would cause him pain, but that any immediate agony I might cause would be the bone setting back in place.

"Will you allow me to feel your injury?" I asked him.

"You are the doctor, are you not?" he said angrily.

"I must hurt you to cure you," I explained. In fact it was not the head of the radius but some little way below the elbow, where it had snapped. I clicked it back in place, as swiftly as I could but his screams were terrible to hear. Phoebe sat with him until the pain subsided somewhat. He would make a complete recovery, but made more noise than men who were much more severely injured.

Still, I remembered some words of Ben. "Every man and woman has a different way of withstanding pain. Some rant and rave, others bite their lip and clench their fists and are silent. And it is their pain, not yours, so allow them to fight it in their own way." We were all heartily glad on that terrible night, however, when the broken radius dropped into an uneasy slumber.

The endless night wore on. The rest of the injuries were not complex but time consuming and desperately painful for the poor invalids. Happily we were able to remove the balls before putrefaction began. Good Master Pares, whoever he was, had his lotion used and blest again and again that night. When I had completed the removal of the foreign bodies, I began to think how we could best keep the men clean. Men are fortunate over women in that they can aim their urine and chamber pots, or.... the rogue with one ear who lives beneath the bed.... the delicate lady's description.... sufficed for that. I decided that if they needed to excrete we would carry them to a jakes, just outside the back door.

I dismissed the whores about two hours after midnight. When they had finally understood that the money Sir John had given them must be returned, unless I was satisfied with their endeavours, they had worked after a fashion. "You are to return here in eight hours time," I told them "You will be needed to help feed and wash these poor men whom you have so neglected." They sidled away and Phoebe raised her eyebrows at my unmannerly speech. She had not been present when I had discovered their activities.

"They are harlots, pure and simple!" I ranted like a Puritan pulpit banger.

"Harlots are never pure, and if they are simple so much the worse for them! May I remind you, Tom, that it is men who make women into whores. If men did not pay them for carnal pleasure, harlotry would not exist."

"Yes, Phoebe," I said humbly. I was too tired to differ from her and indeed on reflection, she was right, as she so often was.

I sent her and Elijah to their beds, as soon as I had dealt with the last injury. Elijah would relieve me an hour or so after daybreak and I would sleep for a few hours during the morning. There were two rooms bespoke for us in the Hartshorn. On my soul I could not remember where my clothes were. In the George, the Close, or at the sign of the Barrel...the Magpie's new nest? I tried to ask Phoebe but could not somehow frame the words of the question. I sat in a corner chair that had been brought in from the dining parlour, Jackie drew forth a chair from the "brothel", and we dozed. Apart from requests for water or for the means to urinate, the patients, who were dog-tired after their hard vigil on the bare floor, fell into uneasy slumber.

In the morning all lived although my hopes for the man with the stomach wound were not high. As I did my rounds I suddenly found a slight figure at my elbow. It was Zacharius. "That's my Dad!" he told me, pointing with his crutch to a man who had had a dreadful slash to his leg.... the musket ball had entered and left his thigh.... and he was weak from loss of blood.

"Where have you been then?" I asked him.

"They let me sleep in the kitchen, d'you see?" he told me, his most expansive statement so far. And then: "Is me Dad for Parson's Piece, Master?"

"Is that where you live?" I asked in innocence.

His reply was scornful and grisly, but to the point. "Nay, that's where bodies are buried. No-one lives there 'cept dead'uns, d'you see?"

"If your Dad has rest and good food, I think and hope he will live," I told him.

"Then we can go home?"

"I hope so indeed."

"I don't like it here, master."

I was forced to agree. "I've been in happier places."

He retired to my chair where he watched the proceedings like a solemn judge. When Elijah returned, tousled but refreshed, Zacharius was kind enough to vacate the chair.... for his personal saviour, his crutch-maker.

I asked for bowls of bread and milk to be distributed with a sweet wrinkled pippin for each man, who could chew, and told Elijah to take responsibility for the tasks of feeding and washing the men where possible. Zacharius wished to know if he could try to walk without his crutch, but I expressly forbade it.

"Your bones need time to come together again, d'you see?"

He nodded sagely, but then I bethought of a useful task for him.

"All these poor souls will need an aid like yours. Go out to the inn stables.... carefully now...." (as he was already hopping to the door), "and see if there is a supply of wood that your good friend Elijah can fashion into crutches for them."

He was gone. I went to my room, lay on the bed for a few moments and suddenly it was evening.

I hastened down to the sick rooms but all was peace and calm. Elijah had conducted the proceedings excellently.

"What of the ladies of the night?"

"They returned for a short time according to your instructions, but seemed more intent on plying their trade with the potboys. I do not have your authority over them, Tom."

I was silent. That "authority" came from a vicious violent slap. I was not proud of that.

"Have the potboys and Jackie helped you?" He nodded, as Phoebe came to find me. She had some cold beef, bread and pickled cucumber for me in the inn parlour where I ate like a savage. It was over twenty four hours since our meal at the George. Whilst I crammed food into my mouth, Phoebe crammed news into my ears. She had gone to the Sheriff's house with Peabody and Gabriel. She had done well as she had met the agent of the Earl of Essex, one Richard Drafgate. The Earl was the Lord of the Manor of Lichfield and Phoebe made much of the fact that Essex was in my debt. Whatever doubts Gabriel might have had with regard to his suitability to act as Guardian for the little ones, when he heard that he would receive a substantial sum for their upkeep, from their father's funds in the Guild, he became strangely responsible and avuncular. He and his dependants were to have rights of tenancy over the Barrel until Hodge was sixteen. Hans had already hired a pad-nag in preparation for his journey to Hull, whence he would sail for Amsterdam. Cornelia would have liked to have seen her poor father on his way, but Gabriel forbade it, desiring her to remain with him, as the children's foster mother. "And in truth," said Phoebe, "she seems to have a genuine affection for them both.

"As for Ralph and Eleanour," she continued, "it seems they will continue to produce diurnals, news-sheets, corrantos, call them what you will, Tom."

"Nay, Phoebe, I call them the devil's arse wipes." Under stress of medical tasks, my language became something fundamental and scurrilous. I had noticed the same with Ben. I begged Phoebe's pardon for my coarseness

She laughed but then sniffed dismissively. "It seems for Ralph and Eleanour to be their mission in life. When anyone questions the morality of what they do, it is always the same. "The people want news." That is always their answer. When I left, Ralph was writing the story of Hodge and Lizzie as the Babes in the Wood, by which he was at pains to explain he meant a barrel."

"Do you think Sergeant Peabody would escort you to Henley tomorrow?" I asked. "I've paid your ransom with Sir John. I doubt it was worth it though."

She aimed a good natured cuff at me, and I caught her hand.

"There is something I must ask you to do for me."

"Oh, Tom, hasten if you please. I have very little time. I have forestalled you. I have already asked the good Sergeant for his protection. He's asking Sir John if he may leave the town. And I must try to get all my possessions into those small bags. And I have bought farings for Joan and a warm woollen shawl for old Gill. What is it you want me to do?"

"Marry me." I raised her hand to my lips.

Her large green eyes, which had been darting everywhere with impatience, widened in surprise and came to rest on my face. "Do you mean that?"

"I was never more determined," I said retaining her little hand.

"There is much you should know, before I can consent, Tom"

"Yes, indeed!" I agreed gravely "I have sent to Parson Worthington and Elijah's mother for tutelage."

She shook with laughter, but then frowned, "All I can say now is that you must think of this. It seems unlikely that I will ever conceive. It has not been seemly or necessary to inform you, but my courses have only recently become regular."

I retained her hand and gently kissed her lips. "Dearest Phoebe, I will think of it, I promise you. In fact I doubt I will think of anything else until we are together again. Life will be drab and dismal without my sparring partner and governess."

"Governess?" she giggled. "I am younger than you by two years, and you are the master in our establishment."

"And you are high borne. Nothing has been more obvious since you were reunited with your great-uncle. You have a way of speaking that commands instant obedience."

"And you have not? Tom, what sort of modesty is this? When you are roused you are a despot!"

"Only to prevent suffering." And when I reflected I knew this was true. I was indifferent to the War of Ideas, which waged around me, but hated its vicious and violent outcomes. "No, Phoebe. I am only a middling sort of person, from a humble background...." but we were interrupted by Elijah.

"Tom I think you should be with us. The stomach wound is breathing fit to burst his chest."

"Oh, Jesu! I feared it would be so!" His wound was perilously near to the base of his lungs. Somehow he had moved in such a way and jolted himself so that air had entered from his stomach wound. Or possibly a broken rib had finally penetrated his left lung. There was a little blood frothing from his mouth and a blueness about his skin and nails, that had not been there before. I needed to cover the wound as tightly as I could. But with what?

"Come now Tom! Improvise!" Ben used to say. What material did we have that did not allow air to penetrate? I made a clean linen pad to cover his wound, having sat him up and suddenly thought that a large patch from his buff coat, bandaged round him securely in place, might prove resistant to air. Water did not penetrate those coats.... at least not for many hours in a downpour. The inside of his coat seemed quite clean, as I cut a piece large enough to cover both wound and pad. I smeared Pares Lotion on it to defy infection, placed the patch over the pad and with Elijah's help, bandaged him tightly so that his waist and middle were quite rigid.

There was a bustle at the door and the Landlady came in with Sir John.

"Why Doctor Tom! These rooms smell quite wholesome now. Tell me," he lowered his voice, "What's the butcher's bill?"

"Alas, Sir, I know not. Do you wish me to pay for their food? I have put them on a diet of bread and milk and apples."

He looked at me as if I were a drivelling idiot. Then said softly but plainly: "How many dead?"

"Why none, since I have had charge of their care!" I told him with indignation.

"There, there, Doctor Tom! No need to climb your high horse.

Tell this good lady what more you need, as I speak to my poor boys."

I asked her for goose down pillows to pack round him with the punctured lung. He could not now lie down but must sit and sleep upright, skewed slightly to the left. "You see he can only breathe from one side, so we must not jeopardise his chance." She nodded and went her ways to bring back several soft cushions. Truly though I had little hope for him.

Sir John seemed well pleased with our sick rooms. "According to my poor lads you are something between St Luke and Aescul....Ascul....that Greek varlet. Most thought they were for the Parson's Plot, but you have dragged them back from it somehow. How do the two young hoydens?"

I was in a dilemma. Elijah had looked very doubtful, when I asked how they had helped us. I called him over. "Sir John wants to know if the two ladies were of service to us."

"The service they wish to offer is extraneous, Sir John," said Elijah, "Their concerns are carnal not caring."

Sir John and I gaped at him. He sounded for all the world like some Puritan Pulpit Ranter. "Alas, I fear that is to be laid at my door," said Sir John. "I thought as my boys were all near death, a little saucy sweetness would ease their passage."

It was decided that Sir John would pay them off, by leaving a sum of money for them with the landlady. I was to regret my inhumanity. When I think of these events, I should have remembered the advice of two wise men. My father always told me: "Make friends, not enemies, wherever possible, son Tom." And then the Earl. His words were to ring in my ears, spoken as we contemplated the body of the dead midwife. "Something more of charity, my son, and perhaps less of over niceness."

Phoebe left with Sergeant Peabody the next morning. It was Wednesday the 8th of March. They would stay at the Swan in Henley and I was sure Walter would send Nat the rest of the way with her, if the Sergeant heard of King's men who needed his services, in Warwickshire. Phoebe had enough money in her purse to pay for bed and board for herself and her escort.

So Elijah and myself were left, doctoring the men of Parliament. Although when I questioned them about their reasons for rebelling against the King, all were uncertain about their loyalties. "Well,

King's a damned Papist, in't he?" said broken radius, who as I had surmised, was first out of his bed. He was helpful and cheerful, once he was out of pain, and knew his arm would mend. Zacharius' Dad had been recruited because Sir John Gell had ordered him to become a soldier, and paid him too, so young Zach had trailed along as well. They had no more notion of the reasons behind the conflict than they had of flying. I found it disturbing that they had sustained these injuries for a cause about which they knew almost nothing.

But perhaps I too was guilty of a lack of conviction. I did know the issues now. A year ago at eighteen I would not have recognised a political notion if it had leapt up and buffeted me about the coxcomb with a cudgel. What seemed the most outlandish circumstance was that simply because the King was no tyrant, for that he was opposed? When one heard the horrors of the past, when during the eighth Henry's reign, one day a piece of mouldy bread was the body of Our Lord, the next day it was not, and either before or after its unsanctification, one could be burned alive for claiming the contrary, then surely this King could be indulged and his prayer books and his Divine Right philosophy tolerated. For Christ's sake, what harm did his notions do? Live and let live.... a good maxim.

The two men whom I had thought were close to death had rallied and were making a little progress every day. Sadly, and somewhat to my surprise, one of the young men who had had a ball taken from his shoulder had died, three days after its removal. There had been no putrefaction. He had taken bread and milk, seemed to be content and recovering but had suddenly left us, with no warning, no words of Farewell. One moment he lay there, smiling and thanking Elijah for spooning sippets into his mouth, the next he was gone. "It had seemed as if a pain rose in his chest and carried him away," Elijah told me, and we felt personally bereft, as if our caring had been deficient. I wished I had an older more experienced physician to consult, but all we could conclude was that his poor heart had slowly weakened and broken.

A few days after Phoebe had left, and I missed her sorely, when I came down to take my turn, (for I had taken to sleeping during the day, Elijah during the night,) I found four or five citizens of Lichfield waiting patiently to consult me. To my consternation they seemed all to be suffering from a rheum that caused nose and eyes to stream. I was afraid that this might be some sort of fever that they would pass on to Sir John's "boys", but they had no other symptoms, no hot brow or languor and felt well. I saw them one by one and gave each, eucalyptus oil to sniff. The weather had become somewhat warmer and blossom floated in the air. I surmised that they were alike suffering from the inhalation of some small seeds that were irritating the delicate workings of their noses. They all seemed happy with their bottles of oil and went their ways. I collected a crown from each of them. They were wealthy men and as my services belonged to Sir John I gave him the money, when he called by later. He was very pleased in equal measure both with my earnings and my honesty.

After that every day there were some few enquirers after "Master Doctor". A woman had a distorted finger. She had fallen on her hand some months before, and "This here finger don't seem to want to sit straight no more," I sighed. I would have to set the bone. I explained that the pain would be desperately bad for several minutes after I had set it, but the finger would "sit straight" again. She listened and asked leave to return in half an hour, which she did, now helped by husband and friends and roaring drunk, with a stoup of Master Frogspawn's best brandy wine, clutched in her good hand. Even so, her scream when I finally set the finger was terrible to hear. We all had recourse to her aqua vita, and sat round for an hour or so, bumpsy as you please, like so many of her gossip pint-pots, until she felt she had the strength to go home.

With each passing day, the new patients, waiting for me, grew more numerous. I realised in Worcester Joan had seen patients first before I had been exposed to their demands, and hopeless cases and trivial complaints were alike dealt with by her, so that my time was not wasted. What a jewel of a woman she was! At least now she would have Phoebe to help her. I had told Phoebe to send Roger to Lichfield with our money after about a fortnight, so that we would be able to ride back at once with the minimum of delay, our fines paid and our three week work penalty completed. Elijah in fact resented his "imprisonment" more than I did. "We didn't choose to be in the Close!" he grumbled. "Why does Gell treat us this way?"

"Because we are wondrous useful to him, Lijah. Would you have had these poor fellows die, at the hands of those wanton bawds?"

We had seen neither sight nor sound of them, since the Landlady of the Hartshorn had paid them off. Zach told us that he had seen them standing at the corner of the market "makin' up to all the men what passed 'em," and then the stable boy came to tell me they had approached him, to ask which was my horse. I felt great relief that no-one at the Hatshorn knew that I had a horse at the George, but then forgot the matter.

Zach was a ready and immediate purveyor of news to us. I sent him to the sign of the Barrel to see how they fared. I thought at the very least, Gabriel or Ralph would visit us in the Hartshorn and after our villainous treatment at Ralph's hands, would attempt to amend matters by buying us food or drink, especially as through Phoebe's good offices they now had a regular and substantial income. But it seemed Ralph and Eleanour had drifted away from the family home. There had been a difference of opinion between Eleanour and her mother-in-law as to who should wash the children's clothes. Gabriel, who had I think the vestiges of goodness and morality about him, promised to visit us one evening in the near future, when he realised that we were unable to leave the Hartshorn for any length of time.

Zach hopped up to the Close at one point. He associated it as the place where one might be given a sugar plum. He came back with some disturbing news. Lieutenant Colonel Russell had it seemed no respect for the sanctity of the Cathedral. I had seen horses being led into it, as into a great stable, but Zach had seen worse desecration than that. A soldier from the Colonel's regiment had called to tell him in friendly fashion that there would be good sport in the Cathedral if he liked to enter. Even Zach, never oversensitive, was somewhat dismayed to see a cat let loose behind the altar and a pack of hounds freed to chase poor Puss. However on this occasion the cat fled through a tiny crevice at the base of St Chad's shrine. If any hound put a nose through the gap, the cat scratched it, so that the dogs were leaping away howling in pain. Eventually they were called off rather than they should continue to be molested by their victim. There was talk, Zach told us, of smoking the cat out but the cavalry captain would have none of that, as the horses might have suffered. Elijah was greatly distressed to hear of such rude blasphemy in his beloved cathedral. For me, my sympathies were with Puss.

"But it would seem that St Chad works ever in defence, both of the helpless, like the cat, Elijah, and of his great edifice," I told him

151

partly to comfort him. "Consider, if the Earl had been able to re-main there, the granadoes would have destroyed the whole fabric of the building."

He nodded. "Let us hope one day it is restored."

"Amen!" I said piously. "Come, Elijah, there is game stew for us in the parlour, by Sir John's special command."

The wounded men continued to make good progress. Nobody else was for the Parson's Piece, and I began to allow the men whose injuries were in their upper bodies to leave their beds. I did not know how further to treat the man with the punctured lung. All I could recommend was stillness and rest. Then one day Elijah told me he thought he had seen both sides of his chest, gently rising and falling. I wrote down what I had done and when I heard that the Lichfield doctor had returned escaped for half an hour to ask him if I could do more. In fact he was a poor ornament to our profes-sion. All he could say was that if a lung was pierced the patient was worm's meat. When I asked him if internal tissue will not mend just as skin will, he clearly thought he had a madman on his hands.

I returned to the Hartshorn perhaps somewhat complacent, happy that Francis Cotton,(the punctured lung) had at least been treated by someone who did not instantly wash his hands of a cure. Indeed all the men were wonderfully grateful to us, as when they had first been brought to the Hartshorn and laid on the floor, they had thought death was imminent and had been prepared to give up the ghost. We had had one addition to our number from the Close, one of Russell's musketeers had cut his hand in sword practice, and had come to us for bandaging and calming words. I kept him overnight to be sure that the cut was free from poison.

The next day, Friday 17th of March, I came down after my daily sleep, in the mid afternoon somewhat earlier than usual. All seemed calm, Elijah and I had finally decided that Zach's leg was straight-ening well. Elijah was helping him change to a stick. They had de-cided to practise in the inn yard. After I'd examined everyone and promised the broken radius that he could return to his home in Kirk Ireton, after Sir John had decided that with a weak right arm, it would be foolhardy to expect him to continue to be a Corporal of pikemen, I sank down in the large chair that commanded a view of all the beds and wondered when we would see Roger. Phoebe had been gone a good fortnight now. We were doing nothing for the men, that clever women, well versed in the arts of healing, could not do. I began to feel great anxiety lest Roger had fallen foul of some troopers of either faction, but reflected there was nothing I could do. At least next week we would have completed our agreed term of work. Perhaps Sir John might allow me after that to keep my fees.... so we could begin to pay him off....

I had drifted into a doze. I woke suddenly, a sharp pain at the side of my neck and a strange weight on my feet. There was a confused shouting and I sat up in alarm, blood oozing over my hand from a cut in my neck.. Elijah was on the floor beside me, pinioning the arms of a woman who lay face down, powerless in his grasp. Zach's stick lay beside them and he was standing beside me, screaming foul names at the woman on the floor.

"She were trying to kill you, Doctor Tom. See, that nail! She were going to drive it in your throat, when I saw her and threw my stick at the bitch."

Elijah jerked her roughly to her feet. It was the harlot whom I had hit and who now began to scream at us, blaming me for losing her employment. The landlady and the potmen entered, horrified by the blood on my neck and clothes.

"She tried to kill 'im!" Zach was shouting.

"Put her in the cellar till Sir John gets here," the Landlady decreed. They bundled her to the door, and as they opened it, she twisted in their grasp and spat at me as I sat amazed and silent, blood leaking between my fingers.

The broken radius whose name was Peter Wright came over to help me. He dipped a clean rag in a bucket of pure water and bathed my neck. For an ex-miner he was very gentle and tender and he bandaged me in excellent fashion. Whilst he was attending to me, we could hear raised voices outside. Elijah was telling someone to wait and then I seemed to hear Sir John's outraged tones. A moment later he was beside me.

"Oh, Doctor Tom! How is the biter, bit! How does your neck? I will remove the strumpet to meet her just deserts. Some wretched child out there has a splinter in his foot. I say splinter but half a tree is more to the purpose. Are you able to remove it? What say you?" He turned to Peter Wright. "My good Corporal Wright, you look as good as new. The pike will not do, nor the musket, so what I propose is that you think of yourself as a quartermaster, do you see?

153

Think about it, my good lad."

Elijah returned, followed by Zach, putting his foot carefully to the ground.

"They've taken her, sir. Not without objections but she is tied and bound and in the midst of four troopers."

"Where are they taking her?" I asked.

"Why to the Close, of course!" said Sir John. "You do not want her, thrashing and banging about the cellar."

"No, indeed!" I agreed heartily with that. "Let's see the half tree."

A small boy was brought in, supported by his mother and an older women, perhaps his grandmother. He had chased out into the family's garden with his ball, half dressed. His toy had lodged in the branches of a tree and he had climbed up to retrieve it. The splinter, which had penetrated the sole of his bare foot, had been further pushed in by his jumping down. He was in great pain but for all that tried to hold back the tears, before all the soldiers. Enough wood protruded from his little foot for me to get a purchase without callipers. I gauged the direction that the splinter had entered, tilted my head to the same angle, took the end of the splinter in my teeth and jerked my head back.

The wounded were treated to the spectacle of their doctor seemingly about to swallow a two inch splinter. Happily the whole foreign body had come out cleanly, leaving no small shavings to vex him later. The child bled, which was healthy. I had a tincture Phoebe had made of Comfrey, Herb Robert and Marigold with which I anointed his wound and gave the rest to his mother. I then bandaged his foot carefully and suggested that he returned as he had come, hopping with his mother and grandmother on either side. He would feel pain for perhaps eighteen hours, but not nearly so much as he had already endured. There would be slight swelling when they dressed his foot tomorrow. If the swelling or the pain became unbearable, they must bring him back at once.

They were very grateful and thanked me effusively. Their gratitude was tempered somewhat when upon their leaving the inn, they encountered Sir John who explained that my fee of a crown would go to the fund he administered for the great cause of Parliament. The grandmother was particularly vociferous when she learned that I was not to receive a penny for my trouble.

"Roger should soon be here," I told Elijah. "And then.... freedom! Zach, you are a prince among Derbyshire soldiers. You saved my life...."and then for good measure, I added his favourite expression.... "Do you see?"

"Aye, well we don t want you dead as mutton when me Dad's not full better yet," he told me sagely. "Eh, Lijah, what'll they do to that murdering girl?"

"Hang her, of course!" said Elijah.

"What?" I shouted.

"Come on, now Tom. What other course of action does he have? Far, far worse than theft! She is a murderess.... where are you going?" as I was hastening to button my doublet and straightening my hose.

"To the Close, of course." I was out the door and through the buttery before he could say another word. The quickest way was up Bridge Street and I ran like a madman, the wound in my neck throbbing somewhat. I ran in through the West Gate, ran round the West front under St Chad's disapproving eye, and into the wide area before the Bishop's Palace. A hideous sight met my eyes.

There was the Sugar Plum, Sir John's moveable gallows, in the centre of what had now become to all intents and purposes, a parade ground. To my horror, I saw that a woman had already been hanged. But her garments were not those of my assailant. I forced myself to go closer. It was the other girl, her body swinging gently in the light breeze, the word "Theef" on a card round her neck, the usual foulness of excrement polluting the air. Sir John and the Colonel sat at a small table near the gibbet. The Derbyshire men, mostly in grey with Brooke's purple coats, here and there, were drawn up in formation. Behind them were the Colonel's men, scores of them, laughing and jeering, as my attacker was led, the halter already round her neck, from group to group. She shrieked abuse at them, spat at them, as they sneered and snatched at her clothing. The thought that this was to atone for a slight cut on my neck caused me to feel bleak despair. Phoebe had said, "It is men who make women into harlots." No doubt some few of these soldiers had used the creature carnally whom they now delighted to abuse.

I approached the table and bowed. Sir John smiled his sidelong smile. "My Lord Colonel, this is the young doctor who has brought so many of the ambushed back from the dead." Lord Russell inclined his head and politely indicated that I might sit.

"You have come no doubt to see this murdering strumpet receive her punishment." He had a pleasant voice, and I took heart from that.

"I have come to plead for mercy for her. I began the enmity. I struck her when I found her wasting Sir John's money and good offices. If I had not struck her, she would not have sought revenge and she would not be here now."

The Colonel said dismissively, "You did right to strike her. Why do you now wish that she should be reprieved?"

Perhaps St. Chad inspired my answer. "My Lord we should exercise forgiveness, if we would seek salvation."

Sir John sighed and gave his long drawn out "Hmmmm!" and the Colonel continued to regard me. Then he said, "As her victim, perhaps you above all others, have the right to ask for her life. But how would you tell these gathered here that they are to be denied their sport?"

St. Chad again inspired me. "My Lord, it cannot be a gentlemanly or a Christian act for these men to delight in the shameful death of a woman. Even though we are at war, the great cause of Parliament must surely hold to the modus vivendi that every Englishman holds dear." As the noise of the men's constant shouting and jeering grew in volume, I had to shout to be heard. The Colonel's captains were even then taking down the corpse of the dead woman from the Gallows, whilst the living harlot was being led towards it. She was placed on the box and the noose slung over the crosspiece.

I turned to the commanders but the Colonel said passively, "They will do nothing until we give the word. But what's this?"

A group of about twenty troopers were suddenly reining in alongside the north wall of the Cathedral, surrounding a young cornet. He rode forward and dismounted. The legend on his black standard read "Deus Nobiscum." At the sight of the strangers the roar of the bloodlusty Midlanders diminished, and silence fell. The Cornet came to the table and bowed. He felt in his doublet and passed over a pack of letters to Sir John Gell.

"This is from Brereton," said Sir John. He read one page and then passed it to the Colonel. After he had perused another page he turned to me. "Well Doctor Tom you have your wish. But it is Sir William Brereton, Major General of Cheshire, Staffordshire and Lancashire who is the Saviour of this tun dish, not you. Wait for me in the porch, Doctor Tom, where we spoke before."

Captains were at the table, receiving orders. As they went to their respective troops, silence fell and orders were rapped out. The men marched back into their quarters, some angry and sullen that they were deprived of their sport, some, I judged, relieved that they had been spared the spectacle of another death, all apprehensive at the prospect of further warfare. The whore's eyes widened as the noose was removed from her neck. Her disappointed executioner jerked his head in my direction and then ordered her off the platform.

I walked round to the west porch under St. Chad, and paused to pay him my respects, wondering whether I caught the trace of humour in his grim expression.

"Why?" said a voice.

It was the woman. "I don't like hangings," I told her. "My father was hanged."

She laughed. "So was mine." She went her ways. As she came to the west gate, she turned and looked back. "But I thank you," she called and was gone.

Sir John turned the corner in time to see our short encounter. "Well, Doctor Tom, are you arranging a carnal meeting to reward your generosity? Make sure the wench has no nails about her person."

"No, sir. I prefer to retain myself in good health. And I think I might well be a bridegroom in a few weeks."

"May I ask who is the most fortunate lady?" he asked, the light of lascivious interest in his eye.

"I do not know if she is fortunate, but it is Lady Phoebe, who holds my heart in her little hands," I told him.

"Hmmmmm!" said Sir John "Well, she can always stand on a chair, I suppose."

I glared at him. He clapped me on the back and once again drew me into the Cathedral.

"You understood Sir William's request? Nay 'twas a demand, I vow. We are to march to assist him to gain Stafford for the great cause of Parliament."

I wondered if I dared hope to be released from my parole. "And I, and my journeyman?" I asked. "We may return to Worcester?"

He gave me a sidelong smile, half over his shoulder. "Alas, Doctor Tom, I fear your parole extends to Monday 27th of this month. I cannot spare so gifted a Sawbones and your man too. I hear only good reports of his skills. I cordially request the pleasure of the company of you both to Stafford. What is it that Shakespeare varlet says? You are too good, my son. I fear you are "hoist with your own cannon" Nay, not cannon either. A smaller gun. I have it. Doctor Tom, you have shot yourself with your own petard!"

10

I pleaded with Sir John that at the very least he would excuse Elijah.

"Like myself, he is not drawn to a military life. We cherish our neutrality and will cure anyone, anyone who needs medical help. He had to endure Edgehill and hated it. The guns alone affected his hearing for some days." A lie but I was beyond honesty.

"No, Doctor Tom, master and man, you are both a good hand in a dead lift. I cannot spare you. This far I will concede. If I can, I will release you from parole, prior to the date you agreed."

"I agreed nothing," I was almost shouting, forgetting wisdom and diplomacy. Sir Edward had tutored me in how to behave to Sir John. I controlled myself, with an effort, remembering that I should appeal to one of his over-riding appetites. "Your pardon, Sir John. If I pay twice the price, will you excuse Elijah? He is his mother's only son. Without him she has no-one. He has already been exposed to danger whilst he has been with me in Lichfield. Sir John," I went on desperately, "name your price for his freedom."

For a moment I swear he was tempted. His large eyes seemed to widen still further but then he remembered the welfare of his "boys"

"It cannot be, Doctor Tom. Dawn at the west gate. I will have mounts for you.... for both of you."

I trudged back to the Hartshorn, completely cast down, despairing and angry. At the sight of my face, Elijah said, "So they hanged her then."

I had forgotten the wretched whore.

"Jesu, no, they did not. They hanged the other harlot but she was spared. Sir John.... Sir John commands us to go to Stafford with him and his army. It seems the Royalists hold it and Parliament wants it. I pleaded with him to excuse you."

"Tom, at least we will be out of these gloomy rooms. Who cares for the "boys" then?"

"The landlady? Jackie and the potboys? Sir John'll find us mounts."

"At least we'll see the lambs and the blossom. I felt I was imprisoned here for ever."

The zeal and spirit of youth. I would be twenty in two months time and already felt…. not old beyond my years but too experienced and worn. There was a knock at the sickroom door. It was Captain Cross.

"Sir John sent me to assist with the arrangements for these wounded who must remain and to see if I could be of service in your preparations."

I thought that perhaps I knew something of Sir John's thinking. He was anticipating that we might make a bolt for freedom. Something of my doubting expression must have been obvious. The Captain laughed.

"No, no. Sir John trusts you…. with good reason. Is there anyone here from his Derbyshire regiment who is well enough to march tomorrow?"

"Indeed not!" I almost shouted, "Unless all is to do again. Peter Wright here is well recovered but may not use his arm for some time, and Zach is still using a stick. Sir John surely does not wish him to court danger. He is far too young to go for a soldier."

The Captain passed among our clean rooms, stopping from time to time to question one of the wounded. Zach who had heard the conversation asked to go to Stafford, but the Captain was of like mind to ourselves. "Next year, good lad," he told him.

"Surely you will not want to leave your father, Zach," I reminded him. "Jackie will be reliant on your help and good offices." Elijah had been teaching them both the elements of herbal medicine and both were attentive students, especially Zach. I had found that what he lacked in courtesy, he more than compensated for in native wit.

The Captain looked round again and shook his head. "This reminds me of the scenes my grandfather described in a monastery when he was a boy. The monks used to care for the sick something upon this fashion. The provision for the destitute and the dying is now haphazard at the best of times and nonexistent at the worst."

160

"Very true, sir," I agreed with his assessment but not with his diagnosis. "But my patients here are not destitute, thanks to Sir John's charity, and nor God save us, are they dying. All improve a little day by day. There used to be a place in Worcester, such as you describe where the monks cared for the dying. But 'tis a rich clothier's house now."

"But what of your own men, Captain?" I drew him into the Buttery where we sat down, and I asked for small beer. "Does the masquerade that Lord Brooke still lives continue to be upheld? Why have you deceived his men?"

"They so revere him, that they would have absconded to a man," he told me. "Few saw the killing shot, so we judged it best to deceive them for the great...."

"Cause of Parliament," I finished his sentence for him. "Well, Captain, I saw that killing shot. His death was instant. His killer is a formidable marksman!"

"Would you know his name?" he asked me, smiling politely.

"Alas, Captain, I would not," I told him, smiling equally politely, "and truly I am very sorry for his Lordship's death, for he seemed a humane and generous spirited commander."

He said simply, "The best of men!"

I gave Jackie very careful instructions. Francis Cotton continued to progress but very slowly. Any exertion would kill him, I explained. Before Jackie fed him or helped him to the jakes, he must listen to his breathing and watch his chest. If the left side had ceased to rise and fall he must not exert himself at all. Rest and wholesome food might be his salvation. The man with two leg wounds must not under any circumstances attempt to walk, (Only I, and Elijah knew that his left leg was reinforced with a piece of wood. Desperate times called forth desperate measures!)

So on the morrow, we came to the west gate. Sir John was bidding Farewell to Colonel Russell, who was smiling broadly, (at the prospect of Sir John's absence, perhaps?) and bade him God speed, with great cheerfulness. Great carts of provisions were trundling past us into the Close.

The horses were good cobs and after a few miles Elijah whispered to me that his mount was of excellent disposition, a great improvement on Mercury. I had to admit that he was right in that it was pleasant to be riding through the early Spring countryside. The regiment from Derbyshire, about one thousand foot and four hundred horse, together with Lord Brooke's purple remnants, had started ahead of us. As the morning mists dispersed, there were wild daffodils and lambs aplenty. Elijah brought our little cavalcade to a stop as he laughed delightedly at a group of about ten of the little woolly creatures, scampering about playing King of the Castle. Sir John smiled benignly and indulgently at Elijah's pleasure. "Sir John likes the young," said Captain Cross. I thought to myself, "Aye, preferably female, and preferably in his bed," but to have voiced my craven sentiments would have blighted the March morning.

As we passed his regiment, Sir John called out to his sergeants and captains by name, sometimes stopping to encourage pikemen who found their long weapon a tedious burden. He was clearly a generous commander. His men were well clad in their grey coats. He had with him a few stoups of wine and if a man seemed downhearted would pass him a drink. To speak truth the men did not seem to resent him or take advantage of his kindness. Riding some little way behind him, on more than one occasion I heard a Derbyshire voice call out "You're a good 'un, John" - a rough testimony of local popularity.

I did not admire or feel affection for Sir John.... for me he did not inspire loyalty like the Earl of Chesterfield, but I could not find it in my heart to dislike him. I tried. God knows I tried. I kept reminding myself how despicably he had behaved to Phoebe's parents, and what a villainous turncoat he was, to have taken the King's favours for the County of Derbyshire for the last ten years and at the last to have received Essex' commission when the King raised his standard. There was something about his sidelong glance, however, and his wry humour that made him a pleasant and entertaining travelling companion on that Saturday.

We were housed and fed royally in a large inn in a village I think was called Haywood, north of a larger place called Rugeley. Sir John had sent one ahead to bespeak good beds and a fine dinner, although the foot soldiers and many of the horse and artillery had to sleep round fires in the fields. It seemed a strange coincidence that one of the cavalry colonels was a knight also called Rugeley. I mentioned this to Sir John who laughed and agreed and hoped it was a good omen and that even more singular and curious was the fact that the place where it had been determined we should meet Sir

William Brereton on the morrow, to march on Stafford was known as Hopton Heath. Sir John's home in Derbyshire was Hopton Hall, near Wirksworth.

"And Doctor Tom, I hope that one day I shall have the honour to dine with you there and pledge you again in a fine Bourdeaux as I do now." He raised his goblet and drank my health. I returned his good wishes. He seemed to like to talk with me. Although he was a good and careful commander, I think he found his companions in arms something tedious. Encouraged by his friendliness I wondered if I could ask him why he had become a changefoot; some would say a traitor. I hoped my first question was of sufficient craft to deceive him.

"I would think my Lord of Essex was well pleased to welcome you to his fold, Sir John. Is he a pleasant courteous man? When I encountered him, he had just hanged my father and was thinking of treating me in like manner."

"Pleasant? Courteous? I cannot say that I found him a man in whose conversation one could take any pleasure, Doctor Tom. He was overjoyed that Derbyshire could be a bulwark for Parliament. He did not penetrate my true purpose in declaring against my King. I had to ally myself with the Parliament side of the matter, for unlike you, Doctor Tom, I do not believe.... nay, I know.... the King will not win the conflict. Expediency is my Goddess, and I had to decide how best I could save Derbyshire lives. The best of all possible evils. And may I say, dear Doctor Tom, we are blest and thankful that Essex was deflected from his original design of hanging, and sons of Derbyshire who would be dead and gone now but for you, are like to go back to their houses and hovels in our best and loveliest of shires."

My curiosity was still unslaked. "Why do you know that the King will not win?" I asked, gulping back another draught of claret.

"I fear that he carries his notion of divine right far beyond what is acceptable. You think I am a turncoat. Believe me, I thought long and hard on the matter. And Yes, I changed my mind. I am not proud of some of my previous actions. The King will never, can never say that. Every mistake he has ever made is tinged with his foolhardy divinity. What of Strafford? Black Tom was his best servant. Evil as the devil, but loyal, loyal as the wife of his bosom. If a King can turn against his best friend and sign his death warrant, what hope for the rest of us? What hope for the poor men of my county? I will keep Derbyshire safe and I will keep us fed. You are a good boy, Doctor Tom and I have respect for you."

I in like manner told him that I appreciated his confidence and was becoming so cupshot that I must needs seek my excellent bed, unusually exhausted I told myself by good fresh air, but in all probability by good strong wine.

I woke the next day Sunday the 19th of March, something low in spirits and tired in body. Stafford was in fact to our west and so on our left hand but Sir John proposed approaching the meeting place from a village called Weston to the north. We reached it before eleven and crossed the Trent here and then turned south-west. His scouts were able to tell us that Sir William was hastening towards Hopton Heath from a place called Sandon and that, hearing of our approach, there was much military activity in Stafford itself.

"Who are the Royalist commanders?" I asked the Captain whilst we were some little way from Hopton Heath. He sighed. "Harry Hastings and the Earl of Northhampton. Spencer Compton from your part of the world.... Compton Wynyates is it not? Do you know it? He was Lord Brooke's rival in the Midlands. Now there is none to hold his arrogance in check."

"So the men that follow him.... they are men from Warwickshire?"

Captain Cross seemed somewhat reluctant to reply. He frowned and scanned the horizon, muttering "Where is Brereton?" At last he said, "I am ordered to ensure that you are kept well back from the enemy should they seek a fray. Some of them from the Stafford Garrison are lately come there. Many were with Chesterfield in the Close. They may recognise you."

"And if they do?" I asked with a faint heart.

"They may think your support of Sir John, the action of a traitor."

"Then Captain Cross if you please, ensure that Elijah and I are kept well back, very well back. We have no interest in dying for Derbyshire."

We were swiftly at the area called Hopton Heath. For a man with little military training Sir John had considerable insight into strategy. He placed his foot soldiers and guns along a ridge between the land of a large house and a wild moor called Salt Heath. Before them was a rabbit warren, and flanking the foot on the house side were his dragoons.

I turned to look behind over the land whence we had come and gasped. It seemed as if a wild army had suddenly appeared out of the ground to our rear. One moment there was empty heath land and the next, ragged men armed with scythes, spades and bagging bills were everywhere on the ground we had recently covered on our march from Weston. It was the legend of the dragon's teeth come to life. Captain Cross was directing us to an area away from Sir John's pikemen at the rear of the great house and I asked who were the strange scarecrows who had suddenly risen up from the ground.

"They are the countrymen of Staffordshire, who do not like the invasion of the King's armies."

"So they are for Parliament?" I asked him.

He looked doubtful. "I think all they ask is to be left alone." My heart warmed towards these poor peasants, clearly desirous of a life free of guns and drums.

"Who leads them?" I asked him.

"Some Captain Queernabs they call the Grand Juryman, though from what assize or court no one can say. They are lamentable poor, as you can see."

We set up our station with some benches and a trestle, behind the house. Before it a line of guns were emplaced and there were more along the ridge. Two or three of the Moorland men came over and asked in their rough way if we had food. They had a pungent smell about them, of damp earth and graves. Elijah had not eaten all the bread and meat, Sir John had issued earlier, and willingly gave it as much from fear as from charity. It disappeared with a speed, miraculous to behold.

Still Brereton had not arrived. However before us from the direction of Stafford, there was a confused noise, the shouting of many men and the neighing of horses. Before Edgehill I had been a boy, a child, thinking that I would be invincible, wanting the excitement and experience of battle. Now my stomach seemed to have vacated its usual position and taken up residence in my knees. I remembered the thunder of the guns at Edgehill and Fielding's terrifying retreat and Wilmot's charge. I could see that Elijah was afraid also and busying himself tearing up bandages. We would be safe out of the line of fire behind the house, which I learned was called Heathyards.

The words "Brereton's here" were noised along Sir John's ridge battle line. Certainly we could see companies of dragoons dismounting in the copses to our north, in Salt Heath. I took a few moments to comfort our horses, which we had stabled near our station at the back of the house. The scouts must have warned the inhabitants that a battle would be fought as the place had the air of having only recently been inhabited. In fact our mounts were happily munching the remnants of hay left in the feed boxes of the previous occupants. I gave them each an apple, checked that they were securely tethered. At least here was our means of escape, should we need it.

I left Elijah and looked carefully round the corner of the house. Now I knew what the horrors of a battle comprised, I had no illusions. The hardened warrior did not leave the field covered in glory but in gore. If he was lucky, it would be the blood of others. If he was not fortunate…. I shuddered. The King's Men were drawing up now facing Sir John, his guns and infantry. They had not much in the way of ordnance but one huge cannon was positioned at the fore of their cavalry, its great mouth pointing directly to the Parliament front line.

At Edgehill there had been nearly twenty eight thousand men. The battlefield had been spread over some miles, and there had been a remoteness and detachment about the whole episode. For every one of those twenty eight thousand there had been a different story, everyone's Edgehill was unique and individual and there were great swathes of tedious time when nothing had happened near our healing station. Here the area we covered could be walked around in ten minutes. I did not think Sir John's army numbered more than two thousand men.

There seemed to be some sort of hiatus whilst the Royalist army and Sir William Brereton's dragoons arranged themselves to their liking. I would have thought the lack of preparedness on either side could be used to the advantage of the other, but it seems there was a method in the madness of battle. But there was a moment sometime around three in the afternoon when both sides simultaneously indicated that they were ready for slaughter…. and slaughter indeed began. The Royalist dragoons started with rousing attacks on their

Parliamentary counterparts. As Sir John's dragoons had stood ready since eleven I considered that they were perhaps relieved to have action at last, but one could see it did not go well with them. Perhaps they had stood patiently in readiness for too long. At the same time, the huge gun, a demi-cannon, which I later learned was laughingly called Roaring Meg, roared in good earnest, ploughing huge lanes through Sir John's Derbyshire boys and causing hideous carnage. It was, as I had heard described in the Low Countries, fountains of life blood and the tearing apart of delicate human bodies. I hated to watch but felt that I must. I had a good vantage point, peering round the protective corner of the house.

Sir John's guns were wrongly aligned. It was pitiful in one way to see the cannon balls arching completely over the enemy. We needed Ferdinand's engineer, proficient with the quadrant to readjust them. Sir John had not, I think expected the enemy to come so close. This was in itself a good strategy on the part of the Earl of Northampton as they charged like demons into the pikemen after Roaring Meg had taken her toll. Pikes need to attack en masse. One man with a pike unless he is exactly at the killing angle to his enemy's horses's breast, is a liability to himself and his fellows. Northampton cunningly used the lanes made by Meg to confuse and destroy the poor fixed pikes. As the King's Men retired from the charge, I saw that they were rolling away one or two of Sir John's precious cannons.

Dead and dying from both sides lay between the armies, and suddenly a few of the wild Moorlanders leapt through Sir John's severely tried foot and seized muskets that had been dropped by the fallen. They were overjoyed at these prizes and once they were back well behind their fellows discharged them in great glee. But there was little time for respite. Northampton was preparing himself for a second great charge. Alas, on that fateful afternoon Compton Wynyates lost its owner. Northampton was fully armed, like a knight from the old stories of King Arthur. His great horse caught its hoof in one of the rabbit holes, and toppled him off. Seemingly undeterred he fought on his feet. I suddenly saw Sir John's standard, a gold ground with five blue stars diagonally under the cross of St George, pressing closer to the Earl's iron clad figure. Then I saw Sir John himself. For all his nice habits he acquitted himself like a lion. But the Earl, his adversary, was fearsome. He roared as loud as Meg at the sight of Sir John and as I think slashed at him with his sword. Sir John seemed to be hurt but did not fall. Yet I could see a gash of red at his neck.

Sir John and his standard bearers drew off a little and the Earl seemed to be alone. He shouted for his followers to support him and his horsemen hastened to surround him. But they were too late. Some of Sir John's stout Derbyshire yeomen, foot soldiers wielding wickedly long swords were swiftly behind him. In an instant his helmet was off and the Earl was down. They offered him his life, but he shouted, (and this I clearly heard), "I scorn to take quarter from such base rogues and rebels as you are." These were his last words. The Derbyshire rams resented his discourtesy. His head was horribly broken open, by a halberdier.

The men from Derbyshire bundled the Earl from the field without ceremony, just as his horsemen and standard bearers drew near. Although their commander was dead, the King's Men had undoubtedly the best of the day. They regrouped for one last attack and just as they did so, Sir William Brereton's foot arrived. There was another of those strange pauses, which sometimes occurs in battle. The newcomers to the field were not certain which were the enemy, and Northampton's men, knowing him dead and seeing fresh opponents, had had more than enough by this time. Sir John Gell's horsemen were nowhere to be seen, and the Moorlanders had long since disappeared.

However, a young dark haired red coated officer would not cry, "Hold! Enough!" He called out, "To me, brave fellows" and the red coated horsemen pushed through from behind, over running the Earl's green jacketed troopers. He rallied his men into a fairly tight formation and they attacked Sir William's foot, who although they were fresh to the field were clearly not well breathed. I later learned they had run all the way from Sandon. This last Royalist charge held for some moments and yet another of Sir John's guns was rolled away. But then the red line seemed to falter. The young officer screamed suddenly and slumped in his saddle. One close to him snatched his rein and pulled him away from the melee, followed by the rest of the troop. Both sides were sated. Sir John's poor boys had taken the worst of the carnage. They outnumbered the King's infantry, but had earlier suffered grievously from Northampton's and Hastings' horse, and now had no stomach for this new onslaught. The guns Sir John had been so proud of, had been all but useless, and several of them had been neatly captured by the Royalists.

I was suddenly aware I had been standing at the corner of the Heathyards for nearly two hours. The March sun was setting. I had done nothing for the wounded. Had any found their way to our station? I began to feel deep burning shame. I had watched the battle as a spectacle, as a theatrical performance. I turned, walked round the house and head hung down prepared to make my humble apologies to Elijah.

He was not there. No-one was there. The bandages he had been coiling were on one of the benches, but there was no sign of any treatment for the wounded. My wooden case of medicaments was on the trestle table unopened.

And then I saw Elijah. He was lying face down, behind some tussocks of grass, perhaps ten yards from our station, facing towards the land where the Moorlanders had taken their stand. I gently turned him over. A musket ball had shot most of his chest away. He was quite dead.

I think I cried his name aloud. He had been lying, his head and outstretched hands facing towards a pikeman who lay some distance from him. This man had a sword gash across his thigh, but had also stopped a musket ball in the back. He too was dead.

No Royalist could have secretly crept behind the house to kill them. Absorbed as I was in the action of the battle, I would have seen such an incursion, and Sir John's dragoons would have made short shrift of such a trespasser. Then I remembered. The Moorlanders who had snatched up the muskets of dead men, after the first charge, had rushed through the Derbyshire lines, and had discharged the guns merrily anywhere.

The pikeman had been staggering to us for help. Elijah had seen him and run to help him and had stopped a musket ball full in the heart. I lifted his stiffening body and carried him back to our station. I think I must have been moaning and crying like a madman. One or two poor invalids came or were carried to ask for help but I could do nothing and when they saw my distress, and the corpse that I was mourning, their faith in any doctoring of which I was capable, must have faded and gone.

I kept chafing his hands, calling his name, begging him not to leave me. My head knew it was useless but my heart kept seeking signs of hope.

There were none. He had been dead perhaps an hour and a half, and rigor mortis was apparent. His hands were cold, so cold. He had been to me the brother I had never had, and yet we had only been friends and companions for about five months. I laughed aloud. We had met at the battle of Edgehill and been parted forever at Hopton Heath. This was Gell's fault, I raged. Why had he made us come here? Where was he? I scanned the battlefield. It was full dark but the Parliament men must have been planning to sleep another night in the open, for many small lights had appeared. Fires or lanterns? I wondered what I could do to find Elijah a fitting resting place. I turned back to his sixteen year old corpse and cradled him in my arms, trying to warm him. The realisation that this embrace was something I would never have done in life, and that perhaps such an action was shameful caused me to set him down again and seize his hands. I cried and howled and wept for some time longer and in this state Captain Cross found me.

"Jesu, Tom. What ails you?"

"Look at this!" I shouted. "The only child of a widow. Why did Sir John make us come with him?"

"Did he stray into the firing line?" he asked me. He crossed Elijah's hands across his broken breast and smoothed his fair hair. Tow coloured the Earl had called it. I tried to explain what I thought had happened, and told him of the dead soldier that Elijah had been hurrying to help.

"I can tell you, Sir John will be heart broken when he hears of this. Listen, we are for Utoxeter. He has a precious burden that he wants to use as a bargaining counter for his guns. I am charged to invite you thither, and into Derbyshire or to tell you, your parole is at an end if you so wish it."

I began to beat my hands on the wall of the house. "This is all Gell's doing. Where is he? I implored him to leave Elijah in Lichfield."

He forcibly stopped my senseless banging. "What purpose now to damage these healing hands? Tell me, was Elijah where he wanted to be?"

I nodded in misery.

He went on. "In my experience I would say this was a clean swift death, much as you described my Lord Brooke's. I tell you, Tom, before this conflict is over, men will be broken and maimed, both in body and spirit, and envious of such deaths."

I remembered Joan's words after my father died. "A lady, not my mother, but her friend, told me when my father died, that the best thing I could do was live for him, now he could not do so for himself."

"A wise lady, indeed. There are some few who wait for bandaging. Will you tend them?"

I nodded again in despair. What else could I do?

"But let us go into this house," I suggested. "They will need warmth and I need light."

By the light of the Captain's lantern, we found candles and a ready laid fire in the kitchen. I laid Elijah on the trestle we had brought with us and used the great scrubbed table to examine the men who had waited patiently, and in pain. As they had walked and stood, hoping for my attention in silence, I expected that their wounds were not grave matters. As I made preliminary examinations, the Captain told me he must leave me.

"How can I get him to his mother in Stratford?" I asked somewhat churlishly, attempting somehow to shift my responsibility.

"Tom, if that is your wish, then I cannot help you further. Have you money?"

I nodded. I had the remnants of the guineas Ralph had stolen from me. At the memory of Ralph and Eleanour, I groaned aloud. That worthless couple! If it had not been for her parents' anxiety, I would not now be trying to clean a sword slash across the ribs of one of Brereton's dragoons. The doctor in me was aware that the man's heart must have miraculously escaped fatal piercing. Why had I not followed my father's profession and become a butcher? Both he and Elijah would be warm and alive, had I done so. I choked back a sob.

When I had leisure to survey the kitchen again, the Captain had gone. There was one last poor invalid to treat, a man in a red coat who had sat apart from the others. I guessed he was a King's man, as I thought from the Prince of Wales regiment, led by some man from Nottinghamshire called Byron.

He showed me his ankle, swollen to twice its size and told me simply, "That accursed rabbit warren!" I had a bucket of cold clean water and plunged his foot into it immediately. The relief was instant and palpable and, sighing with relief, he offered me a sup of wine and bread from his snapsack.

I could not accept his hospitality whilst the other injured men sat or lay in various stages of recovery. One man, with a gash on his thigh which I treated, had a painful arm which I feared was broken, and needed sustenance urgently before I set the bone, and I asked if he might have the food and wine. There was a moment's hesitation.

I said crossly, "I make no distinction. You have a Royalist sprained ankle. He has a Parliament broken arm. If I set it for him as I must after I have further examined you, the pain could cause his heart to fail through lack of strength. Oh Jesu! Do your will! I no longer care." And I wept again, and went over to Elijah and chafed his hands, crossed over his wound.

When I looked round, the broken arm was eating and drinking. The sprained ankle had a servant who had given food and wine to all in the room. They were watching me warily, afraid perhaps that my grief might cause me to undo my doctoring somehow. I laughed at their faces, apprehensive and afraid.

"I ask your pardon, everyone." Finally some vestige of sanity returned to me. I indicated Elijah. "This was my journeyman who was killed in error. He has...." I corrected myself, "had no interest in making war on his fellows but was slaughtered none the less by a stray musket ball."

There was a murmur of sympathy. I rather relished my audience. "So," I went on, "Indulge me. In my surgery, there is no Great Cause of Parliament or King's Men. All are equal. A broken bone has no politics."

It seemed fitting at this point to re-examine the broken arm to see if I could set it. Nothing easier for me, but for him, a pain like the worst pangs of Hell. I explained what would happen, that there would be unimaginable agony for two or three minutes after I had done it, which would fade gradually, and that he could whilst the pain was at its height, abuse and curse me and call me what he would. In spite of my peroration, his screams were terrible to hear, making me feel like a torturer in the Tower. The Royalist with his foot in the cold water turned pale and seemed about to suggest that my treatment could perhaps be forgone, but I insisted on feeling his ankle, which was now of a more natural size.

"As I thought," I told him. "Nothing broken. A good firm bandage now, but do not put your foot on the floor for some days." It seemed he was a captain. He ordered his servant to seek his lieutenants who had promised to wait for him with his horse before returning to Stafford.

But before the servant could leave, the door was suddenly flung open and six more red coated troopers rushed in their swords drawn. As I was the only man on my feet, they surrounded me with swords drawn, as if to cut my throat.

"Leave him!" roared the Captain with the sprained ankle. "He is the surgeon, and a good one at that."

They had peered through the window when the screaming had started and had thought I was abusing their leader.

I had never thought on that dreadful day to see anything that gladdened my heart, but after the troopers came two corporals and a sergeant who stopped in his tracks, grinning broadly. He came over and clapped me on the shoulder. "Doctor Tom! I was never so pleased in my life to see a whoreson sawbones!"

It was Peabody.

11

"Peabody!" I cried out, "Look here."

He drew in his breath in horror at the sight of Elijah, cold and still on the trestle and touched his hair lightly. He stood for a moment and then said heavily, "Poor golden lad." Turning to me, he asked, "Today?" He glanced at the Parliamentarians and stroked his sword hilt. They sat silently, shifting uneasily, displaying their bandages, somewhat diminished by this incursion of King's Men.

I explained as well as I could what I thought had happened. He nodded and turned to his red coated captain with the swollen ankle, who seemed as much in awe of him as the Parliament men.

"Doctor Tom'll see you right, sir. I should've known that toad Gell would have made him come with him from Lichfield. He's off with his tail between his legs, sir, and we think he's taken the Earl with him. Harry Hastings wouldn't release his drakes. May we return to Stafford now, Master Miles? This good surgeon here, a friend and a trusted doctor needs my help. The men could get you onto your horse."

He smiled graciously at the Parliament men, sitting and lying as still as statues. "The owners of this house will be back tomorrow. You can pay them to help you to your homes. Your friend, my friend, everyman's friend Sir John Gell, seems to have forgotten about you poor fellows. Still there are some few hundreds other of your friends, lying outside on the field, who are in much worse case than you.

Alas, Sir John lost today. My advice to you is, think carefully before you support a rebel. There, I have done. Tom, can they be left?"

His polemic over, I did what I could to make the Parliamentarians comfortable and we went out to find my horses. I had decided that since Sir John Gell had left me, alone and friendless on a battle field, whither he had insisted we accompanied him, at the very least he had wished me to have the horses.... as a gift. The Royalist captain, a young relation of the Byron family who all called Master Miles, was heaved up onto his horse with his foot sticking out at an angle. He could not, must not try to put it in the stirrup, I ordered. We decided that the best way to transport Elijah was for me to carry him. I mounted and Peabody gently passed him up to me, and he lay, face upwards, before me across my horse, supported by my arms. Two of his troopers took my reins on either side and so we travelled, trotting slowly, the two miles to Stafford Castle. I will not forget that strange ride, through the moonlight, clasping Elijah's stiff corpse before me, gazing on the white oval of his dead face, praying that the cob would keep his footing. But the track was wide and smooth enough, the two troopers each side of me, good horsemen.

I was relieved when we trundled into the inner bailey of the castle, but somewhat disturbed to see that we were in a tumbledown ruin. I sat on my cob whilst Peabody took Elijah from me and took him into a carpenter's workshop at the side. I dismounted, like one in a waking dream as he returned and he told me he had arranged for Elijah to be coffined. "Will you see if 'tis to your satisfaction?" he asked me and I followed him towards the building.

But at that moment a voice cried "Where is Peabody?" and a large man appeared out of the darkness. Disquietingly he seemed to have only one eye, sparkling in the moonlight.

"I'm here, Lord Harry," and Peabody paused and turned.

"Any news of a surgeon? Where's Miles? Sir Thomas is not like to live. Bleeds like a stuck hind." He glared at us with his good eye.

"Where is the wound, my Lord?"

"Who's this, Peabody? Do I know you, young man?"

"Alas, my Lord I do not know you but I confess I often heard you, penned up as we were in Lichfield Close, with my betrothed's great-uncle, Philip Stanhope." Perhaps it was desperation that made me saucy but I was learning that with those who think themselves great, it does no good to mop and mow. Circumspection is a diplomatic virtue but sometimes straightforward boldness saves the day. Also, I knew I had a very marketable skill. I was growing tired of bowing and scraping to persons who were no more gifted than I was, but who rejoiced in noble lineage. I unfastened my box from my other cob, a docile good creature who had followed me obediently from the battlefield.

Peabody clapped me on the shoulder. "My Lord, if anyone can save him, this young surgeon is your man."

"I ask again, my Lord. Where is the wound?"

"Come on, come on. Follow me! In the thigh. Can you save his life?"

"It is to be hoped so, my Lord." We were following him up the narrowest of staircases which twisted round and round, lit by sconces on the wall. I wondered idly.... How did they get a man with a damaged thigh up these stairs? We came into a large bedchamber, once of considerable grandeur, but now open to the sky in one corner and below the starlit hole, the floor also was missing in that part of the room.

On the bed lay Thomas Byron. He was the young man who had led the last charge this afternoon, and whom I had seen scream and collapse in the saddle.

It must have been a point blank shot, from the musket of a Parliament man who suddenly found himself in the press of battle, alongside the Royalist commander. The fleshy part of his upper thigh was bleeding copiously. The bed clothes were already encrusted with blood. No matter how serious the wound, if speedy action were not taken he would die, but from loss of blood, not from loss of leg. I propped his leg on pillows so the wound was at an angle that would discourage bleeding.

"Candles, if you please, so I can see what I am about. Boiled water, as much as you can bring up here, and clean bandages. A laundered bedsheet will suffice, torn into broad strips by one whose hands have been washed in boiled water. Hurry if you please. Has he had food since the battle?"

Sir Thomas' personal servants hastened to do my bidding. I continued with my examination of his leg. We were in luck. I had a glimpse of the femur, gleaming white and clean amidst the wreckage of his flesh. It seemed to be undamaged. I resisted the temptation to begin to extract the shreds of cloth with my callipers, still unwashed after being snatched up in the kitchen of the Heathyards. The servants brought bowls of water and I washed firstly my hands and then my instruments, much to the impatience of Lord Hastings.

"Peabody, I may need you to hold a candle very close to the wound. For Jesu's sake, ensure no candle grease drips on him or....!"

"Or what?" asked the saucy villain.

"Or quarter staffs at dawn. And be assured I will win. Worcester Kings School Champion, remember!"

"Oh, for Christ's sweet sake!" interposed the King's Colonel General of the Midland Counties.

"My Lord, forgive me. I need to feel confident, at ease and without stress. This will certainly be painful for Sir Thomas. Would one of your servants who is not troubled by the sight of blood hold back the flaps of skin for me?"

None seemed to wish to volunteer. "May I ask you to fulfil that service for Sir Thomas then, my Lord? It requires a strong stomach. The sight of the excavation of a musket ball is not pretty."

I could see that he wished to damn my impudence, but care for his friend prevailed.

I began to move the tendrils of cloth that blocked my vision. In the movement he had endured since his shooting, the exercise had disturbed the material of his breeches and hose trapped in the wound. I worked patiently until I had the ball revealed. Again I thought we might be lucky. It was lodged between muscles which seemed to be undamaged.

I drew it out and laid it alongside the shreds of cloth.

"Does all this matter?" cried Lord Harry, his one eye agleam, and his ruddy complexion somewhat pale in the candle light. He turned his face away to retch into a white silk handkerchief.

"If you wish him to retain life and mobility, my Lord. The wound must be cleaned, lest it become infected."

"But why all this when you must needs cut it off? Where is your saw?"

"Cut what off, my Lord?" I asked in wonder and growing dismay.

"His leg, of course. Are you some kind of a numbskull?"

I was something taller than my Lord Hastings. I stood and looked down at him.

"Let me tell you sir, there is a good chance that Sir Thomas will survive. His bone is undamaged and his muscles seem in good order. If you wish to cut his leg off, then I pray you do so, but you will have to cut mine off first because he is now my patient, and I will die rather than he should have such barbaric unnecessary treatment."

Lord Harry swore at me, but I was beyond caring. After I had removed all the foreign matter, I allowed a little more blood to ooze out but then applied Pares Lotion and bound him up comfortably as I hoped. Through all this the patient had lain with his eyes closed, possibly moving in and out of consciousness, but now he opened his eyes, passed his hands over his bandaged leg and grinned at me.

"Don't heed him," he whispered.

"How do you, Tom?" asked Lord Hastings.

"Better than I would have been, had you had your way with me, you dog ape! Chop off my leg, would you, you crude hackum? I'll chop off your genitals and feed them to my favourite bitch."

"Why, Tom you sound clearly better I think. Do as the good doctor tells you. I must get me a cup of wine. This has quite unmanned me! Peabody, bring the good doctor to the refectory. I must pledge him after my rude unmannerly humour."

He snatched up a candle and took himself off down the spiral steps.

"He is my best friend," said the patient, "the best of men. We were born in the same year. Even so, I do not wish to have only one leg to counter his one eye. Friendship has limitations." He seemed to fall asleep again.

I gave instructions to the servants to feed him broth and sippets of bread and chicken flesh, and then returned to the bailey with Peabody.

"This is madness," I told him as we stood in the dark courtyard. "How can I disport myself like master doctor, as if nothing has happened, with Elijah lying cold in a coffin?"

"What else is there to do?" he asked me gently, (For all his bulk, he could be a most gentle man). "Young Elijah would have been proud of the verbal trouncing you gave Blind Harry."

"Peabody, I must get away from here. I must take him to his mother in Stratford. It has been delay after delay, mainly because great men think my doctoring skills should be at their disposal. I am a conscience salve. As far as they think, it is justifiable to beat and batter their fellows because a fool like unto Doctor Tom will always patch them up." I imitated Lord Harry's proud tone. ""Do I know you, young man?" No, nor do I wish to! Can you help me?"

"Go to Stratford?"

"Aye, with Elijah. It must be soon because...."

I could not voice my dread at knocking at her door with a corpse too putrified, for her to look on her son's unblemished bright face. He read my thought.

"I'll see what can be done. Lord Harry is the Commander here now. I'faith he will want someone to ride to Rupert with the news of this sad victory."

"All victories and all defeats in this mad war are sad, tragic and without purpose. I curse myself that I was caught up in the lunacy today. I am no better than a common ruffian who loves to spar and spur on others on the village green."

"Yes Doctor Tom." he said meekly. "With quarter staffs!" I laughed in spite of my distress, and he went in search of Lord Harry. Elijah was lying in a good elm coffin. He was, alas, one among many. Hastings had had the King's Men removed from the field in carts, and now they lay, some peacefully supine, some in stiff anguished posture. Remembering Powick Bridge and how there had been some few crushed there but not killed, I examined each one, but all were worm's meat.

The carpenter now had to perform the laying out of the dead, prior to burial, much to his dismay. When he learned I was a doctor, he asked how he should get these agonised limbs into some shape like unto that of the usual coffin. I tried to bend back the contorted legs and arms and finally suggested that his apprentice sat on each coffin as he nailed them down.

"How, though, at the Day of Judgement, will they be able to stand before their Maker when they are all bent and broken?" asked the apprentice, an imaginative youth.

"The angels will help them," I told him piously and he seemed content with this.

I paid for the coffin and wondered how we could transport it. Peabody returned. Lord Harry was content to allow him to travel south with me and return to him with news of Rupert. It was decided that the coffin should be strapped between my two horses, whom I would lead on a good pad nag that Lord Harry had given us. The dragoon who had owned it no longer had need of it. Peabody would follow behind on his own large tried and trusted

Cleveland Bay, known as Warrior. We could leave early in the morning. But then came the request I had been dreading.

"Would you, could you before retiring," asked a courteous and affable Lord Harry, his one good eye politely lowered, "look to our wounded?"

I bit back the response that I was too much of a numbskull and would lend him a saw, but as ever the sufferings of my fellows prevailed on me. There were broken legs and ankles, due to Sir John's judicious placing of his foot soldiers above the rabbit warren, some slashes, on arms, chests and legs and a few musket balls to be removed. In all I dealt with about twelve but as I worked I taught Lord Harry's servants how to care for them, causing one to write down the specific treatment for each invalid.

At midnight I was shown to a fine bedchamber. Peabody told me later that Lord Hastings had vacated it for me, having decided that I had earned such noble accommodation. I am glad that I did not know, as I did not wish to be beholden to him. In my view he was a rude one eyed Cyclops, a veritable hog in armour.

In any event I could have slept on a washing line. Peabody woke me early with new bread and small beer, and within the hour we were away, before most of the castle was stirring

"Who lives here?" I asked as we picked our way across a rotting drawbridge.

"Lady Stafford, a venerable widow."

"Do I know her?" I asked him in Lord Harry's arrogant manner.

How it was that in spite of our terrible burden and tragic errand, I could still jest and be a little merry, I know not. Perhaps Death, the great equaliser, loosened our tongues. It was a warm Spring day, and we stopped once or twice to water the horses and slake our thirst. I remember as we came to Rugeley, we were discussing the best way to preserve a body, speaking generally, not just of poor Elijah. I remembered that the Duke of Clarence had been drowned in a butt of Malmsey.

"As well we did not choose to bring the poor lad to his mother in such a way, or we would have drunk his preservation fluid by this," said Peabody.

I could not forebear laughing. "And Peabody, my father told me of an old uncle of his who was drowned in a cask of best French brandy wine. But my father said he had to be rescued twice to pass water!"

I asked him how his journey with Phoebe had progressed. They had stayed the first night at Coleshill and then had been royally treated at the Swan in Henley. Nat had brought them to Alcester the next day, where they had heard that the Earl of Chesterfield's loyal musketeers had taken themselves to Stafford. And thither Peabody determined to make his way, after he had brought Phoebe to Worcester.

"And what an emperor you are in Worcester, Doctor Tom! Two fine houses and large households in each. I tell you this. Roaring Blind Harry would think himself blessed indeed if he had a quarter of your wealth. If Money Makes the Man, you are he!"

"Well, consider!" I said, turning the subject slightly. "Then he is doubly unfortunate for, alas, if Manners Maketh Man, he is sadly deficient there also."

We were to sleep at Lichfield so that I could collect Jupiter and Mercury, and pay for their stabling. We made good progress and were riding down Bacun Street past the little houses and under the walls of the Close by six o'clock in the even. Peabody took the horses round to the stables of the George and I found the good landlady. Yes, she could accommodate us this night and yes, Elijah could rest in the parlour, although she was stricken with grief and horror to hear of his death. As I walked through the dining parlour, a voice I knew well called out.

"Tom! Tom Fletcher! Here I am and here are you at last!"

It was Roger. I had totally forgotten we had arranged to meet at the George and that he would bring the money to buy off our parole. I didn't tell him he was a forgotten man but brazened out my carelessness.

"Roger!" I cried and clasped his arms. "I am so rejoiced to see you, but Roger, such sad news!"

I told him of poor Elijah and he was quite cast down. He had had hopes that in a year or so my journeyman might prove a likely Trojan to face out his mother with him after being initiated into the ways of the Worcester ale houses. He came out with me, and Peabody to the stables and insisted on carrying the coffin through to the parlour, something to the dismay of the Lichfield topers who had met to damn Colonel Russell to perdition. (In much the same manner as they had condemned the good Earl) There was a com-

181

plaint voiced to the Landlady, in that Elijah's presence something blighted the merry meeting. But she would have none of it.

"The good young man stayed here and paid his turn, and here he stays with our best respect. He is to be taken to his mother in Stratford tomorrow, poor soul. A credit to her, he was, and so you may tell her, Doctor Tom. He was always pleasant and courteous. That was before he died, of course."

I bespoke a good dinner for the three of us, and excused myself and went to see my second good hostess at the Hartshorn. She was an honest woman who told me that there was still payment from Sir John for the invalids in her coffers.

Here now was my difficulty. Elijah had been everyone's favourite in the Hartshorn. I had to tell them. Better by far that they heard from me than that they should discover by chance after I had gone.

The landlady whose name I never discovered wailed aloud and sobbed into her apron upon hearing the news. I left her with the potboys and went into the first sick room. Zach was before me instantly. "Where is he?" he asked in his aggressive manner. I think he could see my terrible news in my face. He went back to hold his father, who was sitting up on his bed. I told them as calmly as I could, but Zach howled aloud like a dog and scuttled out into the stable yard where he began breaking his crutch on the walls. I went out to try to stop him, but to no avail. He began beating me instead. Jackie whose worth I would never have guessed, told me softly, "Best leave him. I can make him another crutch. He taught me that skill." The "He" in question was Elijah. It seemed he had also taught them their letters whilst I slept in the afternoons.

I told them I would call in betimes on the morrow to bid them all Farewell, and in truth was relieved to return to the George. It was clear that Elijah like St Luke had been the beloved physician.

But as we were clearing our plates of her daughter's excellent apple pie, Dame Emily told me that a young woman wished to speak with me.

"Well I say a young woman. Mayhap she is a lady, the young lady who you treated before with her good family. She's been asking for you these past two days, since you went to Stafford." It was Eleanour.

I could not pretend to be pleased to see her. Her hair was

dressed far more fashionably than previously, with elaborate blonde ringlets cascading around her sharp face. The dirty white dress, which she had worn ever since I had seen her in Lichfield, had been exchanged for a blue brocade, something soiled but new for Eleanour. She burst into the dining parlour clearly with some complaint or request on her lips, but at the sight of Peabody and Roger, she bit back with an effort what she had planned to say.

I invited her to be seated, gave her a cup of wine and asked her news.

"How are Hodge and Lizzie?"

She frowned with impatience. "Who? Oh the children. Well enough I think. Cornelia cares for them, and Gabriel. Yes, they are well."

Peabody enquired, "How is the old Dutchman? Did he take ship for the Low Countries?"

Again she frowned and seemed almost not to know about whom he was speaking.

"And Ralph?" I asked politely "How does Ralph? Is there much news from Colonel Russell in the Close?"

"Tom," she burst out, "Tom, I must speak to you. I must speak to you alone."

I could see that Roger was much intrigued by this. He had heard of the fair Eleanour of Ledbury, before he and his parents had come to live with me in Worcester and then had heard much, much more from her mother on her visit to us in February, that fatal visit that had caused all our inconvenience, grief and distress.

"Eleanour," I said gravely, standing facing her, my back to my friends, "You have clearly not been told. Poor Elijah is dead. A terrible accident befell him at Stafford. He was shot during the battle at Hopton Heath by a stray musket ball. Would you wish to see him? His face is unmarked."

"I would prefer not to do so," she said dismissively, "After all I hardly knew him. Tom, when may I speak with you on your own? It is imperative, Tom, that I do."

Behind me I heard a muffled sound, like a stifled laugh. Then Roger said in a feminine undertone, "Imperative, Tom!"

I led the way outside into the inn courtyard. She followed me. We sat uncomfortably on the mounting block. "Well?" I asked her.

"Tom, you must take me back home tomorrow. Back home to

Ledbury." This was said with a sob choking her voice. "I want to go home to my mother."

"I can't," I said, "I must take Elijah back to his mother and, at the very least, attend his funeral."

"No!" she cried, "That will not do. You must take me home at once."

I quoted a line of Shakespeare that floated into my head. "On what compulsion must I? Tell me that."

She was crying in good earnest now. "Ralph has left me!" she wailed.

"Left you?" I repeated stupidly. "Why is that?"

"Because he said he could not stomach the quarrels between myself and his mother. She is a witch, a Dutch witch!"

"But when I saw you all together in Cabbage Court, you seemed to be on good terms although your conditions for living were somewhat straitened. Why when life is better could you not live in accord with the lady?"

"When we had nothing she asked nothing of me. Now I have to use a brush here, a cloth there, wipe this urchin's nose, comb that infant's hair. In short she wants to make a household slave out of me. I can't endure it"

I said slowly, "And yet many women, aye and men too, "endure" their fates in much worse conditions than you. Do you think, perhaps, you ask too much?"

"Look" she said, her mouth set in a straight line, "I can't stay with the Dutch hag. I don't care about all your mealy mouthed preaching. If you won't help me I shall end it all in the Minster Pool one night. You must take me back to Ledbury tomorrow."

"I can't!" I cried, seriously disturbed by her threats. "Elijah must be taken to Stratford to lie next his father. That's the least I can do for him."

"Can't you do that after you've taken me to Ledbury?"

"Eleanour, you know I can't." It was difficult to know which was worse, her ignorance of practicalities or her selfishness. "You must know how quickly human flesh decays. I must get him to his mother, tomorrow or the next day, so he can be buried without that further distress."

She was silent, chewing her lip and darting glances at me from under her lashes. Finally she said, "Very well, I will tell you. I am ceratain...well,I have firm suspicion that Ralph is paying court to a rich widow"

"Does his behaviour surprise you?" I asked her.

She began to weep again and then gazed at me from under her lashes. "Has care made me then, so desperate ugly?"

"Listen, Eleanour." I stood up. "After I have taken Elijah back to Stratford and attended his funeral, then I will return here for you. So hold yourself in readiness. I cannot say how long it will be. Perhaps a few days, perhaps a few weeks. But know this. You and you alone are responsible for all that is ill in my life now. If you could have written to your mother and told her you were well, I would not have had to come here with Phoebe and Elijah, and he would still be alive. Oh, you can twist your story how you wish, but I tell you, you are a selfish harlot and I feel pity for Ralph that he is saddled with you. He is a trickster and a thief but even he does not deserve to live with a woman who can think only of herself. I do not believe your tale of a rich widow, but if he had found a woman who was compassionate, I would not blame him." I was shouting by this. "And you stole Phoebe's gown which my poor father gave her, the last thing he did. You are a strumpet, Eleanour, and I will return for you, but when I have taken you back to Ledbury, I never wish to see or hear of you again."

I turned and left her and went back to my friends. I think they must have heard my last outburst. They seemed somewhat confounded at my vehemence, and even Peabody seemed reluctant to engage in our usual pleasant jocular conversation. I sat with them trembling with wrath and regret for some time. She must have taken herself back to the Barrel eventually for when I looked in the stable yard it was empty. "Or perhaps she has drowned herself," I said to my good friends. Peabody laughed inordinately. "Not her! My wife was like that, God rot her. What hour tomorrow, Doctor Tom?" and so we parted for our beds.

Roger had ambled to Lichfield on Hector, so there were now three of us and seven horses. It would have been senseless to have taken them all, particularly as I was now pledged to return to Lichfield. I suggested that Hector stayed at the George to rest but that Roger rode Jupiter and I rode Mercury as both were in dire need of exercise. I had christened Sir John's cobs, John and Mary, the stallion after him and the mare was simply Mary. They had the sweetest and most patient dispositions of any horses I had ever known, moving smoothly after Warrior and Peabody, bearing their sad burden uncomplainingly between them. We left the horse Hastings had given me with Hector. I did not know his name but as he was something long in the tooth, I decided Old Harry would do. But he was a good enough pad-nag for all that.

Elijah had always been somewhat reluctant to ride Mercury and I was to understand why in good earnest. He was infuriating, would buck at a butterfly and shy at a flower. Eventually Roger offered to change mounts with me, saying that he understood recalcitrant creatures like Mercury, having sometimes helped his younger brother break horses for the saddle or the shafts. He was certainly a more vigorous disciplinarian than ever I could have been. Whenever Mercury was saucy, Roger would turn in the saddle and beat him twice across the buttocks with the flat of his hand. As he did not use the whip, I did not object, and Mercury seemed to respond by behaving more civilly.

Wednesday 22nd of March broke wet and cold, as if we had lurched back into winter. We left Coleshill somewhat affronted by the bad weather but made good progress and were at Henley by mid afternoon. Marion was deeply distressed by our sad news and as she knew of Elijah's parents, offered to travel with me to Stratford next morning, in order to offer womanly comfort to Mistress Bridges. I thought, however, that this was a task that I must perform. She and Mistress Bridges were after all only distant acquaintances, not full hearted friends.

"It is the lot of mankind," said Walter as we sat at a gloomy board and ate pork collops with apple sauce, after I had described for the third time how poor Elijah came to be in his coffin.

"Aye and womankind also," said her mother, God bless her, placing a quaking pudding in front of Peabody, who smiled so graciously at her, and smacked his lips so lasciviously at the sight of the trembling white mould before him that she ran back into the kitchen, giggling like an untried virgin.

"Alas, I cannot concur with your fatalism," I said in the grip of logic, sententiousness and very good claret. "Men who are told they are great and noble impose their ideas or ambition on poor men and tell them that these same poor men should die on the battlefield for the ideas and ambitions of the supposedly great and noble men.

It could all have been avoided."

"How so, Tom?" asked Walter curiously.

I had not thought much about what I was saying but warmed to my theme. "Is it so heretical for each man or woman to worship God as they wish? Does it matter what I believe or what he believes?" I pointed at Peabody who said, "I do believe I have never tasted so good a pudding."

We laughed and I went on, "I swear I will never raise my hand against a fellow Englishman for an idea, be he never so misguided."

"Well Tom," said Walter heavily, "Amen to your principles. I am with you. But if your great and noble rich man insists that you fight for him and he has two hundred lusty musketeers behind him, let us hope you can persuade him of the right of your convictions."

We retired to bed with my convictions in our heads and rare good claret in our bellies.

At breakfast I held little Thomas on my knee, and took some comfort from his round blue eyes and hair, close to the shade of a gold finch. I reflected that he had had independent life for the same length of time I had known Elijah. I had delivered the babe but three days before Edgehill. He interrupted my reverie by offering to feed me a hard crust which he had already chewed on to encourage his teeth, an offering valued no doubt by the giver, but somewhat unappetising to the recipient. It became a game as he tried to insert his rusk into my mouth, and I tried to escape his generosity. Her mother, God bless her, swept him from me onto her knee and fed him bread and milk interspersed with snatches of "Cock a doodle doo." She was vastly successful as an entertainer, and little Tom laughed and showed every sign of enjoyment both at her talented performance and with his breakfast. I had the impression that Peabody who had joined us was something jealous of little Tom's privileged position. There seemed to be a sort of understanding growing between him and Marion's mother and I thoughtfully strolled down the path to look at the horses. We would be in Stratford before midday. I was not relishing my task, but it had to be done.

I made myself enquire courteously before we went, as to Marion's mother's given name. I could not continue now to think of her as, "Her Mother, God Bless Her." This was rude patronage in the manner of Harry Hastings. His flagrant discourtesy and arrogance put me in mind by contrast of my father's philosophies, and of his care and value of every man and woman. This good soul had cooked for us, waited on us, given us packs of food to carry away, been ever welcoming and I had not even had the courtesy before to ask her name.

It was Cecily, she told us with a blush and a downward glance of her eyes.

"Mistress Cecily, I believe that I have never thanked you for all your kind care of us. For myself alone before Edgehill, (your pack of food was most welcome), and on the last occasion when I was here with Phoebe and poor Elijah."

"And my heart bleeds for his poor mother. I have some excellent honey and shall send her two jars, by your good self, Doctor Tom, if you will take it, and my blackberry cordial, hardly strong at all. A babe might sup it."

The day was cold and blustery as we gathered to say our Farewells. John and Mary submitted with patient good grace to the carrying of their sad burden yet again. Mistress Cicely, somewhat flustered, questioned our early departure. "Could you not give us a little more of the pleasure of your company?" said she, with a blushing sidelong look at Peabody. He grasped her hand between his two great red fists, bent low and kissed it soundly.

"Dear Madam," said he "Nothing would give me greater pleasure than to dally longer near the lovely Swan of Henley."

Roger, already mounted on Mercury, gazed at the horizon and made a strange noise akin to vomiting in his throat. I sat on Jupiter and exchanged glances of wonderment with Marion and Walter, whilst Cicely giggled like a green girl and told him, "Be sure you return to us as swift as you may, Master Peabody."

She was joined in this kind invitation by Marion and Walter. Nat had an errand in Stratford so we waited as he trotted round to join us, and then amidst heartfelt thanks and sad Farewells we moved off, Peabody leading the cobs on Warrior.

Our journey to Stratford, perhaps thirteen miles, was accomplished far too swiftly for my peace of mind. The town seemed calm enough as we clattered through the narrow streets towards the Avon. The citizens gazed at us with some curiosity but at the sight of the coffin seemed to accept that we were returning a son of Stratford to his birthplace. I saw one or two older men and a woman

188

make the surreptitious sign of the cross. There were no troopers on either side of the river.

John and Mary could not cross the bridge alongside each other, so Peabody dismounted, led Warrior over, tethered him, and came back. Roger silently handed me Mercury's reins, dismounted and he and Peabody carried Elijah's coffin over Clopton Bridge, the bridge which Elijah as a child and as a youth must have crossed so often and knew so well. He must have fished from it, swum near it, hidden under it and now he crossed it for almost the last time.

Nat helped me encourage the horses over. I dismounted and gratefully handed him, Jupiter's reins. The horses stood, somewhat dejectedly with Nat, together in a little group, their heads down. Even Mercury was calm and did not complain. It had begun to rain again, and the river smelt dank and unwholesome.

I went over to the cottage, followed by Peabody and Roger carrying the coffin. The moment was upon me. I knocked on the door.

12

S he opened the door and smiled broadly at the sight of me.

"Why, Doctor Tom!" she cried out with joy. "Where is…." She caught sight of the tragic burden, shared by Roger and Peabody behind me, and looked in vain around us for the beloved face of her son. She leant against the door. "Is that…. is that my boy?"

I could do nothing but nod and wish I were a hundred miles away. She stood for a moment, her eyes wide in disbelief and then she began to weep, terrible grinding sobs that seemed to rise from deep within her and to shake her whole being. I guided her back into the house and Peabody and Roger carried the coffin in after me. They placed it on a bench near the fire and she tried to raise the lid. Peabody performed this sad service for her and we all gazed on poor Elijah's white face for the last time.

She turned to me. "How…. how did it….?" I explained as well as I could that it was a terrible accident, that the man who fired the musket had no knowledge of his crime, but was, with others, excitedly waving about his new ill-gotten weapon. She nodded, but wailed aloud, "Why does God punish me so? What evil have I done?" At this, Peabody, sore distressed himself, prevailed on her to be seated and produced the blackberry cordial so kindly provided by Mistress Cecily. She sipped it and becoming a little calmer, moaned in abject misery that now she had no-one, that her poor husband had died lamentably young and now her poor boy was gone also.

The cottage door opened and Parson Worthington came in. At the sight of him, Mistress Bridges cried anew, "Alas, look at my poor boy, Sam. Dead last Sunday of a stray musket ball. Why does God punish me? Who have I harmed in my life? "

The parson, in black coat and bands, immediately suggested

"Then let us all pray," and poor Mistress Bridges dropped to her knees. As the parson remained on his feet, so did we, and he launched into a great diatribe on the evil of mankind, aye and womankind, and how we must accept that the punishment of the Lord must be visited upon us for our sins and evil actions. This went on for some minutes. He had clearly forgotten that I had witnessed his own "sins" when I had stood in this cottage a scant month before. I became impatient with his homily.I knew, God knew how, that his piety was only skin-deep. Roger and Peabody caught my eye, and helped Mistress Bridges to a chair and some more of the blackberry cordial. I covered up Elijah again and we moved him to the brew house where the warmth of the fire did not penetrate. All this we accomplished whilst Samuel played his part of Oleaginous Reverence and continued to address his Maker; I even went out with a cup of cordial for Nat.

When I returned he was still in full flow, describing in painful detail the pangs we could expect to suffer in Hell. Finally I decided that we had suffered enough on Earth for the present, coughed loudly and interrupted firmly, asking, "Well, Samuel, who must I see to arrange his burial?"

He opened his eyes, and in outraged tones declaimed, "Sir, I had not completed my orisons!"

"No, sir, but I had!" I replied waspishly. "This young man often told me he wished to lie next to his father. How may we accomplish this?"

Mistress Bridges wiped her eyes. "Alas," she whispered "Master Henry Twitchet was our beloved vicar of Holy Trinity, but he went to serve the King when Lord Brooke came here, when you were here last Doctor Tom, about a month ago. I do not know who decides what should take place at church now."

Worthington shouted, "That Twitchet was a malignant, a Popish traitor, as so many of them are, in this Devil's town."

Peabody said in shocked tones, "Shame on you, sir. To raise your voice and in a house of mourning!" I shook my head in sorrow more than anger and said in patient tones. "I ask again, sir and I pray you show respect to this bereaved lady and mother. Who must I see to arrange this ceremony?"

"Well if you wish it I could perform this sad duty," ventured the hypocrite.

"Could you indeed sir? And are you free of carnal urges and the fulfilment of fleshly delights? Is your heart pure?" I asked him with unction as slimy as goose fat.

He looked at me in amazement at the barefaced impertinence of the question and then, as he gazed angrily at me, I saw the light of memory kindle in his eye. He looked downwards. "No man is totally free of urges of the flesh," he muttered.

"So, with that truth in mind, spare us your lengthy prayers and fallacious sermons," said Peabody. "Our task here must be to comfort and support this dejected lady in her hour of need. If you can help us with practical assistance, that is well. If not, I pray you Master Break-Wind.... Oh, Your Pardon.... Master Break-Pulpit, then go your ways from here! Go, go along!"

"Amen" said Roger, grinning broadly.

"I fear I cannot assist. The recusants in this town despise me. I will bid you Good day," and he went hangdog slowly from the house. "Make friends, not enemies," said my father in my head, and I suddenly saw a way out of one small difficulty. "Mistress Bridges," I asked her, "Does Parson Worthington have a horse?"

"Indeed he does not," she told me. "His old nag died last October, and he has not replaced her as he feels he must give his money to the poor."

"Then I have a goodly gift for him from Elijah," I told her and ran from the cottage. The parson was walking in a downcast manner, towards the Banbury Road. I called after him. He turned as I thought in fear at my approach.

"If you please, I have a gift for you. Elijah hoped you would care for his mother. She is friendless and alone now." I ran to the group of horses and detached Mercury.

"He goes well, but is something skittish. You may discipline him with your hand only on his rump. He is a good young riding horse and will serve you well, if you treat him with respect and firmness, and demand the same from him."

He plainly had been a horseman. He ran his hands over Mercury's hocks and fetlocks, looked in his mouth, and surveyed the creature's glossy unblemished hide. He turned to me.

"This is generosity indeed. You might get upwards of twenty guineas at a horse fair. What is his name?"

I told him, and Mercury pricked his ears and looked at me, as I said it.

"Mercury!" said the parson, "The messenger of the Gods. Well, you are a good stout fellow, Mercury. Shall we be friends?" He stroked his neck and the horse who had had scant attention for nearly a month, pushed his nose into the parson's hand, as much as to say, "Yes, Well enough. Stroking is good but apples are better!"

"Have you a stable for him?" I asked, afraid lest the gift should prove an embarrassment.

"Aye, indeed. There is a stable where I lodge. Dry with good straw to lie on."

As it had been Elijah's horse, I hoped that his mother might also benefit.

"You can see his back is broad. When you ride out, you may carry Mistress Bridges before you. Would you now help us, sir?" I asked him, "Would you ride out and tell this sad news to Elijah's uncle? Do you know where the farm is? You would help me greatly if you would perform this service for us. This horse stayed there, I recall during December and January."

To my surprise he stripped off his black gown and in shirt and breeches, nimbly mounted. The girth needed adjustment, and he also seemed to feel the bit was too tight. He pushed his black gown into the saddle bag and turned to me.

"You cannot know how much I rejoice to be again on horseback. I will be back with news of his uncle within the hour." He trotted off.

Roger came out and suggested that he and Nat found stabling for the horses, and that he would accompany Nat on his errand. I told him to bespeak accommodation for us all. He still had the ransom money. I thanked Nat for his patience and help, and they set out together, Roger on Jupiter, telling Nat he had escaped a sore ear battering from Master Parson.

I was suddenly assailed with doubts as to the parson's honesty. Was he in truth a man of the cloth? I returned to the cottage. Peabody was sitting listening to Mistress Bridges, and holding her hand. I helped myself to some more blackberry cordial.

"Master Worthington has gone for your brother-in-law, mistress," I told her. "May I ask you, was he always a parson?"

She sniffed, rubbed her brimming eyes, and looked at me. "I think he was not, Doctor Tom. I think he has come to God's grace but lately."

She served us some thick and wholesome mutton broth, and I mentioned to Peabody that I had found a grateful and experienced horseman who seemed glad to take Mercury off our hands. And true to his promise, he was back within the hour, calming my fears. Elijah's uncle would be at the cottage later in the day. A precious cow was calving and could not be left.

"But he is sore afflicted," he told us. "He has a fine ham for you, Patience, so you may serve your guests."

"Indeed I would wish to do so. How merry we would have been had but Lijah been here."

My spirits sank again. Activity physicked grief, and I suddenly felt I must be doing something. "Mistress, where is your dear husband buried?" I asked her. "If I may, I will go and sit beside his grave for a little. I must try to make arrangements."

"God bless you, Doctor Tom," she said and told me where Holy Trinity was. In truth, I felt that I needed to be alone. Much though I cared for all the company there, now the worst part of my task had been accomplished, I needed some time to remember Elijah in his own surroundings and to mourn him alone.

She had directed me to a path, across the river and I wandered along, realising that Elijah must have so often wandered these meadows by the Avon. I saw now with my living eyes what he must have seen so often in the past. The moorhens, a noble and royal company of swans, a statuesque heron, spearing fish.... these were Elijah's memories and I felt blessed that I could share them.

Daffodils danced by the path through the churchyard. But the church was locked and the place deserted. The grass near the church had been cropped by some ewes with their lambs, and I sat down gratefully to wait for some worshipper who might tell me who now conducted ceremonies. The sun broke through. It had been a grey day with spots of rain but now the sky cleared and I must have dozed in the sudden spring warmth

A woman's voice.... "Young man ! Young Master Doctor!" A woman was standing in the path, smiling in recognition. It was the shot silk lady, though today her gown was in warm shades of crimson and bronze. Her plentiful hair, white as snow, was again fashionably dressed. It was possible that the delicate colouring of her complexion owed as much to Art as Nature. I leapt to my feet and bowed as low as I could.

"Come sir, none of that. You must know we are equals. You are a surgeon, I am a surgeon's widow. No need of time-wasting courtesies. I owe you an apology and as a woman who is old enough to be your mother, I must counsel you against the foolishness of sitting, aye and sleeping on damp grass. Will you enter the church with me?"

"Most willingly and perhaps, madam, you could advise me on another matter." I managed to reply. She smiled, selected a key from the bunch at her belt and unlocked the church door. She went straight to the Chancel where she stood gazing at a monument. It was a bust of Shakespeare. The lines below exhorted whoever should read them to forbear from moving his bones. "He could not stomach the idea of ever resting in a charnel house, so he rests below the chancel, as shall I, when I am called."

"He is your father?" I asked her.

She smiled, "Yes, indeed. Was ever a woman more blessed, Master Doctor? The greatest writer was my father and the greatest physician was my husband. I feel I must give thanks every day. Could I ask you to bear with me for a few short moments?"

She knelt down, her head in her hands and prayed for some little time, though whether to God, her father or her husband, who could conjecture. I walked softly round the church, admiring the memorials, including one to her husband John Hall, and the handsome rood screen.

Finally she rose and invited me to sit with her near the door at the back.

"You wish me to help you, advise you on some matter."

"If you would, Mistress Hall." I asked her if she knew the Bridges family. She offered immediately to show me the grave of good Christopher Bridges in the graveyard and was sorely distressed to hear that Elijah was no more.

"My difficulty is," I explained softly, "I know that Elijah and his father favoured the old religion. I would wish that his funeral could reflect his beliefs. For myself, Mistress, I fear that these terrible wars have diminished what little faith I ever had. But Elijah's religion was a clear burning light for him."

"And he must be laid to rest in the sure and certain knowledge of the resurrection of the body and the life everlasting. Doctor...."

What is your name? I heard it once but I forget. Doctor Thomas Fletcher. I can help you, but such a ceremony must not be noised abroad. Can you bring him to lie in the crypt along the river path tonight? Next Monday, I will have one here to say the last rites over him and administer the mass and he shall be buried out here, in sound of the river, next to his good father, mourned and lamented by grieving like minded neighbours."

I seized her hands. "Mistress Hall, I am ever in your debt. I have good friends who will carry him with me tonight. How may we enter the church?"

She gave me her key, which she asked me to return to New Place the next day. Then she showed me the entrance to the Crypt, a deathly cold underground chamber.

"Is Mistress Bridges content with this method of the disposal of her son? There have been rumours lately, that she has allied herself with one of that Puritan sect that rant and rave."

"The poor lady is delighted that he should be buried in the manner of his father and lie beside him. I know the man you speak of. I think his Puritanism is only skin deep."

"As well to say little of our plans in his hearing. The Town Council are Presbyters, every one. But now Lord Brooke is dead, I do not know to whom they can complain. But they could rule that the ceremony is illegal."

We locked the door and I pocketed the key. I walked back with her to New Place and went down Sheep Street to the river and so back over the Clopton Bridge. Elijah's uncle had come by this. He was sitting when I came in, turning his broad brimmed hat between his fingers, but stood to greet me and thanked me for my patronage of his nephew.

"The mischief is with so many of my own, I couldn't help him. But if I had scraped to do so, we should not now be in this sorry state. What a poor help I have been to my brother's son."

"None of us could know that, brother." Mistress Bridges was in somewhat better case than when I had left, and displaying good sense. It is no use to indulge in "if only" fantastical notions. Amos Bridges was like Elijah, broad across the shoulders and hair so fair, it was almost white.

I drew Mistress Bridges out to the brew house where Elijah lay, under the pretence of looking on his cold marble face again. I told her that Mistress Hall would help us, but that it would be wise to place poor Elijah in the crypt that night and that we must be secret. I showed her the church key and asked her if she agreed.

She wept a little. "It is frightful to think of my poor boy in that dark cold place." In truth I found it hard to withhold my own tears.

"Alas, madam, it is the common lot. My dear friend is beyond light and warmth now. If you want him interred in the old way, I fear we must be secret."

"What will Parson Worthington think?" she asked.

"He may think what he wishes, so long as he keeps it to himself. I will be speaking with him tomorrow perhaps. As Elijah's friend, your welfare is now my first concern."

She grasped my hands and began to cry again and told me I was a good young man, and my parents would be proud of me. Then she said, "I think the Parson loves me."

"Indeed, madam, I think so too. But can he support you? Has he any means?"

She shook her head sadly. "We have lived on what my husband left and what Elijah was able to give me. But now...."

I pressed her to agree that we could lay Elijah in the crypt that night, and promised that the three of us would stay for the funeral on Monday. Both Peabody and Roger had known Elijah and they felt that it was fitting that they should help and support us now.

So that night as soon as it was full dark, we carried my poor friend along the field path to the church. We met no-one but a vixen carrying a rabbit, who stood boldly in our path, her eyes agleam in the lantern light, but then quite slowly, with a certain dignity, she moved aside for us.

"Thank you, Mistress," I said to her as we passed her.

We placed my friend in the crypt. It was terrible indeed to leave him, but better that he should lie there, ready for the ceremony on Monday, than that the ceremony should become common knowledge. Mistress Hall had told me that, as she had the only key, none could disturb his rest.

I stayed with Mistress Bridges, lying on Elijah 's bed. The next day the three of us called on Mistress Hall to return her key, and to tell her that the coffin and its occupant were in place. She served us Sherry wine and little cakes such as Phoebe liked to make, tasting of caraway which she called Knot Biscuits.

"I should advise you, gentlemen," she told us, "that word is already passing secretly amongst the true believers. You will find there will be a goodly congregation to bless poor Elijah Bridges. His family was well liked and respected."

"That is excellent news, Mistress Hall. He was a fine young man and a good and resourceful student." Then she suggested to my joy that perhaps I would like to look once again at her husband's notebooks, as my perusal of them had been rudely interrupted before, when I had been bound for Lichfield. I told her such a study would bring me great satisfaction, but wondered if I could attend her on the morrow, as Roger and I needed to order new shirts, breeches and doublets. I was wretchedly poorly clad, threadbare even, and it seemed to me that Roger, who was after all of my household, needed new clothes.

She agreed to see me the next day, which was Friday the 24th of March, and so we bowed like courtiers and grinned like yawning cats, and went our ways in search of a mercer. We bespoke what we needed, though the tailor who worked there, cross-legged in the back room, told us if the clothes were ready for Monday, he would by then be both blind and deaf, blind for sewing our clothes all of God's hours, and deaf for his wife would nag him those hours simultaneous. I thought that perhaps Mistress Bridges might be in need of a new gown so caused the mercer's man to walk back with us, carrying some rolls of cloth from which she was to choose. She was delighted with the gift, and rain and sunshine chased each other over her countenance in swift succession. "If only Lijah could see.... Such kindness Doctor Tom, sure woman was never more fortunate...." I asked if Parson Worthington could be spared for a little, to walk along with me to visit Mercury in his new home. I had bought apples in the market.

His lodgings were in a ruinous farm on the Banbury Road. In good faith Mercury's stable was in a better state than his room as it was draught free and dry. But the house had damp running down the walls and that particular odour that pervades rotten wood. I had not thought that anywhere could have been more pitiful than Cabbage Court. I was mistaken. It was no wonder that he liked to spend his days, aye and nights too, with Patience Bridges. Her cottage though not rich was comfortable and snug.

There was a field at the back where he had been told by the

farmer who had recently moved out of the ruin into a fine new farm house, that he could freely run a horse if he could afford to keep one. We led out Mercury and walked him around to give him air and exercise.... and apples.

"You had better tell me your history, Master Worthington."

"Praise the Lord, Doctor Thomas. I came to his gracious mercy but last year. Before that I laboured in the courts of the ungodly, a sad untutored fellow, but with my conversion, I have received great gifts from the Almighty who now enables me to speak with divine inspiration and convince my fellow men of the true way of the Lord."

I stopped in my tracks, causing him to stop also. I touched him on the arm and he turned to face me in alarm.I said three words,"Samuel,my arse!"As I had thought it would, a gleam of humour played momentarily about his mouth and eyes. I continued, "I mean no disrespect to our faith or to true believers.Come on, Parson Worthington, the truth if you please. You do not make a good living as a pulpit banger, that is plain for all the world to see. You are dressed as Jack Out of Doors, and Out at Heels and Elbows also. Remember, if you please, that I know your liaison with Mistress Bridges is not based on spiritual inspiration, but to an extent on carnal attraction. I do not condemn you for that, but I feel I must take some responsibility for her now, so some honesty if you will. For a start, where are you from and what is your name? I cannot believe you were christened "Parson"." He remained silent, and seemed reluctant to speak. "Come on now, man, the truth if you will. I know I am something younger than yourself but I must leave Patience on Monday, clear in my heart that you are not out to exploit her."

"No, no!" he said hastily "Never that! I.... Well.... I love her. Her son disapproved of me and he was right to do so. I am a vagrant, a beggar. The preaching was a means to keep the wolf from the door. I saw these black crows sermonising in the market place in Evesham and crowds gathered round them. It is difficult to believe but some people are grateful to be told they are damned. We all have guilty secrets but women particularly seem to relish the knowledge of their own wickedness. It seems to give them confidence. It is strange how simple folk yearn to be told what to believe. I sat under market stalls and ate cheese parings and old parsnips and observed how these charlatans used the knowledge of human weaknesses to purge the credulous of pence."

"I am sure you are proficient to some degree in this career," I told him, "I think, though, that you did not choose this calling.... the calling chose you. Who and what are you? The truth, please, or I repossess Mercury." (I would not have had the heart to do that, as the recalcitrant Mercury was thoroughly relishing having one man's sole attention.)

He started in horror, but saw I was joking. He smiled himself and we paused on our amble round the field and let the horse crop the new spring grass, while he stroked the horse's mane and patted his broad back.

"Do you know the Lenches?" I did of course. A group of the sweetest villages, all with the name of Lench.... Upper, Lower, Middle, Inner, Outer.... all to the North of Evesham.

"My father was the steward of Lench Priory. He died four years ago and as was expected I became the steward in his place. I was named for the old Lord, a good old man, Sir Samuel Morton. My name.... Samuel Price or Sam if you will. I was raised as companion to Sir Samuel's only son, Denzil Morton, you will have heard of him. He is very strong for the King."

"And you are not?" I asked him.

"I confess it freely. That I am not. The reason? Because I found at last I could not stomach the arrogance, the cruel pride, the conviction that noble birth dictated the right to command. Doctor Tom, I was educated alongside this barbarian, Denzil Morton. Non modo did I help him construe his Latin, sed etiam I helped him translate Homer. Our schoolmaster did not believe in sparing the rod, but Denzil escaped many a beating because I, the steward's son, helped him with his tasks. I studied my calling. When my father died, I had planned certain drainage schemes of some water meadows, which after I had effected them, enabled us to increase our flocks. I organised repairs to the Priory roof. If I had not done so, it would all be in ruin now. I rebuilt the stables and learnt to doctor horses. I was Yeoman of the Horse as well as steward. You will not find a better farrier in the Midland Counties. And all for a pittance. We were expected to be grateful. My mother still lives there. She acts as a laundress. She was a parson's daughter, but Denzil and his bitch of a wife allow her to remain, and think they are monstrous charitable

She is two and sixty, too old to go a wandering with her wayward son."

"So then why did you leave?"

"Can you not guess? When he asked me to take up arms for the King. Why should I try to kill men who believe that Parliament would be a better ruler than a popinjay who deludes himself that he is divine? I could not do it. And I have a deep distaste for killing my fellows. Murder does not appeal. Am I unnatural, do you think?" I shook my head, smiling. "They turned me off for my views after I had worked for the Priory estate for twenty years, and earned them much money by my enterprise and efforts. I am thirty six. All they would give me was a horse near as old as I was. She brought me to Evesham, poor jade. There I learnt to do the preaching you dislike so much, Doctor Tom, and with my last guineas bought a worn gown and bands, from the widow of a vicar. I was able to bring some willow wood to Master Bridges from a carpenter in Evesham who paid me a little money. I walked, and the mare carried the wood. Christopher Bridges had died when I got here, and poor Hepzibah died also, her head on my knee in that stable. You are right. The preaching is play acting but Patience does not know that, and sometimes I think I can convince myself. What made you suspect me?"

"Because somehow I liked you, in spite of myself. I am not a man for breast beating and pulpit pounding. If God exists, he is in my heart...."

But my attention was suddenly caught by the horse. His ears were pricked and he had turned his head towards the south where the sun was westering in a sky streaked by rose coloured clouds. I strained my ears but there was no sound but blackbirds and thrushes beginning their evensong. I continued, "I am of a mind with you but the mischief is that there are good men who care for their tenants and dependants among the King's supporters. Lucius Carey is just such a man and the Earl of Chesterfield is loved...." But now I too, could hear what had caught Mercury's attention. In the next field poor men were planting potatoes, arduous, back breaking work. Their rags were as I had observed before indistinguishable from the soil. But in the far corner of the field, a hunt was returning from the woods, which lined the nearby hills. They had clearly had good sport. Two deer were tied on poles, The hounds clustered round the bearers lapping at the dripping blood and were beaten or kicked away. The farm workers stood as two or three riders, one wearing the red sash, which denoted the King's man, rode across the field, careless of whether they disturbed the work of planting. The workers bowed, all but one man who stood for a brief moment as if merely to ease his back and then returned to dibbing holes in the wet soil. One of the riders interpreted his lack of servility as calculated impertinence and rode over behind him, his horse's hooves scattering and spraying mud everywhere, and caught him an almighty crack across the back with his whip. Then shouting, "Damn your impudence, Palmer!" he rejoined his fellow riders, and laughing they rode out to the road.

I wanted to ride after him, drag him from his horse, and encourage his face to embrace the rough surface of the road after my boot had made close contact with his bum, but I pushed my hands into my pockets and remained calm. I remembered Adam's precept, "Think first, fists second." Samuel was tense and grey with rage. This was exactly the oppression he loathed.

"I think you have a convert, Samuel. Shall we help him?" I asked him. We led Mercury through the field gate, and went towards the poor young man who was slowly picking himself up from the wet and clinging mud. His clothes had given him scant protection. A portion of his upper back was visible through his torn filthy shirt. Already a great weal was beginning to bleed. I was concerned lest the soil to which he was in such close proximity might cause the wound to be infected.

"Come, Sir," I told him as we drew near, "I am a surgeon. Let me at the very least treat your wound."

He stood and looked at us, but could make no reply. One hears in stories of heroes whose eyes blaze in extremity. His fists were clenched, his whole being was rigid with hatred, and for a moment I feared he might attack us. An older man approached and told him, "Go with the gennlemen, Davy. It can't hurt to get that dressed."

He nodded slowly and relaxed somewhat. We led him back to the road and walked the quarter mile to the bridge. I sent Sam ahead to warn Mistress Bridges and to ask her to boil water. When we reached the cottage, and we were able to strip off his filthy shirt, I could see that his back held the evidence of previous whippings. After I had bathed and cleansed the wound and smeared a cooling unguent on it, to reduce the terrible stinging, Patience gave him an old shirt of her husband's that she had been keeping for Elijah.

He curtly nodded his head to me and with a "My thanks, mistress" to Patience, he left us. She confirmed what we feared.... that the poor yokels who worked for the landed gentry in these parts were in worse case by far, than those who worked for a yeoman farmer like Elijah's uncle. I suddenly remembered. I had inherited two farms in Herefordshire, part of Ben's bequest. All that I knew about them was that a large sum from both was brought into Worcester every quarter and kept safe by Joan in the Newport Street coffer. William Brindley the ironmaster in Kinver had said to me after hearing my careless profession that I did not know what I owned, "These men know what they own," pointing to his poor manufactuary workers, who had almost nothing.

Ownership was responsibility. What was I doing, drifting about Warwickshire and Staffordshire, involving myself in actions and factions, when I should be at home with my household.... with my two households, working to determine that all was well with the enterprises I had inherited. I should be ensuring that all who worked for me had the best conditions and that the managers in the farms were not using the day labourers who tilled the soil as little more than slaves.

This whole sorry confused situation was the fault of Eleanour Lloyd. How I could have deceived myself last year into thinking that I loved her. She was a shallow heartless hoyden and I wanted nothing more to do with her. She could not hold a candle to Phoebe, who was beautiful, clever and kind.

I was suddenly brought to myself. I had been sitting, gazing into the fire in Patience' cottage, and Sam was asking me if I wished to share a roast fowl that had been on the spit, some inches from my nose. I was aware that I was hungry but did not like to intrude or impose on them and took myself off to join Peabody and Roger, promising to return to sleep. Roger through discreet enquiry had found an alehouse that sold hum, the monstrously strong ale he loved, and which his mother claimed was known as "hum" because after one pint that was all the drinker could say before falling fast asleep.

In the morning I asked Patience for hot water, found some oatmeal soap in my chest and went out into the brew house yard, stripped off and washed myself thoroughly everywhere. I had not done that since I was at the Hartshorn, caring for the wounded. I had the notion that patients trust a doctor who does not smell as rank as they do. Ben had stripped off and washed every day. Even Sir John Holte had confided to me that he had a man pour a bucket of water over him, every morn, rain or shine.

I was to visit the tailor to see if my new clothes were prepared. There were shirts ready for Roger and myself, and small clothes also but I had to assume my old breeches and doublet. Patience seized my dirty shirt and asked if she could wash it for Samuel to wear on Monday. I agreed, pleased that her mind was occupied with practicalities.

Then content that I was as fine as might be, I took my way to Mistress Hall who greeted me most pleasantly, gave me cakes and wine and left me with her husband's precious casebooks. What interested me particularly, and what Joan would rejoice to know, was his dependence on watercress and rocket, or as it is sometimes known scurvy grass. His concoction from these two plants, if drunk daily, would cure lassitude, jaundice, frequency of passing water, mouth ulcers "swelling, sweating and wandering pains."

I spoke with Mistress Hall, congratulating her on her husband's enterprise, and she laid one delicate hand on her white cheek and the other on my arm.

"Doctor Tom, I still drink this infusion. If a woman wishes to keep her complexion, my husband used to say, it is not what she applies outside, but what she takes inside in her diet. And Doctor Tom, I will not deceive you. I am sixty years old in May."

I congratulated her on her flawless visage. I wished she could have known Joan, who still stood over Roger at the table, insisting even though he was seventeen that he ate his greens and salad stuff as well as meat and bread.

"But you must know Doctor Tom, my poor husband travelled far and wide to treat his poor patients. He would travel forty miles to Ludlow to minister to the Earl and Countess of Northampton. That is I think what killed him in the end. He was tireless in his desire to help the sick."

"Well," I said, "The Earl of Northampton has no need of a physician now. I saw him die."

"Did you?" said Mistress Hall with a wide, delighted smile.

"Where was that sad event?"

So I told her of the Battle of Hopton Heath, where poor Elijah Bridges was accidentally killed, and the Earl, unhorsed, was offered mercy by his foes, but preferred to retain his pride rather than his life.

We were sitting at her fine oak table. She pressed more wine on me and told me, "Men and women like you, me and my father and my husband, we are the future. They may think they have birth but we have the skills, the talents, the genius if you will. I am not for either side in this controversy but I tell you this. Their pride will avail them naught. Do you know my husband had occasion to go to Ludlow again, summoned by a Mr Powel as I recall and we made a jaunt of it. And do you know, outside St Laurence's, there were the Earl and Countess both of whom my dear husband had cured walking straight towards us. Well we made courtesies, and do you know Doctor Tom, they took not a scrap of notice of us. Not a word! Noses in air, as if we were beggars in the gutter."

"That is shameful, madam," I said.

"My dear husband made light of it. And told me a little rhyme of an Italian doctor, Cardus or Cordus, was it?

> *"God and the doctor we alike adore,*
> *When on the brink of danger; not before:*
> *The danger past, both are alike requited,*
> *God is forgotten and the doctor slighted."*

My father would have liked that. So the Earl is dead, you say. Alas, Doctor Tom! Such times! Such troubles!" But I was well aware that her sorrow was less than skin-deep.

She went on to speak of the arrangements for Elijah's funeral. She had had the grave dug for him, next his father, and "there will be one Mr Brown will say the mass for the poor youth. It would be politick if no-one enquires after him, whither he comes or goes after the ceremony. He is addicted to secrecy. Above all that black gowned prelate that Mistress Bridges knows. He is not welcome."

"He has renounced his Puritanical views, madam. I promise you, he will give no trouble. He too has been the victim of the arrogance and pride of the great. Dear Madam, I will vouch for him. He will not disturb the ceremony and if you permit it will attend, sober suited, like all others, utterly silent, utterly discreet."

She looked at me gravely for a moment. Then she said, "Very well, Doctor Tom, you shall be his surety. I have arranged bearers and after the poor child has been interred, all may return here for refreshment. But I must beg you do not question the celebrant."

"No, indeed," I promised.

Our clothes were ready on the morning of the funeral. Roger and Peabody came to the cottage, and I insisted that Roger underwent the cleansing process in the Brewhouse yard.

"Jesu, Tom, you are worse than my mother!" he told me. "I'd rather be an honest dirty barber than a powdered perfumed pricklouse, all starched up like a Haymarket Hector."

"There is little chance of powder or perfume today," I told him. "Sobriety and dignity are our watchwords."

As we walked up the path to the church, the sheep bleating in the meadows around, I was surprised by how many of the citizens of Stratford had come to pay Elijah their respects. The coffin was already before the altar. Patience placed a bunch of daffodils upon it and I was pleased to remember that it had been these flowers that Elijah had longed to see, cooped up as he was in the Hartshorn Inn for so many days.

We stood at the back and waited. Suddenly, (and I have no notion whence he came), the thinnest man I had ever seen, in black doublet and hose, was before us, greeting us warmly with the Bidding Prayer. He then spoke of how Elijah died, so needlessly but that it was God's will. I did not agree with that, but I held my peace. He said how it was known that Elijah cherished a love of the old church. He had a loud and dramatic voice, but was like a willow wand. I remembered the apothecary in one of Shakespeare's plays, and the description came back to me. "Need and oppression starveth in thine eyes." There was no incense and no bell ringing.

The ceremony slipped from English into Latin and back into English, and then it was over and the bearers came forward, lifted the coffin and followed by the Romish priest, for such I decided he was, we went forth into the sun, to place Elijah in his last resting place. The coffin was lowered, Master Brown spoke the words of Committal over the grave and Patience Bridges was invited to throw her flowers on it. We all sprinkled a little earth on my poor young journeyman, and many there wept at the senseless random cruelty of his end. I confess that I was one of those who could not restrain my tears. Even though Patience had told me she did not hold me responsible in any way, I still felt guilt at the manner of his ending.

I looked round for the priest. He was not to be seen. He had slipped away into the shadows of the trees that lined the graveyard. I never saw him again.

Mistress Hall entertained us lavishly, but Patience was tired and Samuel supported her back to her home. It was noticeable that the people of the congregation did not like him.... or rather did not trust him. Many spoke words of comfort to her; none addressed a word to him. She wished to sleep, and I suggested to Sam that I took Jupiter from his stable at the Bear and we gave our horses some exercise.

We trotted to a nearby field and thence to a common where we put them to the gallop, which was perhaps equally healthy for man and beast. As we ambled back, I told Sam that I had thought about his situation and that his obvious skill with horses would be a sound investment. I had plans for him. Would Patience ever consent to sell her cottage and leave Stratford? If she would, then I might be able to accommodate them in Worcester and find good employment for him.

He embarrassed me by dismounting and embracing my foot. We were outside Mercury's stable, so I leapt down and told him not to be so humble. "You have a most valuable skill," I told him. "In these times, a farrier's profession is a mystery well worth cherishing. I intend to nurture it. Have no fear, we shall both profit from your talents."

We walked Jupiter back to the town. I told him what Mistress Hall had said, that the future belonged in her view to the people with skill, not birth. "A good woman," he observed. I did not think she was a particularly forgiving lady, but as far as I was concerned she was no worse for that. I told him Cordus' little rhyme and he laughed inordinately. I left him at the cottage and took Jupiter to his stable at the Bear, where I bespoke a meal in the evening for Peabody, Roger and myself. Tomorrow would be the parting of the ways.

So it was that as we were sitting over prune and raisin pasties with cream, the peace of the evening was suddenly disturbed. Shots and explosions echoed up the dark narrow streets. My heart turned over. I had forgotten how terrible it was to be in a civil war. After a few days of peace, here were mad riders, galloping into the town, discharging their pistols and shouting and screaming at the Stratford citizens to come out if they were miserable Puritans and fight for their lives. Was it blind Harry Hastings again perhaps with his lunatick horsemen? Peabody went to the window and peered out into the darkness. He turned back to us, his face one enormous grin.

"All's well!" he told us, "It 's young Rupert!"

13

But all was far from well, as we were to discover. We sat for a while over our puddings, listening to the swearing, shooting and roaring outside. To speak truth, I was something concerned for Mistress Bridges. If Sam had decided to go to his lodging, then she would be alone, south side Avon, in the direct path of Rupert and his riders.... or rather raiders, if the noises of destruction were aught to go by.

"Well," I said finally to Peabody, "You have your wish. Rupert is the man you came to find for One Eyed Hastings. Do you know him?"

"Oh, aye. I know him. Everybody knows him. But more to the purpose he knows me. I am Sir Jacob Astley's man. I had to beg a horse of Rupert for Sir Jacob at Edgehill."

"You were at Edgehill, Peabody?" I asked in disbelief.

"There were one or two other men there, Doctor Tom, besides yourself. I have always fought beside Sir Jacob."

"Where was that then?" Roger asked, greedy for news and horrors.

"I was with him in Europe, in High Germany, fighting alongside the Hollanders. But before that Sir Jacob was with the King's sister in The Hague, and taught Rupert the management of infantry. He caused me to be at his side during the Bishops' War, and I helped him beat the King's foot into shape. These burbling whisks are Rupert's raw recruits, and I had to teach them sword play in November last in the fencing schools round Christchurch. After Edgehill. You did not see the King's foot fight there, Doctor Tom, being dare I say, some distance from where the real work took place. I' faith, it was their battle. If Rupert's horse had not thought they were out hunting, Essex' villains would be all six feet underground. The King's foot were mauled and maimed by Essex' horse but still they stood, like heroes of stone.

So they sent me from Oxford to aid Chesterfield when the King heard of his stand in Lichfield Close. My present commission is to tell Rupert of any movement of Essex that might threaten the Northern routes. So after I had delivered your lady to Worcester, I followed Hastings to Stafford to learn of Parliament's activities. The King expects the Queen back and Rupert is no doubt looking to ensure she can get safe passage to Oxford...."

He ceased his peroration when sudden screams rent the air. The door from the street was flung open and two young girls, mouths open, cloaks flying, ran, falling and stumbling into the ale house. They were hotly pursued by two mounted young blades, younger than me I dare swear, one of whom tried to force his horse to enter the building. He would have grievously injured the poor creature so I helped him to dismount onto his bum, and the horse clattered off down the street.

He made as if to attack me, but my fine new doublet gave him pause and suddenly Peabody was beside me.

"Do you have a quarrel with Doctor Fletcher, Sir Matt? How is your Lady Mother? Pray give her my best respects!"

"Peabody!"

"Aye, Master Peabody, if you please, Sir Matt. You and Sir Nick here had better follow your horse, had you not? Whither are you bound tomorrow? Did you wish to walk there? Where is the Prince?"

"Still in Oxford. He sent us ahead to clear the way of malefactors!"

"Did he so? And may I take it then, these two young ladies have in some way wronged you, gentlemen? Are they in fact "malefactors"?"

The other boy had dismounted and had led his horse across the road to our alehouse door. He muttered, shamefaced, "Your pardon, Master Peabody."

"It is the pardon of these two young ladies that you should be seeking. A guinea each buys it for them and my silence also." To my amazement each one pulled out a heavy purse and handed over the golden coin.

"Here, ladies!" and Peabody went over to the trembling maidens who were being comforted by the Landlady, and gave each a guinea.

"Now find his horse!" he instructed the hangdog oafs. "Go your ways, a rare pair of Jack Sprats, are you not? God give you good even."

He turned back to us. "Come, gentlemen," said Peabody, "these matters grow something heavy. We had best ensure that all is well."

He paid our shot which pleased me mightily, for most men expect me to foot the bill, and we strode out into the street. The horsemen were all young, wild and clearly high born. One group had decided to race down the Waterside. As we approached, Peabody suddenly roared a word of command.... I know not what it was.... which caused every horse to stop dead in its tracks. A few of the riders tumbled off unceremoniously and one came over to us, fists clenched.

"Get back, Simon! It's Peabody!"

"Why, Master Simon? You wanted something from me? A broken arm, perhaps?"

The young horsemen melted away like hail stones at midsummer. But now we could hear a fearful hobbleshow, coming from across the river. There were screams, shouts and laughter. I realised I had been right to fear for Mistress Bridges. Then we heard Sam's voice raised loud calling, calling for me!

"Tom! Tom! For Christ's sake, Tom!"

"Oh, they're having a game with that damned preacher!" said Peabody peering through the darkness to where some lanterns bobbed across the river.

I set off at a run. "He's no preacher. He's a farrier. The preaching was playacting." I had almost gained the bridge but Peabody was suddenly ahead of me, drawing his sword, and pounding over to the crowd of laughing youths.

Sam was in the middle of the hellish throng and they were pushing him roughly across the circle from one to another, tripping him, beating him and spitting at him. His head was bleeding and his hose were torn revealing bloody wounds. Patience was held by two of them before the cottage door. She screamed at us to help him as we ran towards the riotous clamour. As we ran to the shouting roaring hubbub, one somewhat taller than the others, with a gigantic thwack of the back of his sword, knocked poor Sam finally to the ground. God knows what would have been his fate with these mad Devil's bull-heads, had not Peabody been suddenly astride him, sword drawn, roaring like Beelzebub, and turning slowly, invited them one and all, to approach and be damned.

One youth thought to accept his challenge, but was swiftly pulled back by his fellows. "You fool, it's Peabody!" his friend shouted and the bragging boisterous knaves became so many frightened dolts, weak and puerile. Peabody brandished his sword again. "Come on, you base craven poltroons. Come and taste my sword across your arses. What has this poor farrier done to you? He is commissioned to doctor His Royal Highness' horses on his next campaign. I doubt the Prince will be much gratified by your treatment of this valuable and important man."

"Master Peabody!" cried a bold swaggerer.

"Oh aye, Master Ferrers Dawkins, are you there? What's your will, pray?" This with a mock courteous bow. "Pray, sir, name your pleasure. How may we accommodate your desire?"

"This man you protect is a vile Puritan cornercreeper. He is a preaching grovelling toad. We have that on good authority."

"Oh, aye, on whose authority?" said Peabody. There was some confused talk amongst the valiant Hectors. At length it emerged that the potboy at the Maidenhead had told them that Samuel was given to holding forth at the Market Cross.

"Well, Master Dawkins, there are three matters about which I wish you to ruminate. It is as yet not a crime to speak ones mind in public as I do now, and may well do so tomorrow, at the Market Cross with you in the pillory. Secondly Prince Rupert will be interested to hear that you place a potboy's word above mine, and thirdly come forward if you please, and let me examine your intestines. I have long suspected that your liver is as yellow as mustard. I would dearly love to prove my suspicion here and now." He brandished his sword elegantly, placed his left hand on his heart and bowed. Master Dawkins stood, hangdog, like a chastised dunce in the corner.

"I would speak with one of you who does not keep his brain in his breeches. Sir John Fortescue, if you please, come forward." A tall young man pushed his way to the fore.

"I and my companions have just come from Stafford where, with Roaring Meg and mad Lord Hastings, we gave short shrift at last to Brereton and Sir John Gell. It was hot work, for the Derbyshire yeomen fight like fiends. Oh, Aye, Master Dawkins," he said loudly to the youth who had argued with him. "They were seeking chickens of your colour to spit on their pikes. I was en route for Oxford to join His Royal Highness. I understand, Sir John, he sent you to clear the way of malefactors?"

"Well, something of that, Master Peabody. I think he did not mean we should take the law into our own hands. He said he would meet us here o'Wednesday next."

"And meet him you shall," said Peabody, "all of you. And I tell you this. Any noise, any crimes against the ancientry, any drinking over and above what is fitting, any ravishing of honest virgins, and you will kick the clouds for this outrage to the good farrier here when the Prince arrives. Go a-buttock banqueting and spread your noisome poxes amongst harlots if you must. But the honest citizens of Stratford are secure in my sanction from your idiocies. Go your ways."

And they dispersed. "Sir John, assist me please." Between them they levered poor Samuel to his feet, and somehow pushed him towards Patience. When we reached the cottage, I laid him upon the bed and ripped away his torn clothes. Poor Sam! Flesh, clothes and dignity were in a like sorry state. Patience went straight to boil water, and Peabody began to question young John Fortescue.

"So Rupert comes to Stratford o' Wednesday next, does he? And whither o' Thursday or Friday?"

"I think Henley, Master Peabody. And then I heard he had made a vow."

"A vow? What vow is that, young John? Come there is no treachery in telling me. You know I have given my blood for the King more than once."

The youth paused a moment and then continued "I heard him say to his younger brother that he has vowed to avenge the slights the King suffered at the hands of the Birmingham people."

"Slights? How so, good John?" Peabody subtly continued his interrogation.

"On the way to Edgehill from Shrewsbury last October. They pillaged his last wagons and took bolts of cloth and other haberdasher's items."

"And whither from Birmingham?"

"Stafford was it? Ah, no 'Twas Lichfield. To open the way for Her Majesty and to repossess the Close."

This, for me, eavesdropping from Patience' bedroom, bathing and cleaning poor Sam's wounds and bruises, was grave news indeed. My good friend, Joseph, the brown pedlar, had told me when I was there last October that he lived near the Horsefair. The Horsefair! What of Harry and his cobs? I needed to see him. My scheme for Sam encompassed trading with him.

Sam groaned. "A pox on my life!" he mumbled. "Why do I court bad luck?" Patience came in with a posset, helped him drink, supporting his shoulders, even though there was sore bruising about his back. He winced at her touch but smiled at her gratefully and grasped her hand for a moment. I told him to be cheerful, if he could be. Nothing was broken. He was in like case to myself after Brigstock, and his men had tortured me, and the family at the farm. Bruises, pain and stiffness, but food and rest would work miracles.

Next morning Peabody and Roger came early to the cottage. We had to decide what we should do. Sam was able to leave his bed. He was stiff and sore, furious with the high born wastrels who had brought him to this painful pass. The whole episode had fed his hatred of what he called the aristocracy. He would flourish and prosper in our town where "well born wastrels" had no sway. In one sense.... and perhaps these were dangerous thoughts.... I was beginning to despise the chance of birth and to realise that we can all be "well born," if we school ourselves to think we are.

I had planned this day to return to Lichfield to bring Eleanour back to her parents and to get the other horses, Hector and Old Harry. However, the news of Rupert's plans caused me much disquiet. What of the other Harry, who lived somewhere to the north of Birmingham and who helped his brother breed Welsh cobs? What of Joseph, for whom I felt affection and respect? What form would Rupert's revenge take? I asked myself. What did I want to do? Easy enough... I wanted to warn them. So I would do so. I would go to Birmingham, ahead of Rupert and warn my friends, and then ride to Lichfield.

We sat round Patience' well worn table. The letters "E L I" had been carved in its surface. She saw me looking at her son's half formed childish waywardness and smiled, telling me how she had slapped his infant fingers before he had completed his prank. His absence oppressed me for some moments, until I remembered a scriptural maxim. "Let the dead bury the dead." My task must be to save the living.

I asked Patience if she could leave her home. She looked round bewildered and then at Sam for reassurance.

"I think I can help Sam to make a good living for himself as a farrier in Worcester and roundabout," I told her. "And you would be a valued asset also, mistress."

"I was going to offer to make good my lie of yestreen," said Peabody. "Believe me the King's horses always need attention. They are ridden monstrous rough by some of their brachet owners."

"I could not stomach such an appointment, Master Peabody," Sam told him. "Not after my vile treatment of yesterday. And indeed, Doctor Tom knows. That is not the first I have suffered at the hands of our supposed betters. As I see it, the question is can Patience see her way to leaving her cottage."

We all looked at the lady. She pushed a black curl under her cap and surveyed us all. "What have I to keep me here?" she asked. "My parents are dead. I have no sisters or brothers. Those who were dearest to me lie in Holy Trinity churchyard. Amos would pay me guineas for this place for one of his sons. They live like rabbits in a warren in that little farm. I say, Samuel, we should go and take our chance with Doctor Tom."

Roger coughed, "May I speak Tom?"

"Do you need to ask, my prince among barbers?" I asked him in turn.

"I think Sam and Mistress Bridges, if you intend them for Worcester, Tom, I think they should dwell in the Fish Street house, if they do not mind the smells of the Butchery. Gill is almost past housewifery. She can do a little, but would welcome Mistress Patience' skills and assistance. I say this because although there is room aplenty in the Newport Street house, there is also my mother. I know she would be the kindest of neighbours to Mistress Bridges and Master Price in Fish Street but...."

He had no need to enlarge upon his theme. I knew Joan.

"Roger," I told him from the full extent of my two years seniority. "Well advised. You have quite an old head on your young shoulders, have you not?"

He aimed a friendly cuff at me and went on. "Also, a paddock could be fenced off from the field where the beasts wait for.... a paddock for horses.... sick or for sale."

215

"We could certainly begin that way." I was thinking the situation through as we spoke "But it might be that I could buy more land, and there are your brother's foals. There is no farrier in Worcester, is there?"

He shook his head. "None that I know of."

"Mistress Patience," I asked her. "Can you ride?"

"I am a farmer's daughter, Tom. I have ridden almost from birth."

So all was decided. I prudently asked to see what guineas remained from the store Roger had brought for our ransom, and after giving him a generous amount for his support and enough also for their journey of the morrow, pocketed the rest. I felt some guilt about this but as Roger reminded me, "God's death, Tom! 'Tis your money!"

He would ride John with Patience on Mary, and Sam on his beloved Mercury to Worcester tomorrow. He suggested I wrote to Joan to explain what had transpired, and promised to buy parchment from a notary's in Stratford. Patience had a quill and ink for my letter. Sam rode to the farm to tell Amos that the cottage was his for the taking, and Patience began to wrap her treasures in her sheets and bodices. And Peabody and I looked at each other.

"So, what do you intend, Master Doctor? Will you ride to Lichfield tomorrow? Might you go first to Henley?"

"Ah, Mistress Cecily's charms have entrapped you, have they, Peabody? Would you wish to accompany me or do you feel responsibility for these delicate innocents, whom Rupert clearly felt needed to extend their experience? In other words he expelled them from Oxford for a blessed few days, so the Oxford citizens could have a little peace."

"No-one has asked me to wet-nurse them. That was my task some months ago," said Peabody. "I think, Doctor Tom, I will ride with you to see the silver haired, golden voiced Swan of Henley. Yes, I will wait upon you for one more day, Doctor Tom."

I wrote Joan a fine letter something in the manner of a courtier to his queen. I began it, "To the white hands of my ever honoured Lady Bailey, at the Newport Street residence which she and her beloved consort are pleased to grace with their honoured and valued presence...."

"What a smooth tongued rogue, you are Tom! She loves queening it in the Newport house," said Roger. "God's blood! If I were a woman I would have a care to my virtue, if you were given your head as a wordsmith. You could charm the salmon from the Severn."

"No, let Peabody alone for that!" I told him "He is your ladies' man, Roger. And Peabody you shall come with me now, to Mistress Hall. To warn her gently of Rupert's approach and to bid her Farewell."

I wished to thank her again for her kind efforts regarding Elijah's ceremony. She admitted us but was somewhat overwhelmed by Peabody's bulk and warlike appearance. However he displayed his gentle gallant character and in a few moments we were quaffing wine again and tasting her little delicate cinnamon cakes.

"Madam, I pray you take care," I told her with a sideways glance at Peabody. "We have it on good authority that tomorrow there will be "alarums and excursions" here in Stratford. A noble personage rides through with his army. Or he may stay for a day or two. Pray do not venture out and lock all fast."

"What a good youth you are to be sure, Doctor Tom," she told me. "A good youth, is he not, Master Peabody?"

"I do not think he will ever make a soldier, madam," said Peabody "But as a doctor, certain sure, he shapes well. And at the defunct craft of quarter staffs, he has no equal."

"Ah, yes," said Mistress Hall. "That quaint old country pastime."

We thanked her, and took our leave. And next morning early we took our leave of Stratford. And not a minute too soon. As we trotted singly over the bridge we could hear the shouts of men and neighing of horses coming up from the south. We were over the narrow bridge in good time.... otherwise we would have had to wait while Rupert's force passed over. We hurried through the town and at the market place, Roger and his charges turned west and Peabody and I continued north, on the well worn path to Henley.

We were again welcomed like princes and Mistress Cecily at once began to make a quaking pudding. "Ah, madam!" cried Peabody. "What sad havoc you make of my quaking heart! I have thought of nothing since we were here, but of your puddings and your beauty. Doctor Tom had thought to find me a potion to rid me of the delectable memories of these seductions!"

She screeched with laughter, dumped young Tom unceremoniously onto my lap and ran into the kitchen. Marion brought us Canaries and we took our ease by the fire, chatting with Walter and admiring his first born. But Nat brought us heavier news. We had left Lichfield in happy time on Tuesday 21st of March, a scant eight days ago. As we gained Coleshill, Hastings had been leading three companies of dragoons against the Close from the north. But Colonel Russell would have none of it. His cannons aimed at them over the lanes to the north were so well placed that even mad Harry conceded defeat and skulked back to Stafford.

But Nat had "news" that confounded and appalled me. Such skills of reading and writing which were deemed necessary for the good management of the Swan at Henley lay with the ladies of the establishment. Walter could read but had no interest in ever doing so, and Nat could not read at all, but always brought news-sheets for Marion to read at night to the good company. Now he pulled out a news-Sirsheet from his pocket and asked me if I would read him the contents. I willingly assented and began but ceased immediately. To my horror I was reading my own name.

"Recent news from Lichfield, being the actual copy of a letter from Doctor Thomas Fletcher to his household in Worcester." I paused and looked round in amazement. Then continued, "Dated March 23rd, containing a true account of the manner of the skirmish at Hopton Heath, and how blind Harry Hastings and his minions were given a bloody nose but two days later at Lichfield Close.

Dear Friends, I am well, God be thanked, but others are not, alas. The Earl of Northampton was lately unhorsed and slain by Sir John Gell's pikemen at the Battle of Hopton...."

I threw it down. That audacious insolent mountebank! "This is Ralph's doing!" I told Peabody who picked it up. "He has used my name, the arrogant varlet. Eleanour has told him we were at Hopton Heath. Sir John will have sent messengers to the Close after the battle. Nat," I asked him "Where did your friend buy this?"

"All I know is he came through Lichfield and paid his penny for it there. That is your name? Wondrous strange!"

"Strange indeed to Tom." Marion put in. "Someone has made free with his name and calling."

"This is the cozener who has married the daughter of old friends of my parents. You remember when I came with Elijah and Phoebe in February. I found her married indeed to Ralph Truscott, who seeks out, writes, prints and sells news to any who will buy. Sometimes it is truth and sometimes it is not."

"And is this truth?" Walter asked.

I read it through. "Aye, as far as I know.It is a true account of the battle. But my name has been falsely used."

"But consider, Tom," said Peabody "This shows in what regard you are held in Lichfield. If your name graces a news-sheet, it will sell for sure. You are a man to be trusted, to be reckoned with. You have credence, you could get credit even with that frog-faced vintner...."

He gazed at me, eyes wide and brows raised in mock respect.

"Peabody!" I told him. "You are almost as much a deceitful lapwing as the knave who wrote this. Tell us now, amongst friends as you are. Have you always been a soldier?"

"Curses, Tom, you have found me out. I was once a poor scholar at Oxford. That was when I was young, madam," he told Cecily.

"Ah, Master Peabody, then you are speaking of but one year ago!" she said with a burst of wit. And so they brought me with mirth and laughter from my angry humour at finding my name so misused. But I vowed to myself that Ralph would explain himself.... in all probability with my thumbs pressing lovingly on his windpipe.

As always we had a merry evening, although Marion told me that she had wondered much how Mistress Bridges had fared. I told her of the funeral which had been clearly conducted in the old way and of the skin and bone priest, there one minute, gone the next.

"There are such sad fellows, scratch a living in these parts," she told me, "like unto the fairies or the little people, living on leftovers and scraps put out for them. Sweet Jesu help them if the Parliament men win this conflict."

The Henley gaffers who had come in to sup their ale, kept demanding to know what were the jests that set our table aroar so often. I only half heard the wit and raillery. My mind was occupied with concerns for my friends in Henley and for my vulnerable brown friend, in Birmingham. There could be divided loyalties between Peabody and myself. In the morning I stood outside in the cold Spring air, as he saddled up faithful patient Warrior.

"Do you have a home, Peabody?" a question I had long wished to put to him.

"Not now, Doctor Tom. I follow the King's drum. I have had royal favours and wages aplenty. To do otherwise than fight for the King would be the action of an ingrate. Even so," he straightened himself from adjusting the girths and looked me in the eye. "Even so, Doctor Tom, I will be frank with you. I do not like all that takes place in the name of the King. I do not like this harum-scarum scheme of Rupert's to slight the town of Birmingham. No doubt you will do what you have to do about that, I know you have friends thereabouts and neither of us will say a word of reproach to the other. Is it agreed?"

"It is agreed but would you not wish to warn this good family who have given us such excellent cheer that Rupert's rogues will be a-roystering past this way?"

"We should make our Farewells now. I know one way to ensure their safety. To bespeak good beds for Rupert and his close comrades in arms at no other place than here! His Highness will not soil his own nest and when I tell him that my heart is here, he will show all respect to the house."

"You had best see what Walter thinks of that!" I told him.

Marion and her mother looked somewhat alarmed when Peabody told them of the proposed honour.

"No, I thank you, but to favour one faction or another is to lose half my custom," said Walter. "I can take down the sign of the Swan, shutters up, and no lights showing. That way we should not attract notice to ourselves. I am sorry, Master Peabody that I cannot offer you good cheer when you return with the Prince. It is Good Friday tomorrow, and for reasons of piety and respectful reverence, I will remain closed until he has gone. 'Til Corpus Christi if need be."

"Well, well! With such precious jewels of womankind to cherish and preserve, I concur wholeheartedly with your decision. And if I may, I will return alone, after these matters are concluded. Dear madam, your servant!" and taking Mistress Cecily's little workworn hand in both of his great paws, he kissed it with a lascivious air. She squeaked and giggled and ran off to the kitchen, whence she brought us two parcels of food.

We all went out to wave Farewell to Peabody. It seemed to me that his flirtation with Mistress Cecily was all talk and trifling. She seemed unmoved by his going, and said merely that he was a heart breaker who probably did not change. I warned Walter that Rupert had a grudge against Birmingham and I was afraid lest he should begin his revenge as soon as he reached Henley, a scant ten miles from his goal. But Walter was more concerned for Birmingham.

"The mischief is that there is no one, no great landowner with the men or means, to protect that town. They have answered to no feudal lord for many years. They have a way of trading that takes no account of Princes. The Yeomen of the Holy Cross have the ruling of affairs which they do well, excellent well, but they are yeomen, not gentry, and I would think whilst their word is law for Birmingham, the notions that they hold would be seen as damnable in royal eyes. And also the sword makers, and here's the rub, Tom, men like Robert Porter will not sell their blades to any but the men of Parliament."

"What of Sir John Holte?" I asked innocently. "His great house is scarcely two miles from Birmingham."

Walter spat violently into the fire, something I had never seen him do before.

"That thieving murdering bastard! Do you know it's said he killed his cook? He is the bane of these parts. His son has disowned him for his crimes!"

I knew that to be true but did not enlarge on my acquaintance with Edward Holte. Time was pressing.

Marion spoke, "Tom, if you have friends in Birmingham, best warn them as you have warned us. My mother has a cousin there, a lorrimer. Perhaps you would bear a letter to him and his wife, telling them your fears. How long have we to prepare?"

I said I doubted that Rupert would attack at Easter. "Surely he would not do violent mischief on Good Friday, or Easter Sunday. I think he will mill about here for two days and ride there on Monday." But of course I could not be sure.

Marion set about writing to her uncle. Walter came down to the stable with me and complimented me on Jupiter.

"Well, Tom, we have seen changes in the short time we have known each other. It is a rare man who can claim that another man made him a father!"

"Rare indeed" I replied "and your wife had some small part in it, or had you not noticed! But changes indeed! I will ever hold myself guilty for Elijah's death."

221

He shook his head. "Accidents happen every day! His horse might have stumbled next day and broken his neck! Where will you go after Birmingham?"

"Lichfield.... again! I have two horses there and that wretched Eleanour told me she wished to return to Ledbury to her doting parents. She has more hair than wit, and wantons with the kind feelings of others. She uses her fellow humans. I have come to dislike her much, and yet I feel bound to return her to her home if she still wishes to go."

Walter said nothing for a moment or two. Then he said, "Certainly you need to fetch your horses.... as for the wayward harlot, I hope she is not having a May-game with you, Tom."

Marion brought out her letter to me, which I put carefully in my saddle bag. Then I put my pack of food, at the top of Jupiter's oats and saddled up. All were outside to see me ride. I hoped they would be safe over the Easter Festival. I could hope for their safety but I knew that the next few days would not be the peaceful religious feast time of last year.

I kissed the ladies, "Mistress Cecily," I told her, " have a care for young Rupert. He has an even sweeter tongue than Peabody, and is a great charmer of the fair sex."

"Fear not, Tom," said Marion, "I shall protect my mother. Do you protect yourself. We will look to hear from you."

I turned to the north through the village and waved Farewell for as long as I could see them. At last they had dwindled to little waving manikins, visible only when I screwed up my eyes across the sunny distance.

I had the sun on my right as we passed swiftly northwards with celandines, glowing each side of the track. Sometimes there were sheets of harebells or bluebells stretching away under the elms. I gave Jupiter his head on straight stretches of the road and at length we came to a village from which one could hear the sounds of a thousand clanging hammers echoing up towards us, from the town of Birmingham, which lay before me. I had forgotten how busy and diligent the people of these parts were. We paused to refresh ourselves, Jupiter with oats and water, myself with a matchet roll and cheese, and then I mounted again and we rode down the hill through the fields over a sparkling brook, and along a straight road with ahead of us a spire like a heavenly finger-post. We trotted into the main street, which was like a long market of smiths' shops. I stopped at an inn on my right with a crown painted on its sign. A young ostler was immediately ready to tether Jupiter.

"I am Thomas the Ostler, Master, if you want your horse stabled."

"And I am Thomas the Doctor, Thomas, if you want physic for your pains. May he remain here for some moments?" He nodded his assent and promised to guard him.

I went into the inn, bought a stoup of wine and asked for directions.

"Is this the street known as Deritend, Master? " I asked the landlord.

"Aye, son, this is Dirtyend, right enough," he told me pleasantly with a wink.

"Forgive me. Is there a Master Martin Smith, a lorrimer near here?"

"Who wants him?" said a voice behind me. A tall grizzled workman left the group of drinkers, sitting near the window.

"Is that your horse?" he asked, crooking his head to Jupiter tethered to the bar outside the inn. "Have a care to his throatlash. It chafes him something."

His friends roared with laughter. "Nay, you have a care, young Master, or he'll have all your blessed harness off the nag and his own in place and your money in his pocket."

"Thank you, Sir, for your good and timely advice. It is well taken but are you in fact Martin Smith? I have a letter for you from your niece Marion at the Swan in Henley."

"Oh Jesu, not a letter! Here, read it, pray, Frankie" and he thrust it at the Landlord.

Frank scratched his head, took the parchment in his hands and began to read...." hopes you and all the good family are in health.... they are well in Henley.... blessings on you at the Easter feast.... your loving niece."

I looked over his shoulder. This was a time for a gentle jest.

"Tell me, Master Francis," I said loudly "True it is that since this sad civil conflict began, the world is indeed turned upside down, but whence came the edict that we must read upside down also?"

There was a moment's silence. Then the men in the window roared with laughter, slapping their thighs and one came to the buttery bar to buy me a drink.

"That's told you, Frankie!" But Martin Smith was angry. "I've paid my shot here for years. How do I know you haven't cozened me time and again, Francis Cooper? Here, son!" he thrust the letter at me, "Do you read it."

I drew him outside and read aloud Marion's fears for him and his family

"'Tis said Prince Rupert has vowed vengeance on Birmingham. Dear Doctor Tom, the bearer, our good friend, thinks 'twill take place after the Easter feast. Uncle Martin, I, my mother, Cecily your cousin and my good husband Walter pray you and your family have a care to your futures."

"Oh, Jesu, 'tis cause the wenches took the bolts of stuff from the King's carriages, when they was at a stop here last backend. Here, bullies, here's bloody bad news."

They discussed the threat of Rupert for some little while. Some thought it would come to naught but all were of the view that the Yeomen of the Holy Cross should see the letter.

"What think you, Master Short-Arse?" one of them asked me, "Do you say it's certain sure the bold cur will ride through with his mad cavaliers?"

"I hope not, but I fear he well might. The youth who heard him make the vow is a sober-sides who can be trusted."

"And can you?" persisted the questioner. "Doctor, are you? Are you to be trusted? Is it right down gospel true and no gainsaying?"

"All I can say is how willI profit by lying to you? If he does not come, no harm done. If he does come you are forewarned. My masters, can you tell me where a brown pedlar lives? I think it be near the Horsefair."

"Aye, ka me, ka thee. I owe you a courtesy, Doctor. I'll bring you to Joseph's house, and then take this to the Guildhall. Those varlets from Coventry went back there but a week ago, else they was handy with their muskets. Frankie, run and tell the wench whither I'm bound. She's not to go a-gossiping from home, mind."

We walked towards the spire of St. Martin's church. "Were you named for the saint?" I asked him. "He is one of my favourites. I like the notion of him giving his cloak to a beggar."

"Martin Smith. That's me. You cannot get a better Birmingham name, I think."

"No, indeed," I agreed. "You represent both church and work."

He chuckled, "Ah, that's right. Church and work. What more is there in a man's life?

Marion and Walter have a littl'un now, have they not? Does he prosper?"

So I was able to tell him of how little Tom bid fair to be a poison pated rogue much like his father. "He grows apace", I told Martin Smith, though what relation his grandmother's cousin was to little Tom, I did not know.

"Perhaps you are his great-uncle," I suggested.

"Aye, maybe," he agreed.

We turned westward under the walls of the church and walked towards the Horsefair. Strange emotions and memories were battling in my brain. I had had a joyous restful day with Harry and Joseph here before Edgehill, but it was in the Horsefair that I had seen Brigstock. He must have followed me from there, up to the lonely Rollright stones. I shuddered. Martin stopped and pointed to a cottage, standing a little way up the hill to the west of the Horse Fair.

"Now I think of it, I haven't seen him for a week or two. My lad knows his boy though. He sells him my spurs to sell on their pedlar's cart. He's a good boy and Joseph's a good fellow."

"I'm seeking him to tell him what I've told you. 'Tis all, and then I must strike north east again to seek another friend and thence to Lichfield."

"God give you easy roads, son. Remember what I told you about the throatlash."

He walked away and I led Jupiter up to the little house, which stood alone with a piece of land behind it and a stable to one side. I knocked on the door. No-one answered but I could hear movements inside. Might Joseph and his son think it was some enemy trying to gain arrogant admittance? In these testing times as well to announce oneself.

"Joseph, it's your friend. It's Doctor Tom. I must warn you of a danger that approaches."

The door suddenly opened and a youth pulled me inside, and locked the door behind me. It was Joseph's son who had kept the stall while we had drunk and talked in the tavern, last October.

"You are a doctor. Thank God. Look here."

Joseph lay on a rough bed covered with a caddis. I could see at a glance that he was gravely ill. There were dark shadows, darker than his brown skin on his face, which was emaciated like unto a skull. A white handkerchief, stained with blood lay on the coverlet by his hand. He knew me but was too weak to speak.

"Is it the plague? Oh God I am so afeared, Master Doctor. Will I catch it? Is it the plague? What will they do to us? Can you help him?"

14

His words alarmed me greatly. If there were plague, here and now in Birmingham, what was my best plan? Rupert's men riding in and riding out again could spread the pestilence everywhere. I looked round the room. There was dust on the floor and on some shelves where the pedlar's goods for sale were ranged. There was also the smell of damp, which I was now coming to associate with the homes of the poor. No wonder men who worked for a pittance often chose to sit over their pot of ale in an inn, where great fires roared up chimneys. What of their wives left to exist in cold damp hovels? A late realisation. Health and wealth are close allies.

Why did I stand thinking at such a time and gazing at my good friend? Alas, I could do nothing for him, except perhaps ease his pain a little. I knelt beside him and made myself think with as little emotion as possible. He could hardly breathe.... any breath other than a shallow gasp, clearly caused him acute spasmodic pain. As I drew back the coverlet and moved his nightshirt so that I could see his chest, I saw that there was a swelling near his neck and another under his arm. I began to fear that Joseph's son and myself were doomed. Swellings were symptoms of the plague. Ben had warned me of them. But these were not black and oozing pus, and there was no smell of putrefaction. They were simply swellings.

I remembered Ben telling me of another illness that he had seen where swellings occurred with fever. That was not plague although there had been cases where patients had been abandoned, because doctors were so fearful. But when another doctor had taken pity on them, if sufferers with this condition were kept warm and given cows' milk and cheese and the temperature of their body brought down by extract of willow, the swellings very slowly disappeared and they could recover. But the sounds from Joseph's chest, his terrible emaciation and the dark shadows under his eyes banished optimism. A trick of Ben's, that I often used, gave some indication of the state of the lungs. He taught me to tap the patient's chest and listen. A sense of hollowness, of echoing would indicate that air was coming and going. I put my ear to Joseph's pitifully thin body and listened. There seemed to be no movement at all. I caught his eye and he smiled and shook his head slightly. As I thought about his condition, I realised that his body was starved of air, and because he could not breathe, he could not eat or drink.

Then I remembered another illness that Ben had taught me about, that another doctor had told him of in Oxford. A poor family from the North of Scotland had come to Edinburgh to make more money for themselves, as they hoped. They had lodged in a very poor house. But they had all died within a few months. Now I remembered. They seemed to have caught some pestilence that did not affect their neighbours, which did not spread to others but which.... and I could hear Ben's voice explaining it.... "one by one, ate away their lungs." The whole family, one after the other, had caught this strange consuming illness, and had died with terrible chest pains. The doctor who tried to help them remained healthy, the neighbours living in like conditions were unaffected. A strange mystery.

But if this was the illness from which Joseph was suffering, what should I do to save his son? I should keep him away from his father, for if the pestilence were somehow in the cottage, perhaps it could be averted from the boy.

I turned to him. He was looking at me with such an expression of hope and expectation, that my heart misgave me. "What is your name?" I asked him.

"Ibrahim. You say Abraham, I think."

"Abraham, can we go out into the air?"

He led me into the field behind the house. I found a carrot, which I broke in two, and gave half to Jupiter and half to the Dales pony who ran up in friendly fashion. I assumed she pulled Joseph's pedlar's cart.

"How long has your father been like this?"

"The coughing and the blood began a little in January and has slowly got worse. We have been so frightened by the thought of the plague. We could be driven from the town."

"You could say that there is one blessing. I am as confident as can be that he does not have the plague."

The boy pressed my hand. "But Abraham, you can see that there is no hope for him. Something.... I don't know what.... perhaps a cancre.... eats his lungs away, so that he cannot breathe properly; indeed now he can hardly breathe at all. I don't know what it is and I cannot cure it. I am sure that no-one, no doctor in this land can help him now. But I will find another doctor and get his opinion. I will not let him try anything addle-pated, like bleeding him which would kill him straight away. I might be able to relieve the pain a little so that he can speak to you before he goes. For go he will, I think in twenty four hours, perhaps less. Or perhaps more. But it can be days only."

Abraham stood for some moments, then turned away from me. He went to the pony and buried his face in her mane, his shoulders shaking as he sobbed. I let him weep for a while, and got the pack of food from my saddle bag. I went back in to the cottage for a moment to see if Joseph needed us. He had fallen into a doze. I came back to Abraham and led him to an old bench at the back of the cottage. There was a slice of beefsteak pie, apples and little cakes flavoured with ginger. He needed little persuasion to eat and Cecily's food was as ever tasty and wholesome.

"What is the best thing you can do for your dear father now?" I asked him.

He shook his head. "There is nothing. Wait for him to be taken to heaven. He always followed our prophet's teaching."

"Well, good but there is more. Now you must live for him. I fear for you in that cottage. I do not think I will catch what is killing your father, but I fear that you might. I will do this, Abraham. Your father is a good friend of mine. I will stay with him until the end but it is better that you sleep elsewhere."

"No!" he shouted. "No! I cannot leave him!"

"I am not saying that you should not see him. I think it is dangerous for you to be near him for long nights and days," I sighed. If damage had been done to the boy's lungs, no doubt it would have happened ere this. "Perhaps you are right. He does not have long, and you have escaped thus far I think."

He was not sturdy or robust, but was a handsome youth, of slender build, tall and seemed well fed, with redness in his cheeks and a lightness in his hair that was unlike his father. He was fourteen, he told me.

"So do you feel ill in any way? May I see your chest? Have you any difficulty with your breath?"

He unbuttoned his shirt and stood before me, breathing heartily. There was no swelling, and clearly no obvious problem with his lungs. I asked him to breathe in, hold the breath for a slow count of five, and then breathe out. He could do this perfectly, without strain or stress. He looked back longingly at the food we had left on the bench. "Eat, please," I begged him. There seemed no problems with his appetite.

"I am convinced that there is no plague," I told him. "This disease is an independent malevolent condition of your father's. It may or may not affect you in the future if you stay here. May I ask you, is your mother living?"

He gazed at me silently and then nodded. "But we do not speak about her."

Perhaps she was a drab who had given birth and laid her babe like a foundling at my friend's door. I made up my mind. I would find another doctor and seek his opinion of Joseph. And also.... I must visit an apothecary for the poppy tincture that would help him to live his last hours without pain.

"Tell me," I said, "Is there another doctor in this town?" He nodded and told me. "I think his name is Master Tillam of More Street."

"Why then do I not now seek out Doctor Tillam to see your father, so that if aught else can be done, it will be done. There will be no blood letting, I promise you."

We went back in and Joseph opened his eyes. I took his thin wasted hand in mine.

"Joseph, I want to ask another doctor his opinion. My dear friend, I am sure you do not have the plague and there shall be no blood letting."

He smiled again and with great heart rending effort whispered, "Dear young Master, ever a good help in a dead lift."

Tears filled my eyes and I brushed his hand with my lips. I wanted him to know that he was not friendless and alone, dying so far from the warm sun of his native land. There was a sweet scent coming from him. I knew what it was. It came from his urine. This strange sweet smell is a sign that the patient has not long to live.

"Which way is More Street?" I asked Abraham. It was a little to the north and I left him with instructions to moisten Joseph's lips with water, if he asked for a drink.

I found More Street with ease, and a friendly little girl told me which was Doctor Tillam's house. I gave her a penny for her pains and she ran off with her brother to buy tarts.

I knocked and was immediately admitted. I was asked to sit and told by the manservant the Doctor would be with me forthwith. He came into his entrance hall ushering out a poor old woman, who clutched some simples, clearly of his manufacture. They were in good accord for as she passed me she said to me, "He's a rare good, doctor, son. Do as he bids you."

"I will, mistress," I told her.

He came to me, eyebrows raised questioningly.

"I have no ailments, sir," I told him, "I seek your help. A good friend of mine has a wasting disease and I think, as I am a doctor myself, there is nothing to be done. I found him today. He and his son were afraid that he had the plague, but I am convinced that he has not. His son is healthy and the father has been sick since January." I took out my purse. "I need you to tell me if my opinion is good, Master Doctor. And we need laudanum. Any exertion pains him sorely."

He nodded. "I'll get some doses. Who is it of whom you speak? A Birmingham man?"

I told him and he said thoughtfully, "Put your purse away. It is not needed. I wondered why I have not seen Joseph for some weeks. Will you wait here, son." He returned in a short while and we set off.

As we approached the cottage, he produced two linen masks for us to wear. I held mine before my face, but had little faith in such a measure. But he drew in his breath at the sight of Joseph and said, abandoning his mask immediately, "Not the plague, son."

After his examination, he turned to me in the lane outside and said exactly what I feared, "He has days only. Here is your opium. Use it to douse the fire of his pain, not to kill him. Where is the boy?"

Abraham had his arm on the neck of the Dales pony. Jupiter was beside them. The three stood together in silence. When he saw Doctor Tillam, he came to greet him.

"You should have fetched me before this, son. But I doubt I could have done aught. It's not the plague, but a condition peculiar to himself. He has days only."

So that Easter instead of the contemplation of the Stations of the Cross, I helped Abraham keep vigil beside the bedside of a Musselman.

I encouraged Abraham to stay outside as much as possible. The early April days were mild and I sent him on errands to buy us food. I found a bed down at the same inn in the Horsefair where I had sat with his father last October. I slept there for the next three nights. I saddled up Jupiter so that Abraham could ride him round their field, the little Daleswoman trotting like a pageboy behind. Her name was Shireen, which Abraham told me meant "pretty" or "beautiful". Her disposition suited her name.

Riding my horse gave the boy healthy activity. I told him it was to give Jupiter exercise, but in fact it was to encourage him to expend energy outside that dusty cottage and away from his father's deathbed.

On Easter Sunday morning the innkeeper told me that the Yeomen had sent for a detachment of musketeers from Lichfield. They were likely to arrive later that day. He knew me as the man who had brought word of Rupert's coming and seemed not to know whether I spoke truth or not. "In truth, Master Bryce, I wish I was a liar, with all my heart. I think no man ever wished his words to be as untrue." I paid my shot day by day and on Saturday night stood the good company of smiths that gathered there some tankards of strong ale. So although I was the bearer of evil tidings, there was some compensation to be gained from my fellowship.

Joseph died early on Easter Monday morning. I had left Abraham with him, and had slept at the inn in the Horsefair. I was awake in the dawn listening to the thrushes in the hedges at the back of the inn, when the knock came on my door. It was Mistress Bryce, in her night clothes who told me that Abraham had asked them to wake me. I dressed swiftly and ran up the hill to the cottage. There was nothing to be done. Joseph could not even open his eyes but I think he knew both his son and myself were there.

We sat either side his bed, holding his thin brown hands. To be honest, I did not know when the end came, but the frail fingers curled about mine held for a while a vestige of warmth but then gradually were stiff and cold.

Abraham held him for a while, and then looked at me, stricken and afraid. "I don't know what to do. What must we do now?"

I had promised Doctor Tillam that I would fetch him at once when the end came, so I left Abraham with his father and hastened to the Doctor's house. His manservant told me he would be with us within the hour. He came with a paper, which he signed after he had examined the corpse and received back into his possession the remaining doses of opium. I had used only two. I was to take the paper to the minister.

"Remember, I beg you," he told me, "be certain you go to Master Roberts who is the Minister for Birmingham. Do not let any jester send you to Master Whitehall, who used to be our minister but who, alas, is fallen into a pronounced lunacy. He is mad as a blind bear in the ring. When Master Roberts has signed this paper, then you may take it to the sexton, William Billingsley, who lives near the Crown Inn in Deritend, who must.... take no denial, son.... who must dig you a grave at St. Martins. This is Joseph's parish. He paid his dues or I would know, being one of the Councillors. He is entitled to lie here in our church of St. Martin, heathen or Jew, under Birmingham law. If any man argue or gainsay this, come you back to me and I will teach him our methods."

"This is marvellous liberal and equalizing, Doctor Tillam, to let those who are not Christian lie in a Christian graveyard."

"Not so, son. We judge the health of the living to be more important than the beliefs of the dead. The unburied can cause a pestilential atmosphere, and be a threat of disease to the living. To be brief. Bury poor Joseph. Mourn him but bury him. Today."

Abraham seemed to be content to be left in the cottage. He would sit beside his father for some while and then leap up and rush out to the field, where he would run round with the two horses. I saddled up Jupiter for him again so that he could ride him if he wished, but felt that he should stay in the field. I meanwhile went out to find the minister.

He was from home but expected back an hour or so after noon. The maidservant told me I could wait.... in fact I had the impression she would have wished me to wait.... but I felt I had better return to Abraham. I bought us two pies from a stall in the Horsefair. He ate his in three minutes, and looked so longingly at mine that I felt bound to donate it.

We sat again by Joseph and I asked Abraham about his mother. He said at last, "She had better be told. She is his wife."

"Does she live near here?" I asked him gently.

He nodded and I thought I would cross this bridge when I had seen the sexton and arranged for burial. At about two I went again to the Minister's house. He had just retuned from an Easter visit to his sister in Walsall, but was sorely grieved to hear of Joseph's death. "How is the boy?" he asked.

"Do you know of his mother?" I asked.

"Aye, that I do," he told me "But more pressing matters now, my son. There are musketeers from Lichfield, all round the church. They say they are waiting for Prince Rupert. What troubled times we live in to be sure when they must needs form up in the church-yard. "

So I took my leave and, clutching my precious signed paper, walked around the wall of the Church down to the road they called Digbeth, which led into Deritend. It should not be difficult to find the Crown again. Looking back I could see that there was a company of musketeers gathered in the churchyard, taking their ease.

I strode on southwards, seeking the Crown on my left. It was a fine Easter Monday. There was a holiday air about the stalls which lined the road, housewives bustled about, buying freshly killed lamb, cheaper now than it had been on Easter Saturday I was told, children played Catch as Catch Can, darting into the road and screaming with enjoyable fear, and old gaffers sat outside in the Spring sunshine. Tom, the ostler, called a greeting to me, and I waved in friendly fashion to him.

As I turned into the Crown I paused for a moment. I thought I had heard a shot, coming from the South. I was stooping.... to have stood up suddenly would have meant cracking my head on the lintel.... and I listened again. Nothing. Only the sounds of the Birmingham people enjoying the holiday sunshine.

I went into the tap room to be greeted by a howl of derision. "Here he is! Here's the mooncalf who thinks Rupert's behind every tree!" cried out Francis and Martin Smith rose to greet me, laughing at my discomforture.

"Well son, they fetched the musketeers from Lichfield but Devil a sign of Rupert, or his dog!"

I tapped a table for silence. "If I stand a pot of ale for all, will you forgive me?" I was going on to ask if they would tell me where the sexton dwelt, but my second question was drowned in the chorus of approval which greeted my first. I laid my coins before Francis who busied himself in drawing the ale.

But there was no more convivial drinking that day. There were several cracks outside in the street. Musket shots. And then the low bowed window was suddenly shattered and red wine was spattered all over the drinkers. But it was not red wine. It was blood.

I seized hold of Martin and dragged him down under a table. We could not see what was happening, but there were more shots and a fearful groaning came from the window. I shouted, "Get down! Don't let them see you!" There was the galloping of many horses passing outside, and more discharging of pistols and muskets. I pushed a stool to one side so I could look along the floor. Now I could see the white terrified faces of the drinkers, at my level. The sound of the horses crashing past, reminded me of the cavalry charges at Edgehill, when Lord Basil Fielding rode right over our surgeon's station, pursued by an even more terrifying charge of King's Men. But there my calling had protected me somewhat, and I had had assistance from powerful men of Parliament.

There was a shouting from outside, and two horses were reined in. Their riders clearly intended mischief. They ran into the taproom where we lay and shot once or twice at the walls. Fortunately they must have assumed that the visible man who sat dying in the window was the only occupant of the room. One of them shot him again for good measure and then laughing heartily, they ran back to their horses.

There was the rumbling of ordnance passing now. The thunder of hoof beats had faded. I stole a swift glance and could see the gunners, pushing and shoving and whipping their great cart horses onward. They passed us, and but for the odd straggler, one or two whose horses were lame and must be led, the road was empty. A pause, a hiatus in the noise and then up the road, there was a uniform crack of muskets. The men from Lichfield had been ready for them. There was another volley and I heard voices, the Captains of Rupert's horse, calling on his riders to fall back.

"Can you get out of the back of this inn and get to your house?"

Martin nodded, his face white and strained, streaked with blood from a shattered pot. "I should go there and lock all fast. I am going to cross the fields and try to get back to Joseph's. He is dead but his young son is alone and unprotected."

I suddenly had an idea. "Listen, Masters. If you can get to your houses, put the sign of the plague on your doors. That should turn them away."

He grasped my arm. "What is the sign?"

"A cross, as large as you can. Tell your neighbours."

Outside the ostler, Tom, lay with his neck broken. He had perhaps heard the sound of horses' hooves and thought he could gain custom. Poor fellow. I could only spare him a passing pity, as I sped over the road, deserted for a short space, behind the houses opposite and into open fields. I struck out north-west, having the spire of St Martin's on my right. I made good speed and could see, about three quarter of a mile before me, what I took to be the backs of the houses that lined the Horsefair. Other citizens had also thought to escape in this manner. A man and his wife with a small child were making for higher ground towards the west. As I reached them he called out to me, "What grievous error is this! I have always spoken up for the King. Why does Rupert punish loyal subjects?"

I knew the answer. "I fear it is the blade mill, which makes swords for Parliament." I could not stop to indulge in discussion and now my luck seemed in jeopardy. A detachment of troopers came hallooing across the fields. I could not escape. They discharged their muskets in my direction. I flung up my arms and dropped to the ground, hoping they would not check my condition. One or two more shots came but then their Captain ordered them not to waste their fire. I lay still until all was silent once more and then raising my head realised that there was a river before me. I had been told its name. The Ray as I recall. I looked round for the musketeers. They had travelled far to the south and from the noise of shots and hoof beats, the whole of Rupert's force was returning south along the road.

I turned my attention to the River Ray. It was somewhat sluggish and I wondered if it was perhaps the town drain. The nearer to the town, the closer its banks leaned in together. I did not relish the prospect of wading through it, and thought that perhaps I could jump across it, if I took a good run at it. But then near the town I glimpsed something that cheered me. Some enterprising person had laid a broad plank across it. I made for this makeshift bridge at a run.

Sadly I had not made sure that the plank at the far side was securely set in the mud on the opposite bank. In the instant of being toppled into the stream, another musket ball whistled past my head. I had the wit to stay crouched down and waded in an ape-like posture upstream, and took a furtive glance back across the fields. This troop like the previous one had thought to avoid the road, and were galloping south to whatever prearranged rendezvous, Rupert had instructed. But one or two, more curious than their fellows, rode in the direction of the stream to see if I were dead indeed. They were riding to the position of the plank. Still crouched like a dwarf, I contrived to gain the refuge of some blessed weeping willows that grew thickly over the brook about fifty yards upstream from the plank. I confess in that moment I longed like a helpless infant for Peabody's paternal protection. I had had my fill of the River Ray, and of this wretched town.

I peered through the flickering leaves. As there was no sign of me near the upturned plank, and as their captain was calling them back to their fellows, the whoreson knaves discharged a musket ball into the stream, which achieved nothing other than drenching themselves in noisome water. I knew it was filthy in the extreme. I was standing in it. Magnanimously I did not grudge them a drop.

I reasoned with myself. If I had tried to return by the road I would have been dead by this. I was far from dead. I merely smelt as if I was. I forced myself to wait in my hiding place for another half hour. Two more troops chose the fields rather than the roads, but I could hear the noise of the main body of the army slowly receding along Deritend, southwards. I hoped they were not returning to Henley.

Finally when all seemed quiet, I decided that I would run the remaining distance to what was clearly the back of the inn in the Horsefair. The fields here were carefully tended, small hedges separating the strips. Alas, someone's young beans did not profit from my feet. In fact I seemed to have exchanged my boots of leather for those of mud, which were twice the size.

I came to the back door and had the wit to announce myself before knocking. But it was opened instantly with cries of relief. My progress had been viewed hand to mouth by mine hosts, but they had thought I had died under the willows. Now without ceremony they pushed me into the kitchen in an instant and locked the door behind me. Some of the marauders had found their way to the Horsefair, but most of the citizens in this part had had a degree of warning and had locked themselves in.

I seemed to be emanating some sort of unusual atmosphere. At length Mistress Bryce took pity on me, and as there was no sign of any of Rupert's scoundrels at the back of the inn, I was allowed to remove my filthy hose in the courtyard and wash my boots in a pail of water drawn from the communal well close to the Horsefair. I abandoned my hose.... no woman no matter how thrifty a housewife would have wished to have laundered them. As for my boots.... needs must.

Carrying my boots and something more wholesome in my person, I left barefoot by the front door, crossed the Horsefair, and went up the lane opposite to find Abraham. I was at a complete loss as to what to do. He welcomed me with great relief. He had heard the noise of the battle and had decided I was dead like his father.

"So what did you do?" I asked him.

"Rode your horse," he told me, and then to soften the blow he added, "From time to time." I did not question his method of paying tribute to the departed. He still wept at the sight of his father. We sat either side of Joseph. I hoped his spirit did not blame me for his lack of burial. But plainly something would have to be done.

"Here is what I think we must do," I told him, "I think we should go down to Mistress Bryce and see if she can find us some food." There was no mistaking a gleam in his eye at the prospect of sustenance. "And as the world is upside down and at sixes and sevens, I think if there are no more visits from Rupert this even we should bury your father in his field. I think they will help us at the inn. What say you?"

"I say that I had best follow your counsel.... for want of anything better," he said with truth, if not diplomacy.

I found another pair of hose and brushed my poor feet. To be a barefoot beggar was painful. Abraham assured me that I did not smell, so I put my boots on, and together we went down to ask for the essentials. Some of the smiths whom I had treated to ale had crept out to the alehouse. They all greeted Abraham, clasped his hands and told him of their sorrow, and all agreed to help us bury his father in the corner of his own field.

"Joseph was a rare good neighbour," said one gaffer. "If I needed help, he was there. Better to have aided him living than into his grave, but these are bad times!"

"If his head can go towards the East, then that would be what he would want," Abraham said suddenly. Master Bryce had the wood for a rough coffin and promised to nail it together for the even. They agreed to come up before it was full dark, with spades.

There was a knock on the front door and Master Tillam entered. "Good day neighbours," he greeted us, "though I fear it is far from good. I have come to tell you what the Council fear. Rupert has withdrawn some little way down the road to Stratford with his evil followers. But they have made camp, about a furlong from town. We think they will return tomorrow, as we hear they are bound for Walsall. Captain Graves will hold them with earthworks at the Crown, and his Lichfield men will come here to dig a ditch across the Horsefair."

"Best dig it south end, not t'other, sir," said Master Bryce. "We've Joseph to bury in his field, else we could give the Lichfield lads some help."

"I couldn't find the sexton Master Doctor," I told him. "Rupert struck just as I was about to ask for him."

"You can ask for him till Doomsday," said Doctor Tillam. "He waits for others to perform his office for him now. Aye, well, bury poor Joseph in the corner of his own field. Needs must when the devil Rupert drives." And he was gone. He was a good man in the prime of life well able to advise others.

"May I speak to you with a notion of mine, good neighbours all?" I asked. There was a chorus of assent so I outlined my plan for painting the plague cross on the doors of houses. They agreed that it was worth a try, and one man brought a pail of whitelime from one of the stables, and another found a faggot of brushwood. They set to work.

Mistress Bryce found food for Abraham. I see him now in my mind's eye, seated at the trestle in a carved chair, tears streaming down his face, as he ate apple pie. The wonder was he did not choke.

"Come then," I suggested. "Shall we go and feed Shireen and

Jupiter?"

He nodded and we went back to the cottage. He seemed to get comfort from the horses. The neighbour with the whitelime was diligently painting a cross on the door.

Sitting on the bench and surveying the horses, I asked him, "So what about your mother? Can you live with her?"

He shook his head. "They were married. She, and my father. I am not a bastard, not a by-blow. But they made her go back."

"Go back where?"

"To her father's house. When I was born, they gave me to my father. And I am right glad they did."

"So your mother lives with her parents?"

"Not now," he told me, "They are dead. Her brother keeps her close, mewed up at the back of his house. The Yeomen have told him he breaks the law, but he claims he can imprison her."

"So," I summarised matters, "Your mother was your father's legal wife. She was made to return to her parents' home, where she has been kept confined by her brother, your uncle."

"Yes." he said simply.

"Well, perhaps tomorrow, we shall see what can be done."

About half an hour before sunset the men came from the inn to dig Joseph's grave. I had no cheer for them but told them if Rupert did not return I would see them well served that night in the Horsefair inn.

Master Bryce brought in a rough coffin and together we placed Joseph within its narrow compass. Abraham wept uncontrollably now. I knew why. We had come to the absolute end. Placing a loved parent in the cold dark earth is a dreadful reality to contemplate.

We had crossed his poor wasted arms over his chest when there was a noise of hooves, of musket shots and lewd shouts. A detachment of one of Rupert's cavalry regiments was back. Six of them were racing round the Horsefair like mounted demons. They must have found a tavern on Deritend with unlimited supplies of ale for they were drunk as brewers' dogs. They were in fact so drunk as to be only dangerous to themselves, except for the stray musket shots they were discharging.

Three of them detached themselves and raced up the hill. They reined in near the well and one of them pointed to the crosses on the doors.

"What's that for?" he asked his fellows, giggling like a green girl.

"Dolt! Numbskull!" cried another, "Don't you know its Easter? They are very regi... geril.... devout in these parts."

"They are damned traitors!" said the first, "Come on!" And he spurred his horse up to a door across the lane and hit it a blistering blow with his sword.

I remembered Adam's advice. "Words first, fists later." I walked out and said pleasantly, "Good even, young masters. Were you bringing us alms? We are all isolated here. These are lazar houses. The plague is here."

"What?" screamed the first vandal. "You're a damned liar!"

"Alas, would that I were!" I said sweetly. "The great cross on the door denotes the sickness within. We are about to bury my brother. Bring him out and show the good young masters." I called to Master Bryce. He and Abraham carried out the makeshift coffin. "Here, masters. My poor brother! Draw near if you please! Will you keep vigil with us at the graveside?"

"I'll see you damned first," cried the spokesman, and he and the pious saint who knew 'twas Easter galloped down to the Horsefair like the wind, roaring out "Plague! Plague! Back! Back!"

The third barbarian slid from his horse in a drunken stupor near the well. I left him there as now we had our sad task to perform. As we lowered the coffin down Abraham said holy words from Joseph's creed, in his language, and I managed, "I am the Resurrection and the Life, saith the Lord. He that believeth in me shall not perish."

At least he had been buried with his friends and neighbours and his son around him. Shireen and Jupiter looked on, puzzled by the proceedings. I told those present, I would put up a memorial stone in more peaceful times. The smiths piled up a few rocks to mark the place.

Master Bryce shook his head. "Desperate times call for desperate measures."

When we rounded the wall of the cottage, our third reveller had lowered his breeches. For a moment we could not comprehend his intentions and then I realised he was about to urinate in the well, into the precious clean water of the little community. With a great shout of "No!" I launched myself upon him and knocked him down. But he had already begun to relieve himself and although I saved the well, my hose were ruined for the second time that day.

He lay there murmuring softly to himself and I sat with my back to the well, asking myself what more could happen. I cursed the wretched Eleanour up hill and down dale. Why had I found myself in this unfortunate pass? I held my head in my hands and groaned aloud.

Master Bryce misread my grief. "Come on, son, you did your best for Joseph. And don't fret for this town. You did a great task, warning us, in spite of us making game of you. Without you, they wouldn't have fetched lads from Lichfield."

Then he suggested that Abraham and I should go down with him now and taste some rabbit pie, Mistress Bryce had managed to make in spite of all the disruption to her day. Again, that faint gleam of sensuous anticipation from Abraham. That youth loved his food. I suggested that I paid for a bed for him tonight and we went down and listened to the recital of the good deeds that Joseph had done for his neighbours. I tethered the drunkard's horse to the field gate, and gave it oats and water. Not for King, not for King and Parliament, but for the horse which was both hungry and thirsty.... and exhausted. I gave him enough rope so he could lie down if he wished. Later as we sat in the inn and talked of Joseph, a wake they called it for we were awake for hours into the night talking of him, we could hear the invading army making merry all along the road called Deritend, revelling and roistering.

If we had thought that Easter Monday the 3rd of April was a bad day for Birmingham we had not anticipated Tuesday the 4th, which was like the inner regions of the Inferno. Good Mistress Bryce found gammon and eggs for us. I was learning to eat quickly for if I did not, Abraham's liquid brown eyes fixed themselves on the remnants on my plate with such longing that I had to pass it over to him. I was coming to understand that in the last weeks of his father's life, he had had almost no food. But as he wiped up my last egg yolk with a piece of bread, we heard again the resounding roar of Rupert's cavalry, thundering up Deritend. There was naught for it, but to stay close, to catch glimpses of what occurred through the windows. This time Rupert's Captains, anticipating the Lichfield musketeers in the churchyard, had had recourse to strategy. Before their cavalry came into musket range, they veered off right and left and came at the church from other angles, rather than straight forward. The Lichfield men put up a brave defence but could not hold them. They were far too few. Rather than have his men massacred, Captain Graves sensibly ordered a retreat.

But Rupert's followers were out for blood. They ranged through the town shooting at any thing that they could see. We sat silently in the inn kitchen with Master and Mistress Bryce, expecting at any moment that a musket ball would shatter the windows. We could hear the explosions and cracks, but then there was a smell, drifting through the inn. The shots were no longer those of muskets. It was the sound of fire.

Mistress Bryce ran to the taproom and peered through the window. "Oh, Jesu, they are coming this way," she cried in terror. Soldiers on foot were carrying lengths of match such as was used to fire cannons. Others behind them carried small barrels of gunpowder. I prayed that they would not climb the hill. From all around there was the crackle of fire and the terrified scream of horses trapped in their stables. At least our two mounts were free.

"Here you are, landlord! A barrel of sack!" cried one playful villain. He wedged the barrel under the lintel of the inn and thrust one end of the length of match into the barrel. He took the other end to where another whoreson rascal held a fiery torch. Smoke was already issuing from the house opposite. As we watched there was a sudden explosion and frenzied screams. A child was dropped from an upper window to lie lifeless on the cobbles. Other houses in the row opposite had been fired.

A group of riders trotted into the Horsefair, some smiling broadly at the carnage. One or two were even laughing. All were clearly rich men, fashionably clad, men who no doubt claimed to call themselves gentlemen.

There was a shot amongst them, which caused them no little consternation.

Our arsonist who was holding the end of the match for his companion to light looked towards the group. Then Rupert himself rode into the Horsefair shouting something at them. I seized my opportunity. I unlocked the front door, took hold of the match in the barrel and pulled. It came away easily and I threw it away from the inn, and leapt back inside.

Rupert seemed to be ordering the troopers to cease firing the houses and to follow and catch the marksman who had so grievously injured one of his party. Others had dismounted and were supporting the wounded man. He was older than most of the rude villains who were with the Prince.

A group of followers were beckoned forwards from the road which came from St.s Martin's. One with a drum was ordered to beat a cannonade and he and another fellow with a voice like a roaring bull were instructed to walk round the streets. As they passed we heard, "A Surgeon urgently required. Pray Master Surgeon your assistance please!" Abraham looked at me with raised eyebrows. I shook my head slightly. The drum and the crier passed round the Horsefair and turned right towards St. Martins.

Rupert passed now from my view and after an interval, it seemed the soldiers had disappeared. But the houses opposite still smouldered. Master Bryce now showed the resourcefulness for which his town was famed. "The cooper's!" he shouted "A chain of barrels from the Ray."

The unpleasant ditch into which I had fallen yesterday flowed very near the end of the Horsefair. With astonishing speed the smiths and cobblers, chandlers and lorrimers from this side of the town were manhandling barrels to the river. I ran ahead and was there ready to dip them into the stream. Abraham was soon there after me. A chain of men formed up to pass one barrel to the next and within minutes the flames of the first house began to subside. It was backbreaking work and I began to wonder if I would spend the rest of my life in the malodorous River Ray.

"Stop now then, son!" cried Master Bryce, "Good lad, Abram," and we clambered out the noisome ditch and walked back to the tavern. Our clothes were filthy, our limbs were aching and we stank like the town drain, but some families would not be completely homeless tonight, in spite of the worst efforts of Rupert's men.

But the town was a smoking ruin. The devastation of the smithies and work shops was complete. Smoke rose still from Mr Porter's blademill and I heard that the death toll numbered about fourteen or fifteen amongst the citizens. There were also dead troopers and Master Bryce could not comprehend why Rupert had fired some of the houses of the King's stalwart followers.

"Others might have wished to claim that loyalty today." I observed, though I really could not bring myself to care, I was so lamentable weary. "Has Rupert truly gone?"

"Aye son, off towards Walsall, it's said."

The horses were well and seemed to have been unaffected by the fires. They were some little way above the dreadful scenes. Before we fed them, Abram exercised both himself and them by running round the field with them, uttering strange hunting cries. He was a stout youth for action, no mistake. I felt that I could hardly put one foot before the other.

Mistress Bryce seeing the pitiful condition of my clothes and knowing that I had to ride out soon, suggested that we dried my new velvet doublet and breeches by the kitchen fire, and when the mud had dried, it would easily brush off. As for hose, a mercer nearby whose goods were undamaged, could supply them. Abraham or Abram as everyone called him was in like state to myself but had sensibly thought to remove hose and shoon before jumping in the stream. I, and my boots, spent some time yet again in the courtyard at the back of the inn with a pail of clean water.

Next morning, Wednesday 5th of April, I hoped beyond hope to escape from this unfortunate town. Its citizens called forth nothing but respect, but I had two horses and a wretched proud flirtatious hoyden to fetch from Lichfield. Then I could go home. Abram and I sat at breakfast, Mistress Bryce still contriving to feed us well in spite of the privations when there was a knock at the door. She went to open it and a moment later ushered in Doctor Tillam's manservant, Jake by name.

"Sir, you must come straight to the Doctor's. He is grievous wounded, like to die, I fear, and there are sick men and women all burnt clamouring for him in the street. He sent me for you. Please you, come back and help us."

I looked at the good honest man and groaned aloud. This brought Master and Mistress Bryce to my side, wondering what ailed me. I explained shamefaced that it was only my spirit that ailed and not my body. There was nothing for it. As they were both unharmed and their premises uncharred, due they insisted to my intervention, they would come and assist me. Mistress Bryce had balm from St. John's Wort prepared in her kitchen. I gloomily sent Abram up the lane to feed the horses and to bring back comfrey roots and my wooden box. I told him to come on with Master and Mistress Bryce, and I went back with Jake.

The poor people waiting patiently along Moor Street wrung my heart. I would rather not have known about them, but now that I did, well, I would do what I could. Mistress Tillam, weeping and distracted, called me into her husband's surgery. He had died just after Jake had left to fetch me. I examined the body. A musket ball had entered in the region of his hip and abdomen at point blank range. It was such a wound as I had stupidly tried to treat at Edgehill. No-one could have survived it. The loss of blood alone would prevent recovery. The wonder was he had lived so many hours after he had received it. I saw on the chair beside him, the papers that had contained the opium doses I had not used for Joseph. Clearly someone had eased his pain. I looked at Jake. He raised his eyebrows and nodded slightly.

"We have some balm of St. John's Wort and Abram is bringing Comfrey roots," I told him.

"We have dried powdered Comfrey. Shall I distil it, ready?" he asked.

"Excellent notion. But will not Mistress Tillam need your help with her husband's burial? I can sign the certificate for the Minister."

The Doctor had been murdered like a score of other Birmingham citizens. He had gone to his door to admit one with a sword wound, and a group of Rupert's rapscallions had swept past, shouting and shooting like deranged furies. The poor Doctor was the victim of his own humanity. Better to have stayed close within doors. His patient saw his physician mutilated before his eyes.

Jake was able to help me to great effect and Mistress Bryce worked in the kitchen, preparing her excellent balm of St. John's Wort. She sensibly kept a supply in her own kitchen lest she should burn herself when preparing meals for customers. Abram helped me when he could. I kept sending him to the mercers for clean soft cheesecloth with which to bandage the poor patients. Finally the apothecary came to the surgery and assisted me to good effect.

One after another the poor citizens came in: men, women and children. My task was heart breaking. Young girls whose beauty was marred irretrievably. Showers of sparks had caused lasting damage to their fair faces. Fathers of families who had rushed through flames to rescue their children and whose arms were charred like joints of pork. Women whose skirts had caught alight and whose legs had burnt so painfully damaging in the worst cases both muscle and sinew. They were suffering the most horrifying pain. Burns throb unbearably, and the terrible pangs afflict the sufferer in spasms. But what I found the most affecting was that all without exception tried to pay me, or rather their friends who had brought them, insisted that money must change hands. At length I accepted it for Abram and Mistress Tillam, as both were bereaved.

When he was not out on an errand, Abram stayed close to me, watching and listening. He would usher in the next patient with their husband, wife or parent and was of great assistance. I knew he would rather be chasing round his field with the horses, so I found his help a tender offering.

Word must have travelled that a Doctor was receiving patients in Doctor Tillam's premises as even at noon there was still a line of casualties. I had suggested to Jake that he kept rudimentary notes on each patient so that if they returned unsatisfied he would know what had been tried and failed.

Then at length towards the end of the day, there was a stir outside and word went around that Mr Granger was coming. I felt Abram stiffen and in a moment a thick-set fierce man entered. He was well dressed but with little kindness in his expression. He carried in his arms a slender brown haired woman, younger than himself, clad only in her shift. Jake helped him lay her down on a settle, but I could tell from the stiffness of her limbs that rigor mortis had set in.

Abram had seized my arm. "That's her!" he whispered. "I've seen her once or twice before when she's escaped to come and see me. That's her. That's my mother!"

15

"I had to cure myself of the habit of groaning. It distressed Master Bryce and his good wife. They did not groan even though their town was in ruins. I recognised it in myself as a symptom of fatigue. Now as I examined this poor dead woman I controlled myself and groaned inwardly. The smell of smoke hung about her.

"What happened?" I asked her brother.

"I swear to you she was not locked in her room. The Yeomen forbade it!" he told me with a sidelong glance at the others. He spoke in a short clipped manner. "I came back from the mill an hour ago and the servant told me she had not come downstairs this morning. When I went in there, there was a smell of smoke, and although she seemed unharmed I couldn't rouse her. There was a hole in the rafters and I think that smoke had drifted in from next door and smothered her while she slept. The upper rooms in the next house, a carpenter's, were full of green wood. It smouldered for hours, it seems. It is burnt to cinders." He looked at me pleadingly. "You are going to tell me what I do not want to hear. She is dead, I think."

"I'm afraid she is," I said. "That is immediately obvious by the stiffness of her limbs. But her face is untroubled. It is possible she was unconscious for some time before she died and did not suffer."

"Oh, Christ!" He sat down heavily. "She was my only relative. I have no-one now."

"Excuse me, sir!" I said with a feigned civility, "but I think this youth is your nephew."

He looked up sharply and saw Abram, standing with his head bowed in grief. If truth were told, the poor boy had lost both parents within two days.

Had he gained an uncle? "Oh, yes. I catch your purpose! The Blackamoor's boy! I suppose he will come shifting about, lurking at my door, begging for employment."

"No, I will not!" Abram told him. "I have no need of you. Doctor Tom here was sent to help me. If he does not want to, I can follow my father's trade."

"Well, well! At least he has a tongue that speaks English. Come to me tomorrow, after I've buried the wench, and I'll see what can be done."

He picked up his sister, a light slender burden. Abram spoke again.

"I have one request, and I vow I will never ask you for anything ever again. I would like to kiss my mother. This is my last chance."

He leant and kissed her cold brow whilst she lay in her brother's arms. Then, he stepped back and was gathered to Mistress Bryce' bosom, as he wept uncontrollably.

The realisation that one is an orphan whilst one is still young is a hard load to bear. I felt deeply for him. It was a relief for him to vent his grief in tears. He was mourning too for the lack of family life that he had never had.... He had hardly known his mother's love and now she was gone from him. His sobs were heart rending.

Master Granger stood for a moment, unsure how to proceed, looking uncertainly at Abram and then said to the room at large, "I say again, if he wishes he may come and see me tomorrow." He turned and went with his tragic burden in his arms.

Jake had treated the last of the burns and we stood and looked each at other in that strange moment when activity, which seemed to be about to endure for ever, suddenly ceases. Mistress Tillam, whom I am sure, would have wished to have had solitude to mourn her husband, kindly insisted we sat in her withdrawing room and drank some wine. I asked her if she had any thoughts about whether she would stay in her house here and she explained that now her husband, a Birmingham man, had gone, she might return to her native Herefordshire. Her brother was the steward in a fine mansion, owned by the Harley family. I told her of my direction in Worcester, should she need me. The thought of my home and the tedious fearful time I had spent away from it oppressed me, and I longed to return thither.

"We had best feed the horses, then, Abram," I said rising. "Tomorrow, come wind or weather, I am for Lichfield and then my home."

"And I too," he said and we walked up More Street behind the Bryces.

"What did you mean when you said I had been sent to you?" I asked.

"My father told me. When you had gone down to the inn. He said you had been sent."

"Who by?" I asked.

"Allah, of course. And that I was to stay with you and obey you, and you would look after me."

"But you have a rich relative who seems to be offering you something," I reminded him.

"No, no, I cannot go with him. He has a face like a badger's bum."

I shouted with laughter. It was an apt description.

"Well, well, if you come with me, what will you do?"

"Doctor folk, as you do. Count my horses," He grinned.

"Well, I see I must accept the will of Allah," I said slowly.

"We all must, Doctor Tom. Where are we going tomorrow?" It seemed the dice was cast, though whether by Allah or Abram was debatable.

We went back to the Horsefair, and called in at the Inn to bespeak a final night's lodging. Mistress Bryce warned us there would be little to eat and Abram's face fell, but a boy called from a butcher with fine fresh lamb collops which I bought for us all, if Mistress Bryce was not too tired to cook. There was a stables nearby where they still had oats for horses and we bought some and went up to feed Jupiter and Shireen.

"We can take her with us?" he asked.

"Certainly!" I told him. "She would pine away without you and Jupiter. Horses are only human!"

It occurred to me that the needle cases and the pots and pans of Joseph's trade would buy a good welcome from Joan, and packed a bag which little Shireen could carry comfortably. There was a pile of ballads that for some reason I thought might while away a winter's evening, which I also packed away.

"And Mother Bryce?" I asked him. "I have the notion that this is not the first occasion that you have wheedled your way into her kitchen? A needle case for her?"

Master Bryce promised to see if any who came to the inn, would wish to buy the cottage, but I suggested that the field should remain Abram's. His father lay there and if my scheme of horse trading came to fruition, it might prove a useful holding ground for horses in transit.

"The wench and I were saying, Abram son, that there's a home here for you if you want it. We've no little'uns of our own."

Abram thanked him and was clearly moved by their kindness, and disappointed that he must bid farewell to Mistress Bryce' cooking. He was very clear in his desires, however, orphaned as he was, and told them, "I must get away from Birmingham," echoing my own inclination with uncanny accuracy. I liked, and admired the town, and felt the same about the resourceful citizens whose initiative flourished in spite of Rupert's vandalism. But one could quickly become absorbed by this strange little republic. Absorbed and dead, if Rupert came back to complete his task.

So we set off on that April morning, Abram, I observed, full of the hope of the young. I could view him as youthful, after all next month I should be twenty, a great age. In fact when I contemplated what had happened in the two months that I had been away from home, I was surprised that I had not become an old venerable grey beard. I walked beside Jupiter with Abram on his back, and little Shireen trotted after me. We passed near to Sir Thomas Holte's fine residence.... passed and did not pause. Abram had seen its grandeur before and, like all hereabouts, disdained its owner. He remembered of a sudden visiting the kitchens of the great house with his father to see if they needed aught from the pedlar's pack. They had not, and the memory of their rude treatment of his father caused his tears to flow violently again.

I patted his leg, but said nothing. After a moment he said, "At least I have goods of my father's. When I see Shireen, I see him in my head walking beside her. But I have nothing of my mother's. I should have asked Grainger for a keepsake."

"In fact I think you have a fine keepsake from your mother that none can take from you."

He looked down at me from his lofty height. "And what might that be, Doctor Tom?"

My thought was a suspicion only. "Why do you think you did not catch your father's disease?"

He shrugged. "Luck! The will of Allah!"

251

"Why did no-one in Birmingham catch it? Why, please God, not me?"

"You might still sicken." He told me gloomily.

"I think because I, like your poor mother and yourself was born here or hereabouts, that we carry within us the resistance to some pestilences. Your poor father, borne far away in Egypt, could not withstand the wasting sickness. So, yes, I think you have an inheritance from your mother. Your good health." In truth I was not sure of what I spoke, but knew of no other explanation.

As he rode and I walked in the fine April sunlight I was tempted to sing but did not wish to intrude on Abram's grief. But when he heard me humming to myself, he asked me to sing louder, and when we had reached our goal, we had sung, "Back and sides go bare," together several times. I have to admit to hear him bawling away, "I cannot eat but little meat, My stomach is not good", caused me some little mirth, and he, seeing my wry grin, had the good grace to laugh at himself.

Erdington seemed to have escaped Prince Rupert's attentions. It was a neat hamlet, set in the midst of green fields, the meeting place of six roads. I passed up Shireen's rein to Abram and went into an inn to ask directions to the Welsh Cob breeders' farm. It was nearby. "Ah! You'll see 'em in the pastures." I was told. "Less 'n a mile up road!"

And there were six cobs running freely round a field, enjoying the sun with two fellows standing watching them over the gate. They glanced up at our approach and then looked back at their horses. But one suddenly looked back at us, smiled broadly as we drew to a halt and came to greet us.

"I'd know that rattling good pad-nag anywhere. 'Tis Tom, the doctoring lad from Worcester, George. By the Mass we supped some ale that day in Birmingham Horsefair. I'm powerful glad to see you, Tom."

"Harry, I came to find you as I said I would, and am glad indeed to meet you again." I clasped his arms, and for a moment was speechless with gratitude that he should remember me. We had certainly drunk our fill and he had been concerned for me, when I had told him about Brigstock. "We've come from Birmingham, where Rupert has played havoc with the town."

"Oh, aye, we heard about that. He's at Cannock now, drinking them dry with One Eyed Hastings," put in George "And who's this young gamesmaster?"

Abram dismounted, grinning broadly. "Hey, I know you!" said Harry. "You're Joseph's lad. Pedlar's son, George. Where's your father?"

"It's a long story!" I broke in, "Joseph sadly died on Easter Monday, the same day that Rupert came to Birmingham."

"Allah sent Tom to care for me," put in Abram.

"Who's he then?" asked Harry "One of the Yeomen of the Holy Cross?"

"Higher than that!" I said hoping they would cease questioning. But Abram seemed unperturbed. I was starting to understand his philosophy. He mourned his father deeply, and his mother also, and when grief overtook him would give way to it totally. But when he was not overcome, well, his life was for living. A contrast to my own period of mourning after my father's murder. Grey daggly days had seemed to stretch one into the next. It had seemed disloyal to laugh or smile. Necessity, not love of life, had forced me back into the world.

"I have a proposition," I told the brothers. "We need your cobs in Worcester. I have a rattling good farrier there needs to practise his calling, and this young fellow knows one end of a horse from the other. I can get you good prices and they would not be sold to either King's Man or Rebel to be ridden into the ground, but to good honest tradesmen. What do you say?"

"I say we should get some belly cheer from the wench indoors, and sit over some mulled ale and mull over your plan." said George. "Come on, my masters!"

We spent some pleasant hours discussing my great scheme. I had the money to implement it and also knew that it would prosper both for me, and my dependants. We had a fine meal of beef and carrots and a kind of cake made with lard and honey with currants. At about two after noon I thought that we should be making our way on to Lichfield.

Jupiter could carry us both at a pinch but Harry would not have it. It was decided that Shireen should stay at the farm and they would lend me a riding cob, a good little mare called Babs. After we had passed through a neat little town called Sutton Coldfield, it was a straight road and a steady canter would bring us to Lichfield just before nightfall.

We came in to Lichfield on a road, westward from the one I knew. But there were the three spires, glinting in the evening sunlight, all seeming calm and peaceful in the soft twilight air. As ever we made our way to Bird Street, and Jupiter turned into the yard of the George and Dragon, without my guidance on the reins. Hector and Old Harry were being fed even as we arrived. Hector neighed in pleasure at the sound of my voice and at the sight of the carrot I held out to him.

Mistress Emily was delighted to see me. She had news of my patients at the Hartshorn. All had now gone back to Derby but had left a letter with Jacky for me. She had two rooms for us. Mine was the best one where Phoebe had lodged, and Abram's was my old room. I was relieved she did not offer either of us Elijah's room with its window over the street. How the exigencies of a country at war with itself caused one to move from crisis to crisis. Necessity causes the neglect even of our true emotions. I had scarcely thought of poor Elijah, these last days in Birmingham. I sat down in my room, oppressed by his loss and remembered the talk we had had in this inn about gratitude. I could almost hear his voice.

Abram looked round the door. "There's rabbit pie for others downstairs," he told me, "Might she feed us for a needle-case?"

I sighed and smiled. "No need of that. I still have some guineas, though this jaunt has made my pocket as light as thistledown. We must eat and then I must find Eleanour."

But Fate, or Allah, or Jehovah willed it otherwise. After rabbit pie and spring greens we were just about to taste a fig pudding, when we heard the dreaded sounds of an army descending on the town. Shots, squeals, shouts and screams. There was no mistake. Rupert had come to town.

I permitted myself a groan. My quick escape with the horses was receding into that carefree world of the imagination where I had once had a home. But even as I gazed in horror at Abram across our pudding, I heard a well known voice, which raised my spirits.

"What, dear Mistress? No bedchambers at all? Not even for the Prince's friends?"

Peabody was standing in the hall, trying his usual tricks with Mistress Emily, her hand in both of his. I answered him.

"Nothing for the friend of a Prince, Master Peabody, but with

Mistress Emily's permission, Abram might vacate his room for you."

"Tom, Tom, my dear friend. You cannot know how pleased I am to see you."

That sounded ominous. "Whence are you, Peabody?"

"From Cannock even now and before that Birmingham."

"Ah, Birmingham?" I said airily. "Yes I have heard of that town. But pauca verba Peabody. Is it agreed?"

"When have I ever disagreed with you, good Doctor Tom. Who is this?" he had spied Abram who had finished his pudding and had decided that I had either lost interest in, or had no need of mine.

"This is Abram. When he heard that I was a champion at quarter staffs, he determined that he had no other choice but to throw in his lot with me."

"A wise youth. God ye good even, Master Abram."

It was decided that Peabody could have Abram's room, who could use the truckle bed, in my bedchamber. Peabody had to find quarters this night for the Prince's Captains. I told him of the large rooms at the back of the Hartshorn, but he was most anxious that I should accompany him later to minister to someone who had been wounded in Birmingham, "that sink of iniquity famed for disaffected loyalty", said Peabody studying the ceiling.

I agreed. Abram moved his few belongings into my room and I sat at peace for some while with a cup of canaries. Peabody returned from the Hartshorn, having achieved his object of quarters for various noblemen. Now he insisted I accompanied him to Sir Richard Dyott's house. I asked the Landlady to ensure that Abram remained within doors but he asked if he could assist the ostler with the horses in the stables.

The streets of Lichfield were alive with Rupert's men. "When Hastings arrives, we shall circummur the Close" said Peabody.

"You mean you will surround it?" I said. "Well that was more than Lord Brooke ever did. A strategic policy."

The first thing I saw when I entered the house was a coffin, open and occupied, in pride of place on a gate legged table in the hall. It was the man, shot in the Horsefair when Rupert had entered with other riders, when they were firing the houses. I paused to look at him.

"Who's this?" I asked Peabody.

"Earl of Denbigh," he told me, "shot in Birmingham. Started to get better but fell in his coach and died in Cannock, twenty four hours ago. As I recall you met his son at Edgehill. One of the rebels."

"Did this man not shout out that he would lambast Basil's arse for him, for following Essex?"

"Aye, that he did. He should have done so too. A courteous Lord and a loving father!"

He hurried me along to the retiring room which was richly furnished. A man was lying on his front, on two settles that had been pushed together. I knew him immediately.

"Here is Doctor Tom Fletcher, Your Highness. He is a skilled surgeon, none better. I know he will tend your.... back."

He nodded and groaned and indicated that I should remove his clothing. He had certainly been burned.... across his lower back.

"How did this happen?" I asked. Peabody replied, "As the Prince rose in his saddle and spurred his horse onwards, as we were riding from Birmigham, a burning brand fell from a building and showered his.... Er.... back with sparks. He sat quickly onto his saddle, and rode on in some pain, managing to quench the fire with his hand. The incident went unnoticed by all, due to the Prince's valour and fortitude."

Several of the sparks had clearly smouldered for some little time. "Has there been any treatment proffered?" I enquired.

"No, none!" said Peabody "The Prince would not allow of it until now. The pain across his.... Er.... back is considerable."

"I see it is and the wounds are close to septic. If he is not anointed with a good ointment immediately, the pain will become unbearable. I could not answer for his future."

The Prince twisted round to face me. "Then I pray you Master Doctor, do your best efforts to relieve this unbearable pain and afford me some hope for my future."

Mistress Bryce had given me balm of St. John's Wort. I had enough for one treatment, and hoped that the Lichfield apothecary might have more. But I suddenly remembered the still room in the Bishop's Palace. If I could get in there, I was sure I would find a good supply.

I liberally applied the healing salve to the Prince's back.

"Indeed, the pain of burning can exceed almost all other hurts." I said to make conversation. "Has your Royal Highness heard of twice burned Wightman? He was burned not twenty yards from this house…. twice."

The Prince winced. "Yes, burning at the stake was an efficient way of silencing heretics." I went on cheerfully, gently applying the ointment. "Your Highness may remember that your grandfather James' great uncle, Henry the Eighth would burn a man one year for claiming Our Lord was not substantially present in holy bread and the next year would burn another man for saying that He was present. Something of a riddle, Your Highness."

The Prince heaved himself up to look at me. "You are a loquacious babbling lunatic!" he told me courteously, "but a good surgeon. The pain has gone."

"Does your Highness have small clothes of clean fine lawn?" I asked him. "I would recommend that you lie on your front to sleep as you are doing now, and sit and ride as little as possible."

The Prince drew up his breeches and stood up. I straightened up and we looked each other in the eye, being the same height, his hair still plentiful and black like mine. "I know you, do I not? You will remain in this town to dress my wounds again, for as long as I am hereabouts," he told me graciously. "See to it, Peabody. Not a word of this to anyone, Master Blabberlips."

"Alas, your Highness, I fear that is not possible," I began, but he cut in, "Alas Master Doctor I fear that it is possible because I have said that it is. Take him away, Peabody."

I waited until we had passed William Fielding, lying patiently in death, by the door! Devil an arse he would lambast today! I reflected, but that if he could, his friend Rupert's was in a raw and tender state! And I would give him all assistance!

As we gained the street, I turned to Peabody. "You traitor! I must go home to Worcester. At this rate I will never get home."

"Tom, what can I say? In truth, I did not know his bum had been so peppered by the sparks. Something of the stoic about him you know, Tom. It was clearly becoming unbearable on the road from Cannock. We are in your debt. His humour is lightened somewhat."

"Let me tell you what is painfully light and that is my pocket. I have not the means to stay here until his bum is smooth as butter. If I get him a supply of balm of St. John's Wort, his wounds will slowly heal. A poultice of figs is also very good. I will ask my Landlady to make that up for him. She made a good fig pudding that Abram kindly ate for me."

"Leave me alone for some kind of recompense from the Prince, Tom. Whither now?"

I had resolved to visit Gabriel and Cornelia to find out what Eleanour had decided, and invited Peabody to accompany me, as much to avoid Rupert's civil army, drinking, shouting, whoring. I hoped that they gave Master Froggatt's vintner's store a Birmingham Blessing!

We stepped over some gentleman who seemed to prefer the gutter to the more usual vertical modus operandi. Then several jovial troopers informed us, "We be soldiers three, Lately come from the Low Country, With never a penny of money." I caught a glimpse of the harlot whose life I saved, holding court up an alley. In truth she was in a fair way to make her fortune tonight, if she could keep her head intact. Little chance that her maidenhead could be so described!

The doors were fast locked at the sign of the Barrel. I knocked and called out, "Master Gabriel, it's Tom Fletcher with Master Peabody. May we come in?"

Gabriel's voice cried out, "Tom, you say? It's Tom? "Oh speak again, bright angel." Your dulcet tones again, dear boy!"

"In truth, it's me! Please let us in!"

The bolts were shot and the key turned in the creaking wards, and we were admitted. Gabriel was delighted to see us, and embraced us both, inviting us to be seated at the table. Cornelia who had been singing lullaby to Hodge and Lizzie, swept us a deep curtsey, clasped me to her bosom and graciously gave Peabody her hand to kiss.

"Come and see our cherubs." We followed her to where the children sleepily opened their eyes and smiled. They looked wondrous contented, rosy cheeked and bright of eye, Lizzie clutching her moppet, and Hodge's wooden horse was beside him on the floor.

Cornelia kissed them both again, and murmuring a blessing, she led us back to where Gabriel was pouring Sack into pewter goblets.

"The children are well, God be praised." said Gabriel. "They are our saviours, our redeemers. We think they view us as their parents and our lives would be wretched without them. Not merely Doctor Tom, because the Guild awards us a handsome pension to care for them, but because we love them dearly. Little Hodge comes to me and asks for a story so prettily, and little Lizzie dances and sings her little rhymes. They are our joy and our delight, Doctor Tom. My son, alas, and his lady, found the welfare of the children not to their liking. With little ones as young as this, I fear, that they engross our attention, and Ralph and Eleanour found that assisting with their care too troublesome."

"I think when Eleanour has children of her own, she will understand that the mother must put their needs above all others," said Cornelia, still speaking with her strange accent. When I had last conversed with Eleanour, she had complained bitterly about Cornelia's unreasonable demands. I thought this was magnanimous indeed on her mother-in-law's part.

"Where are Ralph and Eleanour?" I asked bluntly.

Gabriel looked greatly embarrassed. "In the Close," he replied. "When I think how the King had nurtured our little company over the years, I fear 'tis the height of ingratitude in Ralph."

"What are they doing in the Close?" But as I looked round the room I understood. The precious printing press had gone.

"Yes, alas, sadly my role as mentor and occasional scribe is now extraneous. They came with a cart and took all the paper, ink, platens, letters. Of course such items are not suitable for little fingers to examine and Ralph once or twice became quite heated with our darlings. Colonel Russell approves of the Press.... when it is for Parliament of course."

"I saw a news-sheet that used my name, for Parliament, that came from Ralph."

Gabriel looked conscience stricken. "I assure you I was not for that. I warned him you would be.... angry, and that it was not necessary."

I went on, "You were right. I am not for either side, Gabriel, and yet this sheet spoke of me as if I was for Parliament. How could I support Essex? He ordered my father hanged. Does Ralph not know that? I think he does. And some of these Royalist Commanders are so arrogant, proud and despising, enough to destroy good faithful men of the middle sort who try to serve the King."

Peabody coughed to remind me he was there. I rounded on him. "Do you think, dear Peabody, that if you did not possess a genius for teaching men to be soldiers, that these high borne simpletons whom you serve so faithfully, would care an empty hogshead for you? If you were not useful to them, my dear friend, they would discard you like old worn out shoes! I tell you the whole conflict will be for naught. Master Gabriel," I went on warming to my theme, "you are familiar with Shakespeare's plays.... all of them." He bowed his head in assent. "What conclusion did he come to in those pieces that treat of our History? Is there or was there ever any good to be gleaned from our Civil Wars?"

He shook his head sadly. "You should have seen my Falstaff, dear boy. "Who hath this honour? Why he, who died o'Wednesday last!" No, you are in the right of it. The bard could see no rhyme nor reason in civil conflict. The only harvest is death."

"And yet his daughter Susannah told us that the future of our land lies with us, the middling sort of people. I cannot contemplate it. Two factions of great lords at odds with each other for power, and the poor are sacrificed. If God looks on at all, it is with sublime indifference." Gabriel and Peabody were alike something cowed by my outburst. I collected myself. "Forgive me," I entreated them, "Dear friends and good companions, as you are. Forgive me my vehemence. Tell me," I asked Gabriel, "do Ralph and Eleanour visit you?"

"Not lately. There is something of a frost, something of a coolness. My dear good lady wife asked her for assistance in some matter to do with the children and Eleanour who had been at accord with my dear one whilst we were in less salubrious quarters, now snapped that she was not a nursemaid. In troth she loves working with my boy. A strange choice for a woman."

"So, are they permitted to travel from the Close into Lichfield to sell their news-sheets?"

"They stand at the end of Dam Street at noon, every day, and get reasonable good custom. Whether they may continue to do that, now the Prince is here, I do not know. I would imagine that the Colonel would allow it. He might well see such sales as advertisement for the Great Cause of Parliament."

We took our leave and I resolved to be on Dam Street by the Causeway the next day. When I took my candle and crept into my room, Abram was already fast asleep but in my bed. I made the best of the truckle bed. I was too long for it. I had the sensation that Abram had tried it and decided that he also was too tall.

Next day, after I had remonstrated with Abram as to the courtesy of stealing another man's bed.... especially if he is over two yards high as I am.... and asked Mistress Emily for another bed of reasonable length for my companion, the three of us went to call on the apothecary. He had enough Balm of St John's Wort for one treatment, and promised to begin the process of macerating the flowers so that in three days I could have more. I paid him for the treatment that he had and paid on account for the future ointment. There is no equal to this balm in the treatment of burns. It soothes and heals. I resolved that I must get my interim supply from the Bishop's still room.

Peabody met some of his Captains, who insisted that he join them for an hour's talk in an ale house, together with hospitable potations It seems that some of Rupert's army after Birmingham had straggled their way too far to the east and had happened upon Parliamentary spies near Warwick. They informed their Commander, a certain Colonel Bridges who sallied forth from Warwick, took two carriages of provisions and arms, captains and men and locked them all up in Warwick Castle.

I sat below Dean Denton's ravaged Market Cross and waited with Abram. The sun was warm and I leaned back against a slighted apostle and closed my eyes. After what only seemed a moment later, Abram who had listened carefully to my plans that morning and knew I sought newsvendors, shook me gently and indicated the man and woman coming down the Causeway to Dam Street, carrying their news-sheets and calling out that they had news to sell. Well, I too had news for them and it was not for sale. They could have it gratis.

"So Eleanour," I called out to her. She started at the sight of me. "You are ready I take it to return with me to Ledbury. I have come back for you, sweetheart, as promised."

She looked stricken at the sight of me, as did Ralph. "What?" he cried, "Go back to Ledbury? What duplicity is this, you harlot?"

"I assure you, Ralph, 'twas when we were at odds about your mother. In a misguided moment I asked Tom to return me to my parents. Tom, forgive me. Ralph and I are again reconciled."

"But I have travelled here for you specially," I lied in my teeth and for once it felt excellent good sport. "At great personal inconvenience not to say financial cost. I have had to buy a horse to suit you, Eleanour, and now you tell me you are reconciled with this mountebank. And what of the widow?"

"What widow?" said Ralph, in genuine bewilderment.

"I fear I strained at the truth, Tom," said Eleanour, her head cast-down. "Her husband was merely mislaid."

"Tom, good Cousin Tom, let us sit and talk of this." There was the usual trick of scouring of pockets for coin. "Do you have some pence about you which I vow I will return instanter? And let us sit over a pot of ale and talk over this grievous misunderstanding."

"Alas, good Cousin Ralph, I have no pence about me. My means have been dissipated and a church mouse is richer than me. All I have is two horses to enable me to escape with Eleanour. Also, alas, I was badly burned by these whoreson wretches of Rupert's in Birmingham. My legs under my hose are like unto shanks of lamb on the spit. I need balm of St. John's Wort from the still room in the palace. There is a good supply in there. Can you get it for me, please, Eleanour?"

Ralph came up to me. "There is no need for you to take Eleanour, so you can sell your spare horse," he told me softly, "and tonight I will meet you at the North Wall of the Close where I will have something for you that will be very much to your liking."

"The balm of St. John's Wort?"

"Aye, indeed if we can find it!" he promised. "About half an hour after sundown when it is full dark. At the North Wall. There is a point where one can jump down. We must sell our News in the Market now Tom. The Colonel only allows us a scant hour and who knows if these Royalist rogues will want our News."

"Why should they not?" I asked him all innocence, "News is News surely?"

"Cousin Tom." he said "Come to me tonight and we will speak further on this matter."

I insisted that Peabody came with me to minister to the Prince's wounds in the afternoon. He greeted us on his feet and motioned us to a table on which wine had been set out. "Your treatment is good, Master Doctor. I was something less than courteous yesterday. Matters are certainly improving. Now where did I see you before?"

"Powick Bridge, your Highness and then again at Master Brindley's manufactuary in Kinver." And then greatly daring, "I hear there is a Parliament plot to burn Master Brindley's Mill as he makes blades for the King."

"The bastards!" he cried. "There is no villainy to which they will not stoop."

"May I anoint your Highness?" I asked, and I began my doctoring. No doubt of it, the balm was effective, the sores were healing over. And it seemed as if the pain was receding.

"I hope to have another supply by tomorrow, Your Highness." I told him.

"What is your fee, Master Doctor?" he asked me, more gracious than ever.

"Perhaps Master Peabody could discuss that with your Highness at your leisure." I suggested, obsequiously. Peabody could drive a harder bargain than I.

He nodded and thanked me and we took our leave. I noticed the Earl had been coffined over. "He is bound for his last resting place, Newnham Paddox in Warwickshire." Peabody said gloomily.

"Did you like him?" I asked quietly.

"No, but I understood him," said Peabody. He did not enlarge on his meaning, so I did not ask.

I told Peabody and Abram that I wished them to stand guard for me after sundown behind the Close. The weather had been fine and pleasant and this night was no exception. There was a moon rising and the lightest of breezes. We went to the back of the Close, a spot Peabody and I remembered well, and I positioned them in a hawthorn brake the other side of Gaia Lane. I had told them "Do not let me do anything that I would afterwards regret."

I sat under the wall and waited. After a while there was the sound of voices, and suddenly Ralph was astride the top of the wall.

"I am coming down," he whispered, and in a moment he was beside me.

"Have you got it?" I asked him also whispering.

"Yes, indeed I have," he told me with great satisfaction and produced a sheet of paper.

"What's this?" I hissed at him.

"Read it! Read it!" he insisted.

It was the same news-sheet with my name on that I had seen in Henley.

"Look!" he was delighted with himself, "your name is there!"

"I know my name is there," I told him between clenched teeth. "I have already seen this dross that you have circulated! How dare you use my name without my permission? Where is my balm of St. John's Wort?"

"Oh, Jesu! I forgot it!" he cried, forgetting to whisper. "Eleanour? Ellie?"

I pushed him onto his back, clasped his fists in my left hand and knelt on them and pushed up into his throat with my right hand. Eleanour's face appeared above the wall. I squeezed gently.

"Eleanour," I said pleasantly. "If you can go now, if you please, sweetheart, and get for me what I asked you from the still room, balm of St. John's Wort, then your husband will live. If you are longer than, let us say, seven minutes, this worm, to whom you are married, will share the coffin of the Earl of Denbigh and go to Newnham Paddox wherever the Hell that is. Go now like a good little sweetheart!"

She gave a strangled cry and disappeared. I released the pressure and let Ralph take a few precious breaths of air. When he seemed to be recovered enough to speak, I applied my hand again. I do not think Aesculapius would have approved of the exploitation of my knowledge of the limits of the human body. But so we continued, I allowing him to breathe just enough. In fact he was in no danger. But he did not know that.

At last she returned and threw three sealed pots over the wall near to where we lay. I immediately released Ralph, who came at me roaring like a bull. To my surprise he was howling in the same tongue as Hans and his mother spoke. I held him off, and suddenly was surprised to hear the same language spoken briskly and authoritatively behind me.

"What is going on here, mien Herr Doktor?"

It was the Prince. The truth is so often the easiest policy.... most of the truth.

"The Balm of St. John's Wort, Your Highness. With Colonel Russell's compliments, from the Bishop's Still Room. You must know, Your Highness, my legs were sorely burned in Birmingham."

"This man is saying in Dutch perhaps, that you tried to kill him."

"Oh your Highness, these men that sell the news will say anything. If I had tried to kill him, believe me I would have succeeded. In truth he was in no danger. As you can see he is unhurt."

Ralph shouted again, in his mother's tongue.

"He is saying that all he did was put your name news-sheet."

"Is your Highness pleased to see your name in news-sheets?"

"No. I am not. Herr Doctor, I will let you settle this matter to your satisfaction." He spoke again to Ralph and passed on with his Captains. They were surveying the walls for.... circummuration, if such a word exists.

In the end we had made so much noise that any moment I was prepared to have Colonel Russell join the conversation in friendly manner, nodding down at us. Peabody discovered himself and we heaved Ralph Truscott back up the wall. I gathered up my pots of precious ointment. As for the News Sheet, I left it there, dismally flapping over the grass.

And next day all was regular and usual in Lichfield. A Lord with great guns was pounding away at the Close and the poor inhabitants were terrified.... again.

16

It was Saturday the 8th of April. The thunder of the guns from the north side of the Close echoed through the town. A few brave stallholders opened their stalls around the Cross. "What's goin' t'happen if he starts his pummelling, town side o'Close?" asked an elderly farmer's wife who had bundled herself into town on her donkey to sell her butter.

I bought some foodstuffs to carry to Gabriel and Cornelia, lest they were too afeard to leave their home, and took Abram to meet them at the sign of the Barrel.

Gabriel opened the door, delighted to see me again and at the sight of Abram asked me in raptures, "Sweet Jesu, Tom, where did you find such a perfect Prince of Morocco?"

Abram bowed politely and explained, "My father came from Egypt, sir, and we are not Princes."

"But the voice, dear boy. He's a natural. Too young for Othello yet, but what presence! What bearing!"

Abram turned to me with a puzzled expression. "Master Gabriel thinks you would make an actor," I explained. "He followed that profession and so did his son with whom you saw me speaking last night."

The children rushed into the room, followed by Cornelia but stopped in their tracks at the sight of Abram, a stranger. He immediately knelt down to speak to them.

"That's a very good horse," he told Hodge, "What is his name?"

"Dobbin," whispered Hodge, somewhat overcome.

"Shall we see how he goes outside?" There was a courtyard at the back of the house. It had been full of empty hogsheads but now, I suspect due to Cornelia's insistence, was neat and trim. In a few moments he was teaching his new friends, "There was a monkey climbed a tree, When he fell down, then down fell he," with suitable but noisy gestures.

"A most amiable youth!" said Gabriel gazing through the window. Cornelia was delighted with the beef steaks and butter I had bought and invited us to share them, at dinner time later that day. She pointed out that my hose were soiled and it must be admitted somewhat stinking since the incident at the well. Could she wash them for me? I agreed with great relief and stripped them off. She held them at arms length between her finger tips and took them into the kitchen. At that moment there was a loud knock at the door. Gabriel went to answer it. "Father! It's me!" Ralph was admitted and rushed into the room.

"Tom Fletcher! Peabody told me you were here. I ought to beat you to Kingdom Come!"

I looked down at him. "Let me invite you to try!"

"What you did last night, that was not friendly. I, and my parents have ever invited you into our home, made you welcome. True, we have not had much, unlike you, but what we had you were invited to share. My neck is still sore and my hands still so numb, I could not today select the letters for the platen."

His father had poured us both a goblet of sack. I noticed that Ralph held his with all his fingers and then transferred it to his left hand to place it on the table. I did not think my knees had done lasting damage. I asked to see his neck. There was a little chafing but nothing that could not have come from an over starched shirt.

"And Tom, you claimed your legs were like shanks of lamb on a spit. I see them clearly. They are unmarked."

I would have to tell partial truth. "I admit it. The balm was for another person," I simpered. "One very dear to me whose charming identity I must not disclose. She sustained burns in Birmingham and is even now recovering at the George."

"Why did you not tell us of this? Why did you not tell me of the happenings in Birmingham?"

"What and have her name blazoned over your diurnals? With regard to your chosen profession, Ralph, you have neither responsibility nor respect for others. You steal information like a vagrant steals food. You do it to feed the unwholesome curiosity of fools."

"Yes, Tom, but these are fools who can read, remember! You say I lack responsibility. What is more responsible than bringing the information of what is happening in our country to its inhabitants?"

I was about to interrupt, but he raised his hand. "Nay, hear me out. The news-book is the cheapest, the commonest, the most popular product of the printing trade. Do you not realise, Tom, that it is printing that has caused man to raise his head from the gutter and the ditch to question the dictates of those hitherto set in commandment and judgement over them? The simple printing press.... well not simple, but mechanical.... has done more to spread knowledge to the middling and poor people than any philosopher seated in his tower. There I have done. But you should be flattered to have your name on one of our news-books, not outraged."

To speak truth, I was pleased by his tirade. "Ralph, you are justified in your defence of your calling and I salute you for it. I apologise for hurting you last night, though I think it was your dignity that I hurt, not your person. I cannot pretend that I was flattered by the mention of my name in the news-book, however. It was vital I obtained the balm. You did not bring it when I had particularly requested it. I remembered all our goods and money stolen, as your parents will bear witness. I remember Phoebe's gown being altered to fit your doxy. I remember stoups of wine, jugs of ale and meals bought at my expense. And I... Well.... we would not now be here in Lichfield, had your "good little sweetheart" not told me that she wished to return to her parents."

"Well," Ralph shifted in his seat. "We could dispute all day...."

"No, we could not," I told him," because I am not disputing with you. I agree with everything you have said about the power of printing and I respect the fervour with which you defend your profession. I dislike your methods. It pains me to say this before your father. I dislike your morals. But know this Ralph. I do not dislike you. I have learned since the start of these troubles that it is possible to hate a man's opinions, but not hate the man."

He nodded slowly. "Well I am happy about that, at all events."

Gabriel who had looked from one to the other and clearly hated us to be not of accord, now spoke. "Come now, let there be peace between us in these troubled times. Is all well in the Close, dear son?"

"Yes, but Ellie and I grow weary of the enforced leisure. If we cannot travel and speak to people we cannot write the news. I have written my memory of the closure of the theatres, father. You might wish to cast your eye over it."

"Ralph, as soon as I am certain sure I can go back to Worcester without some great lord claiming me as his doctor, I will tell you the truthful account of what occurred in Birmingham."

"Birmingham? The musketeers who returned thence three days ago told us of carnage, arson and rape! Oh Tom, if you could narrate to us your memory of those incidents, that would make us so happy!"

The booming noises north of the Close were continuing. "How are you and Mother enduring this terrible noise?" he asked his father.

"We have the children to think of," said his mother with an air of self-importance. Ralph spoke to her in their language, and then told her that Prince Rupert who spoke a dialect close to that of the Low Countries was, to the best of his knowledge, residing in the town.

"How did you get out of the Close?" I enquired.

He rubbed his thumb against his finger tips. "Knowing which guards can be bribed. Nothing easier. How does the Prince? He seemed to know you last night."

I did not wish to have to answer questions about my patient and prepared to take my leave. Cornelia reminded me of my hose which were now drying before the kitchen fire. She invited us to dine at about four p.m. after noon, as that was their dinner time. I resumed my boots, and asked if there was a mercer's where I might buy another pair of hose. Abram was playing "Ride a cock horse" with the children who were competing for the privilege of riding on his back, each in turn. When they heard he was to leave, they each grasped a leg and refused to release him. Only when they were reassured that he would return later, was he allowed his freedom.

As we walked down Frog Lane to St. John's Street, I said, "You never told me what an excellent nursemaid you are."

"You never asked me," he said simply. There was no disputing with that.

The mercer had two pairs of woollen hose that I could purchase for a shilling a pair, a good brown colour which sorted well with my dark doublet and hose. Abram was mightily taken by beautiful silk hose in bright rainbow colours, eight shillings a pair.

"You are too young to pine for your yellow hose, young master," said the mercer pleasantly, "In these parts yellow hose are worn by the bachelors wanting to catch the maidens' eyes."

I had noticed that Abram had enough good clothes, more than myself in fact. His father had not stinted him.

"You shall have yellow hose when we are back in Worcester, I promise, if they still take your pleasure. Here I must watch my purse." He accepted this, realising that I dressed for necessity, not vanity. As we passed the Hartshorn, I remembered that Jacky had a packet for me. The landlady, whose name I could not remember, was delighted to see me. Sir John Gell's money had covered the cost of recuperation and all the patients who had been here, when I gave them the news of Elijah's sad death, had gone back to their homes in Derbyshire. She called Jacky who asked us to sit over a pot of ale and gave me a parchment packet.

"You was right to stop me going with they harlots!" he told me.

"Only for your health, Jacky," I told him, wondering how much of this conversation Abram should hear.

"You'm right there, master," he told me gloomily, "There's some young sparks and blades in this town, wish they'd never clapped eyes on those girls. For that's what they do have: the clap."

"But you are healthy, I hope," I said pleasantly, vowing to myself that if he told me of venereal symptoms, I would pretend to be ignorant of the treatment of such conditions. It was not a branch of medicine I relished.

He grinned. "Oh, aye. And there's a milkmaid back at the farm, as pretty a prugg as any o'they nasty whores."

"Well, I wish you well, good Jacky, and thank you too for your kind help. I hope to be gone in a few days."

"It was Zach what wrote the paper in that," he told me indicating the packet. I deemed it was courteous to depart, so we made our way back to the George.

Abram's luck was in. The packet contained just such a pair of yellow silk hose, as we had seen in the mercers. My patients perhaps hoped that if I proclaimed myself the bachelor, some young girl would pity me. Or they had noticed that my dress was lamentable plain. They must have collected the shillings together from their pay. Sir John, no doubt of it, took care of his boys, if they could afford such a handsome present. I gave the hose to Abram who immediately put them on.

"Well, you are a lusty fancy monger now." I had to confess I was much moved by the paper, with the hose. It said in wavering script, "YOU SAVED OUR LIFES." Zach had written it for me in despite of the fact that Elijah was his hero.

I suggested that Abram changed his hose back to his good serviceable Kersey pair. He could wear the yellow ones on the Sabbath. I sighed as he obeyed me, as always with a good grace. When had I contracted at the age of twenty to become the father of a boy of fourteen, and with whom? I did not remember. But then I had never expected to be here so long after our February pilgrimage from Worcester. The Goddess Fortuna had me bound on her wheel. Try as I would, always some new crisis arose. Perhaps I should have gone straight home from Stratford. But if I had done so, what would Abram have done alone with his dying father? I had made a mutually beneficial arrangement with my friends who bred Welsh Cobs.

Fortune was not my foe but I was not over confident that she was my friend.

We went down to wait for Peabody who had promised to accompany me to visit the Prince. He came in seeming somewhat flustered and out of sorts. "Why what's the matter?" I asked him as we gained the street. Two musketeers immediately fell in behind us.

"These are!" he told me indicating the men behind him. "He grows suspicious. Your meeting with the Newsmonger, Rafe, last night."

"Perhaps I should have told him what my difficulty was." I said hesitantly.

"Perhaps."

"I'll tell him now."

The Earl of Denbigh had returned to Newnham Paddox. I was glad to see him gone, as for me his mortal remains cast something of a blight in the hall of Sir Richard Dyott's fine house. Peabody took Abram to a pastrycook's nearby, and I, and the musketeers went to find the Prince. But it was clear that he was not pleased with me.

"So, Doctor Thomas Fletcher, you consort with the enemy."

"No, Your Highness."

"What were you doing kneeling on a Hollander in the lane behind the Close?"

I tried to explain making much of my knowing the contents of the Still Room when I had been immured with the Earl of Chester-field. When was that? A lifetime ago.

"So, your Highness must understand it was merely to obtain supplies of ointment for your wounds," I concluded.

"Well, apply it now," he said, removing his breeches.

I did so, noting that only two more applications were needed.

"In fact," he grudgingly admitted, "If I am careful, it does not hurt to sit."

I expressed my admiration. "But" he said, buttoning his breeches and the word echoed like a pistol shot about the room, "I am not convinced. You might be a spy. I am sure that you are a good doctor, but I am not convinced that you think the King's cause is just. So.... I have decided to keep you at my side whilst I am in this town. That is for my treatments and for the safety of our cause. Peabody vouches for you, but I would rather be safe than sorry."

"Your Highness," I said desperately, "Surely last night's escapade proves my loyalty rather than otherwise. Why should I go to such ends to get the balm for your Highness' injuries, if I cared nothing for your cause?"

"Very pretty!" he told me, "Well, my loyalty to my cause is such that I will keep you with me, Doctor Tom. You will be my personal physician and that of my loyal followers for the few days it will take to batter down the walls. You were with Chesterfield. A good man, is he not? In spite of the many calumnies noised abroad regarding his practices in his youth."

"I do not know of any, Your Highness, and am betrothed to his great-niece."

He smiled. "Good. Tell me, do you know of any weak places in these thick walls of the Close?"

"No, but your Highness demonstrates immediately that your knowledge of strategy is infinitely superior to that of Lord Brooke. The walls are lower to the north. He never came there and thence we effected the ambush in Gaia Lane. It is possible for a tall man to drop down safely, but we had ladders to get back. Ladders stolen from Parliament."

"You are a useful man, Doctor Tom. In time you will make a good spy for the King. Now I want you to come with me to see the progress of my guns."

We went out to Dam Street and made our way by a circuitous

route across the fields, followed by a small troop of life guards. Eventually after crossing Gaia Lane we came to the meadow behind the Close, where the guns were emplaced. They were I was told culverins and demi-culverins. The noise they made was terrifying but they were impotent against the thickness of the walls.

"You see, this type of ordnance is very effective against men, but a mortar is needed."

"Your Highness might demolish the walls with such a weapon if you could calculate the trajectory by means of a quadrant, and bring the force of the granados on to the top of the walls." I was remembering Ferdinand Stanhope, word for word.

He looked at me curiously. "Very good. Very good, Doctor Tom. Do you know of such a piece?"

"A mortor? There was Roaring Meg at Hopton Heath."

"But I think I must employ even more subtle methods. Your notion of coming at them from above is good, but I think I must find another angle."

The guns had been shrewdly placed so that the gunners and matrosses were out of range of Colonel Russell's muskets. A group of his men were standing on what was clearly a platform which had been constructed behind the North Wall, and which explained Eleanour's ability to climb and descend with such ease last night.

"Your Highness, have a care. The Colonel will have placed his marksmen there." A pleasant faced man warned Rupert.

"Has he so, Colonel Gerrard? No, by God's wounds and I am a marksman also." He seized a fire-lock pistol from a soldier standing beside him, saw that it was primed, ran a few paces forward, and aimed at the jeering group, steadying his right arm with his left hand and fired.

There was a shout, "Jesu! He's winged me!" and another cry, "It's Rupert!" The Parliament men swiftly disappeared and Rupert strolled back

He ordered the culverins to cease firing.

"You have done well, good lads all, but the walls are too thick, I think." The gunners nodded sadly, and sat down to eat and drink. The Prince and I retraced our steps to the town by the field route.

"Your Highness, may I speak freely?" I asked.

"Certainly, you may."

"What form is the curtailment of my liberty to take? I ask because I have a recently orphaned fourteen year old boy in my care. We were staying with Peabody at the George. In fact I am promised to take the boy to dine with friends."

"What friends?"

"The lady is from the Low Countries, the mother of the Newsbook printer I was speaking to last night. Her husband was an actor, and there are two small children, orphaned by the plague."

He was silent and I suddenly realised why.

"Your Highness, will you accompany me?"

"With all my heart, Doctor Tom. It is a great pleasure to speak my own tongue."

I pleaded with him to be allowed back to the George. I wished Emily to heat some water for me to wash my person in, before we went to dine. I did not like the way I smelled. Cornelia's expression when she had taken my old hose for washing had alerted me to my condition.

"Well, it is true that you stink worse than several dead dogs," the Prince admitted with truth if not courtesy, "These two will accompany you."

So there was another expense for me. Pots of ale for my bodyguard whilst I removed the dirt of several days. It was well over a week since I had washed myself thoroughly. I had clean small clothes and, with new hose, there was not a sweeter smelling youth in the whole of Lichfield, after Emily had brought up several buckets of hot and cold water and I had anointed myself with her strong smelling black soap. Peabody and Abram came back whilst I was combing through the tangles of my hair.

"Jesu, who is this whoremaster from a pushing school?" cried Peabody. I pretended that I had not heard him. It seemed he had been included in the invitation. I was still amazed that the Prince should wish to dine with us, but then remembered he had been pleased to consort with Richard Foley, Master Brindley's son in law, in whose workshops I had considerable financial interest. Where there is good food and wine and even better company, princes think no scorn to grace such tables with their presence.

As we entered at the sign of the Barrel, the Prince stopped in surprise. "It is Prospero!" he cried and grasped Gabriel by his arms, "Oh dear old friend. "Our revels now are ended." This was a terrible blow to close down the Kings' Men."

"Your Highness!" said Gabriel, wreathed in smiles, trying to bow. I was reminded of the scene where Hamlet greets the Players, except it was not a Prince of Denmark we had in our company, but of the Rhineland. Cornelia in her best bronze silk gown, welcoming him in his own tongue completed his satisfaction. I was again restored to her favour. She stood near me, sniffed and said approvingly, "That is better." When I thought how tolerating I had been of their shabbiness when they had lived at Cabbage Court, I felt slightly aggrieved. But Cornelia somehow had maintained a high standard for herself even there. I accepted my clean hose humbly and thanked her, meek as a maid.

After we had dined little Lizzie insisted on being taken on the Prince's knee, whence she surveyed the company like a miniature Queen. Then she turned to him and put her little hand on his face and asked trustingly, "Are you our Daddy?" He replied, "Alas, no, sweetheart. Would that I were!" I found myself gazing at him, having to remind myself, this is the fiend who fired Birmingham.

I was allowed to sleep back at the George, but Rupert told me that from tomorrow a room had been prepared for me at Sir Richard Dyott's. After we had said all our Farewells and were standing outside the house in a light rain, he arranged some kind of rendezvous with Peabody for the morrow at the back of the Close.

"They will be here before dark. Can you arrange quarters?" and Peabody's somewhat less than enthusiastic response, "I will try."

The next day was like unto one of those children's games where everyone changes places. Abram much to the delight of Hodge and Lizzie was to stay at the sign of the Barrel, and Peabody and I were found fine bedchambers in poor Sir Richard Dyott's house. I had wondered where the owner of the house was, and was told he had been imprisoned in Coventry after Edgehill. I was fast realising that Rupert no longer mistrusted me, but that, given the hazards of his enterprise, a surgeon was a useful addition to his household.

As I climbed the stairs with my two saddle bags, containing those few possessions which were not on my back, I was brought to a stop. A presence stood before me, blocking my progress. I slowly looked up. He wore the most fashionable boots I had ever seen of softest leather. The tops were turned over to display lace cuffs. His breeches and doublet were of rose coloured velvet with dark green satin facings. He wore a deep lace collar, which was brushed by his thick light brown hair. A thin moustache adorned his upper lip, his eyes were wide, unusually wide. And his facial expression combined the innocence of the cherub and the steel of the dictator.

I wished very heartily to push past him perhaps administering a sharp kick to his calf in its luxurious boot as I did so, but some better judgement, Adam's advice, or perhaps the example of Peabody's judicious handling of this type of well-born wastrel prompted me to scuttle back down the stairs and to stand at the bottom, bowing like a foppish monkey and murmuring, "Forgive me my impertinence, my Lord!"

He paused at the foot of the stairs and not deigning to look at me, but gazing at some fascinating object over my right shoulder, proclaimed, "No harm done, I think!" and went his ways outdoors. This was my first encounter with George Digby, Second Earl of Bristol. If I had known then, what I later learned of him, and if my heart had been wholly with the King's cause, which it was not, I should have drawn my dagger, run him through the heart and deposited him on the nearest midden, fine leather boots and all.

The rain held off towards the end of the afternoon, and I went with Peabody across the fields to the back of the Close. A familiar figure was before us.

"Peabody!" he called in those strident tones, alike used to command and exact instant submission. It was the wellborn bore, Harry Hastings. I studied the horizon, and saw coming from the westwards, with the setting sun behind them, a troop of poor men, the like of whom I had not seen before. They were walking two by two along the track across the fields, in silence. I heard the sound of their feet, a soft shuffling noise as for the most part they were unshod. The older ones among them were cruelly stooped - these walked alongside younger men: all of them looked about in amazement and surprise, and began to speak pointing in disbelief at the Close as they neared it. They were guided by the Prince's Lifeguards who ensured that they did not stray too near Colonel Russell's musket balls. Some hundred yards behind them came some carts in which were stout staves and spades.

These men were clearly desperate poor. Their clothes were little better than rags, their faces black with engrained dirt. I understood. They represented the Prince's other "angle". They were miners and they had been brought to undermine the Close. But as they came closer I could see they were not only poor. Many of them were ill.

One or two coughed continually and to my horror where I had thought that those who were stooped were old, in truth this was not so. They were young men in misshapen bodies.

Rupert was surprised and to some degree distressed by what he saw. Mad Harry Hastings who had been to Cannock Chase, where coal mining was the main occupation, looked on his acquisition with pride.

"Your Highness," he cried, "here they are! Ready to work for one shilling a day which is twice what the mine owners give them. I promised them bed and board. Set Peabody here to work. Come Peabody! You have been idle long enough. Find them quarters."

"Master Peabody, could you do so?" Prince Rupert courteously requested.

"Yes, Highness." Peabody darted a thunderous look at Hastings. I walked over to accompany him and as I did so caught Hastings' attention.

"Hey, do I know you?" he cried, half recognising me from my doctoring of Sir Thomas Byron. I was taller than he. I drew myself up and looked down at him.

"No, my Lord, you do not know me!"

If he could not remember the man who had saved his friend's leg, then I preferred to forget him, the insolent clown.

Peabody had to move some of the Princes's followers from the Hartshorn and remembering the numbers I had tended there, had persuaded the landlady whose name I still did not know to put up all her trundle beds as she called them. We had accommodated about half of the poor miners and had to travel Lichfield knocking on doors to find more places where they could rest their heads. Few goodwives were willing to house such uncouth strangers, for be they never such good fellows, the ladies knew that the strong smell of coal dust clung to them and to everything they owned and touched. After having accompanied them round the town, I wondered if my serious washing of yestreen had been worth my efforts.

"I had thought you were Master of Foot or some such position. I did not know you were quartermaster."

"Neither did I!" said Peabody grimly.

In the end, he found a large empty stable, a quantity of sacks and some clean hay. Their commons this Sunday night were bread and cheese and small beer, but they made no complaint. "Yon one-eyed fartsy fellow promised us meat but 'tis the Sabbath, and we was not expected, like," said their spokesman. I told him I was a doctor and if any of his men became ill, I would tend them, although I could see that there were a host of respiratory problems with which they could challenge me.

"Nay, master, we'm well set for any working day. Not one of us is ailing!"

He was lying, I knew, but to tell truth was to lose money.... and a free meat dinner.

Next day I went to find the Prince at the back of the Close to see if his.... Back.... still needed attention.

"Later, later!" he told me but pointed out the workings that the miners had begun. It had been decided to try to make more than one tunnel and they were hard at it and already there were four deep pits, with piles of earth growing beside each one.

They had already drained the moat, a most unpleasant and noisome task. Earthworks were already being dug to divert the springs that fed it.

"They do not think it is difficult work. But by the same token if the ground is easily worked as this is, it can collapse."

I shuddered. "How deep will they go?" I asked looking down into a pit.

"They are hoping to find a seam of clay. It seems that gives stability. But they are happy. They do not think they have to mine deep into the ground. Deep in the earth, there are horrible dangers of which we know not, Doctor Tom."

I was not sure that I wanted to know. I heartily disliked the notion of being either high above everyone as I had been with dumb John Dyott on the Cathedral Tower, or deep in the bowels of the earth. The thought of either situation was to me anathema. My stomach churned as I contemplated being below the surface of the world we know. To be aware that there was a hideous weight of soil between my cowardly carcase and the blessed sun would be for me every moment a living death.

There was a call from below. The soil was becoming more difficult to dig as its consistency sswas becoming thicker. It seems there was clay below the pleasant pasture where lambs played and daisies grew. About ten men were now at the base of each hole, filling buckets with the earth which was fast becoming reddish in hue. Rupert's foot soldiers were detailed to carry the earth up from below. I suggested that they could dig steps into the side that had a gentler slope. Peabody clapped me on the back and selected pieces of wood that would serve this purpose.

"How be you, Doctor?" one of the miners who was taking a rest called to me.

"I am well, I thank you. And your good selves?" I strolled over to the group who were munching ruff-peck. My father had loved bacon, prepared in great lumps like this, but I found my stomach heaved at the prospect of it. They offered me a generous portion and I hope I did not shudder as I refused. I asked for a piece of bread from one of their loaves and an older man tore off a portion. I ate it as graciously as I could, coal dust and all.

"Are your sleeping quarters to your satisfaction?" I asked politely. They assented and one said, "'Tis not one's own home, but it be snug enough, master."

"Do you think you can mine as far as the Close?"

"To that gurt wall?" one asked.

"Aye, just so."

"Nothing easier, master. 'Tis no distance."

Then they told me that in the mine workings where they worked daily, they were in constant danger. The workings were old and sometimes the wood of the props that held up the tunnels had rotted which could lead to the collapse of the roof. Sometimes they told me, pockets of noxious air, "choke damp" they called it, could be released to kill men who breathed this poison. And sometimes water, seeping into the mine shafts and tunnels, after heavy rain could cause the collapse of a wall in an abandoned area of the mine. This water could become a fatal flood, pouring along the workings and drowning unsuspecting miners.

"And every day you rise and put your lives in danger so that miserable creatures like me can have coal and be warm." In truth these men were braver than any soldier I had met. They pitted their resolve and courage against the earth itself.

The men to whom I had been talking now deemed that their rest period was over. I followed them and watched them pick up their spades. The tunnels at the base of the holes were starting to take shape. I was surprised to learn that the miners had to be reliable carpenters also, and had to construct the wooden frames that hold up the weight of earth inside the tunnels themselves. The foot soldiers who had been ordered to help the miners, were now a competent chain,constantly removing the buckets of earth.

I stood at the top of one of their workings and gazed at them in admiration. Behind me voices were suddenly raised. I recognised the Prince.

"I tell you, you have already done enough damage. A lesson, a show of strength is one thing, but arson, where women and children die and all go homeless is not in my doctrine. That was ill done, George!"

"I did not know your Highness was so nice in your sympathies to the rebels."

"Did you not? And another thing you did not know. The houses you ordered to be burnt. Some were the homes of good men who had shown themselves loyal to my uncle. Not now. Not after the indiscriminate destruction of their homes."

"Could have been merely a handful, Your Highness. But I repeat. Why use these dirty creatures? Use your guns. Bring them closer to the walls. You have men enough to man them."

"Aye, and watch them stand in line to be shot by Russell's marksmen? These are your countrymen! Thank God, I command here and not you!"

I heard no more as they moved away. I watched the progress of the tunnels each day. Rupert went down every one to inspect the work, and came out well pleased with progress but white faced and retching at the foulness of the air. On Wednesday 12th April, there were a series of explosions behind the walls on the north side. I was standing beside Peabody, who swore pleasantly and kindly explained.

"We can't expect Russell to do nothing, not a seasoned campaigner like him, God rot him."

"What is he doing?"

"We have mines so he is mining too. Perhaps to intercept these poor lads underground. Jesu, what a prospect!" Rupert was nearby frowning at the unusual noise. Peabody told him his theory and suggested that the Prince recommenced firing at the walls as a diversion tactic, perhaps at strategic points all round the Close.

"The bastard needs some alternative pastimes to occupy his

leisure hours, Your Highness. The South Gate, the drawbridge, cannot be strong, Sir. Brooke and then Gell gave it a rare good pounding. Tom and I were behind it, and saw it shake and splinter."

"Why have you taken so long to remember to tell me this?" asked the Prince waspishly.

"My duties as Quartermaster to the Royal Miners have given me little leisure to advise you as to strategy." said Peabody, angrily, taking pepper with the rose.

I gasped and my face must have given away my apprehension, as I waited for the Prince's wrath to fall on Peabody. But he merely laughed and ordered one of the demi-culverins to be wheeled round to Dam Street and set up carefully so that there might be safe cover for the gunners. The other demi-culverin was taken in the opposite direction and set up in the field to the west of the Close, aiming across Bird Street, between a gap in the little houses that lined the road to the North West.

He ordered the largest of the guns to remain where it was and to continue to pound the North Wall. So the thunderous noise of the explosions continued during the next few days, disturbing yet again the peace of the long suffering citizens of Lichfield.

And then on Saturday the 15th, the bombardment met with success.... of a sort. A breach was made, not in the portal, but slightly to the side. Debris showered the road where the causeway ran from Dam Street to the gate itself. Peabody was for continuing the assault as the breach was small and only a very few men would have got through, to their almost certain death. It would not have been possible for many to have supported them as the followers on the Causeway would have been picked off by Russell's musketeers. There was a Council of War of sorts with three of Rupert's Colonels of Horse, Hastings and Lord George Digby. Peabody also was allowed to attend, and brought me in with him, saying to Rupert, "Doctor Tom has a practical head on his shoulders." I think the chamber we sat in was almost certainly the one in which Sir Neddy and I sat blindfold and Sir John tried to deceive us that Lord Brooke still lived.

Lord George was determined that as there was now a breach, it must be utilised. Peabody and two of the Colonels were all for continuing to enlarge the breach that had already been made. "The Walls are gradually weakening, Sir, in the places where they are being attacked." said Peabody.

"No, no, no!" George Digby was not interested in the notion of caution and prudence. "It's necessary to give the men some sort of encouragement so that they are heartened in their efforts."

"So what is your idea, then?" asked the Prince. "I must tell you I am not intending to support a plan that involves needless loss of life."

"Ah, Your Highness!" said Digby, "ever the philanthropist! I say we should call for a "verloren hoop" and there will be a purse of twenty guineas for the first five men through the breach, which I will personally supply."

"What say you, Peabody?" asked the Prince.

"I say his Lordship will not lose his money. They will be dead in seconds, and any that come behind. We must wait for more points of access, Your Highness, before we charge. We must confound them by more than one point of entry at once. It is folly to encourage good brave lads to risk certain death in his Lordship's way. There are bound to be some hotheads that will take up this desperate challenge. I would remind Your Highness it is only a matter of time before the tunnels come to the foundations of the Close. Patience and strategy serve our turn better than greed and heedless loss of life. The odds against this assault succeeding are as naught, Your Highness."

"Hastings?" the Prince asked.

"Oh, I'm with Peabody. Only a fool would ignore his experience." Harry Hastings ascended somewhat in my estimation. Colonel Wagstaffe also counselled caution, but Colonel Usher said slowly, "Well, perhaps there is no harm in ascertaining whether there are men who would do it."

Peabody sighed loudly. The Prince said, "Well, Yes. Let us see then. Perhaps, Peabody, we have no right to stand between our bravest fellows and this little fortune that they can earn."

The enterprise would have to be conducted by men on foot. In the end it was decided that a troop of thirty should storm over the Causeway and through the breach. Cavalry men could join the troop if they wished. Only a handful did so. One of Rupert's regiments was lined up beside the Cross to follow on, if the first thirty got in.

Peabody tried again to dissuade Rupert.

"Sir, this is veritable madness. They have not the ghost of a chance. Do you think Russell has not noticed that there is a breach?"

Digby was standing near. "Come now Master Peabody. We are the foxes, rampaging into the chicken house."

"Do you think so, Sir?" said Peabody courteously. "I fear matters are somewhat reversed. We are the chickens jumping onto the butcher's slab."

"Doctor Tom, will you hold yourself in readiness by the Cross?" asked Rupert. "You are not to venture upon the Causeway. No sense in sacrificing our surgeon."

I was in complete agreement with him.

Finally the thirty men were ready, muskets primed. Ten of them carried ladders but the remaining twenty were to attempt the breach itself. Digby held up the five purses of gold that he would present at the conclusion of the assault.

The whole attempt was a complete failure from start to finish. As the thirty men rushed out onto the Causeway, the firing began from the walls and the tower.

About twenty men prudently dropped back, others lay where they were shot, two or three staggered and fell into the sludge of the Minster Pool, but three foolhardy fellows ran safely over with a ladder, which they propped up against the wall under the breach.

Peabody stood with his eyes closed. "This is bloody suicide." Alas, so it proved. Two of them hurled themselves head first through the hole. God knows what horrors awaited. The third teetered on the ledge and having more thought for his comrades shouted back, "Don't follow!" Unnecessary advice. No-one was following. He fell into the void.

A moment later we saw him again. I had forgotten Sir John Gell's moveable gallows....the Sugar Plum. It was pushed to the gate where there had been the viewing platform built by Lord Chesterfield's men. The brave unfortunate soldier was pushed up onto the platform, his arms tied behind him, and the noose from the gallows swiftly placed round his neck. A sign was given to those who pushed the monstrous contraption from below, it was moved backwards and his legs kicked vainly for purchase and then as his neck broke, mercifully he became still.

We were silent but Russell's men were not. "Shoot him down,

Rupert!" they chorused. "Come and shoot him down!"

Rupert was white with fury. "When I take this Close, not one of you devils will have quarter! May God damn me else!" he shouted across the Causeway. They jeered and mocked, continuing to invite him to shoot the poor victim down.

Peabody and I stood silently whilst Rupert cursed the men of Parliament for murdering swine. Hastings tried to reason with him, saying that the best way of continuing was to widen the breach. The Colonels looked at each other, speechless.

Digby, however, was not given to punishing himself with conscience stricken homilies.

He looked round at the assembled commanders and smiled.

"Well, dinner-time, I think," he observed pleasantly and disappeared in the direction of Sir Richard Dyott's house.

"Why did I not listen to your wise counsel, Peabody?" Rupert cried.

"I cannot tell, Your Highness," said Peabody modestly.

I thought I had better visit first the poor horses and then Abram. The ostler at the George told me that all the horses in town were restless, hating the constant pounding of the guns. Jupiter and Hector nuzzled at my hands as I gave them carrots, but poor Old Harry seemed lifeless and Babs too was not happy at her forced period of inactivity.

Abram was happiness itself with Gabriel and Cornelia. He assisted them with the children, entertaining them and diverting them from quarrels and ill-temper.

"Would you consider allowing him to remain here with us?" Gabriel asked, when he and I were sitting at our ease. Abram had gone into the town on an errand for Cornelia. I did not think I could do that. In one way I had made an unspoken promise to Joseph to care for his son, and although there was a certain temptation in allowing Abram to remain where he was manifestly happy, I felt that perhaps I was more likely to find him a trade than Gabriel and Cornelia. Abram had very little money, a few needle-cases and little Shireen. I had to help him make his way in life.

The problem solved itself. When he returned with his purchases and saw me waiting to see him, his face lit up with relief so that I sensed he would not wish me to leave him behind.

"What happened today, Tom? The chandler said something

about an attack on the Close, and a man hanged. I was afraid…."

"What were you afraid of, Abram?"

"I was afraid that it was you."

I was moved by his youthful concern. "I can promise you one thing, Abram. I will never willingly put myself in the way of being hanged. I fear you will have to continue to accept me as your guardian or elder brother if you wish to throw in your lot with me."

He nodded and Gabriel said, "Well no doubt we shall see you again should you visit Lichfield in the future," and the conversation lapsed.

The next day was the second Sabbath of Prince Rupert's sojourn in Lichfield. Peabody and I walked over the fields to the mine workings. Our path was already clearly trodden just out of musket shot from the Close. Today the shouts of derision from the South Eastern Gate where the poor corpse still hanged, seemed louder and harsher than ever. As we crossed Gaia Lane and came to the workings, the Prince met us.

"Doctor Tom! Thank God! I must tell you what has occurred. Our miners suddenly broke into Russell's workings. There was a battle, Tom, can you believe under ground!"

I stared at him in horror.

"How many dead, Sir?" asked Peabody wearily.

"None, by a miracle. The foot men carrying for the miners luckily had their muskets just in case of such a contingency. Shots were exchanged, and a portion of the roof fell down. Russell's men took fright at this and retired and our lads came out, filthy and bleeding. But there are two wounded miners still in there, Tom. It's thought they are wounded in the leg. They need your skills. How can we get them out?"

17

"I must have two trestles to try to carry them from the tunnel," I explained." If you cannot find those, then make up two moving beds. Two poles with firm cloth tied securely between. In fact they are better than trestles, if you can make or find them."

Rupert nodded. "We can make what you describe." A quartermaster was dispatched to find this method of transporting the sick.

"Where are they to go afterwards, so I can treat them?"

"Oh, Sir Richard's," said Rupert airily.

I had my box with me. "I think," I said "if I shall not frighten them, I would like to tie a handkerchief over my nose and mouth. How high is the ceiling where they were injured?"

"I understand about five feet, and there was a candle burning when the wounded troopers left the place." Rupert had at least discovered what he could about the conditions of the miners. I nodded.

"Can others follow me to pull them out of the tunnel, when you have assembled the moving beds?"

Peabody nodded. "I will do that."

One of the older miners had been listening to our conversation.

"You need to be desperate careful, master, or you'll have the roof down on you all. There was a bit of a fall when they started banging with the guns. One of our fellers was half buried. We'd have gone in to clear it but any moving in there could end it all"

I must have looked desperate. He went on, "Best if you go in on your own. Puts less strain like on the roof."

All I could think was "Jesu, help me. Jesu, save me!" and I was one with little or no faith.

"How far in is it?"

Rupert had asked these questions. "Almost at the wall. Russell's men went under it. Their tunnel creeps up into ours."

I looked him in the eye. I was one of very few men who could do that. "Oh, Christ, Rupert, what have I undertaken to do?"

"I can't leave them to die, a living grave. Forgive me."

I nodded. I forgave him. I would have done the same. I took off my doublet, which he took from me, saying, "I'll take care of that." I removed my shirt, which I tied somehow over my mouth and nose. I picked up the lantern and with that in one hand and my box in the other was about to start.

"Is there a long rope I could tie round my waist?"

They found one but it would not stretch all the way. It was agreed that Peabody should follow me to the point where the rope stopped. He would pull on it twice when the beds arrived and I would come back for them.

"Come on then!" I thought of something. "What's your Christian name?"

He laughed. "I'll tell you in the tunnel."

The rope was coiled in a knot round my waist. I would have to go first, letting it trail behind me. Peabody would follow, at a distance, holding the end. I had to progress with my back stooped at a painful angle. If I attempted to stand up, the back of my head and shoulders came into grievous contact with the roof of the tunnel. And yet there was something reassuring in the firmness of the impacted earth above me. It had held steady for the miners until fools had begun shooting. The lantern showed the walls ever diminishing inwards and downwards. I had to marvel though at the masterly craft that had built this tunnel and had made it safe. We were in clay which the miners had told me was easier to work but less secure than rock.

There was a tug round my waist. Peabody had started in after me. I managed to walk another twenty yards but after that contact with the roof was almost continual. I would have to crawl. I could manage either the lantern or the box in my hands before me. The air was not foul so I removed my shirt, twisted it into some kind of rope and tied my box, through one of the handles at the side, to the rope that was round my waist and dragged it after me. My progress was tortuously slow. It seemed to me that I must have crawled under the Cathedral, below the market, and be nearly at the end of the town.

There was a faint noise ahead of me. I strained my eyes beyond the circle of lantern light. I could see nothing but the noise came again. It was a hiss. A whisper.

"Master, hush there!"

I understood and tried to crawl on as quiet as I could. The lantern light was blocked. A solid wall of dank clay lay ahead. And there they were. An older man half buried from the waist down under the tunnel wall on my left and before me, what seemed to be a bleeding corpse. A young man, very young, little more than a child in fact had an open wound across his thigh. I moved his head slightly. He had also a most ugly injury on his scalp.

"Can you get him out? He's alive," whispered the older man.

"What's his name?" I asked.

"It's Frank, Frank Starkey. Not so loud. Can you get him out?"

I untied my shirt from my box. A strange plan was forming in my mind. If I could get Frank to Peabody, I could come back and perhaps displace the clay pinning down the other miner.

"What is your name?"

"I'm John Starkey. I'm his uncle. Don't pay heed to me. My ankle's crushed under here. I've had more lives than ten cats."

The boy groaned. I spoke to him close to his ear.

"Frank? Can you hear me?"

His eyelids flickered but I could judge, nay I hoped, his condition was far from hopeless.

The ground on which I knelt was hard but it was not unyielding rock. I reasoned that if I could make a blanket of my clothes on which I could drag poor Frank, I could get him to Peabody. I stripped off my breeches and tying my shirt on top of them contrived to make some kind of a pad on which his back and backside could rest. The difficulty would be in pulling him onto my garments. But that was almost the easiest part of all. There was nothing of him. Even cruelly stooped as I was, I could lift him onto my clothes. They would be worn through before I got to Peabody, but with luck the beds would be in the tunnel with him by then. I gave two tugs on the rope. There was an answering tightening round my waist.

"John," I whispered. "I'll leave the lantern. I'll be back."

"Master, don't fret yourself! Look after the boy!"

I had to crawl backwards now with less protection for my knees. At first it was not so desperate hard perhaps because I could see the

288

lantern I was leaving and its gleam gave some comfort. I had travelled perhaps ten yards when there was another sound from the lighted area ahead. It was a sprinkling noise like rain, which grew into something of a rush. It was the ceiling falling again. But the sound faded and the lantern still gave out its comfortable glow.

I remained still for a moment and then risked a whisper.

"Is all well with you?"

The answering whisper was as faint as a breath of air.

"Yesssss."

If my progress to find the men had been desperate slow, returning was like being transformed into a snail. I tugged twice on the rope and received an answering pull. My feet had to be my eyes. I dare not crawl back quickly lest I made dangerous contact with the sides of the tunnel. The light before me slowly faded, and it was not merely my knees that were suffering. My elbows and arms were slowly being scraped raw. I tugged again and felt the rope's tension. Peabody was clearly collecting in the rope at the same rate of progress as I was making.

I wondered what Peabody's Christian name was and hoped it was something fantastical from the old Testament like Obadiah or Habakkuk. I began to think of moments that had amused me in the last few months but so often these thoughts brought back memories of Elijah. My situation was now closely akin to his. That in its way had its own grim humour.

I rested for a moment and tried not to think of my torn and bloody limbs. At least I was whole. I remembered the thought that had sustained me when I had had to lurk in the filthy River Ray. "I'm not dead. I just smell as if I was." Somehow that amused me more than anything. There was pressure round my waist again. I gave two little tugs and continued. After several more moments of tormenting movement, I paused again. I thought I had heard something behind me. I listened. It was my name.

I pulled again on what would have been a light burden above ground and slowly edged us both into the light. Only the rays of another lantern but to me it was like the brightest sun. Peabody and two troopers were waiting where the tunnel became somewhat higher.

"This is Frank Starkey," I told them. They had two moveable beds, and somehow we pulled the poor boy onto one of them. "Listen," I told them, "Go for Jacky at the Hartshorn. He knows my practices with the sick. This boy is to go to Sir Richard Dyott's house. Rupert promised it. Boiled water for cleansing."

"What of the other man?" asked Peabody.

"I hope he still lives. I don't think the air is bad, but he is under a mound of clay and earth. It would be better if a miner came down to go with me."

"We'll get one."

"Yes, only one. Extreme caution is needed or the whole roof will topple. And bring blankets and spades." They set off through the tunnel, just able to walk upright carrying Frank.

I examined my clothes. They were in a fearsome state. Still there was little choice so I put them on again.

I looked at Peabody. I had never seen him look so diminished. He was staring at me with something akin to wonder.

"What's amiss?" I asked him "And what's your name?"

"I'll tell you when we get out."

One of the troopers had left a little bread and there was some ale in a bellarmine. I drank thirstily which was probably a mistake. After what seemed an eternity but was probably only minutes, we could see a light coming towards us from the outside world. A miner came cautiously into our sight, followed by the same two troopers.

"What's your name?" I asked him.

"Stephen Dilkes, master."It was the man who had warned me that I would do best if I went alone.

"John Starkey is lying, his lower half under a pile of earth down the tunnel," I told him. "He told me his ankle is crushed. As I see it, our problem is not getting to him. It is getting him out from under the clay. There is room beside him for the earth now that his nephew has gone, but if we try to move it, will more come down?"

He nodded. "It'll be powerful difficult, master. Can he help himself at all?"

"I don't know. His only injury as far as I know is his ankle. As I brought Frank away, the roof pattered down, but I don't think he is in worse case. He spoke and I could see that the lantern was still lit."

"Well, let's be about it, master. The longer he's there, the worse for him."

The second journey down the tunnel did not seem so painful on my head and shoulders, possibly because my knees and elbows were so sore. We carried the bed between us, rolled up under our right arms. I persuaded myself that I was an ape with hands that brushed the floor. Stephen coming behind me was in better shape as he was not so tall, but like me we both had to crawl eventually. I was overjoyed to see the faint beam of the lantern. By unspoken agreement we left the bed in the tunnel. I edged myself forward into the area past John where Frank had been lying and Stephen a few yards behind me, came to a stop and picked up John's hand.

"How do you, Johnny?" he whispered.

"I been better, Steve."

"We'll have you out, no question!"

"Oh, ah! How?"

Steve stood and softly examined the soil, which lay on John's torso. The roof where I was and where young Frank had lain had held up, but where John was, it had broken free of the wooden struts which hung uselessly down. Steve looked carefully where the roof was good, and came past me to where the tunnel was completely blocked.

"Did the other fellows get out? The fellows you ran into?"

"As far as I know." whispered John, "To tell truth, Steve, I ain't much teased about that."

"This seam might hold." Steve whispered.

"What do you mean?" I asked him.

"Some fool shot a musket ball through the clay. Leastways I think that's what's happened. We're not far from the surface. This soil has come through the clay.

But the clay be holding. It's come down in big lumps here but I don't think there's more to come. Or it would have come. You and me has got to move it powerful slow and powerful careful. I'll start and when I think it's safe for you to move it, I'll rest and you can do it. I have to start at the top. It's not the clay that's our enemy. It's the light stuff, the soil."

He took hold of a great piece of clay and gently teased it out of the pile. He laid it in the clear space between us and then moved to remove the next piece with his back to me. He was right. There was a space where the struts hung free. The layer of clay had come down but the earth above seemed stable and constant.

I began to help him move the clods. I had to be delicate and quiet in my movements and this was back breaking work for me. As I could not stand upright, the pain from my bent spine was as if I had been crushed double on the rack. Steven saw my torment.

"When you rest, lie flat," he counselled me. The first time I rested in that way I had to stretch myself out very slowly. When at last I stood up to help again, my body seemed to have reconciled itself to the searing discomfort. I lit another candle for the lantern.

We were making progress of a kind. John did not or could not encourage us. "You'm fools, both on you!" he said once. "Go whilst you can!" He lapsed into some kind of sleep, but when I felt his neck, his heart was still beating strongly. It must have taken us several hours. It felt like weeks but at last the pile of earth and clay had been painstakingly moved from off his broken ankle.

"Could you ease yourself out on your arms and arse?" I whispered to John. He had woken some time before and had viewed our progress with amazement. "We can carry you, if we can get you beyond the lantern."

He smiled. "I'll see the wench again," and slowly he heaved himself alongside the bed, away from the gaping roof. Steve opened up the bed and John rolled himself onto the linen sheet. I rescued my box, which John offered to carry in his arms. We decided to leave the lantern.

I tugged twice on my rope and was pleased to feel the answering tightening. Peabody was still half way down the tunnel.

"Slow and steady wins the race," said Steve, and we picked up the handles. I went backwards so that Peabody could gather in the rope without it tangling in Steve's feet.

We had gone about twenty yards down the tunnel when there was the same spattering noise I had heard before from the area we had left. The trickling, dripping noise became a rush and a roar and a wave of choking dust came from the place where we had been. The lantern went out behind us.

"That's not the clay falling, son. That's the bastard soil. It suffocates a man. Best stand a moment," Steve advised. So we stood crouched in the dark. I was all for running like a craven pissabreech, but I obeyed. The dust must have settled. I tugged twice and felt the solace of Peabody's response.

"It's started raining!" said Steve.

"How do you know?" I asked him.

"That's what's brought the soil down, back there. The clay was holding, see. I was mortal scared it'd start whiles we was down there."

We picked John up again and shuffled along. I was destined it seemed always to creep backwards through these tunnels. Again I was seeing with my feet. We would have lost the lantern light anyway by this.

"Why is the air not foul?" I asked Stephen.

"Because they broke through to them others earlier, didn't they? There'd be a draught right through. I tell you what, master. I'm a deal happier now than what I were afore."

I could not but agree.

We edged slowly into the lantern light. Peabody and the troopers were waiting, their mouths agape. "What was that roaring noise?" Peabody asked.

"'Twas the roof falling in after we'd got 'im out. It's raining see."

"How did you do it, Tom?" asked Peabody, clearly delighted and relieved to be destined for "the world up atop."

"Quarter staff champion!" I said airily.

The outside world was a rainbow of glittering colour, even though as Stephen had predicted, it was raining. Rupert was waiting for us, the rain running down his black hair. He held me for a moment like a father, handed me my doublet and told me he would hear the details later. Jacky had been sent for and there were pans of boiled water at Sir Richard Dyott's house. The troopers had set off with John Starkey and I followed. My shirt was in tatters, my breeches had been worn through (on both knees and arse) and my hose hung in filthy rags over my shoon.

Who should I meet as I went in the door of Sir Richard Dyott's house, but Lord George Digby, scurrilous Machiavellian politician and popinjay. He stopped. I bowed as profound as I could and murmured "My Lord. You do me too much honour."

"Why?" he said.

"You said "Why?" my Lord. You spoke to me, worm that I am." I passed on, up the stairs, laughing heartily. Perhaps I would not have been so saucy with these great lords if I were not now secure in the friendship of a prince.

Jacky had already achieved a great deal with the patients. Frank had regained consciousness and had been told what had occurred. He would recover. His wounds, a sword cut to his thigh, which had bled copiously, and a blow to his head where he had fallen, had been dressed competently and cleanly.

John's ankle presented difficulty in that there was nothing to be usefully done I thought that the ankle bone had been fractured and also I thought the tarsal bone had broken. He could move his toes which was a good sign. We decided to bandage the foot firmly in the hope that any cracks would be pressed into place. He was ordered to keep his leg horizontal.

"You'm telling me to lie still and not walk? Doctor's orders? By the masskin, Doctor, you'm givin me a gurt merry playtime, an no mistake! You'm been and saved my life to make a gentleman of me."

He laughed pleasantly and when Stephen said if I would come to Cannock there would be a drink there for me, John interrupted with, "A drink? Nay son, there's a whole bloody alehouse, if you can drink it."

"But it was Stephen Dilkes here who saved you. He knew it was safe to move the earth."

They both laughed and Stephen told me, "I only knew it was safe as you'm been in there first, master. I wouldna ha gone in for this gurt lummox, without knowing it be safe. If a two yard bean pole can go there and fetch out Frankie, then there was some hope I'd get out!" They roared with laughter at my expression. I did not know how far this was a serious jest.

I needed to make yet another visit to the mercer. My doublet was passable, but my breeches would have been disdained by a scarecrow. I had other pairs of hose but my shirt was in ribbons. I went to my room and after asking for hot water for myself, washed all parts including my hair with some lavender soap a maid found for me.

A knock came to the door. Rupert bustled in as I was holding up my tattered breeches to the light.

"Devil take it Tom! That was a monstrous great fart ruined those! Do you need clothes? Peabody and you are to eat dinner here in an hour with me, and the others. I have clothes to give you. Peabody says you are something of a goldfinch. Why do you not buy more? What do you need? Breeches and shirts?" A servant was called.

"You are a hero, you know," he told me. "The miners will do anything for you now. Do you think you could find out if they can tell me where I can get gunpowder?"

"Stephen Dilkes is here with John and Frank Starkey, the men who were injured. Why not ask him now?"

He went his ways as his servant returned with white lawn shirts and breeches of the galliguskins style. I was not personally enamoured of this fashion but beggars cannot be choosers, and if these breeches were good enough for a Prince then I was pleased enough to accept and wear them with a good grace.

At the dinner I sat next to Colonel Wagstaffe, a most affable Cavalier. His name seemed somehow familiar and I suddenly remembered the Landlady in Stratford who had been so zealous after Colonel Wagstaffe's gunpowder, and who had blamed me for its explosive disappearance.

"Might you be the same Colonel Wagstaffe?" I asked politely.

He looked at me and winked. "I might!" he replied.

Rupert heard us "Jesu, Joseph. I wish we had that gunpowder now. We will abandon the three workings that are to the west and put all our efforts into the most easterly tunnel. I am convinced that due to the lie of the land and our earth works our efforts there are not visible from the Close. I tell you, Joseph, I shall send you to Cannock with Hastings tomorrow with good Stephen Dilkes to bring back supplies of gunpowder."

"It will be my pleasure, Your Highness," said the agreeable Colonel.

Lord Hastings was staring at me with his one eye. He suddenly remarked, "I do know you!"

"Do you, My Lord?" I replied pleasantly.

"You are the Jack Surgeon who wanted to cut off Tommy Byron's leg, are you not?"

This was preposterous! He could not have insulted me more if he'd said my father was a whoremaster, and my mother a drab. I was so overcome by his ability to twist reality that I could not reply. I merely gazed at him, more in sorrow than in anger. The man was a buffoon! Peabody however, ever my loyal friend would not allow the noble lord to condemn me so falsely.

"Alas, my Lord, I fear that the heat and extremities of battle caused your memory to play you false. Doctor Tom here saved Sir

Thomas Byron's leg. He would not allow it to be cut off when others thought it was the only course of action."

"Ah, that was the way it was, was it? In any event last I heard he was hopping about as merry as a pig in pease straw."

I found my voice, "I rejoice to hear it, my Lord."

Rupert now held court. "Tom, your exploits today have made you a hero with both the miners and my Foot. We should pass round a bumper to your prosperity. How say you, gentlemen?"

"Your Highness," I interposed, modest as a simpering milkmaid, "in fact I did nothing that any man round this table could not have done. The doctoring was done here. It could not have been done in the tunnel. Releasing the men from their underground tomb could have been effected by anyone with an ounce of resourcefulness."

"Strange to say, Tom," said Rupert, "there were no offers from round this table to undertake your task. In fact, my Lord Digby, what was it you said after Peabody had gone in after Tom? Something to the effect, "as well, wall them up now and save the cost of burials," I think."

It was my turn now to restrain and curb my good friend, Peabody, who had stiffened with anger. Others round the table showed signs of distaste and repugnance for George Digby's heartlessness. A knight on the Prince's right hand, whose name I later learned was Will Legge, half rose, his hand on his scabbard

"Indeed, my Lord Digby, I shared your despair and hopelessness at the seeming enormity of the task," I said quickly, "but all emerged alive and like to continue so. Your Highness," I went on, as good a smooth, silver tongued sycophant as any round that table, "may I ask that a toast be drunk to my betrothed, Lady Phoebe Stanhope, and to her great-uncle the Earl of Chesterfield?"

And so the endless dinner, with all its undercurrents of malice and jealousy drew to a close. There was no disguising the fact that Rupert was a consummate politician, anxious to demonstrate the personal enmity of George Digby. The Prince had subtly demeaned him by merely telling the truth. Digby had remained largely silent, aware of his lack of popularity, but unperturbed by it.

Next day we were told a supply of gunpowder had arrived from Oxford with a request that should any remain it might be returned. Will Legge kept the budge barrels in a shed on Sadler Street, closely guarded. I took the liberty of suggesting that the guards were discouraged from smoking. He thanked me for my caution but had already ascertained that that danger would be averted On Wednesday Hastings brought more barrels from Cannock, and on Wednesday afternoon, we were told that the miners thought that they were under the wall in the easterly tunnel. Peabody and I walked round to the field to watch the barrels being rolled down the tunnel. They would be stacked up in the underground chamber which, it was calculated, was under the Close wall.

Rupert was now impatient to be free of Lichfield. His uncle had summoned him to Reading.

"Pray God, these pigeons of gunpowder come home to roost," said Peabody. We were walking home from Frog Lane. We had gone to visit Gabriel and Cornelia, but they were somewhat apprehensive as to the fate of Ralph and Eleanour. All in the town knew that there was like to be explosions and fighting at the Close. Ralph's parents had not seen him since the day he had reproached me for my treatment of him. As far as they knew the printing press had been set up in one of the homes of a curate. I shared their anxiety. Eleanour's safety was the reason I had come to Lichfield. When? A scant two months ago. As we walked back to Sadler Street, in the twilight we were aware of the silent movements of troops, running quietly through the streets and creeping softly into their appointed vantage points round the Close.

"Are you not then on duty?" I asked him.

"Tomorrow morning." he told me." Let the commanders of the Horse bear the brunt. This is the Cavalry, greedy for glory. The Foot stand in readiness as support. I will wake you before dawn."

So I went round to the field at the back of the Close, just as streaks of light were appearing in the direction of Derbyshire. The Commanders and the miners too were gathered round the entrance of the final tunnel. In the half light a figure whom I thought I recognised walked carefully into the tunnel carrying a lighted brand. About three minutes later he emerged without it.

"I've done it!" he shouted. "Get down!" It was Colonel Wagstaffe.

We waited. Nothing. Colonel Wagstaffe had come to crouch beside us. The silence extended, and the first rays of a golden sun touched the trees, along the edge of the field. From the town there were the first stirrings of another day. "Fresh milk, maids" came the sing-song voice of a girl from the dairy, starting on her rounds. There was the faint noise of wheels on the cobbles as market women came in to town to set up their stalls.

And then the world changed! I had heard the thunder of Roaring Meg at Hopton Heath, and the cannonade of the guns at Edgehill had been horrible beyond description. But this was prolonged and appalling. There was one great explosion at first and then as barrel after barrel caught, debris was flung into the air. And not merely shards of stone and wood. Sentries who had been posted by Russell outside the Close met their deaths instantly. Fragments of their bodies were blown everywhere. A headless torso landed some distance before us, and Colonel Wagstaffe, smiling no longer, vomited.

A gaping hole in the North Eastern tower revealed Parliamentarians in the Close, running in all directions. They may have been taken by surprise, but when the order to prepare to charge was given a few minutes later by Rupert when he was sure no more explosions would occur, they were armed and ready. Peabody and the other officers disappeared leaving me with the miners, and Joseph Wagstaffe who was white and shaking. I sat him down facing away from the terrible remnants of Russell's guards, and found him some water. He gulped it down and glancing over his shoulder, muttered, "I caused that."

"If not you, then another." I tried to comfort him.

"No, I must prove my loyalty....constantly."

"I don't think the Prince exacts an unwilling loyalty from his friends." I said slowly.

"No he does not. But there are those who masquerade as allies but who are vipers in his bosom. Let us beware of them, Doctor Tom."

"Were you not at Edgehill?"

"Not for long,Tom!"

I told him, "I learnt there to feel the horror in my brain but not my stomach." I passed him a miraculously clean handkerchief I had about my person.

"There,Tom. I thank you. I am a man again. I must go."

He ran over to a troop, clearly waiting for his commands. I watched them disappear into the desperate brawling that was now proceeding in the Close.

I went over to the miners. Their work was now done. Their

bravery and ingenuity had won the day.

"Have you been paid yet?" I asked them.

"Not yet, master. That one eyed Lord do owe us some coin." Stephen Dilkes stared at the Close whence now the sound of fierce hand to hand fighting could be heard. Shots, screams, shouts, the usual sounds of my countrymen laying into each other and killing each other…. for no good reason as far as I knew.

I looked at the miners and shrugged.

Stephen Dilkes asked me, "Why they'm doin this, Master?"

I paused before answering. Why indeed? "The King wants the Midlands towns to be free for the Queen to pass through, unmolested."

A young boy spoke, "Couldn't she hurry herself through at night, when they'm all asleep?"

His suggestion seemed to the miners to make sense. They murmured agreement.

"Any road up, lads," said Stephen, "ain't we the lucky fellers? Down the mines, there's no guns, nor else swords nor enemies. All's peaceful under the ground in Cannock."

They nodded sagely, happy in their appointed lot.

The fighting in the Close continued for perhaps an hour when Rupert gave the order to withdraw. Most of Russell's soldiers had ensconced themselves swiftly in the houses of the Close where they had supplies of small granadoes, which they hurled at the Royalists without mercy. The effect was two fold. They were heavy enough to cause severe injury if they were hurled accurately at the foe. As they were filled with gunpowder to which a lighted length of match cord was attached they would also explode. However Rupert soon saw the weakness in their assault. The match was frequently still burning. "Hurl them back," I heard him shout several times. There was consternation in the houses of the Close as that which the men of Parliament had thought they would not see again, was returned to them.

Rupert's men were streaming out of the Close, some carrying, some dragging wounded comrades. I promised the miners I would send Lord Hastings to them with their money and returned to the house on Sadler Street. A coffin was already occupied in the hall. It was one Colonel Usher, a man who had assisted with the burning of Birmingham. A phrase came into my head, "And thus the whirligig of time brings about his revenges."

But it did not whirl round fast enough. Lord George Digby had been shot but only in the knee, not in his black heart. I was relieved however that Colonel Wagstaffe had only a cut across his arm, which I gladly treated.

"I do not know how you endured so long underground," he told me as I cleaned his wound.

"But you went under today with your brand to light the match. Why did you do that if you found it fearsome."

"Oh, dear Tom! You do not know my story. I am a turncoat, a changefoot! I must be always proving myself! My saving grace is Rupert likes me, as he likes you. He has a great gift for friendship."

Rupert had emerged from the fight unscathed apart from bad bruising on his left foot. There was little could be done. The bruise would fade in time. He limped about his room, cursing, much concerned for the Royalist prisoners.

Lord Hastings came in to him, to ensure his injury was not serious. I reassured him and told him politely, "The miners would like to return, my Lord. Could they receive their payment?"

"Devil take it!" he cried, "I hoped they had forgotten."

"Is that likely, my Lord?" I asked him courteously. The Prince overheard our exchange, (I had intended he should.)

"Harry, for Jesu's sake go and pay those poor fellows. How much was agreed?"

The final sum was five hundred shillings. The Prince removed the money from the Exchequer and gave it to me. "Go and pay them Tom," he told me. "They did us great service. Thank them for me."

Frank Starkey could now walk but I suggested that he and his uncle rode back to Cannock on one of the carts that the miners had brought with them. Peabody kindly helped me assist John to his friends. I remembered Elijah's skill at making crutches. I did mourn my apprentice and thought of him often but so much had happened so swiftly that pressing immediate affairs so often pushed him from my brain.

The two invalids were whole heartedly welcomed by the other miners. They were perhaps nearly as pleased to see their money. For courage and fortitude I had not seen their equal. I bade them Farewell, promising that if I should travel through Cannock, I would stop and share a pot of ale and a rabbit pie.

When we returned to Sadler Street, George Digby's servants pleaded with me to attend their master. I preferred to leave him to the Lichfield surgeon who would probably poison his blood by using unclean instruments, but Rupert begged me to see him.

"He is a snake," he whispered to me, "but he has my uncle's ear. If the King hears that I withheld my own surgeon, it would not go well with me." He hopped over to a table and poured me a glass of wine. "I must go early tomorrow to Reading. It irks me, for the task is undone here."

That evening, after I had removed a musket ball from the illustrious knee of the Earl of Bristol, a message was brought under a white flag from Colonel Russell. He did not have the provisions to feed his Royalist prisoners. Should he slit their throats or let them starve? Rupert knew he did not hold as many prisoners as he claimed, but wondered if there was a lack of food throughout the Close.

I had told him how once he was besieged, the Earl of Chesterfield's supplies had dwindled alarmingly, until all we had was a keg of fine claret. No-one had been able to bring food into the Close, whilst Rupert had been in town.

But the Prince felt that he must leave the negotiations to others and ride to Reading, as his uncle instructed. Harry Hastings was ordered to offer terms of free quarter to all, so that the Royalist prisoners would be freed unharmed and the Close be Royalist once more. It was a gamble. But it was accepted. In fact we learned later the men of Parliament had no more powder for their muskets. They could not remain where they were and survive. It was arranged that on the next day, Friday the 21st of April, the Close would be vacated in the morning.

I could go home. I went to inform Abram who was sorry to leave his new family but who with the joy of youth looked forward to new vistas. (I too am young, I reminded myself, but I felt as old as the Malvern Hills.) I had offered to tend the Royalist wounded but Peabody encouraged me to go.

"You are dog-tired, Tom!" he told me, "You cannot cure everyone. And Abram is at the age where he needs a stable home. You've done excellent well for the Prince, for all you say you are for neither side."

"I like him. I realise he didn't order the burning of Birmingham. That was ordered by others."

He nodded grimly. "There will be trouble there."

The Prince gave me a miniature of himself to give to Phoebe. Friends to whom it was shown kindly thought it was me. He clasped me to him and told me he no longer considered me a spy.

"I would hope not, Your Highness. The great causes of King and Parliament may look out for themselves, but I hope I am never called on to betray a friend."

"Well said, Tom." He clapped me on the shoulder. "I shall miss you. There are few men I can look on, eye to eye."

I told Abram to be up early in the morning and asked Cornelia and Gabriel if they wanted payment for his bed and board. They refused it, but I sensed that such a sum would be welcome so I gave them guineas to buy farings for Lizzie and Hodge. I told Abram to be at the George with his clothes two hours after sunrise on the morrow.

I went to the George. It was growing late by this time, but Emily insisted that I sat with her and drank a cup of Canaries. It would have been churlish to refuse, given that she had entertained us so well. Again I remembered poor Elijah, round eyed at Gabriel's speeches, his wonder at the craft of printing, his love of life. I confess I wiped a tear from my eye when I remembered him resting here in his coffin. Emily was silent also, and I was grateful for a moment to remember. We mourned his young life together.

The ostler promised to have the four horses, Jupiter and Hector, Old Harry and Babs saddled up and ready for us. I thought Abram could ride Babs and lead Harry. By a miracle all four were biddable and amiable. I paid for their keep and went back to Sadler Street for the last time to say Farewell to Peabody.

"You never told me your Christian name," I accused him.

"Tomorrow morning," he promised.

He walked round with me to the George after we had broken our fast. I was pondering if I could be home in two days. We would have to go by Erdington to return Babs and collect Shireen. But I did not wish to enter Birmingham, as I wanted to spare Abram that pain. I discussed a possible route with Peabody as we entered the stable yard at the back of the George. If we went west from Erdington to West Bromwich we could drop down to Hagley, and thence

302

to Kidderminster.

The ostler was waiting for me with a paper in his hand. I took it, thinking it was the account for all the horses that I had stabled here since the end of February.

But Old Harry's stall was empty.

"Where....?" He pointed to the paper. It was a note of requisition from Colonel Russell. A horse must be supplied to the bearer, payment to be received from Lord Brooke's Exchequer when I should present myself and this paper to the Midlands Headquarters Coventry....

"Who brought this?" I demanded.

"That young man who was here with you, two months back was it? He came first thing this morning."

Abram came running into the yard, panting and stopped when he saw our concerned faces.

"Not this young man," said the ostler. "The fellow who sells the news-books in the market."

I looked at the paper again. It was printed, giving it an official air. It was nothing to do with Colonel Russell. Ralph had printed it. I began to laugh. I laughed at the vagaries of life, at my stupidity in thinking I could ever plan my future, at the terrible pass our country had been brought to, but most I laughed at Ralph Truscott, his pranks and tricks and wiles. Peabody smiled; a tight lipped smile and Abram looked from one to the other of us, totally bewildered.

"He'll kick the clouds, that one!" said Peabody grimly.

"I hope not! Jesu, I hope not! "I cried, still laughing, "As for Old Harry, perhaps by rights he should have gone back to Hastings. Easy come, easy go!"

There was the noise of many feet marching. It was Colonel Russell and his men on the way to Coventry. They were streaming out the western gate and straggling down Bird Street, past the George and Dragon. We stood under the stable arch and watched them go. After the Foot came the Cavalry, trotting along, some sporting still the orange sashes of the great cause of Parliament. The officers put up a brave show, following on excellent mounts. I recognised Colonel Russell. His eyes wandered over me and I knew he did not remember the doctor who had pleaded for the life of the whore. I wondered who would be cleaning out the Cathedral, which was where their horses had been stabled.

303

And then the wounded came past, dragged in carts over the cobbles. They seemed in poor shape and I was sorry that I could not help them. I knew that there were Royalist wounded who had spent the night in the fields with little comfort and treatment. At least tonight they would sleep in the comfort of the Close.

"There are too many of them, Tom," said Peabody, reading my mind. "You need rest. You saved two men from a living death underground and healed a Prince's bum. Be content."

More carts passed, carrying the remains of the provisions. Some barrels, a few cheeses and some loaves and a haunch of venison. Then the weapons. The pikes! The muskets and swords of the wounded. Even some armour.

And the last cart.... contained a printing press. Eleanour, her hair fashionably curled, her face clean and made a little prettier by the judicious application of subtle paint, her gown white and becoming, held the reins. She bent her head graciously towards me, smiling sweetly. Between the shafts was Old Harry. He seemed content to be at work again. At the back of the cart in the lea of the printing press, Ralph was half sitting, half lying on some handsome brocades. In one hand he held a golden chalice from which he was drinking, and in the other hand was a chicken's leg on a silver platter. He saw us and toasted us, holding up the goblet so that it caught the sun's rays. Wooden boxes, that I thought I recognised, were stacked round the printing press, holding it firm.

"The bastard!" said Peabody. "That's the Cathedral treasures."

I remembered. The boxes had been in the Still Room. When Eleanour had gone for the ointment for the Prince, she must have seen them.

I was still laughing. Neither side had won, and the Cathedral treasure would disappear into the coffers of a couple who wrote news-books.

We went back to the stables, and said Farewell, which was a sad moment, as Peabody had been the greatest of friends.

"If you should be near Worcester, you will visit me!" I ordered him.

"In your great gentleman's house! Aye, Tom, I'll visit! I have a great desire to be a gentleman like you, Master Raggedyarse!"

So we mounted, I on Jupiter, Abram on Babs.

"What's your name, Peabody?" I shouted as we clattered under the arch.

"It's Christopher!" he called out. I was disappointed. Not Ezekiel, not Zedekiah and not Habakkuk!

"Is all well, Abram?" I asked him.

"All well, Tom," he replied and we rode home to Worcester.